Justinian's Daughters

Nigel Stewart

JUSTINIAN'S DAUGHTERS
© Nigel Stewart

Nigel Stewart has asserted his rights under the Copyright Designs and Patents Act 1988 to be identified as the author of this work. This book is sold subject to the condition that it shall not, by way of trade or otherwise, be lent, resold, hired out, or otherwise circulated without the publisher's prior consent in any form of binding or cover other than that in which it is published and without a similar condition, being imposed on the subsequent purchaser.

This is a work of fiction and any resemblance of the fictional characters to real persons is purely coincidental and non-intentional.

ISBN: 978-1-7391652-5-3

Cover photography front and rear ©Nigel Stewart, reproduced under license to Provoco Publishing
Cover Design © Graeme Parker at Provoco Publishing
Provoco Logo ©MJC at Provoco Publishing
Interior artwork ©Graeme Parker at Provoco Publishing based an idea by Nigel Stewart

For Dawn, who helped me make this book all that it is

Introit

The bishop looked at the men around him. This Chapter of clerics, priests and canons, who despised him and all he stood for. He knew of their treachery, that report declaiming him as a heretic. It had enraged him. But, now, his smile filled with the strength of a King's mandate.

'It is 1538. These things you venerate - pilgrimage; relics; saints - are superstition with no place in today's world.'

It was true, they hated this weathercock reformer. Gwilym spoke for them all. 'Your Grace, I beg to differ. None of this is superstition. David is the saint of Wales. Kings and conquerors have travelled here to pray with him. His relics are sacred, as are those of his friend, Justinian.'

The bishop's smile grew wider. 'Ah, yes. Justinian. Tell me, Canon, what this other great Saint means to you all and to this place, this land.'

'Justinian came to Wales in the 6th century, your Grace. A Breton who sought sanctuary. When Dewi-Sant visited his hermitage on Ramsey Island, he quickly grew to admire Justinian's ascetism and the way he prayed while standing in the sea, no matter how cold. They became friends and Dewi asked Justinian to be his confessor, then made him Abbot here on the mainland. He was a powerful, faithful force for Christian good, your Grace.'

The bishop bristled at the use of Welsh. From the chatter of weak-willed peasants on his travels, he knew some of this nonsense and didn't care for it. This emigré, Justinian, had soon grown weary of the monks in his charge and rejected David's patronage. Back on the island, with loyal monks supporting him, he founded a stricter, more holy, more spiritual community.

Then reality became lost in mythology. Unable to abide the monastery's codes, the brothers and their servants rose. They attacked and beheaded Justinian, only for his body to pick up the severed head and walk across the sea. Such errant, witless bilge. Yet these fools, this Chapter, sustained it as if it were fact.

Gwilym was still talking. 'Justinian's chapel and shrine were built near the coast, your Grace, but his bones were eventually brought here to the cathedral, where they remain in peace.'

'Until now.' The bishop had heard enough. 'It is time for me to suppress this cult. Your Welsh Saint, and this Saint of Dubious Legends. No one needs these relics. I am going to confiscate them. This stops now, by order of his Majesty.'

Days later, Gwilym looked aghast at the plundered shrine and knelt to pray. 'Lord, help us to forgive these acts and resist the temptation to seek justice through revenge or retribution. Amen.'

But as he walked from the cathedral, Gwilym's prayer became a plainsong chant. 'Revenge. Retribution. Justice.'

REVENGE, RETRIBUTION, JUSTICE

Elementary

They flew in from the sea. Over the island, then up and over the cliffs, resonating and echoing in the coves and caves beneath them, caressing the stones of St Justinian's ruined chapel.

They filled the air over that tiny city, rattling the cathedral's stained-glass windows, then sped onwards to the drawing on the ground. Those three lines. That imperfectly drawn letter A.

They accelerated down the longest line, from west to east, clouds of dusty earth and pollen billowing up as they passed. Then over the quarry, down the river valley, back to the sea.

They dashed through the harbour, skimming the water, and the boats rocked at their moorings. Then back to the letter A and a different line. Barely off the ground, close enough to touch it and feel what was buried. Away over the fields to the sea.

In from the sea again, they flew between those bright, white obelisks atop the cliffs at the entrance to another harbour. They swept down to the letter A, tracking the final line. On to the clifftops and bays with their sandy, rocky beaches and mysterious caverns.

The rippling white-capped waves flowed to the shore, remorseless, regardless, relentless.

They soared over another saint's relics, along the shoreline, around the island then started all over again, repeating the paths they'd flown.

Now, a vaporous sea fret followed them, smothering the land in damp. It seemed that hypnotic, lilting voices were borne on the rolling, boiling mists. 'The last two are coming. We are ready to complete this work.

Come, beautiful child; come soon. We are waiting to help you.'

The land on and around the letter A became dark and opaque, lit sporadically by jagged streams of light.

Erin heard the news and its report of a mysterious fog enveloping parts of Pembrokeshire. There was disbelief in the reporter's voice when he said that zero visibility had caused roads near St Davids to be closed.

She headed west out of London; she knew that the apparently inexplicable fog would dissipate as quickly as it had arrived. She would be there soon. It was time to finish their work. Time to blow out the last three lights.

Act One

ONE

March 2023. Saturday

'You twats. Why aren't you in the car?'

Ben's walking boots took the fifth. He almost always forgot them, nearly left without them, had to go back to fetch them. He accepted, though, that it wasn't their place to remind him. He gave the left boot a small kick, so it fell on its side, then grabbed a bag and packed his recalcitrant footwear away into the car. Loading complete.

He waved at Mrs Brice, looking out at him from number 18 across the street. Her smile in return seemed sincere, but she let the net curtain drop so that her face became blurred.

Back indoors, Ben squeezed the last flavour from a teabag and spooned sugar into the mug. Stirring gently, causing tiny tings of metal on porcelain, he took another look at the newspaper and the page where his face smiled from the bottom left corner. One date on his autumn tour already bore a *Sold-Out* overlay.

A cheeky one-liner would be needed that night. Something with intrinsic local knowledge which, right now, he didn't have. It would probably just be *'Thank you, Reading. You're the best.'*

The tea was just right, and he had a taste for more. Instead, he washed and dried his mug then put it next to others in a cupboard. Ben completed a final roam around the house, checking stuff, switching things off, pulling out plugs, muttering an accompaniment as he went. 'Cabin crew, doors ready for departure.'

Fifteen minutes later, he'd left Clitheroe and was

pointing his car down the A59, wondering if it really would take nearly six hours to get there.

⚔

Erin stared down at the water. Just a couple of hundred metres downstream, this river formed the border between two countries, but that was nothing to Erin. Borders, barriers, lines in the sand. She belonged on neither side.

The journey from London had been what it always was. Slow, then fast, then a frustrating grind, stuttering along the final miles. Perhaps the scenery was notable? Worth a look? But she never stopped. It was a flashing blur.

Erin looked at the map. Her destination was just over a hundred miles away to the west. She expanded the view. As a child, she'd always believed the peninsula looked like the profile of a creature. The small lake near Rhosson, its eye. St Brides Bay, its mouth. St Davids Head, its ears. Ramsey Island, its prey, or perhaps its plaything. Inland, coloured lines linked the places from her history: a legacy of connections.

In the middle of it all, the airfield sat there, stamped like a faded postmark on an envelope. A letter from a loved one with well-thumbed pages. Hidden away, like treasure in a box under the bed.

Erin had work to do, and she began an assessment of what was needed. The slow steady flow of the river Wye helped her concentration.

One of them had travelled to a halfway house, a place he knew from childhood and adolescence. Erin would be there too, in less than an hour, to check on Jacob George Wallis. He was predictable, practical, and liked his plans and to-do lists. His booking at the house had been backed up with dozens of questions about spurious details. She'd let him play his little games, bullying and entitlement made respectable by calling them a negotiation. He would be first, and easily dealt with. Something routine to close that chapter.

The other one was still in Lancashire, going through the motions. He was cautious and easily distracted, often by the lyrical or pastoral. He had choices about the best route to Pembrokeshire and might take any of them. There would be a waiting game. It would be the same when he got to the property. Erin expected that Budd would be difficult to corral into a routine. She would need time and patience. He was the last, and she had more than enough time to enjoy whatever would be done with him.

Erin returned to the Old Black Lion, collected her car and drove away.

He'd meant to stop sooner, but Ben pressed on because he liked the look of the word *Oswestry*. So many ways to say it. Which could it be? He guessed the key would be about emphasis, or stress. He liked emphasis more than stress. His mind settled on Os**wes**try. It had to be that. He loved it.

'Yeah, I'd like a grande latte; extra shot.'

'Anything else?'

'A muffin. The raspberry cheesecake one.'

The young man at the window knew it was him but stayed cool. 'How will you be paying, sir?' In the background, two other baristas had clocked that it really was Benjamin Budd waving a phone at the pay machine.

'Tell me: how do you say Os**wes**try?'

The young man laughed. 'It definitely isn't like that.'

For the next five miles, Ben was grinding his teeth in defeat. Why wasn't it Os**wes**try? Or even Oswes**treeee** would be better than the reality.

Then the road signs included instructions and place names in Welsh, and that was a whole new box of delights.

It was a couple of hours before he got to Aberaeron, where the pretty, multi-coloured buildings made him calm. Ben decided this was a good place to stop and stretch his legs. Perhaps grab a bite. He parked near the beach.

It was chilly, but the sun shone, and the waves made a pleasing set of sounds. Ben hadn't been to the seaside for years. It triggered something. He felt close to these smells and sounds, weaving familiar tunes. A gust of especially cold wind, strong enough to blow spray from the wave tops, drove him away from the shore.

The road through the village was noisy, invasive and made him feel sad that somewhere so pretty was spoiled by the fumes and grinding gears.

But there was still a pleasing bustle, the happiness of people who stopped to talk, listen and learn. As he scanned the buildings, Ben saw a café with an improbable name and fell in love with the word *Cwtch*.

Ben saw the signpost to the place he couldn't say but kept driving. He couldn't check in yet so there was time for shopping and exploration. He parked, then mingled with walkers and other tourists. The atmosphere was relaxed, yet there was purpose in every gait.

He bought basics at the supermarket, and some walking essentials at the outdoor pursuits shop. He liked that no one seemed to know him. This was what he had hoped for.

A steady incline took him up and away from the centre, up past shops selling fine homemade things. Outside one, there was writing on the pavement: *DDLU*; and *LICE*. Ben checked the map on his phone. It told him this building was The Old Police Station and it drew his attention like a magnet. He felt he knew some of its history.

Ben kept walking to the outskirts. There were signs to beaches, campsites and schools. He turned back, down to the city centre and was thrilled to find himself on Goat Street. All manner of notions filled his brain. How could he use this?

'A comedian's bread and butter.' *Boom-Tish. Applause.*

'A capricornucopia.' *Laughter. I thank you.*

'Does your nanny know you're here, Billy?' *What a fantastic audience you've been!*

It took his first sighting of the cathedral to jerk him out of these hopeless ideas. Sometimes his jokes had such terrible provenance.

Ben knew little about ancient buildings, but plenty about beauty. The cathedral was solid and charming, imbued with bold angles and lines that somehow defied the sloping landscape. The neighbouring ruins, once a Bishop's Palace according to his phone, had seen better days. Why had one monumental structure survived alongside the other's tumbledown fate? Perhaps dark deeds once prevailed here?

The sun had gone now, and another sudden gust of chilly March wind blew dust across his face. Perhaps it was time to see if the cottage was vacant.

Ben turned at the sign to Caerfarchell. Soon, he guided his car alongside the building. He'd studied it so often on the website that he recognised it instantly. Technically he was still early, but he climbed out and looked under the doormat. The key was there.

Inside The Wool Merchant's House, he found everything he had hoped for. Space to pace, up and down; a substitute stage from which he would learn to project all the things that would bring the house down. Comfort too. He'd lounge happily on that sofa, perhaps reading his scripts, but more likely watching porn on his laptop.

Armchairs tested. Tick. Cosy.

Views to the side and front. Tick. Charming.

The wood burning stove created an aura: that half-comforting, half-troubling, half-nauseating smell of stale smoke.

'You can't have three halves, you idiot. It isn't a whole.' He re-divided the aura into thirds.

A long wooden kitchen table bore a small, welcoming tray of gifts: wine; Welsh cakes; chocolate. In the fridge, more kindness: milk; eggs; cheese, made from ewe's milk. Ben slit the wrapping to smell the lactic acidity, resisting the desire to guzzle it. He left it to warm up. Something made him feel it would go well with the Welsh cakes.

It took no time to unload the car and dump his things in an upstairs room, where skylight windows delivered brightness. Low ceilings with exposed beams. He'd need to be careful around those silent bastards.

Ben unpacked and put away his things then tried to call his nana. The patio was the only place his phone had a consistent signal. But it was nice out there.

TWO

Sunday

Ben had slept well. The dull morning sky didn't trouble him, and he was soon ready to walk. He had a rough idea where to go and stepped outside, set for anything.

The tiny hamlet was a different community from what he knew. His home in Lancashire had hilly streets and back-to-backs, was Northern and civic, redolent of history, patronage and occasional conflict. Clitheroe castle loomed, silent and forbidding; a reminder that this evolving town had its feet in a violent past.

Ben looked up and down the narrow lane that connected Caerfarchell to other byways and roads. Opposite his temporary home was a large grassy area. It seemed too unkempt to be something as grand as a *Green*, though it had a vague air of consequence.

The Wool Merchant's House was part of a bigger building, but he'd heard no sounds through the walls. He guessed no more than twenty other dwellings were dotted either side of the lane, some in terraced lines, others stately and more aloof. It was, Ben concluded, somewhere with a past, present and future, just like any other place, and its size and humility didn't diminish it despite the lack of any outward statement of why it was there.

These thoughts filled him with the need to explore. Here was a good start. His mind was nowhere near his routine. There was work to do, gaps to fill, jokes to write that would make his show complete. But that was for another day.

High hedges made his progress seem enclosed, and any glimpses of landscape suggested something overgrown, untended, and somehow deserted. Ben went with his instincts and took a left turn signed to Middle Mill and Felin Ganol. He dipped down the lane, once more channelling between overgrown hedges. Cottages came and went. Then another dwelling. These buildings seemed remote yet were evidently lived in.

'Why would anyone live here? In such a desolate place?' He often spoke aloud, and his voice was amplified in an oppressive silence. He increased his pace downhill.

There was a giant scar on the landscape, with a large disused two-storey building ruined at the roadside. Ben stopped then ambled into the compound to rattle the chained-up gates. It looked like many years since industry had been in play.

Ben yelled: 'Ah-haaaaaaa', expecting an echo from the torn face of rock. Nothing resonated.

He realised that Middle Mill and Felin Ganol were the same place, and he had arrived there. It comprised a working woollen mill, a few houses, and a babbling stream which he soon established was the River Solva. A sturdy, quite pretty road bridge spanned the water. He had the choice of three directions.

'You can't come all this way and resist the lure of a road called Prendergast.'

And he couldn't.

A few hundred metres later, Ben passed the sign telling him he was in Solva, and he decided that, somehow, the word *Solfach* was way more beguiling. He was getting a crush on a language.

It was the prettiest harbour he'd ever seen. Ben stood on a bridge watching the river empty itself into the sea. He felt joyously overwhelmed by the scene. Small craft bobbed at their moorings. The tide was coming in. The land reared up on either side of the inlet. Figures, small human interventions, abounded.

'Solfach, so good.' *It's the way I tell 'em.*

He didn't linger and was soon scrambling up a hill, stopping to stare over St Brides Bay. Some rocks guarded the harbour's opening. Pummelled by waves, they stood firm. Moments later, he'd walked round in a loop and was in the village centre. There was a church, a pub and lots of chalkboards about dressed crab.

'I wonder what the well-dressed crab is wearing these days. Something prêt-à-manger perhaps?' *Hilariously unfunny from Budd.*

He decided to have a pint. The pub looked deserted, but he was welcomed and chose a local beer. He took his pint outside to enjoy the sunshine pushing its way through the clouds. He'd walked about three and a half miles but didn't feel tired. Ben was fit and lithe and knew he'd be fine for the walk back to base. Tomorrow's plan was a far longer walk, which he might even dare to call a hike.

⚔

Erin was at a house overlooking Solva harbour. She stood on the small verandah, scanning the horizon, sensing that scenes had been set.

Yesterday, she'd easily found Wallis at Llandovery. His car, parked in the street, was so pumped up with its owner's aspiration and hubris that Erin half-expected it to bark as she ran her hand over its front. Shortly, he appeared at the front door, hands all over a woman who didn't seem sad he was leaving. Erin smirked to herself. It would be the last time he'd get to touch those things.

She'd followed him for a mile then turned off and

headed for the coast.

Budd had also been safely predictable. He'd come down the road from Machynlleth. Erin had known she'd find him, whenever and wherever he stopped. Sure enough, there he was, ambling near the beach at Aberaeron. He was strange in her eyes. She could see he was filled with comfortable sentiment and seemed to have no sense of being a celebrity. Instead, he looked like someone who had returned to a home he had never known. Erin couldn't work out if that was in her favour. It made her journey down to Solva pensive and calculating.

It was unseasonably warm, and she glanced at the deck chair, contemplating sleep. But there was no time to rest and relax. Those scenes, the ones she'd sensed, needed actors who, in turn, needed direction.

Ben felt like another beer and stayed indoors for his second pint. In between his chat about the pub's cute-looking dog, the guy behind the bar bemoaned the lack of custom. The uneasy tension made Ben eye the salty snacks behind the bar, wondering if he should spend more money. There were pork scratchings, and he wondered whether pigs literally used claws to create them.

When a carload of guests arrived, then more on foot, Ben felt less guilty about leaving. He walked up the road to the village store and bought some dressed crab, another pack of the ewe's milk cheese and four bottles of local ale. The process of paying for these items also involved exchanges with the owner that were just a few smiles and fluttering eyes short of flirtation. Ben could not get enough of that accent.

Then he was back to his role as a walking tourist, stopping often to turn and look at the views out to sea. It wasn't a completely clear day, but it was still possible to scan around and see a headland to the west and the expanse of a bay to the south. The views were a wonderful treat.

Ben saw a small, pointed frame and its exposed bell before the rest of the church was visible. It was a simple building, and he took many photos. From here, it wasn't far to the cottage by road, but he set off in a different direction to find a way across the fields. Not far along the lane, he found the thing he somehow knew he'd find: a gateway and signpost to the right.

This was no muddy path. The surface was well-maintained tarmac, and Ben soon saw piles of rubble sitting on a patchwork of concrete rectangles. Was it an old road? Soon, the patchwork line intersected with another road. It had metal fences and cow shit liberally splattered on the surface.

Ben stood in astonishment. The road he'd just followed went on in a straight line for perhaps another 500 metres. The one it crossed disappeared into the distance in both directions, east and west.

It wasn't a road. He was standing on runways. And he suddenly felt as if he was wearing noise-reduction headphones.

Impatient to learn about why the runway was there, Ben got back to the cottage and rushed through a shower, some tea, and an unduly buttered Welsh cake. It took no time at all to find answers, so he made more tea to aid his studies. He'd already learned to be patient about the slow internet connection. The Wi-Fi often dropped and, unless he stood outside on the patio, his broadband signal was rubbish.

What he'd been walking on was RAF St Davids. It had been disused for decades. Its only military operations had been in the Second World War when it had been built and used for Coastal Command.

Nothing he found, however, explained why those rectangles had seemed so full of ghosts. Standing on or striding across the surface, Ben had felt something pulling him into the ground, through the cracks in the runways, down into the hell of uncertain readiness and of flights into the unknown. Towards battle and conflict, mortality unravelled for that mission.

He'd known nothing like it. Ever.

It was cold, but a message from his nana popped up so he stayed outside to chat with her. He sent some photos, and she loved the harbour scenes. Ben promised he'd send more from tomorrow's walk. Nana told him to be careful and asked if he was safe out there all on his own. He called her and said she mustn't worry. She quickly seemed to forget her concerns because she was very excited about her upcoming cruise with the girls from the choir.

'By the time I get your photos tomorrow, I will be somewhere on the deep blue briny. I don't even know if my phone will work there. Will there be internet?'

'I'm sure there will. But you'll be too busy chasing eligible bachelors, won't you?'

She chuckled. 'Let me at 'em. Me 'n' the girls will be unstoppable.'

'Well, I'll send the photos anyway. Maybe we won't get to talk. But that's okay, isn't it, Nana?'

'Of course.'

She reminded him to take care on his walks, and he told her to make sure she knew where the nearest lifeboat was. She chortled lovingly and told him she'd bring him something to remind him of the Fjords. And she wished him well for his plans to finish and fine-tune his show.

THREE

Monday

Ben was up early to down some porridge and a banana before setting off. He'd replaced his original planned route with one in which those hallowed runways would feature. He re-examined the web page about the airfield. It seemed the runways were made from asphalt, and the longest one – from east to west – was a little over a mile long.

He felt the same draught of belonging when he walked along nearly two-thirds of the main runway. Each step seemed to allow something to be planted in Ben. A rippling surge of stories, myths and phenomena traced up through his feet, legs, torso and hips. A seed, quickly germinated by his own fertile imagination. Despite the ghosts, or maybe because of them, he occasionally made engine noises and imaginary communications between skipper and control tower.

Near the westerly end was a large cross – a giant X – then a line across the centre of the runway.

'This was it; I suppose. The point at which still being on the ground meant you'd fucked up.'

He cupped a hand to his face. 'Roger that, skipper.'

A dog walker with an excited, bounding hound hailed Ben, and he offered a muffled good morning, embarrassed that the woman might have heard him talking aloud. But she marched off, leaving Ben to stand at the very end of the runway gazing along its length and wondering what tales were interred there.

'She was only the runway maker's daughter, but she liked her asphalt.' *In aid of Give an Old Joke a Home week.*

Feeling unworthy about this plunge into the very worst humour, Ben turned and headed onwards.

He didn't linger in the city centre and turned where signs directed him to *Capel Non / St Non's Chapel.*

When he reached them, Ben assessed the relics of St Non as vaguely interesting but not all that impressive. The chapel was a rectangle of rubble, obstinately standing despite centuries of neglect. In one corner, a large slab held a scratched circle and cross. It seemed inauthentic. Stones that looked like they might once have been significant were scattered randomly nearby.

The well wasn't what he expected at all. There was no brick-built circle with a bucket dangling from a canopy, ready to be wound down into the water. Instead, a stone arch, like the entrance to a railway tunnel, protected a small pool. Devotions were scattered nearby, and he could see coins, quite a lot of them, in the stone basin. The tinkling of water was relaxing, and Ben considered filling one of his bottles with the well's water.

'Would that be a sacrilege of some kind? Theft of Non's life-giving liquid. Non shall pass!' *Good effort.*

Instead, he stroked his fingers across the surface of the spring then headed to the coastal path, wiping his dampened hand on his brow and cheek.

Ben was much more taken with what he saw from the clifftops overlooking Caerfai beach. The small arc of sand looked inviting, but it was the ribands of white, advancing into the bay like surging remorseless invaders, that struck him most. It meant leaving the coastal path, but Ben had an urge to gambol in the shallows and feel that sand between his toes.

It was deserted. Not a soul in sight. No ships floated across the horizon. There were increasingly noisy waves, some blasting spray up into the air as they smashed onto the earth. Climbing over the rocks Ben found himself in a smaller, neighbouring inlet with angled, jagged pillars reaching up from the sands like a failed building experiment. Somehow this seemed spiritual, much more so than the ruined chapel. There was a dark satanic cave, with a roughly hewn, haphazard vaulted roof. He stood inside and started to recite part of his routine.

'What do we think of these people who have lists of things they'd do if they were made king or queen or president or whatever? You know the ones. The *I'd have people shot without trial for sitting in their cars with the engine running* brigade.' He'd expected an echoing or at least some kind of reverb. Yet as he finished the words, he couldn't even hear the sea. This space seemed dead and resentful of his presence. He rushed back to the main beach.

It wasn't warm, but there was watery sunshine. Ben decided to paddle.

By the time he returned to The Wool Merchant's House, Ben had walked twelve miles. His detours and pauses for photography meant he'd been gone more than six hours. But he'd had two runway fixes, and during those his quick walking pace had been little more than a dawdle. The airfield had been captivating, but Ben was shattered.

He ran a bath, drank several pints of water, drank a mug of tea with extra sugar then made a second, and guzzled the last of the Welsh cakes. As he stripped off his walking gear, he found himself humming something he didn't know.

The bath eased away the aches and tensions in Ben's legs, hips and lower back. As the afternoon became evening, he made himself a simple meal and turned his attention to the work he would do in the coming days. His act and routine were in decent shape but lacked a good opening. Some of the links between sections were tenuous. He had every confidence that these coming twelve days of focus and seclusion would deliver the improvements he needed.

Nana hadn't responded to the messages he'd sent, most with photos or videos attached. Wherever her cruise ship had reached, Ben guessed his grandmother would be happily ensconced with her friends and a very real danger to any man in a tuxedo.

Several beers and two large glasses of red wine conspired to make Ben doze off on the sofa.

He woke up with a start, in complete darkness and with a considerable sense of disorientation. His notebook and pencil dropped from his chest.

There was gentle knocking on the cottage door.

Ben picked up his phone, and it lit up with the news that it was 23:19.

'Hello? Please can you help? There's been an accident.' It was a woman's voice, quiet but insistent.

He was about to switch on the lights, then decided not to. Maybe it would mess up his night vision? The keys were hanging from the lock, and he twisted them anti-clockwise, then pushed down the handle and opened the door.

'Thank goodness. This is the fifth house I've tried, but you're the only person at home. Maybe you should switch the lights on?'

She was tall and slender, wearing a short jacket over a black dress.

'Come in.'

'No. Please. We need to get back to the accident. My husband…' She looked behind her at Ben's car.

'I can't drive. I'm over the limit. Let's call an ambulance. Do we need to call the police?'

'No point. I've tried. My phone's dead.' She held up a handset. Ben looked again at his phone and saw there was no connection.

'Does your home have a landline?'

'It's not my home. I'm here on holiday. No phone, and the internet seems to have dropped again.'

'Please, Mr…?'

'Budd. Call me Ben. How far away was the accident?'

'I walked it in about fifteen minutes. Well, really, I ran.' Now Ben saw she was wearing incongruous trainers. He grabbed a fleece, put on his own trainers and said he had a torch in his car.

'I'm Erin, by the way.'

'Erin…?'

'Just Erin. Follow me.'

They set off towards Middle Mill. The air felt heavy as if a storm was coming, and their fast pace made Ben warm. He soon felt beads of sweat running down his back.

'This way. It's not much further. Down this hill. No: please, Ben. We don't need the torch. Maybe when we get to the scene.'

'What brings you to Wales?'

'Oh, my husband wanted to come, and so… we came.'

'How badly hurt is he? Was it sensible to leave him?'

'You can see for yourself. There's the car.'

They'd reached the entrance to the abandoned quarry. A car was smashed into the open end of the two-storey building. The driver's door was open.

'He's gone.'

Ben lit his torch and walked towards the wrecked vehicle. Its front was massively impacted, and the windscreen shattered. The airbag had deployed and hung from the steering wheel like a condom hanging from a disgorged cock. Fragments of something shiny lay all around the floor and on the driver's seat: Ben thought they looked like tiny beaks, and he reached down to pick one of them up for closer inspection.

'Best not to touch anything. I don't understand where Jake has gone.'

Ben shone his torch on the ground all around the car. There were no footprints, no bloody trail, and no obvious sign of anything untoward. A few more of the metal shards had tumbled out in the immediate area of the door's sill. He diverted his torch back into the car and realised there were no signs of blood in there either.

Around the back of the car, two lines of tyre tracks had churned up the verge. Then a hole in the undergrowth, and more tracks leading to the road.

'Shall we open the boot?'

'Why?'

It seemed a strange answer. 'Don't you need your things?'

'Bring your torch over here, Ben.'

Erin was walking towards the steel gates that closed off the quarry. In the darkness, the shiny rocks Ben had seen on Sunday were just an extension of the night sky.

'Jake must be in there somewhere. Let's try to call someone.'

Ben's phone dazzled him briefly, but there was still no signal. The humidity he'd felt after they left the house seemed stronger now. It was early March and the temperature during his walk earlier had barely risen above 10 degrees, yet it felt like double that now.

She looked across at him and seemed slightly fearful. 'We should go back to your house and see if the internet is working. That way we can get help.'

'I think we should try somewhere nearer. They might not be affected by the broadband problem or have phones that work.'

'I tried them all earlier. No one answered. Same at the cottages up the road, between here and your place.'

There was a rumble, like thunder, from beyond the quarry face. Then a flash. Then a second and third flashes.

'Same with your neighbours; in the adjoining house to yours.'

'I think no one lives there.'

'Oh. Really?' She seemed to be calculating something. 'We should head back before the rain comes. And in case Jake has gone that way too.'

Ben couldn't hide his exasperation. 'What the fuck do you mean?'

Erin stared at him, and, in the deflected glow from his torch, Ben could see a hint of anger mixing with the fear. And something else: confusion; uncertainty. Shock, perhaps.

'I mean, he might have recovered consciousness and followed me.'

'Then we'd have passed him.'

'Yes. In which case, we must check the ditches and areas off the side of this road. But we should head back. Come on, please.'

She walked purposefully away and up the hill, back to Caerfarchell. Occasional heavy drops of rain began to tap on Ben's head. He set off after her.

They found no sign of Jake and the storm intensified during their walk. When they reached the cottage, it was causing the electricity to fluctuate. The internet hadn't reconnected.

'Maybe you could take me to a hotel?'

'I told you, I'm over the limit. I suppose you could drive my car then come back in the morning. There's a hotel in St Davids. There might be more than one.' He held up his phone to check the time. 'It's not too late to check in.'

'I can't drive. Can I have some water, please?'

'Sorry, of course. Would you like a hot drink too? Or something stronger.'

'I don't drink alcohol. Water, please.'

Ben filled a glass from the tap and sensed she was standing very still, watching him. She seemed to have lost any concern about her husband and hadn't mentioned him since they'd left the scene of the accident. It was very odd indeed and her whole demeanour was unnerving, those dark purple eyes constantly appraising him. Even during the occasional flickers in which the lights dimmed to nothing, he could feel her gaze on him.

'How about food? Would you like something to eat? I've crisps, bread, some cheese. Really nice cheese, actually.'

'Nothing, thank you. Ben.' Her use of his name sounded like an afterthought. As if she was learning it, convincing herself. 'Do you have any tea? Herbal tea, as a preference.'

'You're in luck. I do. Some of those ones to help me sleep. Chamomile and vanilla, I think.'

'That would be nice. I've stopped you from sleeping. Why don't you have one too?'

'This storm would have woken me. It seems determined to hang around.'

'It does.'

When the tea had finished brewing, Ben handed the

mug to her, then took a sip from his own. They were still standing in the kitchen, the uncomfortable air of strangers with nothing to say hanging between them.

'Do you think you're still over the limit? After so much time since you drank?'

'I can't risk it. Especially after seeing your car smashed up like that.'

'I understand.'

Ben sighed. There was no choice. 'I think that all we can do is get some sleep and hope we can raise the alarm in the morning. You better stay here.'

'You're right. Thank you. Ben. I will sleep on the sofa. In case Jake comes to the door.'

'There's a bedroom with two single beds. You'd be more comfortable up there.'

'Really, it's more appropriate if I stay downstairs. It reduces the potential for any misunderstanding. But maybe you could get me some bedding? I'll make more tea.'

Ben brought a duvet, an under sheet and pillows down from the second bedroom and scattered them on the sofa.

'I'll go up and leave you to settle down. The bathroom is downstairs, just there. I hope you'll be comfortable.' They finished their tea and said quite formal goodnights.

Ben lay, drowsily listening to the small sounds from below his room. Footsteps, running water, doors opening and closing, the click of switches. As he finally succumbed to sleep his last thought was that, in the morning, he must ask Erin what tune it was that she kept humming. He'd been hearing it all day, and it was driving him mad.

FOUR

Today

Ben woke to the noise of his own breathing.

It was loud and through his nose. It didn't feel right like that.

Nor did the fact he was sitting up, tied in that position. Each foot was bound to the bed frame. One of those plastic ties, the kind you pull so they lock tight, secured his right wrist to the bed head, about six inches above the mattress. A crinkling sound, like a squashed-up carrier bag, came from under him whenever he moved. With his left hand, he could feel there was no cotton sheet, just the slippery smoothness of a plastic sheet. The handcuff around his left wrist was tied to a thin chain, in turn, secured somewhere out of sight. It meant he could move his hand, but not far enough to remove the tape covering his mouth. The tee shirt and shorts, ambitiously called pyjamas by the supermarket where he'd bought them, were missing.

Ben could move his head fully to left and right and could lift or lower his chin. He saw that the window to his right had its blind closed while the skylight was partially open, allowing a slit of sunlight and chilly air to sneak inside.

A tall chest of drawers sat with the bedside lamps on top, their mains lead's unplugged, dangling down the front of the unit. The bedside tables had been pushed together against the wall to his left. On top, from left to right, was a troubling collection: a hammer; a wooden spoon of some sort; two scalpels; a packet containing what looked like syringes; a small crystal figure; some small phials, like the ones he'd seen whenever he had a vaccination. So, those must be syringes. Then at least five leather straps in a range of sizes; one of those massive rolls of blue perforated paper towelling; and several bubble strips of pills.

The door was ajar.

Ben's breathing intensified with his heart rate. He made a roaring, humming noise through his nose. It hurt his throat.

Shouldn't his throat be drier?

He could lie back slightly, as a series of pillows was stacked behind him, also wrapped in a plastic covering. Realising this, he relaxed, even though that really wasn't the right word for the movement he made. It was more like a submission. Ben couldn't think of anything rational.

Then he tried.

The woman at the door. This was something to do with her. Or with her husband. Jason. No. Jake.

Was it Jake?

It wasn't Jason.

Jake then.

Why the fuck was there a hammer?

Ben felt tears well up in his eyes, and his breathing resumed that faster rhythm. Then he tried some more coherence.

There was no source of pain anywhere on his body. Now he closed his eyes and tried to remember what an injection hole felt like after giving blood or having an inoculation. Nothing. No pin prick of pain in either forearm or bicep. Or his thighs.

He sat up again and looked down between his knees. The restraints around his ankles allowed a small amount of travel for his legs and he could raise his knees a few centimetres. That movement caused an involuntary one further up. His shrivelled cock fell to one side. His balls were up tight, like an unusually large monkey nutshell; but pink; and stubbly. The carefully coiffured line of pubic hair looked ridiculous. Ben tried to move his left hand to give these manhood members a reassuring clasp, in the hope that perhaps they could be shielded. They were out of reach.

He plunged into another vacuum of blanked out incomprehension.

No really. Why the fuck was there a hammer?

Then he heard the humming. And running water. Something was being filled, and soon the kettle boiled and clicked off. Something got stirred, noisily, followed by smaller sounds of exertion and effort.

There was footfall on the stairs.

It was her. The woman who'd knocked on the cottage door last night. Erin.

She was carrying one of those squeezy, clear plastic bottles like people use in the gym. It contained a light pink liquid. A long, thin tube was attached to the top. She placed it next to all those other accoutrements to his left.

She was wearing the same clothes as last night. Or was it last night? How long had he been asleep?

'Hello, Ben. You slept well, didn't you?'

He tried to make his eyes appear angry and made more nose shouts, one of which petered out in a whimper. His stares and those noises made Erin look at him with pity.

'You poor thing. I was sure you'd slept well. In fact, I made sure you slept well.' She looked around the room. 'Otherwise, how could I have done all this? Are you warm enough?'

He remained still and silent. Something was making Ben feel he shouldn't respond, nasally or visually.

Erin looked up and down his body, her eyes resting on his groin. 'I think perhaps you are cold. That particular arrangement of bits and pieces looks in need of some warmth.' Her eyes returned to meet his. 'Maybe later, Ben. It is Ben, isn't it? You're certain of that?'

He maintained his dumb insolence.

'Maybe that's a question for us to answer another time. When I've finished telling you a story or two, or more. Yes. Then. But you'll need some strength for what's to come. I've brought something for you to drink. In the bottle.'

Erin turned slightly and Ben tried to lash out at her with his left hand, but she was beyond the limit of where the chain would let him reach.

'There's really no need for violence, Ben. And if you don't want the liquid food I've brought for you, then you can just lie there and become dehydrated. You'll die in about three days. Is that what you want?'

Ben eyes showed defeated compliance.

'Good. But, just to make sure you're not lying, I need to do this.'

She bent to the floor, and he heard the chain pulling tight, in turn clamping down his left hand. Erin held up the end of the chain and showed him the metal grip in her hand, like the ones on resistance machines.

'I'm going to put the bottle in your left hand. Once you've got hold of it, and so long as you don't try any silly attacks, I'll loosen the chain slightly then feed the tube into your mouth. There's a hole in the tape. When you need to drink, you just give the bottle a squeeze.'

She pulled hard on the chain then placed the bottle in his hand.

'Got it? Good.' Ben watched with a kind of respect. Erin was dextrous, helping her keep tight hold of the chain's grip, while reaching across to his face. He simultaneously felt and heard something adhesive being unstuck. She held up a strip of sticky bandage, her eyebrows registering a gleeful *Ta-Daaaaaa!* for his benefit. Ben could feel the small change in the sensations near his mouth. Now he was able to expel small amounts of breath from his mouth through the hole she'd uncovered.

Erin kept the chain pulled tight. 'And now, we insert the tube. Mmmmm, Ben. Nothing like parking a pipe, is there?'

He felt the tiniest push in towards his lips and parted them slightly. There was a taste of plastic.

Erin had stepped away and he heard the chain being slackened. 'Now you can move your hand more freely and squeeze for some liquid.'

Ben did nothing.

'Oh, Ben. You must try to have this sustenance. I promise you it's completely unadulterated. Yes, okay, I put something in your tea that first night. But not now. So, please; squeeze; and suck. But not too hard.' She looked down at his cock again. 'We don't want you to drown or anything.'

Ben squeezed slightly, then a little harder on the bottle. The liquid that eventually trickled into his mouth tasted a bit like those crazy energy drinks.

He tried not to let his eyes register fear and anxiety. 'The liquid is high in nutrients and will keep you both hydrated and sustained.' Erin's dispassionate eyes bore into Ben's, and he was gripped by their dark purple determination.

'And now we begin. It's going to be a bit like one of your shows. I'm going to tell tales, connected by cords and ending with a flourish. A standing ovation, if we can get you to stand.'

She looked across at the makeshift work bench and its assorted tools. 'And we have things here to make sure you listen and to ensure that you can stand up at the end, or whenever I'm ready for you.'

Erin let out a long, bored sigh. 'This really will be just like one of your shows, Ben. Eerily similar in fact. Because your routine isn't remotely funny, and all I'm about to tell you is deadly serious. There is plenty that is good, but too much that is bad and ugly. I think it's best if we start with some history.'

FIVE

June 1915

The lifeboat swung gently on its davit as the SS Strathnairn steamed west off the south Pembrokeshire coast. Ava hummed a tune in time with each sway, knowing the sound ran through her arms and hands as she rested them on her stomach. The baby would never want for a song in her heart.

It wasn't cold, and she was dry. The sailors had left a blanket. Her bag, filled with the meagre bundle of clothes and inessentials she still possessed, was under her head, neck and shoulders. She could cope like this until Glasgow.

Ava had received good fortune during those last days in Cardiff. There was no money for a train, but even if she had it, the trains were smelly and vile. The journey she'd made had been fine at first. But, after Glasgow, it wasn't just the smells that were vile. The looks were too, as they absorbed her simple clothes and stretched belly. These judges were abhorrent in their outlook and manners.

The return had to be a sea voyage, probably in hiding. Ava needed to be inventive.

The boarding house where she stayed had quickly used up her last few pennies. The search for her child's father had failed and Landlady had no empathy with Ava's plight. She wasn't welcome.

In a speech that combined long, accusing stares with her curt lack of manners, Landlady told Ava to leave. A guaranteed income was needed, and sailors always had money. Ava clearly didn't. Preferred Welsh sailors, she did, but might allow other British. That was patriotic, but Landlady took no risks with anyone that might be a Hun. Or any nationality from other shores. They were all the enemy. Safer like that. Landlady would play her part in destroying that mad brute.

Ava nodded and smiled during this rant, then watched Landlady turn away four men. Their weathered skin and tough physique marked them as sailors and, as they shuffled sadly away from the boarding house, Ava followed; curious; impelled by chance.

One of her men saw she was following, smiled in welcome and told her his name was Chang Hong. She walked with them to the docks; Tiger Bay, they called it. All four sailors were kind and asked about the baby, the father, her home. Ava told her tale, and how she needed to get back to her island home, near Scotland. Things fell neatly into place. Her four new friends would be sailing tomorrow, June 15th, bound for somewhere in Russia. The ship would call at Glasgow, about thirty hours after leaving Cardiff.

In the end, these four sailors had no defence against the silent but insistent appeal in Ava's dark purple eyes. She explained she had no money, and they said it didn't matter. They would help her to stow away. The crew's quarters were unfit for a woman. Even these men, used to hardship, avoided too much time down there. Only the British officers had comfort. There would be space, shelter from the elements and concealment in the depths of one of the ship's lifeboats.

The deal was done, and her men talked between themselves, noises rather than words: sibilant; percussive. Then they agreed they should escort her back to Landlady to enjoy a final night of bed and board.

Megan watched her sister lock the door with habitual painstaking care, accompanied by a muttered wish for all to be well in their absence. She looked across the fields. The day was warm and sunny, but the breeze would help the crossing.

Walking along the lane, the twins enjoyed the silence between them. There were small interventions: gulls and choughs; sheep, bleating. They stopped to look at the ruined chapel and held hands while Bethan murmured a prayer to Justinian. In the distance, across the sound, the island glowed green and basked in the sunshine on its contours.

'Quick now, Beth. We need the tide to be right and the sun to be up for as long as possible after we get there.'

The steps down to the sea were steep. It took them several minutes to reach the lifeboat slipway. Their boat was tied up on the small arc of pebbly beach and they dragged it to the rippling shallows. Megan helped Bethan step on board and, while one sister waded and guided the boat further onto the softly undulating sea, the other readied the sail. When the water reached halfway between her knees and hips, Megan jumped up, and Bethan pulled her on board. After a few seconds of turmoil, the sail filled, and the boat levelled.

'This breeze is good for us. We will be there quickly, and the sun will still be high.' Bethan used a paddle to steer the boat, so it tacked through the south-westerly wind. They exchanged no instructions. Each controlling action was completed at the right time, so that, as predicted, they reached Bae Ogof Hen in ten minutes. It was slower round the northern coast, slower still sailing south and into the small cove on the western side. Once ashore, they took out the pails and began their search. This close to the summer solstice, there were several hours of sunshine left.

⚔

Under her tarpaulin parasol, Ava sensed danger approaching. There was hissing, like someone sucking breath through their teeth. The fear of something cataclysmic overwhelmed her. Her enclosed space was alive with tension, anxiety and the slowly mounting dread from that unknown, onrushing, malevolent threat. It was out there, coming. Ava was powerless, imprisoned and immobile.

The detonation of high explosives was deafening, followed quickly by a different, equally loud eruption. Her lifeboat refuge swung alarmingly, and she heard shouts of rage and terror. Then of determination.

Ava hummed again, loudly now, and she put both hands on her baby to caress her through clothing and flesh and fluids.

Something held the lifeboat steady. The tarpaulin cover was pulled back. Vivid yellows and pinks glowed in the sky, and Ava glimpsed, blinking, at the sun low over the sea to her right. Chang Hong's face looked in, fearful but reassuring. He told her to stay hidden. She heard barked instructions about the lifeboats as the crew prepared to escape. Ava felt the boat held steady while someone climbed in to join her, then it swung loose again. Chang Hong was soon on board, and others joined him, eventually using pulleys to lower the boat. To their left, the ship was leaning towards them, and she sensed it was slowing down.

A shout of *Let her go* went up, followed by yells,

then a piercing scream of horror. She asked what had happened. Chang Hong shook his head. They reached the water and Ava saw another lifeboat shattered on the surface, bodies in and around it, unnervingly, shockingly devoid of life. Then her sailors began to row and paddle, driven by a frenzied instinct for survival, away from the ship's hulk. Into the setting sun, then round in an arc behind the ship's stern. They saw the starboard boats capsized in the water, not a soul in sight.

Then a warning shout went up, and they veered to the right, away from the ship and from any opportunity to find fellows in the water. Ava saw a glassy eye then a metal pole raising it above the waves. There was some sort of machine, or beast, rising from the depths. She felt a surging sense of the fear around her and the urgent renewed rowing to put distance between these survivors and that metal leviathan. She looked again. Human figures were visible on top of the tower, apparently surveying their work. There was a letter and two numbers on the beast's body.

U-22.

The twins heard the sounds. A repeated thump, faint but significant.

Boom. Boom.

They looked to the northwest, then scanned around through ninety degrees. The sounds came from somewhere out there, but no source was revealed. The sea was calm, bejewelled and bright.

The sun was dipping down, but there was light enough for another hour or so of labour. They set back to work, looking for those stones with the tell-tale signs of hidden value.

⚔

The lifeboat steered through the gentle swell. Ava felt increasingly uncomfortable. They'd passed rocky isles, small and insignificant, a few times since leaving the stricken ship. None was a safe place to land so the crew kept with a south easterly heading and seemed torn between getting to land and returning to look for survivors. There was disgust and hatred that the Germans had done nothing to help fellow sailors. They were merchantmen, not military.

Cowards, they were. Huns.

Killers. Merciless. Pitiless.

There was a larger mass ahead of them, but it bore no lights. A dark shape with two raised humps. As they turned into a small bay, Ava let out a cry. Something was happening inside her. It didn't feel too wrong, but she knew it was a little soon.

Then a cry echoed back at them from the shore, perfectly attuned to Ava's voice.

Megan and Bethan had been sleeping just above the pebbly beach at Aber Mawr. Their work had been fruitful with plenty gathered to take back to the mainland. The cry from the darkness made them instantly awake and watchful. Beth's response was instinctive and involuntary.

Ava could see the shoreline and, without telling Chang Hong, her face showed she needed to be taken there, to be on land. The lifeboat pushed on through the water, and Ava saw the outline of a small boat bobbing near the beach. Once the lifeboat grounded, many hands helped Ava stand. Men jumped into the shallow water, and she was passed to them and carried to dry land. Chang Hong brought her bag. Ava rummaged in it and found the pouch of tiny runes and symbols. She gave one to him, along with two farthings. He took these with a muttering she didn't understand, but there was something there between them. A power. He touched her hand one last time, a barely tangential intimacy.

The twins watched as the woman was helped to the beach. These were good brave men, soon back in their boat and rowing hard into invisibility. Then Ava wailed, and they knew there was work to do.

Ava's baby was coming. She was anxious but not scared. The three women exchanged words, confirming each was confident about what to do and what would happen. Satisfied that Ava could manage a short distance on foot, the twins helped her away from the beach and up to where they'd been sleeping. There were rudimentary coverings on the ground, and two threadbare blankets. Bethan gave Ava their flask of water and told her to drink all she wanted.

'When did you last eat, Ava?'

'I had some bread on the ship. And an apple before we sailed.'

'We've no food here. Will you be all right?'

Ava confirmed she needed nothing to eat, then placed her hands on her stomach and hummed a repeating tune. She had no idea why these sisters were here, nor what might have been in the pail that Megan emptied so she could fill it with sea water. The summer night was warm but offshore breezes freshened the air. Ava's dress was damp which made it easier to roll up and away from her hips. She could feel the soft mossy grass on the skin of her lower back and bottom; it felt reassuring and gentle.

'Is this your first, Ava?'

'Yes. But it doesn't matter.'

'No. It doesn't. Is the baby coming on time?'

'No more than a fortnight early. She was...' Ava gasped then cried.

The sounds she made became frequent and regular; then, they intensified. Bethan watched over Ava's legs, scanning from the raised knees to the mound of her belly. Then back again. Megan placed her hand on Ava's stomach, took hold of her hand and smiled into her eyes. She hummed the repeating tune and smiled down, perhaps hoping Ava would join in.

It was still pre-dawn, but light enough to take in every detail. Ava was outwardly calm, but her face showed moments of pain as the contractions came stronger and longer.

'Keep tight hold of my hand, Ava. I'm here. Do you feel like pushing?'

Ava shook her head. Megan wasn't finished. 'Maybe if you sit up slightly it will be more comfortable. Can you do that?'

Using Ava's bag and some of the twins' own materials, they helped her to sit upright. She agreed that it felt better. The twins resumed their watching and waiting.

Each time she gripped Megan's hand or wrist or forearm, Ava could sense a sinuous strength. It seemed to make her pain drain away, as if this nursemaid was absorbing all she felt and then conducted it: up, away into the air; or down through the rocky ground.

Then she felt the fluid flow from her, and Bethan raised her head into Ava's line of sight and nodded.

'It's time. She's coming soon. Try to push. If you can.'

The twins exchanged a glance. Determined and capable, they sensed nothing was wrong, but they were alert to any and every danger.

Ava's breathing was powerful now and she was wracked by the exertion and bouts of pain. Every time she screamed; the twins echoed the cries.

'Her head is here now, Ava. Not long to go. Don't rush.'

Megan affirmed her sister's suggestion that Ava should breathe deeply and push less hard. Then she began to undo the buttons down the front of Ava's dress.

Both twins were humming the repeating tune, and Bethan had her hands ready. 'Your baby is nearly here, Ava. Now I have her head. Give a push, and she will be yours to hold.'

Ava's final shouts filled the air, relief mixed with agony and expectation. Now, the twins remained silent. The tiny sound of a baby's first cries seemed somehow louder than all the noise that had preceded it.

She was soon silent on her mother's breast; her body held safely by Ava's right arm while her left hand rested on her baby's head. All the while, she hummed the repeating tune. Gentle. Persistent. The twins joined her. The baby was calm.

Megan cut the cord when it seemed right and, once the final contractions pushed out the placenta, both sisters bathed Ava with seawater, gently washing away the blood.

'Look, Beth. She's suckling.'

Mother's milk was irresistible.

∡

The light rose behind them, and they saw the sun glinting on the bay. The sea was calm, and they could leave soon. But now there was time for a good look at Ava's baby.

'She is beautiful. And strong.'

'Hungry too. How are you feeling, Ava?'

'Tired. And, like her, more than a little hungry.'

'Did you get some sleep?'

'Moments. Nothing to help me rest.'

'You look awfully tired, Ava. Do you feel any pain?'

'A little. But bearable.'

'Do you feel able to go back on a boat? The crossing isn't long but the steps at St Justinian's will be hard for you. Then it's a short walk to our home where you can rest properly. Can you cope?'

Ava nodded.

'What shall we call this adorable newcomer?'

Ava looked at her baby's face, nestled between her arms and chest. Baby's eyes were open, their colour indeterminate, but fixed implacably on her mother's own dark purple eyes.

'I think she should be named Justina.'

The sisters looked at each other and nodded. Megan spoke first. 'Then welcome to our world, baby Justina.'

It took two trips each for the twins to move all their effects to the beach, then they both helped Ava walk to the boat. Megan held the baby while Bethan helped Ava on board. Once Justina was safely back in her mother's arms, the twins began to push and pull the boat into the shallows where it soon bobbed gently. It took several minutes for the two women to join Ava and several more for them to get under sail.

The breeze took them quickly away. Ava was quiet in the boat's prow, holding Justina and looking back at the twins as they navigated. Occasionally, she seemed to drift into sleep but jerked back to wakefulness whenever any larger waves slapped the hull. The baby fed, as she had often done.

The wind freshened and caught the sail. The craft zipped over the surface. There was still some way to go when Megan realised something was wrong.

'Drop the sail, Beth. Ava. AVA.' Their frantic movements made the boat rock. While her sister pulled down the sail, Megan scrambled forward to where Ava lay, oddly slumped and still. She deftly gathered up the baby, who began a distressed, primitive mewling. Another lurch of motion and Megan passed the baby to Bethan before swiftly turning back to examine the motionless body. A large stain was spreading out on Ava's dress and there were a startling number of crimson drops in the murky bilge water. With increasing alarm, Megan patted Ava's expressionless face then pinched her cheeks with mounting urgency, but those dark purple eyes remained behind their lids. A trickle of blood appeared at the left side of Ava's lips and, as she fell to one side, a more significant gobbet of red spattered out.

'Tend to the baby! Why is she silent?' Megan's voice was quaking between urgency and alarm. 'Check her. QUICKLY.'

Bethan hastily examined Justina, the stress rising from within causing her hands and head to shake. She found a ruddy complexion. Justina was breathing steadily.

'She's all right Megan, well wrapped and sleepy. She'll need her mama soon. We must do all we can to save Ava. Megan. Please.'

Megan ran her hands over Ava's face and head, neck and wrists. There was nothing. Her limbs flopped. She was still.

SIX

De Profundis

The twins were in a solemn and quietly spoken conference about what to do. The profound sadness that engulfed them needed very few words. Their priority was baby Justina, and that plan was easy. The boat bobbed gently in a passive summer swell, but it didn't create gentle or compassionate notions of what they should do with Ava.

Taking her body ashore was neither the right nor the wrong thing to do. Pledging her to the deep also had its complexities.

One required a story, facts and evidence. Then weeks, perhaps months of engagement with inquisitive authorities.

The other, a simple act of committal.

Justina slept but would soon be hungry and they had nothing to feed her at their home. This single fact drove their decision. They needed to give her nourishment. Then they needed to find a family where this baby could be safe and loved. Neither necessity was simple, but both were achievable. They needed to get ashore, but not near the lifeboat station, where they might be observed. They reset the sail and steered away from the island.

About five hundred yards off Caerfai bay, they turned in to the breeze and dropped the sail once more. The water here was deep. The pails of stones would drag Ava down and prevent her from drifting ashore. While Bethan kept Justina warm, Megan began to fashion small loops to ensure Ava could be attached to at least four of the stone-laden pails. She reverently and gently eased off Ava's clothes and pushed them in to her bag of belongings. Her child would need these things. Their smells and aura. Comforts. Legacy. Finally, Megan took out a knife and sliced a handful of hair from Ava's head. She dipped one end of the hair into the blood on Ava's legs and under her body, then folded the clump into a ball and secreted it in her pocket.

As Megan pushed Ava's body overboard, Bethan began to chant. Sounds that might be words, interspersed with a repeating tune. The four pails of stones, one tied to each leg, one to her left wrist, and one around Ava's throat ensured the body lacked buoyancy. Megan released her grip and, as the naked body slowly sank into the sea, Justina's eyes opened. A wail of elemental intensity broke from her lips.

The trip to shore was quick thanks to the incoming tide. The twins hid the boat in a cave then took it in turns to carry Justina and her mother's bag of belongings to the clifftop. They crossed the fields, and the warm sunshine made them sweat. They were hungry and thirsty but that was nothing compared to the need to do right by Ava.

When they reached St Non's Well, Justina was asleep.

'We should let her sleep.'

'Yes. But we must bathe her, then get to Tyddewi. Are we agreed on it being Cissy and Owen?'

'It can only be them.'

'What of Owen's injury?'

'The arrival of the child they want, that they need,

will quicken his recovery.'

'Then we need to get to there soon. This will make Cissy and Owen happy, but we must be sure they understand where their blessing has come from.'

'And how their blessing must be tended. She must be a secret, yet a cause for hope and joy.'

They took Justina down in to the hollow and unwrapped her swathes. With great care and love, Megan held the baby above the well's pool then immersed her in the water. Bethan chanted words using simple plainsong: 'Dial. Ad-daledigaeth. Cyfiawnder.' It made Justina wake and cry, but more of the hummed repeating tune calmed her and she was soon bound up again in warm materials, including a scarf from Ava's bag. Megan soaked a rag of cloth in the water and held it gently to Justina's mouth, so a trickle of liquid wet her lips. It made her react, but she opened her mouth and seemed to drink.

The twins also drank from the spring and quickly bathed their faces, necks and arms. It refreshed them but both knew they were tired, almost to the point of exhaustion. Something would keep them going until these matters were finished.

*

The June day was hot and Tyddewi was busy. A small shop had fresh ewes' milk and while they waited for it to be poured into a bottle, the twins chatted to another customer and learned there would be a bus soon. They went to sit on the steps of the cross, and Bethan pulled Ava's dress from the bag, then tore off a section from around the neckline. Patiently, she formed a tight knot in the material then dipped its end in the milk. When she trickled it on Justina's lips, the baby's head shook slightly, and a tiny fleeting frown passed across her brows. But slowly, with each dab of the milk, Justina seemed to adjust to the taste and fed contentedly.

When they heard the approaching bus, the twins gathered their things and walked to the stop. They stood back-to-back, facing up and down the High Street; watching; alert; eyes and minds assessing all they saw. The bus had *Hwlffordd* on a small sign inside the front window and, when the whining, smoking machine pulled up, Megan, Bethan and Justina were the only people to climb on. They joined five other passengers and paid the conductor when she passed. Two passengers left at the first stop. The other three remained on board when the twins stepped down at Solfach. The omnibus, gears grinding and motor straining, made its way over the bridge and they soon heard it make still more struggling noises as it encountered the hill up out of the valley.

※

They set off to the left and were soon passing the small terraces of housing on Prendergast. When they passed out of the village, overarching trees provided some cooling shelter and their pace quickened.

Felin Ganol looked pretty, the grassy area and bridge dappled by light and shade. Megan stayed near the river, in the lea of the bridge, holding Justina and occasionally testing her with more dabs of milk.

Bethan found the woollen mill was open. Cissy James' smiling face was a welcome sight.

'Is Megan not with you?'

'She is down by the river, soothing her feet and tending a precious parcel. Is Owen here?'

'He's at the house. His wound has been troubling him, so I told him to rest. We have a collection later so I will be walking back soon.'

'We will walk with you.'

'I need to work, Bethan. Why don't you bring Megan and her precious load and the pair of you can have something to drink and a rest? You look tired. There's nothing to eat, I'm afraid.'

Megan already knew she was needed when she saw her sister hailing her from the mill's entrance. She climbed to her feet and walked to join Bethan. They whispered to one another about Owen's absence and agreed what to do. It was better for Cissy to tell her husband. He wouldn't dismiss her needs. They were his needs too.

A child.

They had tried all this time, but neither of them knew which one of them was incomplete. Perhaps it was both.

'Hallo, Megan. I told Bethan: help yourself to some water. Or make some tea. There's no milk.'

'We have milk. And tea would be a treat. We've been busy. On our feet. But we're nearly done with today's work.'

Cissy was busily working the loom, and her voice sang out over the sounds. 'And you have a precious parcel, I'm told. Something to trade, perhaps. What tricks are you bearing?'

'When you finish your labour, you can see for yourself. I think you'll see how very precious this parcel is.'

Cissy and Owen James knew the twins well. They'd been helpful before the war, either fetching and carrying things, or quietly providing sheep's wool taken in the fields near their home. Since Owen's return from the Marne, his left hand missing and a seared stump at the end of his arm, the twins had helped the couple to organise their lives: to carry on with their milling and tailoring. They brought Owen up from the depths of his despair, in which he believed his life and skills couldn't be rebuilt. They showed him that he could still do his trade, and that Cissy had learned what to do. She'd been in charge since he went to join up. They'd expected him to be gone for years, not months.

In the end, Cissy told Owen that having him home with one hand was better than him being somewhere he wasn't safe, using both his hands to kill. He'd wanted to fight in a war he knew was coming. But she wanted him to be in their home, fighting for their lives.

Justina woke up and cried out. It was barely audible over the sound of the loom, but Cissy still heard it.

'Someone here wants to meet you, Cissy. Come; say hello to Justina.'

'Your parcel is a child?'

'A very special child. Here.'

Megan held out the bundle to her friend. Cissy's curiosity quickly transformed into a look of adoration. The small head, with its fuzz of dark hair, was all she could see. And the tiny ears, a stub of a nose and eyes gazing up at her from Megan's clutches; flickering between the two women.

'Take her, Cissy. She's yours.'

'How can she be mine?'

'Maybe you shouldn't ask that question, Cissy. Within just a few days, you and Owen will be all she has. And her love will complete you. Make you a family.'

Cissy took hold of Justina. She weighed next to nothing. 'But where is she from? Whose child, is she?'

'She's Justina. The child of Owen and Cissy James.

And her father should meet her. Can we go now?'

Cissy needed time, a quarter of an hour at most, to finish what she'd been doing. Then four souls, one carried, three on foot, began the climb up the hill. Their ascent was accompanied by the tinkling of the river to their right, solid rocks to the left and by the story they created to explain this baby's birth as Justina James.

SEVEN

Today

'You seem to be enjoying my story, Ben. Which bit did you like most? Oh, wait. You can't answer my questions, can you? And that will have to remain the case, unfortunately. I'm going to assume you liked all of it, because it was sad, but heroic and Justina was so well cared for, wasn't she?'

Ben felt tired. His eyes fluttered. Yet as he sensed the approaching comfort of sleep, the fear and anxiety of this situation jerked him back to consciousness.

'Yes, Ben. It's as well if you stay awake while I proceed with the tale. Especially since, now, there is much more that is bad than good. Bad men, Ben. Women too. They are all around, always at large; then; now; forever. You'll need to pay attention because the cast list is growing. Would you like some more to drink?'

Ben nodded and Erin worked through the refreshment process again. It was still light outside, but the silence was like night. As he sucked on the tube, Ben listened harder to what he could hear. There was nothing. Just that calm, relentless voice.

'Good. I think you will stay awake for a while now, Ben. Let's get on, shall we?'

THE U-BOAT CAPTAIN

Kapitänleutnant Bruno Hoppe looked through the eye pieces of his periscope. His touch had deserted him in 1916: just five kills. He'd been unstoppable in U-

22. Some of those hits in 1915 had been big ships: three in two days off the coast of Wales.

He'd earned his Iron Crosses.

But those medals had been like anchors until he moved to this new command, when success was instant. 1917 was going to be his year.

The ship in his sights was a merchant vessel. British. Steaming around the south of Ireland from the Atlantic.

On board that vessel, the Farnborough, a watchman alerted the bridge that a torpedo was approaching. When it struck, all hands executed the drill. Abandon ship. Board the lifeboats.

Hoppe watched the explosion and ordered his crew to finish off the stricken ship. Scanning the horizon, he saw a storm of some sort. An opaque darkness raged where there should have been the light of a watery February dawn.

Much later, the Farnborough's Captain noted in his log that a sudden storm had descended: darkness; powerful gusts; arcs of lightning. But his officers and men were busy, distracted by their furtive mission. This German was theirs, regardless of a storm.

U-83 surfaced and pulled in close alongside its damaged victim, whose lifeboats were safely away. Then hidden gun crews opened fire, pummelling the German vessel.

The Farnborough was a Q-Ship.

On the submarine's conning tower, its second-in-command saw dashes of intense light in among the bullets. It didn't seem like normal gunfire. The Oberleutnant watched as Hoppe's head was sliced off.

U-83 sank without survivors.

David Morgan, Dewi to his family and friends, couldn't sleep so he lit another cigarette. He'd been exhausted since withdrawal from the front line. In fact, he'd been exhausted ever since his regiment landed at Boulogne two years earlier. He'd fought, and he'd killed, and he'd survived. Then he'd done it all again. Ad infinitum. Ad nauseam. Some charm had prevented him suffering anything worse than a scratch when a bullet grazed his upper arm. Even that had been a British shot. He was lucky.

Others were not, including his kid brother. Poor Hywel. One of the first over the top at Fromelles, snagged and trapped on the barbed wire, then shot to pieces as he hung there. Dewi had been granted no time to grieve and he was hardened to Hywel's loss. It ended up that it meant nothing. How could anyone mourn one life alongside the millions of others lost?

But Dewi fought viciously to avenge Hywel.

That most recent triumph had come at the usual cost. Victory always did. But this lack of sleep, lying behind the lines, felt like crushing defeat. He wanted to be a casualty of sleep's sting. To dream of his beloved Fishguard. And, in his dreams, he could still call it Abergwaun. Too many of his pals in the Welsh Regiment didn't speak their country's language. The lads from the English and Scots regiments didn't even know where Fishguard was.

He'd be back to the front soon. And, if his luck held long enough, back to the French coast and across the channel, home to Cymru and Abergwaun. One day.

Another cigarette seemed necessary to cement together the stones of his defiance.

Eventually sleep came. David dreamed of home, of

policework, of being called Dewi, of watching the steamers and sailing boats in and out of the harbour.

Most of all, he dreamed of Claire and how he would marry her when he returned. His heart was set on 1920, even if this war still raged.

Predictably, reliably, David returned to the fighting. Back to the Western Front, to the trenches and stenches. Back to Passchendaele, then on and on, time and again. Cambrai, Albert and elsewhere in the second battle of the Somme.

In November 1918, he was back at Étaples. But, this time, what kept him awake was the news that the war was won. The Welsh lads in the camp sang Land of My Fathers. They'd all be there soon: back to Wales; brave warriors; splendid patriots.

And then Claire would be back in Dewi's arms.

THE LANCE CORPORAL

George Cottam looked along the line, then up at the trench ladder. He'd climb it soon, and then he'd be a man. Here, now, at Bapaume, he was set to start killing Germans and bring victory for his country. Then he'd stay a soldier in the mightiest army in the world. There'd be more wars and next time he didn't want to be kept waiting.

He'd joined up on his eighteenth birthday. When the clock ticked over in to 1918, his excitement and pride were overflowing, for he had become a soldier in the Loyal North Lancashires. His journey to the front started at Kirkham & Wesham station. The family was conditional in its pride. Father hugged son then stepped back to come to attention and salute. Grandpa Cottam joined in with the salute, his old, mottled face sagging with suppressed tears. Nana Carlton stood and watched. Ma was too upset and scared, broken by the constant news of death and disfigurement; she reluctantly kissed George's cheeks, left, right, left. For all that she might never see her son again, this mother couldn't bring herself to hold him in her arms.

They waved him off with many last-minute checks that he had everything packed.

George watched these four people with a kind of contempt. He felt no sadness at leaving them here in their home town with its dying trades and tumbledown mills. Their sadness and despair were weaknesses. He'd be back, but when that homecoming was done, he had no intention of hanging around.

THE SPY

It was unbearable. Heinrich Brandt felt the pain flowing from his mother's every word and movement. He had felt it too, back in 1917 in the aftermath of Vati's death near Lviv. Killed by a stinking communist Russian soldier, running away from the fighting. A Russian who hadn't even wanted to be there, who despised his own country, yet still found the means to kill a proud soldier. Vati loved his country and believed Germany would win this war. A man who loved his family; an adoring wife; a favourite daughter; a devoted son. A man who believed in the honour of battle and who would have died happily in a fair fight. The essence of Prussian chivalry ran deep in Vati's heart and soul.

News of his father's death arrived at their home just days before Heini's 12th birthday, the last one he had celebrated. Now he was fifteen. His life, his family, his country - all defeated, torn up in to scraps then reshaped in a fashion he didn't want to recognise. What had Germany become? Governed, controlled and abused by the French and British with their treaties and rules. Festering from within, the cankers of socialism or Marxism – or whatever it was called - invading the veins and arteries.

Katrin left home but returned from Lübeck every month, bearing nothing more than smiles and warmth. These provided succour for Mutti who returned a muted maternal pride. Heinrich loved his sister and listened intently to her tales about life as a nurse. Katrin was playing her part in rebuilding the nation's people, restoring the lives of the injured.

He matched her calm determination to be the best with his own zeal for progress and change.

At school there had been rumours about what was happening in München. The battles between left and right. Uprising and momentum. The birth of a new way to live that would erase all the causes of a nation's despair: capitulation; defeat; the contempt and disrespect of the French and British.

It all seemed, metaphorically and literally, to be many miles away from his corner of post-war Germany.

Yet Heinrich believed.

EIGHT

Justina

She was loved. Ava's adoration for the precious baby she held too briefly was never lost. It hung in every word and caress given to Justina by Cissy and Owen James, and in every moment that they hummed the tune they learned from the twins. A new family came to be.

Megan and Bethan were now surrogate aunts, inexorably linked to Justina. Later that day, after leaving their niece in the loving care of Cissy and Owen, they'd trudged wearily across the fields towards home. It was slower than the lanes, but more direct and, anyway, there was one last thing for them to do in Ava's name. Her bag of belongings was with Justina's new family. But the twins had kept the small leather pouch and soon paced out the distances between the places where Ava's runes, coins and the clump of her bloodied hair could be buried. With bare hands, they dug deep, and, with each tiny interment, they chanted small hymns to Ava's memory. When the work was done, they walked the remaining few miles to their home.

Over time, Justina was often in the twins' care. She was lively and learned quickly, her dark purple eyes always filled with curiosity for the things around her, and for what was said. She learned words and, eventually, called herself *Stina*. So that became her name.

Stina's arrival in the James family was presented to the world as unexpected. Cissy had not shown but it didn't matter. They were believed and respected. No one doubted their integrity. The tiny community around them was discreet. There was no carping gossip in the rural family's voices. No one doubted that Cissy and Owen had been overcome by joyous news. Everyone accepted that Stina was a blessing.

When the raging war ended, Stina was three and almost impossibly active. She played in the fields and demanded things to do that would help mam or daddy. Every morning she walked with her parents to Felin Ganol. She was more likely to need a lift on to daddy's shoulders for the journey home. All this activity helped her to grow strong and love being outdoors.

She learned quickly and deeply. When she started school, Stina spoke Welsh and English with confidence. She could sing tunefully and read books whenever she could, yet still craved the narration of grander stories by her parents. The classroom was a relatively happy place and she made friends among her peers.

At school, she was good, but by no means a saint and sometimes suffered a strap across her palm for words spoken out of turn in class.

At home, she stayed within the boundaries of any discipline imposed by her parents.

At school she learned the beginnings of friendship, education and knowledge.

At home she learned about the value of hard work, good manners and listening.

When Stina asked Owen about his missing hand, his answer showed her the power of forgiveness. He'd forgiven the enemy. He'd forgiven the establishment. Both had subverted his passion for a just war into a sense of being a victim of its murderous folly. He needed to move on, to improve and to be content. Her daddy showed Stina how the weight of unhappy, resentful memories can become a terrible burden and it was best to shed them. It also made her love, deeply love, her father's compassion.

From Cissy, Stina learned to be direct and unambiguous. Her mother would never remain silent if something needed to be said and was forthright in her words. She was truthful and honest in all she did. Stina learned how powerful Cissy was in the business she ran with Owen. Her mother walked alongside her father as an equal in all things. Their recovery from Owen's injury had been rapid and effective because of Cissy's willpower.

What both parents instilled in Stina was the maxim that, when work needs to be done, there is no place for frivolity, laughter or fun.

Her aunts were hugely influential on Stina's development. In their presence she could be more free-spirited. They encouraged her to have no fear, but to know the value of caution. They took her with them to Ynys Dewi and showed her how to spot the pebbles and rocks that might bear quartz. Stina could set a sail and navigate their boat before she was seven, and by the time she was ten, the twins often left her to sail alone. At the beaches of Caerfai and Porth Mawr they threw her in to the water, so she learned to swim in and cope with the powerful waves and tides.

Pre-eminent in their teaching was that it's better to be alone, flying like a bird, than hemmed in by a company of dogs.

When she passed ten, Stina realised something was missing. It started with dreams: movement; voices; water; nameless faces and places. Whatever was absent, her mind couldn't assemble the pieces. They remained ephemeral. It meant she couldn't express it aloud to anyone, least of all herself.

Stina was never troubled that she often spoke aloud to herself and enjoyed it. She could resolve any number of complications like that. But this new problem seemed to have no solution. It made her withdraw and seek time alone to think and assess what was happening.

The dreams kept breaking in on her sleep then became supplemented by visions. Her walks home from school involved a climb up the hill out of Solfach. Some days she went via the mill. It was during these walks that she began to see vivid revelations that were much more than dreams. A ship, sailing. Hemmed in under partial darkness. An undulation. The sounds of the sea, and that tune she knew so well. Some undefined underwater menace. A crashing tumult, like the end of the world. In darkness, a face gazing down at her, filled with such love that Stina could feel it coursing through every fibre.

That same face, deathly pallid. Gone.

What was this?

The warm summer afternoons of 1926 caused her to want more time outside, on the land among the cattle, sheep or crops. Stina started to take a different path. In the fields her visions became more detailed. Each step towards home seemed to create clarity.

One afternoon, she arrived at the house to find Megan and Bethan talking to Owen and Cissy. That evening, Stina learned her real mother's name and fate.

THE LANCE CORPORAL

George Cottam was home, cut off from the things he had grown to love. Those battles in the summer and autumn of 1918 had been life-affirming; the kinship with most of his fellows; all the bloodshed and explosions; a weapon of one kind or another constantly to hand. But it was ended without fanfare in the wet chilly mess of a November day.

Thousands upon thousands of soldiers, from all over a shattered landscape, began the long slow adieu to the Western Front in the homeland of a despised ally. George made it known that he wanted to remain a soldier. He thought they weren't paying attention, but someone had.

His homecoming was happy but tempered by news that his grandpa was close to death. Influenza. It was everywhere. No one was allowed to go and see the old man. It would be over too soon.

His teen sweetheart, Sheila Kirby, was pleased to see him but kept breaking down in tears. It irritated George that she was still overwhelmed by grief for her lost brothers. He could understand her upset at the loss of Peter so close to the end of the conflict. But she'd been crying about Andrew for years, which was pointless. It was getting in the way of what he wanted from her, and he realised he might get nothing unless he forced it on her. He was a man now, fresh from the trenches, with heroism in his backpack. Men get their women to comply. This was what he had learned from that body of men over there in France.

His efforts failed.

Rejected, he turned to the national news, such as he could understand it. He read what seemed to be nonsense. Why would the politicians take money away from a victorious Army? Surely what Britain needed, more than ever, was the ability to wage war? On the Irish. On the Hun. On the hordes in Palestine and Anatolia. And, in fact, on anyone. Especially those despicable millions all over the Empire, where treachery abounded and disloyalty to King George -

their Emperor – was rampant.

Something went his way, and the Loyal North Lancashire Regiment gave him the papers he needed. He was soon overseas again, in the Allied Occupied Territories, to get those Turks in order and assert the power of Britain and all its Dominions. A fight was imminent.

Then so-called allies said *no*, or *non* or some such. And something called public opinion suddenly mattered. The generals backed down and lesser politicians defeated the hawks in Parliament. The Turks won without a shot being fired. The regiment stayed but as a police force. No killing. No joy. George was not yet twenty-five and his life as a soldier was over.

What a waste of money.

George wanted a bloody war. He wanted a bloody fight, and he wanted bloody hands.

The regiment returned to base and soldiering felt like nothing more than parades and shoe polish. Sheila finally returned to his life, provided the favours he craved, and they married in 1930. Then Joseph was born, and they were soon calling him Jack, after Sheila's grandpa. Two years later, a second baby was stillborn, and that was that.

Just after he was thirty-six, George was discharged with honour and a glowing testimonial. The CO used his personal grapevine and George joined the Corps of Military Police. He couldn't remain at Preston Barracks and his first assignment took him to Yorkshire. Sheila and Jack remained in Kirkham, building the home they needed. George would be moved from base to base. That was no life for mother and son.

Surrounded by the massive volume of men and machines at Catterick, George still wanted a bloody war. Otherwise, what was the point of all that ordnance just sitting there in sheds?

THE SPY

Frau Brandt never recovered from her broken heart. When she died, ten years after the fighting that killed her husband, Heinrich was twenty-two and worked whatever hours he could muster. One or two employers were reliable and honest. Others were smiling one day and looking down their noses the next.

Katrin said she couldn't come home, and they had a dispute about where he could live. Lübeck was the sensible option but Heinrich didn't want to move to a city he didn't know. He especially didn't want life in a tiny apartment with his sister and another nurse. How could he sleep there? In a place where those two young women would be with the young men they brought back to fuck. He'd be on the floor listening. That wasn't right. He had nowhere near enough money to pay the rent on the apartment their family had once called home. Heinrich asked the landlord if he could pay in other ways, and he became a rent collector and enforcer. That worked for a while.

While the British and French played their games to keep Germany in line, ticking the boxes that rules were being followed, the Americans went a step further in the Fatherland's annihilation. Their futile capitalism had collapsed in on itself, a system failure whose deathly tentacles now stretched out to poison other nations. The trickle of income Heinrich relied on soon dried up and he turned to crime. He stole from some of the shops that had once given him work. He attacked defenceless people in the unlit streets. He still didn't have enough, felt permanently hungry, felt terminally angry.

One dark morning he became the victim. With rain lashing down, Heinrich was attacked for money or food he didn't have. He fought back and one of his assailants ran off. The other punched and kicked and scratched with a kind of venom. Heinrich was losing. He hadn't fought since he was a child. Maybe he would die in this mêlée? The man was neither bigger nor harder than Heinrich. He just seemed better equipped to win. There was neither rage nor scowls of hatred. His attacker was carrying out this work as just another routine task. It was quite chilling.

With a small surge of strength, gathered from somewhere unknown, Heinrich pushed the man away then, when three paces brought his foe back in range, Heinrich butted him hard on the nose. The man reeled noiselessly backward and received a kick, hard, into his groin. The shout of pain this caused was the first sound the man had made. It was the final act in the bout. Two police officers saw Heinrich's actions and determined them as belligerent. He was taken away to be charged with assault.

In the cell he received more blows. It made no sense. Why was this happening now? They could have kicked him to death in an alley or side-street. Was this what punishment had become? Something meted out arbitrarily. Retribution without the constraint of justice? Heinrich kept his head up and, in between each volley of punches, spoke quietly and respectfully of where he lived and worked, how he had been assaulted by the two men and was in fact their victim. He told them his mother was dead. His sister many miles away. His father had died fighting the Russians. Heinrich told them he had been, and remained a scholar of mathematics, literature and languages. The beatings continued until someone intervened.

Heinrich was moved to another room where a uniformed woman patched him up, gave him water to drink and a piece of bread no bigger than his hand. She left the room without speaking. The man wore a suit and wanted to know if Heinrich was all right. The man admitted there was no excuse for the behaviour of the police. No excuse. But no apology.

Would Heinrich care to tell his story?

THE POLICE SERGEANT

Dewi Morgan strode into the Police Station to begin his first day as sergeant. He was welcomed by the divisional inspector, there to assure a smooth transition to Dewi's tenure. He met the three constables, was given a briefing about the town and finally shown the bicycle he would use to enforce law and order at a distance. Great things were expected from Sergeant Morgan. He deserved his promotion. The move to St Davids would be good for the force, for the town and for David and Claire.

They'd married in 1920, just as Dewi had planned. David Junior came along five years later. It had been a wrench bringing Claire and the boy away from Abergwaun, but there was a tied house in Tyddewi. It was no distance for them to travel back home when duty allowed. They'd go back to see his sister get married. Dewi would walk Lizzie down the aisle, proud to act as their father and honour their late brother. Hywel's death had made Dewi and Lizzie closer than they'd been before.

The Inspector jumped into his car to drive back to headquarters. Dewi watched the tiny machine struggle up the road. He could overtake it on his bike, for sure.

Assured that his men had work to do, Sergeant

Morgan grabbed his helmet and stick. He'd been here before, but today he would conduct a thorough review of the streets. With a last look at the three chevrons on his arm, Dewi donned his helmet and set off.

With the town conquered on foot, he went further afield by bicycle. He took the bus out to Porthgain, then walked all the way back down the coast. It took him all day. Back on his bicycle, he ventured down the small lanes to see the beaches, the lifeboat station and the ruined chapel of St Justinian.

Dewi saw a great deal on his travels, none of which was cause for police intervention. This was a peaceful, law-abiding community. Petty pilfering and trespass might be the worst offences, usually not involving locals. He'd barely met a soul on the trips away from Tyddewi. A friendly couple and their daughter. Innkeepers. Two garrulous women, twins by the look of them, hanging washing on a line. A young couple, the man on a boat in the harbour, the woman helping it cast off. He'd stopped to talk to all of them and those affable smiling exchanges helped him learn names. Back at the station he spoke to the constables about those names, learning that all were pillars of the community.

But perhaps those sisters down at Rhosson might need watching?

✕

Stina left school at fourteen and started working at the woollen mill. She already knew how to operate the machines and often worked alone, trusted by Cissy and Owen.

She wasn't sorry to leave school. Being there, together with children of any age between five and fourteen, created a void. Everyone was just a child. The needs of a young woman were no different to those of an infant. It made her mildly resentful and disinclined to learn.

She loved Cissy as mother and Owen as father. The revelations about Ava had shocked Stina, despite the dreams and visions she'd had.

And what of her real father? Ava had either been deserted by him or had chosen to be a family without him. To think that her father was unknown, his identity locked away in the mind of a dead mother, was difficult to bear. Stina knew she wouldn't search for him, nor conjure a comforting, fanciful image. It gave her a kind of peace. It wasn't that her father didn't exist. He simply didn't matter.

Instead, she formed a bond with Ava's memory, finding time to see that face, all its contours and brightness. The repeating tune she'd learned before her birth was a foundation for their bond. Ava had given her those notes, improvised and unique; sung as a key to motherhood. There had been tragically scant time for baby to have truly known mother's eyes, smile and breast. Yet Stina knew the lines and shadows around Ava's slender face. Lips forever smiling. Hair swept back, dark and rich with waves. Eyes arched by brows filled with questions and answers; eyes that pierced in to Stina's heart and soul with the intensity of their dark purple eloquence. And Stina knew the warmth of a rounded breast, filled with milk, that hardened nipple giving life through its perforations.

Ava's constant subliminal message to her daughter was that Stina must love Cissy and Owen with all her heart. In them she had the living, breathing embodiment of a dead mother and immaterial father. Stina complied with Ava's guidance. She had no questions or doubts.

Owen James had been more hesitant than Cissy about the need to tell Stina. He saw the occasionally troubled soul in his daughter's face and argued she might be broken by the news of her real mother's fate. He didn't want to lose this perfect child. Cissy, forever a more pragmatic hardened character than her husband, knew it was necessary to reveal the truth. In this she was supported by Megan and Bethan. So, it was Owen that told Stina the patchwork of facts about Ava's journeys. He held her hand as he spoke, felt a sudden squeeze when he spoke of Ava's death and saw his daughter reach to take Cissy's hand. She slept with them in their bed that night, insistent on the rough blanket the twins had saved from Ava's belongings.

Where school had been ultimately complex for Stina, the work she did for her parents was comfortable. She'd known how to operate the looms since she was ten. Now she was engaged full time and her facility for negotiation and design became strengths. Owen and Cissy had never bowed down to the mill's owner but tended to know their place as managers and guardians. Stina was less inclined to accept that and often confronted the owner with things he needed to fix or update or provide.

At the shop or in the market stalls, Stina's customers were often beguiled. She always sold something extra and never accepted anything less than the asking price. Business thrived. Not enough to make them rich. Enough, though, to keep them fed and to be a family with a wealth of love, commitment and unity.

After the small celebration on the morning of her 17th birthday, Stina left the house and set off down the lane to work. It was a bright morning, warmed by the sunshine phasing in and out of abundant white clouds.

While walking, she couldn't shake off a growing sensation. It was the same as she'd felt in the build-up to her youthful visions, but more powerful. As the road descended into the river valley, Stina was disoriented. Her steps were like the kicking of legs under water, keeping her afloat. Her movement down the slope wasn't barred. It progressed. But it felt like she was being channelled through rapids, not walking on earth.

Some distance before she reached the mill, Stina had to stop. Her bewilderment was unbearable. She sat on the grass verge and held her head between her hands, staring down between her feet to restabilise. When she looked up, the sunshine had been blocked by an opaque darkness. It pulled her up in a rushing headlong flight, ballistic and accelerating away over the fields. As she passed over the coastline, two lines of light soared up and flew alongside her. Megan and Bethan took her hand. Their path was seemingly a tunnel protecting them from great conflagrations of flashing light, leaving her no sense of distance or time. The sea raced underneath, then land appeared to the right. The flight slowed to a glide then a circling around a scene: small boats moving away from a larger vessel; a small grey shape emerging from the deep, becoming larger; a long slender pencil of menace closing in on the stricken vessel. As the grey shape drew close to its victim, a tumult of bangs and flashes erupted.

Stina's flight re-accelerated into a descent, straight at the protruding tower on top of the grey marine pencil. In concert with the twins, she flashed down, faster and faster, uninhibited by the fusillade of bullets streaking at the same target. Down, hard and unremitting at the uniformed men on top of the tower. Down, then level and straight at the neck of the U-boat commander, her flight slicing clean through the flesh and bone, taking off his head.

On the grass verge, she found herself intact and inert. Behind her eyes there were still flashes of white, curiously shaped. A long line. Then a second shorter line, bisecting the first and rushing to a turn where it flashed back across the long line once more.

NINE

Today

Erin was agitated. Almost as soon as she stopped talking, she stood up and left the room, then Ben heard a slammed door. In the silence, he tried to make small movements to test how tightly he was bound. It took no time for him to realise he was powerfully entwined.

Tears welled up in his eyes. This crazy bitch meant him harm. And she must have harmed whoever had been in the crashed car. He was going to be a serial killer's victim.

Part of Ben just wanted her to stop her ridiculous stories and end it all.

He heard the front door open, then the sound of things being dropped on the tiled floor in the living room.

'Been getting kindling for the fire, Ben. Oooh, isn't that a lovely word? Kindling. Mmmm, Ben. Where were we?'

Ben shook his head.

'Owen is lovely, isn't he? A good man. So kind, despite his own fears and pain. To give all that love to Stina. Another good man was soon on his way here. You see, Ben, something seems to bring people here and so many of them are wonderful.'

THE LOVER

When the doors opened, Thomas Harty strolled out from the school. The younger, excited kids were rushing, and he liked that. They were kids. Running was their sole purpose. But this was his last day at school, so his exit had an air of important calm and resolve. He was a man now. A fourteen-year-old man.

Some of the lads invited him to play football in the park and he havered. Thomas loved to play but preferred to watch. Five times during the season just ended he'd seen Millwall. They'd finished seventh in Division Two: not quite London's finest; but better than fucking Palace down there in the basement. There was a kind of football joy in the capital, for London could boast The Arsenal as league champions. Thomas secretly harboured a bit of love for the Gunners. He'd get his head kicked in if he ever told anyone. You just didn't like the North in this manor. That was worse than liking the rich. But even so, he had that picture card of Cliff Bastin and had sworn he'd see the great man score a goal, one day.

He walked to the park and, for fifteen minutes or so, watched them kick the ball and each other. Then, with ribald words of dismissal from his mates, Thomas made his goodbyes and headed away and on to Malabar Street. No one was home so he sat on the step to wait. The Thames, flowing less than 150 yards away, created the aura he had known all his life. How could something so magical and life-giving smell that disgusting?

Later, they all said grace then ate tea in silence. His dad's prayer was different every evening, but always carried the same core messages: we are lucky to have our health; we are lucky to have work; we are lucky to have this food. It didn't matter that the meal was simple, nor that it was meagre. It would sustain them. Sometimes, mum or dad took out an astonishing treat. Chocolate. A pastry. A banana. Whatever form the treat took, it was divided equally between the brothers with nothing for the adults. It was an equality Thomas took to the bed he still shared with James and Peter.

His first day of freedom from school was also his last. Joseph Harty returned from the docks that evening with news that he'd seen a market stall advertising for a lad. He'd agreed for Thomas to get a trial. It would be a good place to work. Billingsgate always needed people. Something like that would tide him over until real work could be found in the docks.

Thomas passed the test and, that evening, it was he that supplied the astonishing treat.

The things Joseph prayed for, and his thanks for what they had, rewarded the Harty family with good health, wealth from hard work and a happiness borne from their self-belief in family and community. There was talk of romance between Peter and Bella, a beauty from the other side of Millwall Park.

There was also talk of war.

It was the Germans again.

Jennifer Harty threw protective arms around her men. She knew Joe was too old to be called up, but her handsome boys would be taken. She didn't want them to die in France or Germany. James and Peter calmed her nerves. Their jobs unloading the ships laden with trade would be a reserved occupation. All four men would remain at home, winning a war on the home front.

Thomas broke her heart. He listened to the stories he heard about Hitler and the Nazis and saw something that demanded defiance. As soon as he was old enough to enlist, he would go to stand alongside others defying that threat.

George had been promoted but the celebration he tried to create fell flat. He was home on leave and found Sheila's struggles with baby Jack had evolved into a constant battle. George tried to resolve this with military discipline. Within a week of his return to base, a letter from Sheila revealed Jack had got worse.

That news, and the brief renewal of family ties, almost prompted George to leave his job and work on civvy street. But work was hard to find. That grass wasn't greener. And anyway, his latest posting to Aldershot had cemented his view that there was trouble ahead. Everyone knew war was coming but George no longer wanted it, especially not with the Germans. He'd fallen squarely behind appeasement. What he saw while policing the soldiery indicated a soft underbelly that could easily be defeated by a determined foe. These young men lacked the powerful self-belief of those he'd fought alongside in the trenches. They complained about things: the food; the equipment; the lack of pay; their poor accommodation. Listening to them, in the barracks and pubs, George couldn't see how Britain would stand up to the powerful forces being mustered in Germany. Re-armament had come too late. Years of being passive had made the training and investment ineffective.

If this lot end up on the Continent, he thought, the Wehrmacht will swat them aside.

He proposed this point of view in a discussion with a colleague and got a punch. This was treachery. Shame on you, Sergeant Cottam, for doubting our lads and country.

It got worse. George received a dressing down, then demotion and docked pay. Within a few weeks, he was given a posting that felt like a punishment. A new airfield was being constructed and he was needed to liaise with the local police to ensure there was clear demarcation between their roles.

George looked on a map to find Pembrey. It took him several minutes. Swansea was the only place he'd heard of near there. Why on earth was an airfield needed so far from civilisation?

The Spy

Heinrich walked along Prinz-Albrecht-Strasse every morning from the small house where he was quartered. He wore unremarkable civilian clothes and carried a briefcase containing the work he'd been given the previous evening, mainly a series of scenarios and fictions that he was required to read and memorise. His days started with a de-briefing, conducted in English, French and Flemish.

The rest of each day consisted of more routine. Heinrich was being converted into an intelligence operative, skilled in unarmed combat, surveillance, sabotage and communication devices. He learned how to codify messages, use knives and handguns, and many ways to kill: silently; with or without a weapon. In a gymnasium, Heinrich was coached to build strength, power and endurance. In a swimming pool, he developed the ability to stay underwater for as long as possible. Some days he was taken out of the city and given tests in which he had to move silently and invisibly through undergrowth. Any noise resulted in a massive reprimand, and a fresh start on the course. Other days would be spent trailing around the city, trying to spot a tail or evade any follower.

As well as making him a lethal weapon in Germany's

future, the organisation also turned Heinrich into a Nazi. That was how the organisation assured compliance with its founding principle, namely the continuous supervision of everyone in Germany to root out the filth that might destabilise or undermine. Heinrich learned who to hate and, basically, it was everyone. The Party, the SS and the SD were his triumvirate masters and assured his obedience with a constant dialogue of bewitching paranoia. Germany was already at war with itself, and he was taught that its enemies sometimes wore smiles of belonging. It was essential to detest and distrust. Otherwise, sentiment would rule, in turn leading to forgiveness. Heinrich was required to banish forgiveness.

However, his training also ensured that his political indoctrination could be contained within an ice-cold sense of logic and cunning. Survival was more important than prejudicial subjectivity, especially since his training was focused on a role in which he would be overseas, remote from the filth.

He was part of *Department III - Ausland SD*.

As the machinery rolled on through annexation, smiles with Britain's foolish leader and the inevitable march on war, Heinrich saw clearly how unstoppable it was and what glory sat on its shoulders. The reoccupation of the Rheinland had proved, if ever proof was needed, that the French and British were craven and weak. They had been submissive at München. Now they were ripe for invasion and destruction.

Heinrich's training changed when he was moved to Section B. It confirmed that he would conduct espionage in the West. There were intensive briefings about the geography of England and Wales. His entire routine was now conducted in English, and a linguistics expert taught him idiomatic elements of the English language as well as regional accents. At a naval base he set sail on a submarine to create familiarity with the cramped quarters. He was released from the submarine via an airlock and learned to surface and assimilate in the cold water. Back in Berlin, he was given an identity and the paperwork needed to become a citizen on that Island, nestled smugly on the periphery of Europe.

His final days in the Fatherland were spent back in the forest at Grunewald, surviving in a wilderness for days on end. By the time that finished, Heinrich was ready. They gave him a few days to relax at a luxurious hotel. But he didn't relax. Not even the woman they sent to provide unknown, carnal pleasures made him forget his mission.

In the darkness and misty murk of a November night, the U-boat surfaced off West Angle Bay. Heinrich boarded the dinghy and, in silence, watched the two Kriegsmarine paddle the craft silently across the calm waters. They left him to wade ashore and, on the beach, Heinrich Brandt found a remote place to bury his wetsuit and the material that had protected his small sack of belongings.

During the middle of the following morning, he stood at a bus stop, still in unremarkable civilian clothes. But now he was Huw Morris, resident of Paradise Row, Pembroke. He walked with a pronounced limp, the legacy of a terrible accident down a mine. When the bus pulled to a halt, he struggled up the steps then took a seat near the front. He watched the clippie come towards him to politely enquire about his destination, Huw held out a crumpled return ticket and his faultless Valleys accent explained he was headed home after visiting his old mam. He smiled endlessly at the conductor as she clipped a second hole in the ticket.

THE POLICE SERGEANT

Dewi Morgan was bored. The life of a police sergeant in this remote place lacked excitement. Not that he wanted gangland killings, or organised thieving, or brutal street violence. They could keep all that in Swansea and Cardiff. But he sometimes wished there was something more wicked to be investigated or stamped upon.

What made the frustration worse was the knowledge that he himself had been involved in some wickedness.

Claire was a doting mother to David Junior. It left her husband feeling ignored and undesired. They shared a bed and occasional, momentary passions. It seemed they both wanted this, but it was clear to Dewi that Claire's willingness was driven by duty, not arousal. His desire was diluted.

By the time David Junior was seven, his father was still a relatively young man and his needs had become unstoppable. The young woman he'd often seen at Porthgain was in his thoughts, especially when he learned that her relationship with that seafaring young man was tenuous. Invigorated, Dewi began a daily trip to the tiny harbour, sometimes in the police car they'd been allocated. Her name was Alwen, and they became lovers. She was nearly half his age but seemed twice the woman Claire had become. There was no romance. This was purely, simply, utterly about sex and their respective needs for as much of it as possible.

But the affair began and ended in one summer. Alwen eventually made the decision that their dalliance was a dead end. She'd enjoyed every moment of what they'd shared, those wild times on the cliff tops above the harbour. Once, she'd made him push his truncheon inside her, then licked it to taunt him. Dewi had laughed and said he loved her. That was when she knew. It could not continue, regardless of how good it made her feel. A married man's love was never true.

A week after she ended it, Dewi returned to Porthgain and they rushed up the path away from the harbour to engage in one final, frantic, spontaneous act of desire. Satiated in equal measure, they knew this wasn't enough. It was over.

Alwen was reunited with her partner, and it meant she could pass off her pregnancy as his work. David Morgan's bastard child was born the following spring.

Unaware of his paternity, and increasingly unconcerned about Alwen's existence, Dewi embroiled himself in the important work of upholding law and order. The town was an occasional destination for holidaymakers, some bringing the potential for misdemeanour or felony. There was also the matter of those twin sisters.

Dewi quite liked Bethan and Megan, whose increasing age hadn't changed them. They'd even managed to obtain a small cart and a pony to draw it. It wasn't possible to call his curiosity an investigation, but he tried to find time to check what they were up to and assess whether dirty work was afoot. Dewi met them at St Justinian when they landed their boat. They happily let him look in the pails. He took their word that they would sell these pebbles for a pittance. They offered to take him over to the island, but he declined. He felt that a small sailing boat could be an unsafe place to share with the twins. When they rode their cart along to Solfach and beyond, Dewi followed at a discreet distance on his bicycle. The only thing that wasn't a mystery about these trips was his knowledge that they gave wool to the Jameses. Back in Tyddewi, he flagged them down and asked about the wool. It was a simple trade, they told him. The farms around Rhosson had surplus. Cissy and Owen's mill needed the wool. Megan and Bethan moved it from supplier to manufacturer. Quite simple, really.

Nothing they did seemed to be in any way wrong or illegal. Yet Dewi could never quite shake the sense that they might be hiding something.

What couldn't be hidden was the sudden change in Claire. After years of cold sexual reticence, she began to show Dewi a new flowering of desire. With David Junior at school, and with hardly any crimes for Dewi to solve or prevent, the couple spent each lunchtime sating this newfound appetite. It was a welcome return to a neglected act. They both desired it, wanted it, used it, discussed it. They agreed it was wonderful and made them happy. They were in or near their forties but felt a spring of youthful vigour.

There was more. There was love. Whatever had been lost was found. Ten years after David Junior's birth, his parents gave him a baby sister. They named her Mary, in honour of King George's Queen. Lizzie and Stephen came to visit with baby Gareth. These were good days, and no amount of war talk could spoil them.

Family life became special again. David Junior was tall and powerful like his father and showed signs of being a fine flanker for the school team. Mary was a healthy baby and grew to be a pretty child with a head full of curls and smiling, happy eyes.

TEN

Today

'He was a bit of a rogue, wasn't he? Suddenly not such an upstanding officer and gentleman, at least not in the traditional meaning. Imagine it: a truncheon up her cunt. And then in her mouth. The dirty bitch. But perhaps I shouldn't be so cruel and condemnatory. The poor woman might be someone's dearly loved, silvery haired great granny by now.'

Erin was grinning at him and reviewing his naked body. 'Are you a rogue, Ben, on the quiet? Have you ever fucked on a remote clifftop? I bet you haven't. Would you like to, though?'

Her manner changed. 'Hold that thought, Ben. You need to stop thinking about sex with me and make yourself calm again. This next bit is terribly sad.'

THE POLICE SERGEANT

Policework remained uneventful.

Then, one day, it was touched by tragedy.

Inside the Police Station they heard the shouts and screams. Dewi and two of his constables rushed into the street. People were pointing down the slope at a receding bus, going too quickly for Dewi's liking. Someone shouted *runaway*. One of the constables was sent to call for support and to bring the car. The other officer and Dewi set off at a sprint. When he saw a group of concerned people gathered around a prone figure on the pavement, Dewi gave a wordless gesture of command to his constable.

Up ahead he saw the bus veering to left and right, then watched in disbelief as it jerked hard to the right before crashing over. It slid along at a slight angle to the roadway with screeches of metal and sparks flashing back towards Dewi. He had nearly caught it, when a final sound of bending metal, and a loud crash, indicated it had come to a halt.

Its engine cut off after a whining diminuendo. The shocked silence was worse than the sounds that had preceded it. All around the scene, people were staring in disbelief and horror. Dewi reached for his whistle, then realised he wasn't in his tunic. He shouted at people to stand back. There were sounds of pain and yells for help from inside the bus. Dewi looked in through the front windscreen. There was a crumpled figure, the driver, lying in the footwell of the passenger doorway. Beyond that he could see the tilted passageway between the rows of seats, and people who'd been thrown on to what was now the floor of the bus when it fell over. Dewi ran around to the rear of the vehicle and looked in through that window. He counted eight people inside, all of whom were moving. He heard a car pull up and moments later Dewi had a plan. With the car parked as close to the bus as possible, Dewi helped Constable Thorburn climb up on to its roof then on to the side of the bus. It meant he could pull open the emergency door and it was clear they needed more help. Dewi shouted to the onlookers to try to find a ladder.

The constable was shouting a commentary. The driver had groaned, so was alive, but he looked in a bad way. The eight people, five women and three men, were all able to stand between the seats with their feet on the inside of the windows. They were staring up at the constable, faces imploring him to get them to safety. One of the men had a badly injured arm. All bar that person said they were able to climb out of the emergency door unaided. The arrival of a ladder meant Dewi was able to climb up then get inside the bus. The two officers told everyone to move towards the emergency door so they could be guided up and out. From outside, the second constable confirmed he had called for ambulances. The same constable also relayed the news that someone was saying it looked like there might be people crushed underneath the bus.

It took a while to get the able-bodied passengers out. Each one eventually reached the safety of the High Street. After some cajoling by Dewi, the man with the injured arm agreed he would also try to climb clear. That took many minutes and by the time he had climbed slowly down the ladder the first ambulance had arrived.

Dewi couldn't take much notice. He'd climbed slowly over the seats towards the middle of the vehicle checking the ground beneath the bus. There were two figures lying down there. They were bloodied and crushed. This must have been why the bus lost control. The driver had been swerving to avoid pedestrians. The bus's slewing momentum caused it to topple over, trapping the two bodies.

He had seen repulsive sights on the Western Front. Headless torsos. Lifeless, limbless souls. Bodies so irredeemably snared by wire they seemed to be sliced by its constraints. Bloated dead, stinking and oozing. The foaming mouths and bloodied eyes of the gassed.

It was nearly twenty years since any of that, and it had hardened him to death and injury. But what he saw under his feet made him vomit. A warm stream of fetid half-digested food gushed out onto the bus window.

Then Dewi told the constable who it was lying smeared beneath the bus. Owen and Cissy James.

Stina was packing away at the shop when the car pulled up outside. The constable climbed out and donned his helmet, an act that lacked enthusiasm. His actions seemed to be in slow motion.

Five minutes later, she knew her parents were dead. The police officer was shaking uncontrollably so she made tea, which didn't really help either of them. Stina's stunned silence was matched by the shudderings this young man was unable to restrain. He thanked her for the tea, and she thanked him for being brave.

As the police car drove away, Stina heard the clip and clop of trotting hooves. When Bethan and Megan enveloped her in their arms, she broke down. Her tears and sobs were uncontrolled. The twins' silent huddle created a receptacle for her grief, and it flooded out to be consumed by those twin souls. Wherever there was space between the three women, the spirits of Ava's love wove their way, expanding and soothing as they travelled. Invisible bonds soon tied them, tightening, squeezing more grief from Stina's being.

The twins encouraged her to lock up and travel with them to the coast. Above one of the beaches, Bethan unharnessed the pony so it could roam with the other horses in the fields. When they reached the sand, Megan built then lit a small fire and they gazed into its flames. As the evening melted into night, they rekindled the fire and it erupted with new sparks and flames. Stina's tears hadn't dried but she found her voice and spoke of her feelings. The twins were all she had now, a link to the mother she'd never known, and to the parents she had known. All loved. All lost. The twins had cared so much that they created a brand-new family. Now Stina's greatest fear was that she would lose these aunts and could never live without them.

They lay together above the tide line, rough blankets under and over them. Sleep came with difficulty, even with the repeating pattern of Ava's tune humming on the air. Morning brought the crashing of waves, angrily battering the rocks and roaring at itself as it ebbed and flowed. Stina had woken first, undressed, and started walking into the water. They saw her standing against the chest-high waves, arms aloft. The swell should have knocked her down. Maybe she wanted that. Three times, as they waded out to rescue their niece, a wave pushed one of the twins onto her back. But Stina stood firm. When they finally reached her, Stina had brought her arms down then folded them. Eyes closed; she started walking further out to sea. It took both twins all their strength to stop and turn Stina around. When they reached the shallows, she collapsed.

What ensued, the days and weeks of grieving misery, made Stina feel that she'd never left that place. Face down in the soft wet sand, her hands clawing at that mix of earth and sea, the contours of her body imprinted. The rushing water, streaming up between her legs and under her arms, was a reunion.

At Cissy and Owen's funeral, Stina held hands with Megan and Bethan. She felt Ava within her. It seemed the whole population, from every surrounding community, had descended on the tiny church of St David at Whitchurch.

When the service was done, the twins took Stina back to Rhosson and on to the ruined chapel of St

Justinian. And there she finally found sleep.

THE SPY

After his arrival in late 1938, Heinrich Brandt had been inactive and had settled well into his role as Huw Morris, the pensioned miner from up near Merthyr. He lived a modest, carefree, tee-total life near the sea and doted on his mam.

It had been an easy part to play.

He knew his time would come.

He'd made Huw a quiet soul, but no one doubted him. It meant he wasn't questioned when he headed back to watch the Scarlets, staying with old friends for a few days either side of the match. Those same friends were his make-believe hosts whenever he travelled.

His activation code had arrived eight days after Britain and France declared war on Germany. That provocation in Poland had worked, as everyone had said it would. And, this time, there would be no mistakes. Heinrich was thrilled by the news and readied himself for action and for victory over these foolish people and all their so-called Allies.

His journeys to Llanelli continued and no one could have imagined that he left the bus or train early to spend time gathering intelligence about the new airfield at Pembrey. Loose talk could be elicited with patience, and Heinrich reported that the base would soon be home to fighter squadrons.

When heightened security was more apparent, Huw's trips were curtailed in favour of observation of Pembroke's military bases. He limped along the roads or sat reading books, listening to whatever he could learn and capturing sights in his memory. During 1940, and on into the early part of 1941, Huw was what he had always been. The kindly ex-miner who'd moved here to be near his ailing mother and to benefit from sea air. Inside that shell, a malevolent cuckoo was itching to take over.

During the Spring of 1941, Huw's landlord arrived with an instruction for Heinrich. He was told to make it known his mother had taken a turn for the worse and he would be going to Angle to share whatever time she had left. During the following days, Huw bade farewell to neighbours whose concern for him and his mam was heartfelt and sad.

With a small suitcase of innocent belongings, Huw limped to the bus station and boarded a bus to Haverfordwest where he alighted to await the connection to St Davids. Another return ticket was clipped and, when the conductor asked Huw why he was headed to the coast, he pointed to the sign on the partition behind the driver saying, *Careless Talk Costs Lives.*

Back in Pembroke, all trace of Huw Morris was eradicated. The assortment of tools he had used was locked in a trunk which was stowed, neatly and innocently, under a shelf in the scullery. The landlord locked up and walked to the train station. In the gentlemen's toilets, he dropped the keys to 14 Paradise Row into one of the cisterns. Eventually, a train arrived and took him east.

Heinrich left his second bus and walked up Prendergast to number 41. He looked down the tiny street before opening the front door of his new home. This sly, furtive survey revealed no one in either direction. If someone had been out walking, he would have hailed them and stopped to chat. With his routine of checks complete, he let himself in and prepared for the next day's inevitable inquisition from his new neighbours. It wasn't hard to spin the same yarn. His limp and his convincing accent were more than enough. He was too badly injured to be of use to the armed forces, so Huw had fled from Wales's industrial heartland. Here, down by the sea, he'd be able to live out his days in relative peace.

One evening in the Autumn of 1941, Huw sat in the King George Inn listening to the locals. What he heard confirmed the reasons for his instruction to move here. Construction would begin next year on a new RAF airfield, bisecting the land between Whitchurch and Caerfarchell.

In the immediate aftermath of her parents' deaths, Stina found it impossible to consider any notion of work. Going on, continuing with Cissy and Owen's business, seemed impossible.

But she had to work, and, in the end, she made a fine job of keeping the Wool Merchant's shop running.

The mill's owner wasn't patient and soon demanded she hand over its operations to new managers. It simply could not stand idle, tragic though the circumstances had been.

Stina reached agreement with the new couple running the mill that she would work there for nothing, and this would be part payment for their continued supply to her business. She also agreed to sell other products from the mill, such as small rugs and bedding.

She made just enough money to pay the rent and continue to live in Cissy and Owen's house. She couldn't bear the idea of leaving, so her ability to stay was comforting and, ultimately, healing.

But it was sometimes lonely. Mother, father and daughter had seemed to fill every space in the house. Now, sometimes, being there alone made her feel that she was like the last coin in a money box: of value; but making all the noise. The lack of company was oppressive, and the memories of a happy childhood and strong parental bonds were sometimes impossible to bear. It made Stina sad beyond words. Yet she knew this was the right place for her to live and, thanks to its silent remoteness, Stina grew to love it as a safe haven.

Megan and Bethan came to stay with her once a week. Their status as aunts had shifted so they were more like nannas whose presence banished Stina's loneliness. They had happy, fun-filled evenings whenever they stayed.

At first, Stina resisted their teasing prompts to find a man. It seemed so unlike them: they had always told her to distrust men and feel no pressure to be with one. Stina tended to win their friendly arguments by pointing out that not many young or eligible men were to be found these days.

But news of the plans for a new airfield filtered into the discussions. Some parts of it would be so close to her home that she'd be able to walk along the lane to its perimeter fence in ten minutes. It would be much less across the fields. Megan and Bethan said that any number of eligible young men would soon be in her clutches. One of them was certain to be perfect.

George Cottam climbed from the front passenger seat with a smile of thanks to the driver. The trip had been enjoyable. As well as the pretty coastal scenery and countryside, the two men had enjoyed lively exchanges about life in the north of England. George rarely met fellow Lancastrians, so it was a treat to hear those wonderful vowel sounds. They agreed to meet when this lot was over.

He looked around St Davids and quite liked its sunlit visage. The smell of the sea occasionally filled his nostrils. George liked that. In front of him, the police station seemed solid and reliable. With a quick check of his watch, he noted that it was twenty-six minutes past two, and he was slightly early. Nonetheless, he donned his Military Police cap, picked up his bag then walked briskly into the building.

Dewi Morgan quite liked the look of this new arrival. The Oxford blue on his cap and two stripes on his arm were borne with a pleasing military gravitas. He was probably between five and ten years younger than Dewi, so he'd probably been in the last lot. Lance Corporal Cottam of the Military Police (Vulnerable Points Wing) seemed like someone to be relied on now things were hotting up here in Tyddewi.

After a salute, a formal exchange of greetings and confirmation of identity, George stood easy then followed Dewi into the small office. He too had been impressed by Police Sergeant Morgan who, for his age, was a powerful, fit looking man. George recognised the signs behind the eyes; the knowing look, still flickering deep inside, of a fellow Great War infantryman; the unyielding respect for the uniform; the silent antipathy of a killer. How ridiculous that neither of them could still serve. They could be and do so much good for their country.

Once George had given his summary related to the new RAF airfield, and his role liaising with the local police, he handed over an envelope addressed to *Police Sergeant D. Morgan, Pembrokeshire Constabulary*. Dewi noted, with increasing respect, that Lance Corporal Cottam's verbal précis of what was written in the letter had been concise and accurate. Dewi had been anxious about the need to host a Military Policeman, but now felt these next few days would be a pleasure.

After dropping George's kit bag at the police house, the two men headed out towards the airfield's proposed site. The way Sergeant Morgan referred to places by their Welsh names amused George. He couldn't imagine how you spelled the word, but it sounded like Treegoyz. As they drove east along a lane that would effectively be on the southern border of the airfield, Dewi spoke of the low crime rate in the area and how there were unlikely to be problems with the locals; they kept themselves to themselves.

George didn't doubt it. Since leaving the town, they'd not seen a soul. He knew the locals wouldn't cause difficulties. It was the influx of personnel to the area, to construct the site, to enable its logistics and then, ultimately, to make it operational that would be the problem. That's why he was here. To work with the local bobbies so they kept the populace under control, leaving George and the MPs to control any incoming miscreants amongst the fliers, their ground crews and, especially, the RAF Regiment. Fancied themselves a little too much, that shower.

This initial trip was reconnaissance, enabling a report up the ranks before construction started. While they drove, Dewi established George's regiment and battle honours. They'd come close to being in the same theatre near the end, and the Loyal North Lancashires had a reputation to be admired. Fighters as good as any in the British Army. Yet George seemed envious of Dewi's time on the front line. Perhaps he resented it? Dewi made a mental note to find Kirkham on a map. He vaguely knew where Blackpool is, and George had mentioned it was near there.

George asked Dewi to stop so they could stretch their legs. All around them was undergrowth but Dewi pointed his hand to indicate the locations of a small hamlet, a river valley and a woollen mill. The coast was no more than a mile to the south. George took out his map and identified these places. He took out a pencil and lightly sketched an approximate location of the runways planned for the airfield. It would need to be rubbed out back at the station, George explained; and Dewi agreed. This was secret, and therefore privileged. Neither of them could be careless. The triangle looked, to Dewi, like a strange letter A.

On reflection, Dewi felt a nagging concern about this. George shouldn't have drawn that symbol on the map. Dewi would insist the Lance Corporal did erase it after they returned to base.

Back in the car, Dewi drove on to a place so small George couldn't believe it had a church. They turned into a lane that fell and wound then rose gently into another tiny place. A horse and cart, small and still, stood outside a house opposite a grassed area. Two older women stood talking to a younger woman outside what looked like it might be a shop. Dewi asked George if he'd like to meet some locals, but he declined. Then he cast a lingering glance at the dark-haired young woman.

Thomas Harty spent his last weekend with the family in London. He was leaving, potentially for weeks. He'd volunteered to join the RAF and they'd accepted him, but not as a flier. His eyesight was weak so there was no question of him flying ops. Instead, he was recruited as ground crew. Thomas wanted combat but would be unable to fight. Not in a meaningful way.

This exclusion frustrated him, but he learned to live with the disappointment. His part in the battle would still be important. He would make those aeroplanes ready and safe, and he learned to speak of it with pride. And in so doing, he calmed his upset about being just an erk.

He was ready for war and would soon be at training base. Then he would travel to join a squadron up North: he wasn't allowed to say it was in Yorkshire.

This news was the final straw in Jennifer Harty's dismay about her son's decision. It made her question what benefit could possibly be gained from having aeroplanes up there. Everyone knew that, any time soon, the capital would get pulverised by the Germans. Why wasn't every single plane, tank and gun down in the south; protecting their city; its vital artery of trade; and its people?

Thomas deflected his mother's worries with his unflinching certainty. Every city, town and village in the kingdom needed protection. At every airfield, port and barracks there would be people like him who, regardless of rank, would play a part in defending the nation.

Jennifer remained unhappy. In the days and weeks before his departure, there was a reproachful, bewildered, protracted farewell. Thomas's parents and siblings exuded no pride in his mission. He could have stayed here with family, friends and workmates. A community at the heart of their mighty city. What he'd chosen wasn't bravery or honourable. It was a kind of cowardice: turning his back on home, in its hour of need.

These things, feelings and expressions, didn't come in a flood. Instead, the household engaged in a steady drip of grievance. Whispered, shouted, embittered words didn't deter Thomas. Nor did they set him against his family.

On the day he set out for the muster station in central London, there was a relenting, reluctant truce. It was a working day for them all, so no one could join him on his journey into the city. But like a real family, and as a family, Joseph, Jennifer, James and Peter Harty stood in the street and hugged Thomas. They all kissed him too. The men clapped him on the back. His mum stroked his hair and face and neck. Their boy, the baby of the family, was going to make war on the Nazis. As he walked away down Malabar Street, voices spoke words of encouragement from windows. People came out to shake his hand. Thomas left the street and soon reached the bus stop. The bus took him away, gazing out on the sprawl of docks to his right, and a rushing, simmering Old Father Thames to his left.

It took several buses, and more time than he could ever have wanted, to reach the building near Waterloo station. A process, some instructions and a transfer of papers took place. Then, in a group of fifteen, Thomas was escorted to the expanse of platforms and on to a train bound for Hook, the nearest station to his training base.

With the dirty old river still winking at him as the train steamed away past The Oval and Battersea Power

Station, Thomas realised this was a London he didn't know and had never known. His life and family were back there at the docks. That was his London. Ships. Cargoes. Tides. Market stalls. Football. Millwall. It had taken a war to move him between the zones in his city. It seemed so ridiculous. Would he have been welded to E14 forever? Had Hitler and his rabid bastards actually freed him?

The train gathered a bit more speed, and it seemed no time until London, whichever version of it that he knew, was gone. The factories, workshops, businesses and streets became fields, interspersed by the stations for places that might as well have been on the moon.

His training went well. Thomas was adept with the machines he would use and the processes in which he and those machines would be deployed. Then he travelled north to join the squadron and was soon supporting bombing missions. Quickly gaining promotion, he led a team, then another so he was effectively second in command of the squadron's ground crew personnel. Like many of his fellows, he heard the news about the Blitz and sometimes struggled to get news about loved ones. London was burning, and his family lived by the river. But he learned from his mates, and all the personnel stationed on the base, that many cities were also a target for the Luftwaffe. This united them as a team and as combatants.

The squadron switched to Coastal Command and moved to a new airfield in Cornwall. Thomas didn't move with them. Instead, he was flown to RAF Pembrey in South Wales and then driven to St Davids where a new airfield was about to be built.

With other ground crew from squadrons in Coastal Command, Thomas would be instructing and liaising with the workforce constructing the runways and buildings. Their mission simply to ensure fitness for purpose.

ELEVEN

ENSEMBLE

During the early part of January 1942, Dewi Morgan set out into the chilly midday air to walk a beat around his manor. As he strode up the High Street, out of the town, the bus from Hwlffordd crawled past in the opposite direction and he noted the passengers on board. Ever since that terrible accident, Dewi had stopped to watch the buses if he saw them. He hoped maybe he could <u>will</u> them not to become runaways and, on this occasion, his will did its job.

Satisfied, he walked on to the town's boundary. It wasn't possible to see it; not quite. But he knew that, just under two miles away, work had started to prepare the ground for the construction of RAF St Davids.

Huw Morris alighted from the bus and limped the short distance past the cross and on to the pub where he could watch the activity in the High Street and listen to the voices around him. He enjoyed these visits to the town. It had a pleasing charm and, even though it was an enemy stronghold, his German alter ego admired its pretty simplicity and the understated nobility of its cathedral. Huw had seen the two old women several times in the last few months and always wondered what purpose they served. Today, their cart and its tiny horse came up from Goat Street into the square and, for the first time, Huw realised that their purpose might be to bring something beautiful into everyone's lives. The slender, dark haired young woman sitting alongside one of the old crones, chatting amiably it seemed, was a sight for the sorest eyes.

Megan reined in the horse as they drew up the small slope alongside the cross. It was a default for them to stop here and spend a while in the square, either seated on their cart or on the steps that held the monument. It was quite busy, so Megan said she would wait with the cart while Bethan and Stina took some time to touch the cross's stonework.

In the small memorial garden below the monument, some young, uniformed men were standing silent, hats off in respectful commemoration. The two women went and sat with their backs to the cross, and Stina could see the young men in their blue uniforms.

Dewi found all was quiet. In the distance he could hear the low putter of a motorcycle engine and knew it would be one of the Military Police returning to his digs after a morning at the construction site.

Thomas Harty and his three peers had enjoyed a half of watery weak wartime beer in the Farmer's Arms. It was their first day on leave since the new year and they'd agreed to spend time in the town. Then it would be the walk back to the bivouac at the construction site for another night of discomfort. This detached duty made some sense, when written in standing orders. But its practical uses were lost on the four men. Their squadrons were up there in the skies, killing Germans, defending the island, at whatever cost. Checking the work done with fuel dumps and storage depots and building positions was something others could have done. Like the blue-capped MPs who strutted around with their sticks, apparently knowing everything about nothing.

George Cottam climbed stiffly out of the motorcycle sidecar and took out his cap, briefcase and cane. These contraptions were horrendous, and just two miles in that tube, with its noisy, rattling hardness, were enough to send his spine and hips into spasms of discomfort. The local police had made a tied house available for him and his fellow officers and he would soon be comfortable inside. More comfort than he'd known at any time since leaving home to join the Regiment twenty years ago. The door opened and his colleague, Corporal Lewis, emerged. They exchanged a short sit rep about activity at the site, then Lewis squeezed down into the side car and left. George looked up and down the road and decided he needed to stretch his legs, get some air and perhaps a look at the old Cathedral and its neighbouring Bishop's Palace while it was still light. He walked into the High Street, emerging at the southern edge of the War Memorial where he saw the four erks.

Dewi had seen nothing of note. The town seemed quite busy but that's how it could be. As he walked up the hill back to the station, he stopped to speak with one of the old twins and noticed the other one at the cross with Stina James. Dewi admired Stina. She'd coped so well with the death of her parents. Looking at her now, he saw how confident she seemed even just sat there with her back to the old cross. He had never understood her connection with the twins, but he categorically knew that it was a powerful, unbreakable bond. Dewi's brief discussion with Megan was how it always seemed to be. Light, filled with a kind of fun. Yet strangely unfulfilling.

It was Heinrich Brandt's eyes that squinted in troubled distaste at the four RAF uniforms. He vaguely approved of their act of remembrance, but their presence meant something he needed to log and report. He drank the watery, warm flat British beer and wondered if he could stand the remaining few centilitres. It was not beer. This was brown ink. Something made him want to be outside, hearing their discussions and perhaps getting closer to the beautiful young woman sitting facing him from the cross. Then something caught his eye, away to his right. There was the strange one. Military Police, they were called – and more specifically, this one was called George. That most English of names. From their German King's ancestry. He nearly spluttered into his glass. Heinrich told himself to be disciplined. There was no question he could go out there now. So, he watched. And he saw the most embittered expression imaginable on the face of the English King's namesake. This was pure gold. A motherlode. That Military Policeman simply hated those four blue-clad fliers. Huw asked for another pint.

Stina watched the four RAF men and envied their simple emotions as they reflected on Tyddewi's war dead. If only they knew that her mother had no memorial. Probably, by now, the loss of SS Strathnairn's brave sailors was commemorated somewhere, and rightly. Yet Ava was not. She had been a stowaway, thus a non-person. She was other. Her life had been erased by an act of war. Her death had been erased from any memorial, except the one in the minds of Stina, Megan and Bethan. She felt these four young men wouldn't understand it. Perhaps one day she might be able to explain it to them. In fact, to that one. Second from the left. He was tall, but thick set. His spectacles set him aside. They lent a kind of beauty. He was weak. But perhaps the strongest of them all.

George put on his cap and regretted leaving his cane at the house. Those four should definitely not be here, but his dilemma was considerable. Any open display of discipline by him while they were honouring war dead was clearly improper. Yet George wanted them out of the town and back to the camp. This was *his* place. And he also wanted them away from the lovely Stina. He was captivated by her. Those legs beneath her habitual long skirt. The twin bulge of her breasts under her cardigan. Her broad shoulders, slender neck and beautiful face. That mass of tumbling black hair, sometimes loose, sometimes arranged. And her eyes. That dark purple magnificence. He'd tapped up Sergeant Morgan for some basic details and learned Stina was well respected for her business sense. No one understood why she was single. But sorrow was deemed the likely cause. George decided on a softly-softly approach. He'd go and talk to the lads. For they were only lads.

Megan listened to Dewi Morgan and smiled at his efforts to be an authority. But something was flickering across the air between the twins, and it made her more interested in the goings on to her right.

Look at Stina, was the first flicker. Look at how she is besotted by that blue-clad warrior, broad and bespectacled. He might be the one. The Lover.

Don't ignore The Police Sergeant. That was Beth's next surge of knowledge. He isn't stupid. Be careful.

Third – this one, here to my right in his puffed-up khaki attire topped with that strange blue hat. Like a power-crazed hydrangea. But poisonous too. The Lance Corporal. Beware, my sister. Beware, everyone.

Finally, if you can, without drawing attention. Look behind you. Him again. The miner from Prendergast. He is not what he seems. There is ice-cold, fanatical hatred within him. Can you see? He combines this with calm, unyielding determination in his movements and scouting. Like a spy. The way he checks his surroundings is terrifying. That limp isn't real.

We should go.

Megan saw Bethan touch Stina's arm, then they both stood and descended their steps.

Heinrich stood on the pavement below the memorial garden and was glad of the unsolicited discussion with a stranger. He loved this. People said hello, how are you? And they meant it. His training enabled him to chaff with the man, while tuning in to the scene beyond. The Military Policeman had joined the four RAF men and addressed each of them by their names. Henrich's face registered distaste when he heard the name Harty. His interlocutor didn't notice and carried on with his review of the scandal they all faced about reduced bus services. So: one of them is a Jew; Harty; a Jewish name. That would require both care and attention. Heinrich would need to rein in his need to snarl with loathing at this Harty. He must not get side-tracked by those needs to do harm. Now he noticed the fräulein and her hideous old escort were preparing to leave. It troubled Heinrich that he couldn't follow them, but the cart would whisk them away. He could ask for a lift, at least part of the way. His next few paces involved an especially painful looking series of limps.

Dewi bade a cheerful goodbye to the twins and made a vow to find a way to recognise which was which. After all these years policing the streets and lanes, he still couldn't tell Megan from Bethan. He suspected they played on that by never using their names in his earshot. And he compounded it by never insisting they confirm the right names, ideally with some sort of documents to prove it. That miner, Huw, was limping painfully up the slope after his pint and a natter with old Gwyn Major. Huw seemed a kindly type, with time to talk and listen. And here he was now, giving Dewi a hearty greeting and asking after his family, his Valleys accent guttural and smoky. His bus would come along soon. Dewi called out to the three women on their cart. Maybe they could take Huw?

George had engaged with the four erks who were deferential but vaguely insolent. As they explained that they would be walking back to the site shortly, George looked through them at Stina whose eyes were locked on Harty, even as he stood with his back to her. What could she possible see in him? His cocky cockney demeanour should put anyone off, especially someone as lovely as her. George was glad when one of the old hags took her away, but his elation was brief for she cast a lingering glance back towards Harty who had turned to watch her. Perhaps he smiled back at her, for Stina's face, and especially her eyes, lit up with pleasure. George's softly-softly approach didn't last any longer.

Thomas Harty was astonished by the sudden abusive manner of the MP. He'd been mildly authoritative, but friendly in his way. An off-duty enforcer, casting an eye and lending an ear. Quite happily answering their questions about his home, family and brief life in the trenches. It wasn't fun, but nor was it discipline. The eruption of rage in Cottam's eyes was violent and ghastly, caused by some deep-rooted problem that Thomas might never understand or know. The anger and spitting orders to stand to attention and get back to the site appeared to be for all four of them but Thomas sensed he was the primary target. He saw hate in Cottam's whole demeanour.

Dewi saw it too, but it was a military matter. Even if things turned nasty, he couldn't intervene, regardless of it being in his jurisdiction.

Stina saw it too. What a vile little man the Lance

Corporal must be. So coarse. She saw how the young men stood formally upright as this unilateral dispute took its course. She saw no respect, and, on the face of her favourite, she saw contempt. Good for you, my perfect young soul.

Heinrich saw it too, but it was Huw that commented on it to Bethan as they made ready to leave the square. She was sitting with him in the cart and his chuckling remark about that crazed bluecap made her turn to look at the scene. Heinrich's eyes squinted into slits. So, the Military Policeman hates the Jew, too. And it was because of this beauty seated to his left, holding the reins and occasionally making encouraging noises and saying simple words to the pony. Later, when they dropped him at Middle Mill, to walk the last few hundred metres of his journey home, Huw bade them Noswaith Dda before Heinrich walked away. His head was full of plots and intrigue.

George marched the four erks up to the edge of St Davids then told them to head straight back to the site and report to Corporal Lewis on arrival. He didn't regret his outburst, and the looks of shock from those four wet-behind-the-ears young fools had proved he was right to assert himself. The reason for doing it was wrong, but it had done its job. He stood, almost to attention, and watched them till they were out of sight. It was growing dark when he turned back into the town. As he passed the police station, he heard a familiar voice call his name. If you're off duty, it said, perhaps we can have a pint?

Thomas couldn't stop thinking about the woman. He guessed she was older than him, but not by much. The look she'd given him as she walked away had made him smitten. He'd been unable to stop himself smiling at her and felt a surge of something rushing from his smiling lips, down through his throat and the pit of his stomach to end up pulsing down between his legs and into his thighs. He wanted her. He needed to find a way to be alone with her.

Stina said Nos Da to the twins before handing the reins to Megan and jumping down from the cart. As they always had, Megan and Bethan held their cart steady until they saw her bring the oil lamp to the window to wave that all was well. The sound of Dylan's shoes clipping and clopping away lulled her into a fantasy about the young man in his blue uniform. She had rarely considered beauty in any context. But he was beautiful, and she found herself smiling as she lay down with time to spare before sleep.

Dewi didn't doubt that Lance Corporal Cottam was slightly out of control. There was a curious madness in him and the scene in the square was not the first time he'd seen it. As they walked down the High Street to the pub, Dewi spoke of inconsequentials, but he wanted to understand whether he needed to intercede. Not directly with Lance Corporal Cottam. More likely via his own senior officer. To suggest that something might need to be done. As they stood drinking, Dewi could see things had calmed down behind Cottam's eyes and in the mannerisms of his gestures and the tone of his words. Maybe it wasn't Dewi's business to do or say anything.

Megan and Bethan saw the two policemen, one civil, one combatant as they walked the last few paces into that twilight alehouse. The twins exchanged a glance but remained silent until Dylan had pulled them up out of the valley and begun the last leg along to Rhosson. Then they spoke of that troublesome coalition of law and order. No good could come of it. Their man - Morgan - seemed all right, despite his uniform and prying. That other one, in his blue cap and preposterously polished boots, was rotten.

Huw Morris let himself in and locked up. He was home and done for the night. Twenty minutes later, he extinguished the lights and, after another ten minutes, left the house. Clad in dark attire, Heinrich prowled, with feline fluidity, into the wooded area above the lane. At his destination, after sitting in silent stillness for fifteen minutes, he slid out the small transmitter and tapped a short message to report on his latest intelligence and to request approval for a proposal.

TWELVE

Stina & Thomas

After that encounter in the town, it had taken Thomas a matter of days to learn that Stina travelled twice weekly into St Davids to trade with her customers and suppliers. It meant that Thomas was able to ensure he was there to coincide with one of her visits. They talked and smiled and talked some more. The young women he'd encountered back home were sometimes coy and difficult to know. Stina was uncomplicated, direct and quite publicly tactile. They walked back along the lanes, past the increasingly busy construction site and on to her home in the place he couldn't pronounce.

After their next meeting, their walk home took a new path. A short distance outside Caerfarchell, Thomas pulled her to a halt, and she turned to face him. He thought she might resist, but before he could suggest what was in his mind, Stina kissed him. They stood in a gathering dusk and enveloped each other in sensuality. Their mouths were pressed in harmony, their hands explored and, in so doing, discovered how things feel when you touch someone in the places they need you to touch them. Hard things. Soft things. Wet things.

The only words they spoke were confessions. This was new to them. They knew neither what to do next nor what skills might be needed to succeed together. Touch, for now, was the one thing they could do with certainty.

This debut of intimacy was over too quickly. There was a reality in which Thomas could stay no longer and Stina needed to finish some last-minute tailoring.

Come back tomorrow, she said.

I can't wait, he said.

Thomas had known he would end up alone with Stina. Now, here she was. Naked, her eyes hypnotising him. Earlier, when Thomas arrived at her house, Stina had made a pot of tea for them to share. She asked if he was given nice food and, when he told her it was terrible, she took out and gave him some ewes' milk cheese and a piece of bread. Thomas said he'd only eat it if she joined him, so they shared a first meal together and she taught him how to say Caerfarchell. When they finished the bread and cheese, Stina brought some small flat disks to the table and said he should try a Welsh cake. She'd got them from her grandmothers. Then she explained that Bethan and Megan weren't really her grandmothers, but were a special part of her life, and had been since she was born, all through her childhood and forever. Thomas watched Stina telling him these things and felt like he was party to a secret; a grand tale; imaginative and evocative; peerless. When night started to fall, she'd taken his hand and led him up to her bedroom and they'd undressed without ceremony.

Tell me what to do, he said.

We will find out together, she said.

Thomas left at first light and walked across the fields to the site. He had reckoned on no one having missed him, and he reckoned right. Stina got up with him. There was no heartfelt farewell. She told him to come back that evening. They would keep finding out what to do.

⚔

Megan and Bethan set out across the bay to the

island despite the choppy waters and a gloomy, chilly day. The wind was ripping down from the north west, so they took the longer route around the south of the island. As usual they travelled in silence, but they sensed something; knew something. It was unclear and unusual, but their sense of it was mutual and real.

The weather closed in. It was too stormy for them to land. They had to go back with nothing.

As they turned to sail around the north of the island, the winds caught their sail and blew the little boat fast across the waves. Low cloud and driving rain, together with the spray from the crests of waves, made it almost impossible to see the mainland, just a few hundred yards away.

The twins felt no danger. But they sensed the intangible once more. The mist blowing around them was opaque and Megan struggled to keep their course straight. When they landed at the lifeboat slipway, on the meagre sands below Justinian's chapel, a tiny line of white light appeared, tracing the cliff tops above them.

Now they understood what they had sensed. There would be another daughter soon.

The white line scanned down the walls of rock, flickering as it moved across the pitted surfaces, glinting off the rails for the lifeboat station. It reached sea level then passed under the twins' feet before submerging in the shallows, turning the water many shades of blue, grey and purple that faded to darkness once the line was fully submerged.

Soaked to the skin, the twins secured their boat and trudged up the steps to the cliff top. Their bones, aged and weakening, seemed to ache and crippling pains pulsed through them. But Megan and Bethan had thanks to give and stopped briefly at the chapel to give thanks to the Saint.

George Cottam watched the tiny car pull up. It seemed almost impossible that Police Sergeant Morgan could fit inside it. It was as if parts of him needed to be folded so he could get in and out of the vehicle. Once clear of the car, Dewi stretched ostentatiously before walking to salute, then shake hands with George.

Construction of the airfield was in full swing. Beyond the gates where Lance Corporal Cottam greeted him, Dewi could see buildings and, to his right, a strip of patchwork asphalt.

They briefly discussed the work they were about to do. Still not on first name terms, the two men nonetheless asked after the wellbeing of their wives and children.

But they needed to get things done. They'd agreed to start in Middle Mill and squeezed into the police car. Soon they were knocking on randomly selected doors, delivering short speeches to the good people living in communities near the airfield. A series of unsmiling warnings was concluded with a stark threat about the consequences of non-compliance.

Heinrich had walked across the fields from his house, unencumbered by the need to deploy Huw's limp. When he got to the stone wall bordering the church, he knelt and watched. After fifteen minutes, no one entered or left the church. No mourners came to lay flowers or bow their heads in memoriam. He vaulted the wall and stole across the ground towards the far end of the church. Another wait, in which he rested on his haunches behind a gravestone as a car drove along the road. Moments later, Heinrich reached the hedge bordering the western edge of the church grounds. Another crouching survey, then he scurried on.

It was dry but overcast, with that customary chilly wind. This was the most risk Heinrich had taken since being activated and all his defensive instincts were heightened. He had a cover story, should he be seen, but hoped he wouldn't need to explain he was here to search for an old friend's grave.

He squatted down, took out his field glass to scan the terrain to the north and west of his position and soon located the airfield's newly constructed gatehouse, with its sentry boxes and barrier.

There were the two police: the big one; and the weasel. Best of friends, or so it seemed.

Heinrich watched the ridiculous car approaching, many times more gigantic in his field glass, then lay flat until it passed. Back on his haunches, he refocused the lens on the apparently ceaseless work on that damnable enemy airfield.

Thomas and Stina lay in each other's arms as the clock ticked on past one o'clock. They'd been together in her bed so often now that in just two weeks they'd helped each other learn more and more about what to do. They were some way from being experts, but this was no longer the uncertain activity of novices.

They both knew that what they did, the tactile things, the searching lips and tongues, the lurching grabs of intense need, and all the kisses wherever they took place was beautiful. This wasn't a mucky, end of evening affair in some field or alley. The kind they'd heard others boast of. Stina loved Thomas. Thomas loved Stina. It should never have happened to two strangers, cast together thanks to a wartime posting.

Heinrich's next errand from Prendergast saw him set off before dawn and track carefully up the riverbanks, then across fields to the eastern edge of Caerfarchell.

The tiny village, with its oddly scattered collection of dwellings, was of moderate interest because of its proximity to the airfield. He sensed this could be important once the British had planes flying there and his proposed mission had been approved. He was well hidden and waited in the undergrowth. From here he could scrutinise many of the houses, the lane running through the village and perhaps catch sight of the fräulein and her endlessly long legs. Heinrich was smitten when he saw her greeting a customer with smiles that were soon reciprocated. But his pleasure was quashed when he arrived: that bespectacled man in the RAF uniform. That Jew. Harty. She greeted him with a lover's smile; he seemed polite and restrained. But thanks to Heinrich's field glass he soon saw them at an upstairs window. It was the briefest glimpse.

His training almost cracked. That internal voice dictating orders, demanding restraint and patience, requiring logical, calculating ruthlessness was silent. But Heinrich's discipline prevailed. He set aside his jealous rancour and slipped away from his post to check other vistas in and around this strangely named place.

Thomas opened the door to leave. They stood apart and Stina's grip on his hand slipped away. They tried never to be seen publicly, especially here at her home.

As they climbed from the police car, both Dewi and George saw the emotional intent of that slowly dwindling touch. George immediately donned his cap and told Thomas to come to attention. Then at Dewi's suggestion, the two military men moved several yards down the lane for one to receive the other's admonishment. Thomas was off duty but was not supposed to be fraternising with civvies. He was told to stand to attention again.

George marched, left-right-left-right-left-right, back to the whore's house. And in the hob-nailed clamour of his steps he realised this explained everything. Harty's cocky manner and brevity. He was getting his share, perhaps the only share of this bitch's cunt and George hated both of them. She would need to be taught a lesson and he intended to give it to her, over and above the scripted lecture they were supposed to deliver about the perils of loose talk and wariness of strangers. Loose talk. Loose morals. Loose drawers. What more could be expected from this cockney shit and that woman? Nearly thirty and no husband; the filthy slut. George spun round to see Harty sneaking a glimpse back at his whore and he barked at him to get his eyes front, or he'd be on another charge, this time for insubordination.

Dewi hadn't seen this for a while, but there it was again. The loss of control over nothing. Except perhaps this wasn't quite nothing. It was because of this young woman and her madding eyes, and shapely frame. Jealousy's gripping compulsion, with its green eyes and sly face. Dewi understood the lure of a younger woman. It had once been his own brief joy to share those times with Alwen. Comforting, in its way. A time to exhale, then breathe in new pleasures, wrapped in the certainty of having no commitment. It had been necessary and helped Dewi and Claire regain stimulus for their own pleasures and needs. Dewi understood Lance Corporal Cottam's obsessions but saw them as impulsive and greedy. George always spoke with great fondness for his wife and son, back there in Lancashire. It seemed peculiar and complicated that he should consider replacing that with an impossible wish for someone so young and unattainable.

Dewi kept things simple and explained to George that he'd told Miss James why they were here. Now, perhaps, it was time to take Mr Harty back to the airfield. They could revisit the hamlet another day to do more houses.

Stina watched these two men, both saturated by the authority of their respective uniforms, neither able to shake off the faded glory they'd once been part of. The way the khaki one had screamed at her lover wasn't frightening. It was a fop, a gesture of futile power. He didn't own Thomas. All he owned was his little cane, and that blue banded cap. She knew the other one better, in his blue/black uniform. Morgan, the man from Abergwaun, too big for the black carriage that bore him hither and thither. He played fair, but something in his soul was unwholesome.

They had incarcerated her lover in that carriage. As it crawled away, Thomas looked back at Stina through the glass of his cage, his eyes framed by those spectacles. That defiant wink told Stina he would be back.

In the silence of their short journey to the gatehouse,

three men reflected privately about Stina James. Two of them considered her unnerving dark purple eyes and her habit of speaking carefully and succinctly.

One of them smiled at all he knew of her, and she of him.

Dewi had known her since moving here more than fifteen years ago, but now he wondered if Stina was somehow tainted by those two old sisters: a cause for his attention; a potential felon. Had he missed something all these years? Was Stina James crooked? Could he have taken advantage somehow?

Thomas was still smiling as the car drew to a halt at the airfield's entrance but needed to suppress those gleeful signs as Cottam hauled him from the back seat.

George bade Dewi an abrupt, icy farewell and rapped on the car's roof with his cane to instruct its departure. Glaring in through the lenses of Harty's spectacles he saw mutinous layers; contempt; dislike; defiance. Deeper still, he saw something lurking; Harty's desire for the James woman. George felt a surge of lascivious voyeurism. Through Thomas's tender passion for his lover, Lance Corporal Cottam captured an image of a woman to be used, hurt and oppressed.

Megan needed nothing more than a glance at Stina to confirm it. Twenty-seven years after Ava's fateful encounters there would be a new chapter in her tale. Bethan saw it too. These were reminders, not revelations. Those moments on the stormy waters off St Justinian had been the testimony.

Sitting peacefully together in the cathedral close, Stina and Thomas were happy, oblivious to the scandalised chattering that had seared through the community since her pregnancy became known and was unconcealed. Word travelled around the lanes and roads, pulsing into and out from the beating heart of the town. The conversation often centred on poor Cissy and Owen: their memory shamed by this terrible godless act; a daughter, for so long their pride and joy, now making bastards to fester amongst them. To make matters worse, the father was from England.

How could she? And so brazen! How dare they walk arm in arm near this most sacred cathedral?

The young lovers, now parents to be, kept on learning what they needed to know. Nothing else mattered.

The warm sunshine was the perfect excuse to grab time resting here, under the ancient gaze of the window arches and pinnacles of the cathedral's south transept. Thomas had a morning off-duty and Stina some deliveries to fulfil. It was a regular treat to share these moments together. They both loved every moment.

As the twins strolled past and greeted them, they talked awhile then realised why they'd seen so little of Stina in recent weeks. Her distraction was total. They didn't linger but Megan handed Stina a tightly tied paper package. Stina carefully opened the wrapping to find a small crystalline figure. It was a spiral goddess, cut from rose quartz.

Their stolen time was finite; it always was. Thomas was needed as a cog in the war machine and Stina had stitches to sew. They walked together back to the Wool Merchant's House and kissed when they parted. Within just fifteen minutes, they were working hard in their respective jobs.

RAF St Davids was coming to life, also creating chatter in a community that grumbled about the iniquities of all the disruption it caused. As the main construction effort tailed away to one of routine maintenance and occasional minor building works, military vehicles sometimes toured the area. A small detachment of RAF Regiment personnel arrived to take up residence. Their role, to provide security for and defence of the airfield from either air or ground attack, saw gun posts set up to complement the concertina wire stretched along the airfield perimeter.

Light aircraft started to make occasional flights in and out of the airfield, usually bearing supplies, ordnance and people.

Heinrich watched these things and reported them in safely encoded messages to Berlin. It was intelligence he gained during his continual reconnaissance missions over the fields between his house and the edges of the construction site. But those occasional flights caused him concern. His tracks might be visible from the air, even if the aircrew weren't actively scanning for mischief below. The arrival of personnel whose mission and sole objective were to make the airfield safe from harm also caused Heinrich to make fewer excursions, even in the relative safety of the pre-dawn hours, or those just after sunset.

By day, Huw took his daily bus trip into St Davids. It helped him keep in touch and build a rapport with a small group of local men, too old or too infirm to go and fight for king and country. He learned very little from them but, as the days became longer and warmer, their meetings at strategic benches or inns gave him the ability to smile and nod at his fellows while scanning the streets for military activity. It was increasing, and he noted with satisfaction that his two favourite policemen seemed to have become marginal.

Heinrich wondered if it might soon be time to engineer a chance encounter with the weasel.

Stina James gave birth on the last Friday of November 1942. Thomas couldn't be there, but Megan and Bethan provided the same care they'd given Ava that fateful night.

During the evening, a swirling sea fog crept across and enveloped the land all around, driving people and animals to shelter. At the airfield's gatehouse, the guards heard a muffled boom with confused concern spreading between their glances. George Cottam heard it too and, additionally, saw a moment of diffused light from somewhere the other side of the main runway. For all the world it looked like a lightning strike, but in reverse. He felt increasingly peripheral these days, made worse by being stationed here on the airfield. So, when he heard the crackling of boots on the ground outside his quarters, George decided to leave the problem to others. The noise and flashes were probably one of the gun sections, letting off a round for fun. He should go and do his job; be the disciplinarian his role and rank dictated. Instead, he let it slip, to be resolved in the morning, in daylight rather than in this filthy Celtic mist.

It was more than twelve hours before Stina and Thomas embraced, with their baby between them, and decided to call her Alis. While he rocked his daughter to sleep that night, Thomas asked Stina to marry him. He wanted to stay here forever with the woman he loved and with their daughter and innumerable other babies. Even if the war, or family or his duties took him away, Thomas Harty would return to be with them.

Stina's dark purple eyes bore into him during this speech. She had doubts. What if she accepted and he took her and Alis away? Could she cope? This tiny place and her life in it were perfect. Uncomplicated. Protected. Unsupervised. She loved Thomas and trusted what he said. But what if his sincerity was diluted by an unseen authority? Or by his commitment and loyalty to the family he'd left behind in London? She needed a future in which the only things that caused change would be Alis. Her daughter. Their future.

When Stina didn't reply, Thomas handed Alis to her then went to fetch his greatcoat from the hook inside the front door. From one of its pockets, he took out a piece of wood, two inches wide and about nine in length. It consisted of a series of carefully carved, connected symbols: a hollowed-out heart; then a circle around a Celtic cross; then a solid, smaller heart; then a padlock, complete with keyhole. The final connection was to another heart shape, this one solid but with a shallow bowl.

Thomas had made her a lovespoon.

When they lay together that evening, with Thomas's face nuzzled into the nape of her neck, she said she would marry him but would never leave this place. He whispered his thanks, then gently rolled Stina on to her back to look into those dark purple eyes before they kissed, and he told her they would always be together here.

Within three months, Thomas climbed on to the wing of a small aeroplane and took one of the two seats behind the pilot. A few hours later, he re-joined his squadron at its current location in Hampshire. His work at RAF St Davids was done. Stina's doubts and fears had been realised, but she hung Thomas's lovespoon on the wall behind her bed and comforted Alis with the repeating tune Ava had given them.

THIRTEEN

Today

Ben hadn't been paying much attention towards the end.

She looked impatient. 'Are you following all this, Ben? I think maybe you got a bit lost. Didn't you? I should be more cross with you, but I suppose there has been a great deal to take in.'

Ben looked away from her; those dark purple eyes were too dangerous. To his right, the small window wasn't the conduit to light and sound he needed. Even through the drawn blind, he could see it was dark out there. There was silence: not even a hint of noise; no hooting owl; no barking dog; no windswept rain tapping the glass.

'Let me summarise for you, Ben. The very finest of good men had shown all the love in the world. There was peace in amongst all the belligerent machinery. A new bond was formed, linking this baby with her parents, with love and hope, and with a kind of power. At that moment, nothing mattered about those three malevolent men. Whatever they might say, or do, or think, or decree was all just white noise, Ben. White mischief. Those officials of loathing, made impotent by a new life.'

Ben saw Erin's face twist into a parody of a smile. 'So, it was a perfect, wonderful, joyous irony that one of them should suffer.'

Mary Morgan loved being knocked around by the surf. The broad sweep of sand was her favourite place, and she pestered her mother to take her there each day of the school holiday. Claire liked it there too, but Dewi always said she must ration their daughter's visits. The tide could be powerful and, because her mother couldn't swim, Mary was potentially at risk even in moderately shallow waters.

Mary's insistence was quashed on rainy days and cold days, but when sunshine warmed the air on her eighth birthday, she finally cajoled her mam and dad into submission. Dewi took his swimming trunks too and, by early afternoon, this happy family time seemed to exist millions of miles from the killing sands of North Africa. That's where David Junior was. Or would soon disembark. No one was completely sure. But he would be there to finish off the job of driving the Germans into the Med. Mary's excitement was a blessed distraction for Dewi and Claire.

Father and daughter played boisterously in the waves of an incoming tide. Mary loved to sit on Dewi's shoulders while he walked backwards into the swelling sea until, eventually, the most powerful wave knocked them down. There were a few other children playing nearby but Mary wanted to stay with her daddy, as she spent so little time with him away from their home. She vaguely understood that his work was important but couldn't comprehend why he sometimes had so little time for her. Today was special, therefore, and she needed to monopolise his attention.

Watching from the dry sand above the tide line, Claire smiled. She shared her daughter's wish for Dewi to spend more time with her. Mary was the embodiment of the reunion they had enjoyed nearly ten years ago. Claire had known of Dewi's infidelity but spared herself the misery of confrontation. It didn't matter. Once it was clear he was no longer at it, Claire knew she could still beguile and entrance him and he could still be powerful in her arms.

Dewi threw Mary, in a star shape, into an onrushing wave and delighted in her squeals. This wonderful new game repeated time and again. When they heard Claire's voice beckoning them to get dry and enjoy some food and drink, Mary was the most pleased; the game had made her breathless and a little disoriented. She held Dewi's hand as they walked back to the towels and blankets then they all enjoyed wonderful things Claire had created from their meagre rations.

While they ate, Constable Thorburn arrived on his bike. The two men spoke briefly, concluding that Dewi wasn't needed at the station. As Thorburn rode off up the hill, Dewi heard him puffing and panting with effort and made a mental note to get his men to toughen up.

Mary dragged her daddy back to the sea. The sun was warm and made the sea feel much colder, even in the shallows. After thirty minutes playing, Dewi could see the goosebumps on Mary's arms and legs and feel the chill stiffening in his own torso. It was time to finish in the water and spend whatever was left of the warmth with Claire. This was greeted with dismay by his daughter, so Dewi gave her the concession of ten more minutes. With a shriek of joy, Mary leapt back among the rushing waves.

Claire watched her husband walking up the beach towards her and, past him, kept an eye on Mary as she frolicked. She saw Dewi turn to walk backwards for a few yards, so he too had an eye on their girl.

In the short time neither parent was watching, while

daddy dried himself and mammy poured him some tea, Mary did one final dive at an oncoming wave. She timed it badly and the water hit her along the line of her breastbone, tumbling her backwards onto her head and breaking her neck when she landed. Claire and Dewi saw Mary's body floating into the shallows and laughed at her playfulness, right up until the moment it was chillingly clear their daughter was in fact limp and motionless. After his frantic sprint across the fifty or so yards to where she lay, Dewi saw that Mary was also lifeless.

Out in the desert, David Junior was denied compassionate leave and granted limited time to grieve.

The huge turnout of mourners and well-wishers didn't matter to Claire. Her son's absence meant this funeral was in effect for both her children.

Dewi carried Mary's coffin, unaided, from their house to the church and, from there, on to the cemetery. Claire walked alongside them, ghostly pale. The service was short and soon Mary was buried.

Megan and Bethan stood watching, heads bowed, ready to hand a small gift to the mourning couple. Like many in the community they had been deeply affected by Mary's death and spent time at Justinian's chapel and Non's Well, chanting laments and incantations.

When Dewi saw the twins, he made a silent gesture of communication to Constable Daniels.

Moments later, Megan and Bethan were told they weren't welcome. Sergeant Morgan and his wife didn't need whatever they had brought. Go, or spend time in the cells. Soon Dylan was pulling the sisters along the lanes to see Stina and Alis to tell them of this affront.

✕

There was a period in which Claire and Dewi blamed each other: for being negligent; for being unable to swim; for letting a child's demands unravel their otherwise careful parental discipline. Then they found a degree of peace and reconciled themselves with their loss. Mary's death had been a tragic accident, unforeseeable and without guilt. So, they mourned and grieved, turning Mary's memory into a force that might protect her brother.

Dewi became less compassionate in his role as guardian of law and order. His tolerance and goodwill slipped away. His team of constables grew to fear rather than love him. Any miscreant, no matter how trivial the offence, ran the risk of being punched, thumped or given blows by Dewi's truncheon. Having resolved the conflict he felt about his or Claire's guilt, Police Sergeant Morgan now blamed everyone in his path for the loss of his daughter.

THE LANCE CORPORAL AND THE SPY

During the summer of 1943, Heinrich Brandt continued his spying. He knew the airfield was more or less complete and it was a matter of time until operations would begin. It became impossible for him to sustain effective surveillance when spot checks on civilians became commonplace within a mile of the airfield. Security personnel roamed the lanes and would set up ad hoc checkpoints to show readiness to anyone who might pass. Some of the men were cordial to the locals. Most were contemptuous and judging.

This pleased George Cottam mightily. He was sick of the community and of his routine policing at the airfield. But at least, for now, the tiresome ground crew boys were gone, and the RAF Regiment men showed discipline. None of them was sniffing around the local women. Like Harty had done. His bastard child and whore mother were increasingly visible now the brat was older.

Bored, George took out one of the motorbikes, ostensibly to track where the checkpoints had been created. None of them had anything to report. The locals were predictable. No one ever seemed to arrive from further afield. It was easy to consider the possibility that there was something to protect, but there was nothing that threatened it. As George passed through Caerfarchell, there was the usual scene. That stupid stunted horse, the old witches and their horrible little cart. And then she appeared with the Harty bastard. Perhaps George needed to give Sergeant Morgan some made up evidence to get this sinister coven put away.

He throttled the engine to full and roared away, unnoticed despite his combustible, mechanical bluster. He took the left fork down the hill then along the narrow lane towards the harbour. Where Prendergast joined the main road through Solva, just next to the river bridge, he stopped and switched off the engine. Seated on the machine, like a bird of prey on its perch, he scanned the three directions. He wanted something to strike at. A cause. All he got was that limping man with his uncertain smile of welcome.

Heinrich had been unable to believe his eyes that afternoon. The weasel was there on his machine scanning the horizon, his make-believe whiskers twitching with malevolence. Huw nodded with conviviality, unsure if the weasel would bite. And it didn't. But a carefully timed stumble from the kerbstone caused a nibble.

RAF St Davids was declared fit for operations. Coastal Command Squadrons were expected to begin sorties during November and, as Stina arranged a love-filled celebration for Alis's first birthday, the sky became filled by the frequent roars and whines of aviation engines.

Before she reached her second Christmas, Alis got the perfect gift: the return of her daddy.

The planes and personnel of Thomas Harty's squadron arrived in early December. Thomas had precious little time to be with his family for his work as ground crew was constant and arduous. But he was besotted and beguiled by his baby girl and her charming dark purple eyes. Alis smiled and giggled constantly at her daddy and cried whenever he left her.

Thomas cried too.

Stina's eyes also charmed him, and they quickly found they had forgotten none of the lessons they'd taught each other.

Heinrich had taken a huge risk with George Cottam. That encounter by the road bridge had shown him the volatility and menace in the weasel. It seemed to be surging through him, just under the surface of his skin, sometimes erupting like lava. Yet it could just as easily ooze out, in ripples of frustrated silence; sulky; pernicious; closed, and therefore malleable.

Trained to perfection in the art of entrapment, Heinrich reeled George in with a series of gently baited hooks. The weasel's new-found mobility meant there could be chance encounters. One evening, George and another blue cap arrived at the Farmer's Arms to weed out some errant, loud-mouthed absentees from the airfield. On duty and filled with disciplinary righteousness, George still found time to scan the bar and give Huw Morris a knowing nod. Heinrich raised his glass, fractionally, in acknowledgement.

The weasel was also in company and uniform when Huw limped into the King George that night, just after Christmas. Standing at the bar, George was in a friendly discussion with the landlord about their respective parts in battles on the Western front. The other Military Policeman was stalking the inn in a fruitless search for lost souls. Huw waited his turn alongside George, then ordered a half of bitter. With charmingly contrived naivety, he enquired if the Lance Corporal would allow him to stand him a drink. It was declined, of course, but then Heinrich heard perfect music. The other MP had returned, overheard the offer of hospitality, and told George to go ahead and enjoy a half or two. He could drive their motorbike and sidecar back to the airfield. No one would know. Where was the harm? George still turned down the offer, but now with hesitancy. Huw made a submissive gesture with both hands and, touching George's upper arm, approved of his rectitude. It was the landlord that caused a change of heart. Join me in a half, he said. One last spit in the Kaiser's eye. For the Old Contemptibles. George weakened, then capitulated so the landlord included Huw in the offer of one on the house. Heinrich swore inside as they toasted the defeat of Germany, then and to come.

George drank this complimentary half of beer. Then, with little encouragement, took another from the limping Welshman. When the two Military Policemen departed, one of them had proved his discretion was easily punctured by liquor.

Stina and Thomas stole time together that was rightly not his to give. But while their reunion reaffirmed their infatuation and passion, these were dampened by duty and by their love for Alis. Their devotion to her took all of Thomas's off-duty hours, sometimes less than a few hours a week. It was loving, and gave Thomas feelings he never imagined could overwhelm him. Alis had become his reason to survive and, every time he left their home, he told her he would love her forever. Her infant eyes always told him to stay. Tearing himself away was unbearable.

Stina also drove him wild with agonising longing, but it remained thwarted for some time. Alis was a curious, demanding child and there were many barriers to the love-making her parents craved. Megan and Bethan sometimes stepped in to spend time with Alis, out on the lanes or down by the sea, leaving Stina and Thomas to make love, and perhaps to make more babies. But they needed more time to fully rediscover their intimate specialities.

George Cottam had convinced himself that there was nothing wrong with his increasingly regular visits to the King George. For starters, it bore his name and he was proud of his kingly moniker. Plus, he got to spend time with the landlord, whose name he struggled to say, but who made time to discuss 1918 and those decisive times in the trenches. They played an affectionate game of one-upmanship, dropping the names of battles into their chattering: Belleau Wood; Soissons; Amiens; Cambrai.

Call. Raise. See. Fold.

Then, Corporal Lewis made it clear he didn't mind covering for George and dropped him off at and collected him from the inn. George got to hear from his chum, Huw, about life in the mines and about the partially collapsed seam that had crushed his leg causing that limp. And about great days at Stradey Park watching the Scarlets, Huw's beloved Llanelli. It felt good to be able to say someone actually was his chum; a pal; he hadn't had any friends ever; not back home; not in the trenches; not out there in fucking Anatolia; and categorically not in this role as a blue-cap. George even began to arrive in plain clothes so that he blended in and felt like just another local, supping a pint or two and breaking any ice the other men might feel in his presence.

Heinrich had been given a coded instruction to commit the act of sabotage he'd proposed. Anything that would prevent flights, however temporarily, would make a difference to the Reich. The directives told him to expect clandestine exchanges on bus trips in order to deliver RDX and other accessories needed to make an explosive device. If he could get inside the wire, up close to the fuel or bomb dump or even to a bomber, then he could change the course of the war.

Heinrich had no doubt that George could help him with access to the airfield. It might not be willing help.

Slowly, Heinrich developed the plan needed to make that happen.

Megan and Bethan arrived one afternoon much to the delight of Alis, who loved their company and funny faces. Each doted on the infant. It was unanimous delight.

Stina packed a bag with the things Alis needed for a night and day with the twins. Clothes, mainly, but also some scraps of food. When Thomas arrived, his daughter was giggling with delight as she stroked Dylan's nose causing him to shake his head playfully and whinny with what sounded like joy. Thomas took his daughter in a whirl of enchantment and now her giggles were infectiously joyous.

They wrapped her up in warm things, then Bethan cuddled Alis tight as Megan signalled for Dylan to walk, then trot away from Stina and Thomas. They stood and waved, then went inside to release days and days of pent-up arousal.

Heinrich Brandt left 41 Prendergast and limped slowly away; a medium-sized duffle bag slung over his shoulder. Once clear of the houses, and certain no one was in sight, he moved quickly and limp-free to the fields and soon rushed up the hill towards the church.

It had all come together neatly over two evenings in the George Inn.

The first of them combined the innocent temptation of the landlord with Huw's more deliberate coaxing and had seen George Cottam consume several pints of beer. It was already common knowledge to the locals that the man couldn't take his ale.

When the landlord brought two small glasses of whisky to their table, Huw told George he couldn't stand the stuff and watched his Lancastrian pal throw both glasses down this throat, followed by the last half of his pint.

Earlier in the evening, while still sober and cordial, Huw had dropped two names into the conversation.

Stina.

Harty.

He knew it would happen, but he was still shocked by the changes in George's facial expression. There was hatred there for Heinrich to use. So, he drip-drip-dripped little notions of how something should be done about that tart and her London lover. Each droplet increased George's contempt. Each new pint increased Heinrich's grip on the situation. As George slammed down his empty glass, the sixth pint he'd consumed, he looked around then whispered to Huw that he would gladly see the whore and the cocky Cockney cunt killed.

Outside the inn, Heinrich held George steady awaiting the arrival of Corporal Lewis and his sidecar.

I could kill them, he whispered to the rapidly disintegrating weasel. I just need an easy way in and out, something that avoids the checkpoints on the roads. Maybe from the northern edge of the airfield? Quicker to the whore's house across those fields? What do you think? Why don't you help me get in, George? Perhaps in the sidecar of one of your motorcycles? They are just about big enough for me to squeeze inside. Take me to somewhere discreet within the airfield, then quietly leave me to finish the job? To finish that Harty?

Had he not been hopelessly drunk, George might have noticed that Huw's lilting Welsh accent had gone, replaced by a flatter, calmer voice with harsher sibilants and longer vowel sounds. A voice that emitted a highly overt level of uncontrolled loathing whenever it pronounced that word *Harty*.

But it all went in one ear and out of the other.

The next time they met, George was sheepish about the state he'd reached that night and asked for Huw's forgiveness. It was given with a wafted hand and a smiling face. Don't be daft, man! What's a bit of drunkenness between old friends? Let him who is without guilt cast the first stone! Forgive and forget, eh? Next time, I'll join you in a roister. But not tonight, eh?

So many idioms for fake forgiveness.

George agreed and, this evening, he resisted the temptation for excess beer and sipped from a half pint glass over the course of the hour or two they spent together. And he was sober when he asked Huw if he'd been serious about killing Harty and James.

It seemed some of what Heinrich had said that night had clung on between George's ears.

Heinrich reached the southern edge of the church grounds and ducked down to wait for the tell-tale sound of the motorbike. The weasel had believed him. *Das Wiesel.* Heinrich shook his head with contempt for George's pathetic slide into treachery and his passive connivance in the act of terror that was unfolding. The explosives in his bag were all he needed to disable the airfield indefinitely. An event that would reduce the risks for his countrymen in their U-boats and surface ships. It would destroy enemy machines and combatants. But, above all, it would cast a massive cloud of doubt in the increasingly blue-sky minds of the British. This thing he would do was a strike at them on their own territory. Something to cause doubt and panic. This was an attack at an extreme of their hapless island. A remote place, where security could only ever be thin and easily overwhelmed. Then, perhaps, this was a blueprint for many more such acts, driving the British to fear what skulked in their hinterlands.

Heinrich chuckled: how these *Britischers* feared invasions, big or small. If only they knew how easily they could be defeated without an invasion.

The low throb of an engine announced the weasel's arrival. Heinrich bolted away from the churchyard towards a gate and, once there, crouched down to wait.

When the motorbike drew level with the gate, George brought it to a halt with the engine running then unclipped the waterproof cover so Huw could climb feet first into the sidecar. Neither man spoke, and it took Heinrich longer than they'd wished to lie down low enough for George to reattach the cover. It was painfully uncomfortable, but Heinrich now had ice-cold determination in him that overcame any discomfort. He felt the machine vibrate, then move, then speed up. They slowed and turned before accelerating and shaking for several minutes. There was constant noise and changes of direction. Heinrich felt his heart hammering.

He felt their speed reduce to slow, then a right turn and a halt. Voices. Recognition. Welcome.

Back soon, Lance Corporal.

Was she not in the mood tonight, sir?

Better get back to your wanking chariot, sir.

Laughter.

Going to take a look around the field, check on the

gun positions and perimeter.

On you go then, Lance Corporal.

Heinrich swore at them: a stream of mental invective.

The machine crawled forward again then sped up after turning left. There was percussive bumping as if the wheels were progressing over a grid. A lurching, juddering turn, sharply to the right, then another acceleration. He should have been disoriented, but Heinrich calculated they must be near their destination. The weasel had been good to his word. They'd agreed he would take Huw to the northern edge of the airfield, in turn giving Heinrich a six or seven hundred metre dash across the fields to the whore's house.

He had never seen George challenge or doubt the plan. It was clear the weasel was resentful and needed to bite the hand that fed him. This breach of military security seemed to give George a perverse kind of pleasure.

Heinrich smiled. Treachery, like love, is blind.

The motorbike slowed to a halt then the engine was switched off. He heard George dismount then make a heavily theatrical yawning noise. Footsteps ensued, seemingly away from their location then back again. Heinrich was warm and claustrophobic now. The clicking of stud fasteners was a relief, and he heard George say *wait*, then *all clear*. Heinrich extracted himself slowly and painfully. With no further words or glances, George had climbed back on to the motorbike and was making himself comfortable in the saddle.

Heinrich had the cosh in his hand and moved quickly towards George. He dealt a powerful blow into the Englishman's solar plexus, another into his face as he fell breathlessly forwards and finally rapped the cosh across the back of George's skull. His chauffeur slumped, unconscious, over the bike's handlebars.

Heinrich buttoned down the canopy on the sidecar, then dropped into a squat behind the machine to recover his night vision and survey his surroundings.

There were aeroplanes to his left, seemingly parked in readiness, noses up, tails down. Optional target one - locked.

Beyond them, a hangar with a truck outside; one of those with a canvas cover over its rear. Optional target two - locked.

Straight ahead of him was the point at which the airfield's two short runways ended at an intersection. Then to his right, more buildings and planes and, half hidden behind one building, the unmistakable shapes of fuel tanker trucks. Optional target three – locked.

One last scan of the near and middle-distance revealed no sign of life. Immediately behind him was the northern perimeter of the airfield, with a coil of Dannert wire stretched out, left and right. Heinrich emitted a tiny exclamation of patriotic joy. The British were using a German invention to protect their military sites from attack. How profoundly perfect that was. It gave him a surge of elation.

The tankers were his target.

Prime and set the explosives.

Move, and find the place in the wire he knew George had cut. Or hoped he had cut. If not, Heinrich would need more decisive measures to escape.

He sprinted towards the buildings and tankers then, realising he hadn't spotted the gun position, fell flat to the ground and waited. Faint voices filtered across the twenty-five metres or so. He couldn't make out the words.

Options:

1 - keep going in a crawl and plant the explosives
2 - abort and escape
3 - get into the gun position and kill.

Impossible to abort. Which left 1 and 3. He chose 1.

Ten metres more crawling and he collapsed to flat once more. Louder voices now from the gun position. A beam of torchlight. Fuck. Heinrich rolled on to his side and grabbed the machete from inside his tunic. He'd have to kill these soldiers. They were between him and the fence. His night vision was very good now: one soldier was at the gun position; two had walked cautiously away. They would find the bike and the weasel soon.

Fuck again.

Maybe sprint to the tankers, plant the bomb, set the timer to something short - thirty seconds - fifteen seconds - then just sprint away to the wire and hope to cut through in the inevitable confusion caused by the explosion. He might die. But he might not.

No. Fuck. Escape. Fight another day. You won't have the weasel to help but something will come up.

Heinrich crawled on his belly in a line towards the occasional twinkle of metal he could see. It must be the Dannert wire, perhaps ten metres beyond the gun position. He wasn't discovered yet.

If the single man in the gun position became alerted, kill him then hit the fence.

A shout behind and to his right. They'd found the weasel.

Silence. There was static, electronic static from a radio, hissing out from the gun position. An exchange of voices. Urgent. Attentive.

Heinrich reached the wire quickly, crawling on his elbows and knees. The weasel had done his job. There was a small section of wire with cuts, creating a way out. He was through in seconds, on to the muddy fields.

Another ten metres on his belly then up and sprinting, not looking back.

Fifteen seconds at full speed, then turn and drop. Nothing. He wasn't discovered.

Up, fast, turn and sprint again. Then repeat the checking routine. Nothing.

He was filthy and wet. Two more cross checks and no danger had arisen. This time he stayed flat on his belly and waited. He was perhaps 500 metres from the place where he'd crawled through the wire. No barking dog. No searchlights. No shouts.

Ten minutes later, Heinrich stumbled out from a well-worn footpath into the lane heading north out of the hamlet. He was at least a thirty minutes' walk from his safe house and there could be a net thrown around the airfield soon. Patrols on foot and in vehicles. He needed a safe place.

FOURTEEN

Dust

Thomas and Stina were so lost in pleasure that they didn't hear the breaking glass. Ever since the twins and Alis had left, these lovers had been awash with lust, and it flooded out and through them. Unstoppable. Unremitting.

Nor did they hear footfall on the stairs. Nor a creaking door.

Heinrich felt the beginnings of arousal. The Jew and his whore certainly made a noise. As well as their yelps and groans of pleasure, there was the clatter of furniture. He stood at the bottom of the stairs, wet and stinking. The house was in darkness except for a slit of pale light up there on the landing. He imagined a small lamp of some kind, lighting their glistening nakedness.

He calculated. The treads might be noisy. Weren't they always noisy? He took a step up, suddenly mindful of the lump forming in his trouser front.

Twelve slow steps up and Heinrich reached the landing. The tiny light came from under the door to his right, which was minutely ajar. The whore was coming, and panting words he couldn't recognise. The Jew was making a low growling noise and encouraging her to come. Heinrich had left his duffle bag at the foot of the stairs. He held a single implement.

There was no pause to suggest his presence was known. Heinrich knew he could push open the door enough to get inside. It might creak but he doubted they'd hear a thing. He calculated again. Sneak through the door? Or rush in?

Beyond the door, the heightened frenzy of her coming was in tune with his. Heinrich faced the door and took a deep breath. When the *a cappella* finale of passion burst forth, he slipped into the room to see one impending victim collapse on top of the other. Four strides, with no fear of discovery, and Heinrich was at the foot of the bed. In one blow, he plunged his father's bayonet between the Jew's shoulder blades; hard; down through his thoracic and into the whore's chest. Their screams were curtailed, then silent.

He left the blade in its place and retrieved another weapon from his sack. Then Heinrich Brandt made sure his job was finished with slices.

A wail of despair alerted the twins to an unshaped, uncertain danger. Alis was frantic and hurt. Inconsolable. Mouth open, forming sounds that weren't yet words, because she knew few words.

But she knew that the danger was something tragic and terrible. It was dead of night, still hours from dawn. The sisters sensed that one of them needed to be at Caerfarchell.

Bethan didn't get far. As she reached the hill down into the Alun valley, the sound of vehicles reached her. From somewhere beyond the town. It was too dark and too early for those sounds to be normal.

She turned back for the short walk home. How could they possibly get to The Wool Merchant's House and rescue Stina?

The discovery of an unconscious Military Policeman had created havoc. One soldier kept watch over George Cottam. The other rushed back to the gun position to alert the gatehouse. The field telephone began to hiss with rushed, uncertain statements, questions and answers. Everyone was incredulous. It took time for anyone to get a grip on the bits and pieces of facts and evidence. Someone started to make notes.

Lance Corporal Cottam had been out on patrol earlier, but briefly. He returned with nothing to report. He'd openly told the sentries that he intended to tour the airfield perimeter. This information was relayed by radio to the gun positions in a simple message: *MP on patrol*.

One sentry confirmed that the Lance Corporal had appeared quite calm and informal..

The men at the gun position had heard, then seen the motorbike's approach and taken no action. They returned to their scans: of the skies; of the horizon; of the perimeter. The motorbike had stopped about one hundred yards from their position, then the engine was switched off, presumably to allow Lance Corporal Cottam to spend time on foot patrol.

George had regained consciousness but remained drowsy and mute. He hurt in three places. What had he done to deserve Huw's attack? His side of the bargain had been honoured to the letter. However, silence and a feigned trauma seemed his best friends for now. When they got him on a stretcher and into the ambulance, his head was full of revisions and alibis. If that Welsh fucker had still delivered on the killings of Harty and James, he would be happy but not without culpability.

One of George's colleagues was dispatched to inform the local police of a security breach at the airfield. They were required to support the military operation as a priority. Another was told to get some erks to retrieve Cottam's motorcycle.

At first light, a party conducted a detailed inspection of the whole perimeter.

⚔

The twins had some wool, enough to create the illusion that it was a delivery to the mill.

But there was a chill in the air. Neither of the sisters could say Stina's name, nor tell Alis her mammy would hold her soon. Alis was anxious and troubled, needing constant care, hugs and smiles. They couldn't take her on this journey. It was impossible to conjure any sense of normality. In turn, they chanted those words: 'Dial. Ad-daledigaeth. Cyfiawnder.'

Megan knew Bethan was Alis's favourite, so she left them together and drove the cart in to Tyddewi. No checks or barriers prevented her taking the road out of town, and Dylan set a good pace.

The road to Caerfarchell was closed off. Two itchy-looking young men in blue regarded her balefully from behind a barrier. One put his hand on his pistol as she pulled up.

Access denied, madam. What's happened? Nothing, but you're not going to Middle Mill, madam. Even to deliver wool? Not even that.

Megan felt every sinew stretching, almost to breaking point. How could she check on Stina? Bethan didn't respond to her thoughts; Megan needed to head back.

Along the road, Dewi Morgan flagged her down from his car. He was heading to places near the airfield to check on houses and residents, but he didn't say why. It was a friendly discussion, but Megan sensed concern and something more profound in the policeman's eyes. He told her he was sure there would be time to deliver wool soon.

Megan decided to tell Dewi that Stina was at Rhosson with Alis.

✕

Heinrich heard the impolite, insistent knocking on the door. Then a firm confident voice said Open Up: Military Police.

He lay still, damp and stinking. If this escalated into a search of the house, especially at the rear, Heinrich would be caught. And would be hanged, or shot, or both.

More knocking, then a new voice seeped through the air. It was that civil policeman. Morgan. Something about the occupier being away seeing family. Then an exchange too quiet for Heinrich to hear.

He needed to get out. He had to assume they would find the broken open window, his muddy footprints, and the trail of his arrival at the house. What if he stayed and just took them on? Killed them. How many would there be? More than one. Four, maximum. Armed, but not killers. It was a fight he would win.

Heinrich had arrived in darkness and wasn't sure if there was any easy escape route to the rear. He calculated where the British might have reached in their assessment of what had happened.

✕

The cut wire was eventually discovered. So was the absence of ground crew sergeant: Harty, T; 58 Squadron. So were two unfastened studs on the waterproof cover for the sidecar. There was nothing inside, but it was impounded.

The gatehouse sentries were quizzed about the status of the sidecar when Cottam had returned yesterday evening. Inconclusive. His machine wasn't inspected. George was a Military Policeman. What was there to suspect?

Medics reported that Cottam was concussed but lucid enough to be interviewed. Efforts to question him provided plausible results. He'd been on patrol off site. On the road down in to Solva he'd seen figures in the fields and pulled over. Several moments of searching had revealed nothing. He'd returned to base.

How long was the motorcycle unattended?

At least ten minutes.

Was there any difference in the motorcycle's performance?

Such as?

Such as slower speeds or handling, as if the sidecar was occupied.

No. It was no different.

Thomas Harty's fellow ground crew hadn't seen him since the previous afternoon. He was probably with his missus and sprog.

Where were they?

Shrugs from some. Others said it was the village up the road. The one no one could say.

Men in a vehicle were sent to Caerfarchell to check on the whereabouts of Harty and, if found, to bring him back to the airfield.

Meanwhile, bombing sorties continued but planes, machinery and buildings all over the airfield were checked with forensic scrutiny.

A debriefing involving the Military Police, senior officers of the squadrons and the RAF Regiment concluded that an attempted attack on the airfield had been foiled by Lance Corporal Cottam. The evidence suggested that the saboteur might have been brought on to the airfield, unwittingly, in the motorcycle's sidecar. Cottam was then attacked but his assailant aborted whatever mission was intended and cut his way out to escape.

The priority was therefore to identify and neutralise the assailant, and the civilian police would have a part to play in that objective.

Dewi told the military chaps he would check Stina's property if they wanted to look at other houses. He skirted around the right-hand side of the shop extension and looked across at the house from its boundary. Then he walked around the front and down the left side, once more to scrutinise the rear windows and door.

Heinrich was waiting. He'd decided to pull the broken window shut and wait inside the door for any attempt at a forced entry.

Dewi took out his notebook and wrote: *Conducted full inspection of Stina James' property, from the sides and from the rear garden. No evidence of suspicious circumstances. Miss James stated to be with friends in Rhosson. No need for further action*.

When he re-joined the military chaps a few moments later, he told them the same.

Heinrich listened to Dewi's words through the front door and frowned. They were such amateurs. They had done an incomplete job, for reasons he couldn't understand. But this was all to his advantage. He dashed up the stairs and saw Morgan take one last look around before driving off. The others climbed into their jeep and headed off in the same direction he needed to take.

Heinrich calculated that the military group had been sent to find Harty. He was less clear why Morgan had arrived, but potentially it was a coincidence. There would soon be a more extensive search. It was time for Heinrich to get out of this house. He assumed there might already be roadblocks and roaming patrols. His escape route was clear: exit from the rear; cross the fields parallel with the lane until clear of houses; cross the lane; head to the river. It was daylight and the risks were high. If necessary, he would need to kill anyone he encountered. After completing the wide arc around the hamlet, he'd reach the river and could follow it, if necessary, by wading in it, down to Solva.

He needed an hour, perhaps more if he encountered checkpoints.

FIFTEEN

Today

'Such wickedness, Ben. Did you ever hear such a story? And, in case you doubt it, this is real. These things happened here.'

Her words broke a silence and shook him into a state of watchful concern. Erin's latest monologue had been filled with quiet, sullen moments. Now she seemed to be elsewhere, her head lifted and tilted slightly as if listening for a signal or the call of a creature. Then she closed her eyes and hummed that tune.

'There was work to be done. An infant in need. An emergency.'

When she returned her gaze to Ben, he saw something close to kindness in her eyes.

'Do you believe in hope, Ben? Some say there is always hope.'

✕

Bethan sat on the bus with Alis sleeping in her arms. Across the aisle, three rows in front, two young women chatted openly about their problems.

Some were simple. The bus journeys to and from work and the wish for somewhere to live in St Davids. Loneliness at home. The drudgery of their jobs.

Some were sad. They both missed their husbands and feared for their lives. Nicola's was fighting in the far east, Jane's in Italy after months and months in North Africa.

Some were tragic. In the days after his conscription, Jane and William had conceived a child, news that had made William believe he had something worth fighting for. Before he'd disembarked in Tunisia, the baby they'd made was lost. Jane had miscarried. Nicola was the only person she'd told, and Jane didn't know how to tell William because her letters were censored. She didn't want him to be the last to know.

Some were worrying. Jane suffered bouts of mental and physical anguish. She was scared and her anxiety was redoubled by pain, bleeding and a fever. It made her weak, with a profound sense that something serious had happened. When her monthly bleeding didn't return, Jane was plunged into despair. How could she ever tell William that their marriage would be childless and joyless?

Some were cause for hope. Their husbands had survived so far, and sometimes celebrated victory despite the news that this war was years and years from its end. Both women had found work as maids at a hotel in St Davids at a time when it seemed no work could be found.

Bethan listened and approved of the way Nicola and Jane confided in one another. They were young and married, but a war had made them single. It gave them a kind of unity. Bethan was especially interested in Jane. When she and Alis left the bus to meet Megan, the twins talked awhile and knew they had found a mother for Alis. By the time they arrived home, they had a plan.

This would be a distraction for them, because there was unfinished business elsewhere.

Huw Morris was dead, the ghost of his being deflated in the pile of stinking clothes on the kitchen floor. Heinrich now had just one person to protect from harm. Sitting, as clean as he could make himself, he carefully assessed his situation and structured his thoughts about what he must do.

His escape and furtive expedition back to base had passed without incident, allowing him time to ditch the packs of explosives in the undergrowth. Lucky. Fortune that he fully expected to sustain in the hours to come. He formed a simple plan. Identify a safe haven. Send a signal. Await a reply. Gather resources to keep him alive for up to five days, probably unsheltered in the wild. Flee this building and village.

Heinrich looked at the pistol. He had no doubt door-to-door searches would be widened. He had to be out of this house in less than an hour. Otherwise, he might die in it, with any number of British dead in the process.

He knew there was a small island away to the west, and less than a kilometre off the mainland coast. A glance at a map confirmed it.

How could he get there?

It didn't matter. That was the rendezvous. Time to move.

Heinrich was back in less than fifteen minutes. Up on the hillside, in the wooded slope of the ravine, he'd sent the signal that his cover was blown.

He ate some morsels of food then placed the rest in his sack. A flask of water completed his rations. He packed a whistle. What else? Things to make him dark: face and hand paint; a balaclava. Protection, defensive and offensive: a gun; two grenades; two knives; the strip of wire that could be a garrotte. Not much space left now. Warmth. Yes. There was room for a single item of clothing. A woollen jumper?

Heinrich had carefully watched the coming and going at the harbour, such as it was. The one certain departure, when the tide was high each morning, was that small sailing boat owned by Gwyn Harries.

Where did he go?

It didn't matter. Get on board. Hide. Wait for the boat to set sail. Kill Harries. Get to Ramsey Island.

He had everything he needed for that trip. Everything else would just be left here in this house. Clothes. Radio. Weapons. Everything, regardless of whether it was a clue to his real self.

Heinrich slipped silently into the street shortly after midnight, dashed through the gudel to the river and made his way down stream to the harbour.

The terrible scene that confronted the two young Military Policemen left them shocked and disturbed. Neither could function properly, and it was an act of supreme will that one of them was able to radio back to base for help, and for a communication to be sent to the civilian police.

When the news reached the Police Station, via a breathless and clearly upset messenger, Dewi Morgan listened with a troubled expression. Worried that his lack of diligence might be deemed a factor in what had happened, he immediately despatched Constable Thorburn to attend the scene. He needed time to think about what he had and had not done. His mind wandered off to a story where he might heap blame on the twins for what had happened.

What had one of them said? Miss James and her child were at Rhosson. That was a lie.

Why did the twin lie? It was brazen. He'd always

known they were bad and now one of them had proved it. This was the excuse he might use for his lack of proper investigation. With this zealous defence burning in his head, Dewi set off to join his constable.

Investigations didn't take long to link events at the airfield with these murders. The broken window and other signs that an intruder had been in the house didn't leave much room for doubt. Dewi's heart sank, for nothing he saw could possibly have been the act of an elderly woman. Not even of two women. The strength and brutal malevolence needed to drive a bayonet through two bodies could only be the work of a trained assassin. Much as he distrusted the twins, this wasn't their work. His mind began to formulate new excuses.

There was confusion and suspicion between the military and civilian police about who owned the problem. Yes, one victim was a serving member of His Majesty's forces and there was a clear link to an attempted act of sabotage at a military site. On the other hand, a civilian was also dead, and the scene was not in any military jurisdiction. An unedifying dispute seemed to be preventing any form of reason.

The security and intelligence services soon arrived and made it clear that everyone was now working for them. The quarrelling stopped. This was an act of espionage and, regardless of rank, role or department, their common goal was to find a lone, highly dangerous assailant. Once found, he should be captured alive if possible.

Personnel, on motorcycles, in cars and even some on foot, were soon banging on doors proclaiming the right to enter and search.

The twins didn't care for the way Morgan spoke to them. His accusation that Megan lied to him about Stina was wafted aside with a statement that she never said any such thing. And the steady gaze of both women prompted Dewi to doubt his own memory, made worse by the mewling and squawking of that damned infant.

Distracted, Dewi tried to make noises about the need for Miss James's child to be taken into care. Processed. Put into a system. But even as he spoke those words, his doubts returned as he succumbed to the sisters' stares. Baby Alis is safe with us. You've got more important things to resolve, Sergeant Morgan, none of which requires you to be here. Please go and find the person responsible for these crimes.

After a compliant Dewi left, Bethan and Megan were less calm than they had shown him. They hadn't mentioned Cottam and limping Huw, but the twins were sure that pair was the plausible answer to the question of Stina's and Thomas's deaths. But Morgan wouldn't have listened to that logic. He never would.

Then they calmed. Time was running out. Alis needed to be removed from harm and the potential treatment that Dewi wanted. She must become the child of Jane and William Howells. It was an irresistible ending to this tragedy, and to Jane's terrible dilemma. She needed to know this.

That creature of habit, Harries, didn't fail Heinrich.

The yacht sailed from the harbour with Heinrich hidden under the cover of a tarpaulin. When he sensed they were sailing due south, Heinrich acted quickly to emerge and kill his skipper. He laid the body face down in the prow, the pool of blood that had gushed from his throat already dark or diluted and dissipated by seawater.

For around an hour, he tacked westerly, about a mile offshore. With ease, he'd made himself safe from whatever was unfolding at the airfield and environs and Heinrich chuckled to himself. Now he was a pirate and hijacker as well as a spy and assassin. How could he have massaged so many roles into his short life?

Would his father be proud?

And the Führher?

No large ships or boats were close as Heinrich steered towards the island and, after passing the rocks at its southern edge, sailed towards the shore. It was calm enough for him to use his field glass, and he quickly found where he could land and wait for his rescuers.

When the pebbles and sand appeared a couple of metres under the boat, he pulled up the keel and continued to steer towards the rocky beach. As soon as the boat grounded, Heinrich pulled down the sail.

His rapid survey of his surroundings confirmed what he'd seen through his field glass. Two quite high rocks blocked line of sight onto this beach from the open sea. Now he had work to do.

He took down the mast, then lay it in the bilge. He wrapped Harries in the sails and the tarpaulin Heinrich had hidden under. He wrenched the tiller upwards, so it broke away from the rudder.

After leaving his duffle bag safely above the water line, Heinrich pushed and dragged the boat back into the shallows. It required massive effort on his part, but soon it floated, after a fashion, but still occasionally caught on the seabed and stones.

Once he was up to his hips in the water it finally became easier to push the boat to where he wanted to hide it. When the water became shallower again, and the boat started to ground, he pushed it as hard as he could, so it crashed up against the rocks. Heinrich looked around and reckoned it was invisible to passing ships.

Finally, he started to throw the largest loose stones he could reach into the boat. Within half an hour, it was dead in the water, and barely moved in the waves.

He'd been willing to wait, and be drenched by the sea, for at least five nights. But, in the darkness of his third night on Ramsey Island, Heinrich caught the sound. A repeating pattern, blown on a whistle. One, then two, then three short peeps. He returned the call with one long blow lasting exactly five seconds. Then he saw the conning tower and sleek shape of the U-boat. In less than an hour, Heinrich was on board his rescue vessel as it submerged and set a course for Hamburg.

Heinrich Brandt was going home. To Germany, and victory.

SIXTEEN

The End Begins

As she waited for Nicola after her shift, Jane was beckoned by one of the hotel's night staff. There was a message for her in the foyer.

The small envelope wasn't sealed and inside was a card saying: *Rooms to Let, 27 Goat Street. Mrs Haines.* When Nicola joined her, Jane showed her the card and asked if she was also interested. Nicola wasn't but agreed she would go with Jane to see the accommodation and what might be on offer.

It was a house in a terrace of four, backing on to the cathedral close. Mrs Haines introduced herself as Rebecca, was not much older than Jane but seemed harassed and saddened by something that caused lines in her face and a weary, aged demeanour. She told them her husband was dead, drowned in an attack on his ship in the North Atlantic. She needed to pay the rent and letting rooms was the only way to bolster whatever pension she would receive.

On the bus home, Jane worked things out in her head. She would save the bus fare each day and work longer hours. She might get extra shifts. Even if she still sent some money to mam and dad, Jane would be slightly better off living with Rebecca.

A frown darkened her face. Mam and Dad would want to see her every weekend. They wouldn't come to visit, would they? Jane wouldn't be better off.

She was still deep in thought when she sat down to eat with her parents.

Jane returned to see Rebecca with a well scripted

and memorised speech that requested a lower rent in exchange for work around the house. Cleaning. Washing. Gardening. When she got there, the sight of the cart made her worry someone had beaten her to it.

It wasn't Rebecca who opened the door. It was a much older woman, who Jane felt she might have seen before. Bethan ushered her into the parlour where Megan was holding hands with a young girl who gazed at Jane with a curious smile. As she took in those dark purple eyes and flowing black hair, Jane found herself smiling back.

When she left to catch her bus, Jane was beside herself with excitement and disbelief. There was a place for her to stay and a genuine bond with Rebecca. And those wonderful, crazy old sisters had somehow conjured up the answer to her prayers. It was a perfect illusion and meant that, when he was safely home to stay, she would be able to present her lovely William with a daughter.

George Cottam was given a medical discharge and all he felt was liberation. Something he had once loved had become a burden, doubly so for the knowledge that he had nearly been caught in an act of colossal betrayal and treachery.

They told him to be ready to leave with 24 hours' notice, so George packed up his troubles and waited in the barracks, wondering vaguely what on earth he would do back in Kirkham, with a wife and child he hardly knew.

He was given permission to go into St Davids and bid farewell to Sergeant Morgan, who he claimed was a friend. For the first time in weeks, George felt happy.

At the Police Station, George learned Dewi was out on patrol but expected back soon. It was a warm, sunny morning, so he told the constable to let Sergeant Morgan know he would meet him at the cathedral or palace. The constable shook his hand warmly and a second constable came out to wish George well, with an accompanying salute.

He strolled happily away, past the shops and the Celtic Cross where he made a small detour to stand in the memorial garden. George recalled the encounter with Harty and the other erks. That cockney fucker had got his come-uppance. So had that wicked woman with her slatternly ways. The acid of loathing bubbled through him for the first time since his encounters with Morris, or whatever he was really called.

George turned away, knowing he had outsmarted them all and smiling about the killings of Thomas and Stina. They'd been done for him. A victory, by any number of measures.

He strolled jauntily to the cathedral close. The wonderful building sat there, a sandy cross of certainty in a field of green. There was nothing like this back home. Maybe he should stay? Or come back, with Sheila and the boy. What could they all do here once the war was over? George made a mental note that he would check with Dewi about becoming a part time police officer. What did he have to lose by asking?

Down the steps, then along the path past the cathedral. Dismissing the option to go inside, he kept walking and crossed the small stream. George liked the idea of a last look in the Bishop's Palace. He could wait there, in the sunshine, for Sergeant Morgan.

Inside the walls, George gazed with wonder at what confronted him. Such grandeur had once conceived then built this gigantic place. He wondered at what could possibly have happened to see a mighty palace become deserted, neglected then ruined.

He walked up some steps, then through an arch that must once have been a giant doorway into a church or abbey. George emerged into an open roofless space and felt a sudden chill. The huge walls cast shadows across the floor, and it seemed the sunshine was gone. The light breeze became a wind, gusting around George. The arched window frames admitted no light and it seemed that a roof, missing for centuries, now covered the building.

George was disoriented. The gusts felt like tiny, winged creatures bombarding him in waves. He felt compelled to stay, but really wanted to leave. Whatever was diving in and around him now had voices: whispers; shouts; screams; calm accusations.

You did it, George. Didn't you?

Traitor. Heinous, hate-filled fool.

We know. We know what you did. We saw it. You let him loose and he went wild in your name.

Dewi arrived in the sunlit cathedral close, looking forward to meeting up with George this one last time. His anticipation was tinged with regret that he'd sometimes held so many concerns about the Lance Corporal. In the end, he'd turned out to be a hero. And Dewi felt sad that he would never see the Lance Corporal again.

Behind him, to the east, a roaring started up. Another sortie by the RAF. Soon the Liberators or Halifaxes might be overhead bound for the sea and whatever awaited them.

As Dewi walked across the grounds of the ruined palace, he saw George fall from one of the arched windows in the chapel. He rushed across to where George lay and saw that two bayonets had been stabbed into his body: one between his shoulder blades; the other upwards into his chest. The roaring sound had diminished. No aeroplanes appeared. A streak of light flashed overhead, but Dewi was too busy looking with shock at the dead body before him. George's face, his eyes wide open, held terror the like of which Dewi had never seen, not even in the trenches or field hospitals.

A noise above him made Dewi look up into the archway. Two figures stood there, staring down: expressionless.

Dewi still hadn't learned which was Megan, and which was Bethan.

SEVENTEEN

Prosecution

The Germany that welcomed Heinrich Brandt was defiant, especially in its uniforms or when draped in that flag. This bold façade was missing in the eyes of anyone he met in the streets or shops or bars. When he was finally reunited with Katrin and her husband, Rolf Ahrens, he began to understand why.

The voyage back to the Fatherland had taken days. British defences meant that the short route, through the English Channel, was impossible to take. Instead, the U-boat travelled west of Ireland, north past the Outer Hebrides and into the North Sea through the wide gap between the Orkney and Shetland Isles. The first seven hundred kilometres or so, and then the final five hundred, had allowed long stretches on the surface. But all around the Scottish coast, deadly patrols by British ships and flying boats made it necessary to submerge, which slowed them to less than fourteen kilometres per hour. Slower than a bicycle. It was torture.

Cramped living conditions, and Heinrich's relative isolation from the crew, made the time crawl and tested his patience. He felt, but had to swallow, a raging distaste for some of his fellow travellers, especially when he heard so many of them, young Germans to a man, revealing a weary defeatism and dislike for the Party. Once safely cruising along the Elbe, Heinrich was given a short briefing about the horrific damage done by raids on Hamburg. He was told he was to be met and transported back to Berlin. The Kapitänleutnant spoke in a respectful, almost business-like manner but Heinrich saw the contempt in those eyes.

He asked if Lübeck had been targeted by the RAF. It troubled him to hear the news that the old city had been one of the first in Germany to be bombed specifically to kill civilians. Kapitänleutnant Brausch showed some sympathy when Heinrich mentioned that his sister might have been caught up in the attacks, but it was momentary. The U-boat was filled with a crew whose families were affected by the American and British raids. Their job was to avenge those deaths. To blow naval and merchant ships to pieces and destroy their crews. Yet here was his U-boat, a skulking non-combatant in dangerous seas for the sake of a special cargo. A man they had been forced to retrieve. Not a military man, or a fighter. But a spy and Nazi. That diversion from serious military action was one that Brausch and his men despised.

Heinrich left the boat without ceremony. A driver stood on the quayside with an SD staff car and Heinrich felt a kind of welcome, at last. With no further ado, they sped from the city to a small airfield. A little more than two hours after disembarking, Heinrich was in Prinz-Albrecht-Strasse facing a barrage of questions about all the things he had caused to go wrong. It was brutal and shaming.

Heinrich stuck to the story he had memorised during the days at sea. He had successfully integrated. The weasel had been identified and entrapped. No one had suspected him. He'd even found friends in the local police. He'd easily gained access to the airfield. He'd been set to blow up the fuel dump and disable operations, possibly indefinitely. The weasel had turned against him at the last minute, and escape was his only alternative. There was no circumstance in which he could still have blown the fuel.

He'd originally planned, then dismissed, an idea that he should claim credit for killing Harty and the woman. On balance, he saw this was an act of folly. Personal. The right ideological outcome, but one that grew like a weed from the failure of his actual mission.

The questioning was initially fractured. This and that, then that or this, and finally anything that was neither that nor this, but sometimes both. Nice, nasty, normal, numbing. Slowly, it crystalised in to one topic. Given Brandt's success at entrapment, and the obvious gullibility of the weasel, what had caused the Englishman to change his mind, and disrupt the sabotage?

Heinrich had prepared for this and reeled off a well-rehearsed soliloquy. Once exposed to the nearby gun position and its men, the weasel became emboldened and perhaps realised he could face a firing squad.

This problem seemed to be one that obsessed his interrogators. *Waste* became a word they all used, time and again. Years of training. Years of creating the world in which a spy, assassin and saboteur could safely reside. A world that was also secret from other sections of the German intelligence community, especially the hated Abwehr and their treacherous dogs. A whole chain of operatives in Ausland SD was compromised. Stories and documents and connections had to be unravelled, disconnected, destroyed, rebuilt.

Waste.

Failure. Shame. Imperfection.

Heinrich remained calm and disciplined. He dredged up every ounce of self-control to maintain the veneer of a brave fighter, defeated by chance and caprice rather than any failure on his part. For several days, he was convinced he would face something that ended with his expulsion from SD, the Party and possibly from this life.

But eventually it ended. The intensity of the debriefing concluded with a short meeting in which he learned his fate. He would remain at SD headquarters and kept from prying eyes for several weeks. Heinrich Brandt was neither known, nor acknowledged as an operative, therefore no identity change was required. He simply needed to be kept out of circulation until it was safe for him to return to normal life. His role in Ausland SD was finished, though he might have a part to play in protecting the Reich in some other way. It could be anything, but his days operating outside Germany were over.

By letter, he learned the tragic news that Katrin and Rolf's young daughter, his niece Rosa, was dead. She'd been killed in an air raid. She'd been staying with Rolf's parents in Hamburg. They hadn't found any bodies in the house. Katrin and Rolf were safe and well in Neubrandenburg, running a general store and living close to the old family home. Rosa's older sister, Renate, was with them. They were all broken and terrified.

When Heinrich finally returned to his home town in the summer of 1944, the newspapers and radio broadcasts were filled with news that American, British and Dominion forces had landed in northern France.

Twelve men, just and fair, returned four unanimous verdicts of guilty, two each on Megan and Bethan. The circuit judge listened impassively as a foreman confirmed the jury's decree, then thanked them all for their deliberations.

Without further ado, the judge informed the court he intended to pass sentence. He asked the twins to stand then donned a black cap and gloves. With no altered tone of voice, he said Megan's name then stared at her as he spoke.

'The sentence of this court is that you will be taken from here to the place whence you came, and there be kept in close confinement until August 15th, and upon that day that you be taken to the place of execution and there hanged by the neck until you are dead. And may God have mercy upon your soul.' When both twins replied *Amen*, the judge raised an eyebrow and missed a beat as he repeated his sentence to Bethan. The sisters both said *Amen* again, and then some other words that no one recognised.

During the trial, no one doubted the core witness, Sergeant David Morgan of the Pembrokeshire Constabulary. His sworn statement that he saw Megan and Bethan administer the stabbings that killed George Edward Cottam was given under oath. The jury also accepted the written confessions and wholly circumstantial evidence that the sisters had killed Alis James-Harty, whose disappearance was deemed suspicious and without credible explanation. Dewi had impressed the whole court with his powerful presence, and with the gravitas of his testimony. No one noticed that the sergeant never once looked directly at the twins at any time during the proceedings.

During questioning, he had recounted the events from that fateful day. Dewi had seen the unprovoked attack on George Cottam, then acted swiftly to arrest the sisters. Megan and Bethan hadn't resisted and willingly accompanied Dewi on foot to the Police Station. A constable had been despatched to stand guard over George's body until a doctor could attend.

Another constable was told to retrieve Dylan and the sisters' cart, then take it back to their shack, which he was instructed to search and remove any offending articles for investigation.

The constable found nothing.

The twins were formally charged with murder and locked in two of the three available cells.

Dewi made two phone calls, one to the local doctor, the other to his inspector. Twenty minutes later, Dewi met the doctor and they walked to see George's body. A cursory examination was all that was needed for the doctor to declare that death had resulted from two stab wounds; one almost certainly pierced the victim's heart; the other probably sliced through his spine. Either of the wounds would have caused instant death. The combination of the pair was conclusive. As soon as he returned to his surgery, the doctor completed a death certificate confirming the causes of death he had presumed at the scene.

A harassed detective soon arrived and, after interviewing the doctor and Dewi, took notes about the scene. Dewi and DS Williams were old acquaintances and chatted amiably as they walked back to the Police Station.

An ambulance carried George's body away to the mortuary at Fishguard hospital where it was embalmed, ready for onward transport. A constable was tasked with letting the senior officers at RAF St Davids know about George's death and whether any special action was needed. Confronted by a somewhat complex situation, the station commander and Military Police captain engaged in a discreet conflab and quickly concluded that since George Cottam had been discharged, his murder was a strictly civilian affair. His planned transport to Lancashire was cancelled.

Megan and Bethan continued to offer no resistance to what was being done, but also declined to speak. The only thing either of them said to anyone in earshot was a simple statement: 'Neither of us killed George Cottam. But he was complicit, with Huw Morris, in the deaths of Thomas Harty and Justina James. You know that to be true.' When DS Williams queried this with Dewi, he responded that these accusations were false, and a wicked fabrication to cover their own involvement in what had happened.

He didn't report this in court, but Dewi was shaken by the twins' determined repetition of pleas. A worm of worry had started oozing between his ears. No one had seen Huw Morris for months. He'd ignored that. Huw's disappearance was concurrent with the last time anyone had seen Gwyn Harries, whose boat had also been reported missing. Dewi had ignored that too. These were inconvenient matters that could intervene with great consequence for the already thorny problems he was managing.

Once DS Williams drove back to Haverfordwest to get his report typed up, the two men had agreed it was an open and shut case. Megan and Bethan had killed George Cottam and would be found guilty, then hanged.

Dewi cycled out to Rhosson himself, this time to search for birth certificates. Puzzled about where his constable had taken the horse and cart, Dewi reconnoitred the small building and its tiny outhouse. It was all utterly insignificant and nothing he saw inside changed his mind about that. The small, single storey abode had three sparsely furnished rooms and he roamed between them looking for something - anything - that might help his case. There was nothing. No pile, or box full of papers that might reveal where these damned women were from and what they were called. His ordered mind couldn't rationalise a way in which he could correctly conduct a formal process without knowing their names.

As he cycled back into town, something else clicked. There'd been a small bed in one of the rooms. Of course! The James woman's child! Where was she? Had those two also killed an infant? They must have done.

He got nowhere with questions about that, and the twins' mute disobedience made Dewi obsessed about proving them guilty. He phoned in to HQ to report his suspicions and new investigations made it evident that Alis James had not been recorded as born, and no welfare group had taken her in to care.

Within just a few hours of him finding George's body, Dewi had become deranged. His mind corrupted multiple episodes so the strands between them twisted into a tangled web of fakery and obfuscation. He had never trusted those sisters and now he turned that misgiving into malice. No fairness or logic prevailed. He would lie that he'd seen them kill George. And he would find a way to have them tried for infanticide. Somehow, Dewi deemed this to be justice for what had happened to Mary.

At the trial, the twins continued to say nothing despite being warned that their silence was contempt. Even when the court was shown two pieces of paper, each declaring responsibility for the death of Alis James, and disposal of her remains, they said nothing. As Police Sergeant David Morgan told the court that each sister had made their mark on those pieces of paper, marks witnessed by him as theirs, two pairs of eyes bore into him projecting their truth and derision for his acts. It didn't stop him committing perjury.

As directed by the judge, Megan and Bethan were taken back to Pembroke Castle where, within just a few days, and after one final sisterly hug, they were hanged.

A few moments after their bodies became inert, a Halifax bomber taking off from RAF St Davids exploded as it climbed over Whitesands Bay. The crewman in the mid-upper turret had spoken into his mask, questioning if anyone else had seen what looked like lightning. Whatever his six fellow crew had seen or said was taken to their watery graves in St George's channel.

Jane Howells saw what the gunner had seen. Alis saw it too. Looking over her mother's shoulder, she saw a reflection in the window.

For weeks, since the arrest and incarceration of the twins, Alis had been affected by fits of wild, staring anxiety. The flashes they'd both seen caused Alis to shudder, with something close to rage. She had hold of Jane's hair, pulling it hard. Jane moved her daughter so they could face one another and realised Alis's tiny voice had started to sing a tune. She continued to pull Jane's hair, but with a rhythmic pulse that matched her singing. The dark purple eyes showed Alis wanted Jane to learn the tune, and when she eventually sang along, Alis smiled.

It left Jane mesmerised and moved, but also unnerved by what felt like something that was controlling her. She rarely spoke Welsh, yet Alis had made her sing, 'Dial. Ad-daledigaeth. Cyfiawnder'. Why was she chanting about revenge, retribution and justice? That evening she hummed the repeating tune as Alis lay in her bed. It ended up being the first full night of sleep either of them had managed for months.

Heinrich felt an unease, bordering on panic, about the news. Soviet forces were rampaging towards Germany, triumphant every hour of every day. They were terrifying. He told Katrin they shouldn't stay. Poland's border, less than fifty kilometres to the east, would soon be breached. Staying here, in the far north east of a failing Germany, made no sense.

He'd been given work in the gestapo, working with other police to round up then torture dissidents and traitors. But it was a losing battle. People were filled with doubt about the future. Worse, there was scepticism, almost rejection of the recent past.

Katrin and Rolf were disinterested in his paranoia. Their business was far from thriving, but they had a kind of hope. Their future was no better and no worse than anyone else's. They had lost poor Rosa in that air raid, and felt sure their second daughter, Renate, needed the security of a family home. This was enough for them. Renate was still young and frail and needed their love and stability to keep going.

Heinrich didn't feel he could leave his sister behind. She was all he had. There would never be children with a Frau Brandt. He was the last in the line. He was still young enough to find love and a future with someone. Yet Heinrich lacked something, some simple set of rules, that made him want those things. He could admire a shapely form, or a pretty smile. But he found women impossible to know.

His tactic switched from presenting his own fears to one of disinformation. The Soviets are murdering their way through Poland, mutilating Germans and leaving civilians without homes. This was the Party line. The aggressor had become victim, conveniently ignoring its own atrocities.

In the spring of 1945, Katrin weakened. Soldiers from the Wehrmacht were seen fleeing the oncoming Soviets. Bombing, by guns and planes, was audible each day. Renate was terrified, and that was decisive. Quite possibly nowhere was safe, but anywhere would be better for a child. Heinrich fuelled the decision with news of the American and British advances in the west. Much safer to be vanquished by them, for all their faults, than by the savage communist horde.

Rolf and Katrin sold as much stock as they could, then closed the shop. Their small van was loaded with whatever could be taken. Two landlords would be left without rent, and with unpaid arrears, but they assumed that risk was worth taking.

Traveling on minor roads they reached the large, forested area near Lübeck, where Katrin knew a former colleague with space for them to stay temporarily. From there it was a short journey to Hamburg and, despite that city's devastation, Heinrich was sure it was the place to settle. It would be regenerated quickly and return to its status as a major port and trading post for a new Germany.

Heinrich quickly felt imprisoned by the kind goodwill of their host. He told Katrin he was going to make his way to Hamburg alone and find shelter there. They all agreed to meet again soon, and Heinrich said he would write with news, despite knowing letters might never be delivered.

He walked a while, then hitched a ride with an old man with sacks of vegetables in his truck. They spoke little and this silent journey made Heinrich realise the end had happened. Six years ago, their progress along the highways would have been filled with triumphal expectation that Germany was reborn. Now, all they had was a ruined destination and a frugal delivery.

Heinrich gave the old man a few marks for his trouble. The carrot he received in return was probably worth more than the cash.

Barsbüttel was a good place for Heinrich to take stock of his situation. A short walk to central Hamburg, but far enough away from potential fighting or bombing raids. His immediate dilemma was one of identity. He could certainly find and become part of the local gestapo organisation, but was that a future he should have? If captured, it wasn't out of the question that his role as a spy might be uncovered or that he might be identified as a saboteur and murderer. But if he could integrate quickly as a gestapo officer, it meant he would be found somewhere to live and make money.

At the Rathaus he was told to wait for his credentials to be checked with Berlin. Three hours later, Heinrich was collected by the local senior officer and taken to the police station for a briefing. He noticed no urgency or drive in this conference, nor in the four officers he met. But he was welcomed and, late in the afternoon, a colleague walked him to the relative safety of the room he could call home until further notice.

This was a conditional safety, perhaps one that had to be measured in short timescales. Days? Half days? Six hours? Two hours?

He sat on the lumpy bed and formed a plan. Each moment of every day needed to contain a contingency for escape. Heinrich would make sure he was always armed, and ready to shoot and stab his way out of any situation. He would report for duty each morning and conduct himself as a trusted officer. He made it a priority to find and steal an identity from police records. If necessary, he would kill for one. As soon as the wider situation demanded it, Heinrich would disappear into the wastes of central Hamburg and reappear as someone without a deadly past.

The first thing he did at the police station the following morning was to write a short letter to Katrin, confirming he was safe. They would be reunited soon, he promised her.

As the final months of war progressed towards victory, operations in and around RAF St Davids continued. There was still an enemy; still work to be done; still battles to engage and win. Thomas Harty's squadron had moved to a new base, each of its aeroplanes carrying his name on a small sign above the crew's exit hatch.

No one remembered or honoured George Cottam.

In the lanes and villages and towns around the airfield, the shocking events were less easily forgotten. Notwithstanding a war, this corner of the world was peaceful and calm. For it to become the scene of murders, attempted sabotage and of terrible unexplained accidents was a cause for anxiety and doubt.

Dewi Morgan saw it as a duty to create stability. With his team of constables, he began a process in which the police could be seen as a force for good, assuring security. Everyone trusted him. It made Sergeant David Morgan a pillar of their community and he revelled in it.

That sense of purpose and rectitude was redoubled when David Morgan Junior came home. Mother and son had never been parted in Claire's mind. Father and son had used the absence to form a bond in which they were battle-hardened survivors, sometimes shaken by the experience of hostility, but deep down filled with the knowledge that they had done their duty with honour.

They travelled for a family Christmas with Lizzie, Stephen and young Gareth and there were tears of reunion, then tears of remembrance for Mary. When Dewi and Claire left on Boxing Day, David Junior stayed behind. On New Year's Eve, he dressed in his infantryman's uniform and went into Fishguard to celebrate the end of a fateful year and the arrival of 1946. He was a young man who had fought to secure the future. It meant he was bought many pints by grateful souls who slapped his back, shook his hand and saluted him. David Junior had far too much to drink. Another soldier, not in uniform but still feted for his part in victory, realised help was needed. Ably supported by his sister, Geraint Carver helped David Junior to his feet and assisted the long stagger back to Stephen and Lizzie's house.

During the first afternoon of 1946, Kathryn Carver called round to see how David Junior was feeling. After several cups of tea, she left to go home, and everyone knew romance was in the air.

William Howells also came home. Jane stood at Carmarthen station. His face and shoulders appeared from one of the windows and Jane's heart nearly broke with relief and happiness. Alis watched this joyous collision of adults, amused by the scene and the floods of tears her mam couldn't contain. Once she was able to talk, Jane told her husband that Alis was their daughter.

On a warm, late September day, the couple and

their daughter travelled together to St Davids. William was desperate to go and swim in the sea, so a grand day out was planned, better still with a night together in relative privacy at Goat Street. As Alis gambolled in the shallows, Jane held William's hand and told him everything she knew about Alis. When she finished, she also told him the truth about her miscarriage and that she could no longer have children.

Lying in the shallows, tiny ripples of water lapping around her, Alis watched these two people embrace. She was two months from her third birthday, but she knew Jane and William weren't her real parents. Alis didn't mind, and happily accepted that they wanted to be her mam and dad. She sometimes still felt the slash of emotion she'd felt that night, when her real mam and dad were killed. And the turmoil caused when Megan and Bethan had been killed. Alis didn't understand why these things hurt her, but she loved Jane as mam and, because mam loved William, then she must love him as her dad.

The waves were growing more powerful. William walked to be with Alis and within a few moments she was giggling at the games he played with her. Jane joined them and they all played and laughed and swam in the azure waters of Caerfai Bay.

Sheila Cottam and Jack walked solemnly behind the hearse. The clip and clop of hoofs was the only sound, occasionally augmented by a screeching gull. The cortege wasn't long: a few friends had joined them; one of Jack's school friends. But parents were long gone, and there were no siblings. No one who had ever been one of George's pals, in the Loyal North

Lancashires or the Military Police, had been in touch. He was persona non grata in the eyes of His Majesty's armed forces.

She couldn't cry. Ever since the police arrived to tell her George had been murdered, Sheila had felt one emotion: bitterness. Sometimes this evolved into rancour. But mainly she just found herself demeaned by the knowledge that a husband she had barely seen remained her responsibility now he was dead.

Jack had cried. A few times. His boyhood wish for a father and guide had never been lost through the years he'd shared with a living, albeit absent father. The times George had spent at home were precious memories. But Jack's sadness was confused by doubt.

Worse still, whatever light had ever been lit in his mother was now extinguished and Jack had no idea if he could ever change that.

The cortege wound its way towards the town, up and down the hills before turning by the market square. A vicar greeted them, and the service was quickly over. Almost everyone drifted away once the last litanies were spoken, leaving Sheila, Jack, the vicar and some gravediggers to see to the final knockings.

Prayers, dirt, farewells.

Jack stood and stared into the hole and a final glimpse of the cheap coffin. As a soldier's child, he would have found the loss easier if his father's death had been heroic; some tiny part of the greater good; to be celebrated forever as a worthy part of a just cause. Instead, this was ignominy. His dad was nothing, killed by two old witches, or so it seemed. Jack cried again.

Sheila turned from her son and walked away from the graveside. Once she stepped off hallowed ground, she took out and lit a cigarette, sucking lungs full of smoke as if it would reinvigorate and mend whatever was happening. Two more draws changed nothing. From her handbag, Sheila pulled out the flask of whiskey she always carried and drained half of it in one go.

EIGHTEEN

Today

Ben had been phasing in and out of sleep all through Erin's storytelling, listening in an enforced silence to the words about people and places. She kept interrupting her story to look at him, testing his need for more sustenance and, if needed, feeding the tube for him to drink.

He realised he must have slept quite a long time because Erin was wearing different clothes.

'Do you like my new outfit? Ben? Do you? It's kind of revealing, isn't it?'

Another burst of the hummed, repeating tune she seemed to need as an impulse. She stood to his left; the bedroom door closed behind her. With the benefit of that doorframe as a guide, Ben realised she was tall, perhaps as tall as him: five feet ten; and a bit. The dark hair was a mess, as if by design. The face was slender, with high cheek bones. Two dark lines arched above her eyes. Her nose was ever so slightly upturned at its tip. And all Ben could think about her mouth was that it was utterly, utterly cruel yet kissable; lickable.

With a troubled shake of his head, Ben tried not to think that he fancied someone who was going to torture him. Either with drugs, or implements, or more of her serpentine story.

'It's rude not to answer my questions, Ben. Do you like my new outfit? One blink for yes, two for no. Maybe three if you think it's a bit... meh.'

He took in her appearance. It wasn't really an outfit. A tight, sleeveless top - perhaps a waistcoat, and possibly of leather - was buttoned up to her throat. Then shorts, like cycling shorts but with no padding. These were also tight and left nothing to Ben's imagination.

He blinked once and Erin beamed back at him.

'I'm fit as fuck aren't I, Ben? Aren't I?'

He blinked once and felt another wave of nauseating fear. She really was fit as fuck. Her skin wasn't pale, but nor was it tanned or stained. Every inch of her limbs was toned and lithe. On her upper left arm, on the outside of its bicep, he could see a tattoo: a symbol of some kind, but not one he recognised.

'Where were we? Oh yes. We'd just finished the second world war, hadn't we? I could tell how much you loathed those men, with all their wrongdoing and hatred. It was in your eyes. You know they were bad and got away with terrible acts and lies. You know the process now, Ben. Tell me. Yes or no. You hated them, didn't you? Morgan. Cottam. Brandt.'

Ben provided his response.

'I knew it. They were bastards. Absolute cunts. And so were their spawn and everyone who ever loved them. But you also loved the cultured, perfect women didn't you, Ben? The women and their chosen partners.'

She looked at him. 'Another solitary blink. You're learning.'

Ben felt as if he could make a dreadful mistake at any moment. Or perhaps just inadvertently twitch his eyes and tell her something she couldn't bear. To quash this sense of impending castigation, he turned his head to look at the window.

'Which woman did you like best, Ben? Oh, wait. That's quite a tricky one, isn't it?'

Erin scratched her chin, theatrically, as if about to

reveal how she'd solved some terrible crime.

'Let's do it this way. I'll say the names of these important women - hugely important women, I might add - and you blink when I say the name of the one you liked best.'

She started with Ava, Megan, Bethan, Cissy...

Ben blinked.

Erin scowled. 'What? Why? You can't like her best. How could you be that stupid?' The scowl became fixed. 'Answer me, Ben. Oh; playing dumb, eh? Well, that won't do.'

She turned to the table and unwrapped the polythene from one of the syringes. It was a pretty large one: about three centimetres diameter and more than ten long. Making sure his left arm was securely immobile, Erin took two steps so she could sit on the bed.

'Please tell me why you chose Cissy, Ben. Come on.'

Under the thick black lines of their brows, the dark purple eyes were suddenly threatening. Ben felt his bowels move.

Wait. When did I last have a shit?

Now Erin placed her right hand alongside Ben's torso and, as if it was a pen, used the syringe needle to trace a line slowly up the inside of his right thigh. When she reached his groin, she smiled cruelly.

'Are you really sure you meant Cissy?'

Ben tried a new tack and blinked twice.

'It was a lie then? I need you to be consistent, Ben. Please be consistent.'

Now she looked down at the needle again as she traced it back to the inside of his knee.

Ben had never listened much in school, but he knew that if she injected a bubble of air in to one of his arteries, it might kill him. And the needle was very close to one of his bigger arteries. She'd gone back up, halfway between knee and crotch.

'Why is your cock like that, Ben? And where have your balls gone?'

He had no idea. He couldn't tear his eyes off Erin's thumb on that plunger. The humming was constant now. What was that tune? Since he'd started humming it to himself that day, Ben couldn't shake the earworm it had become. But what was it? Two notes. Then four notes. Then two notes.

'If not Cissy, then who?'

She started the list again. He stared at her. At the end of the list, she said, 'You have to make a choice, Ben.' He felt the needle go slightly harder up against his skin. She repeated the list of names, but this time finished with a new option.

'Maybe it's all of them, Ben. Is it all of them that you love?'

One blink.

Erin laughed loudly. 'Perfect. I knew it.'

And she stood up and placed the syringe back on the table, grabbing the bottle with its pink-tinged liquid so Ben could drink some.

'Don't worry about wetting or shitting the bed, Ben. That won't be a problem. But you do need to keep having this wonderful sustenance. And I'm thinking that, maybe, you might soon need something to help your poor genitalia. They look so lost down there, all shrivelled and withdrawn. Any man in his right mind would have a boner looking at me. I mean look at me, Ben. I really, truly am fit as fuck. Aren't I?'

He affirmed it, then also blinked that he'd sucked in enough of the liquid.

'Good boy. Now, we had started to discuss Alis, hadn't we? She was a growing infant and it's time you learned more about her, and some of the things she did in memory of her mother, grandmother and favourite aunties.'

Ben sighed deeply.

'Oh, am I boring you, Ben? Is this tale of wonderful people becoming too much for you? Is it? Two blinks. I see. Well, that's good. But don't sigh again, Ben. I don't like being made to feel like I'm somehow a nuisance.'

Erin's story rolled on to a new, post-war chapter.

Act Two

ONE

Alis

With war consigned to history, the Howells' family life settled into a loving calm, with Alis at its core. The delayed start to married life had caused no harm. William joined Jane working at the hotel. His job as a kitchen apprentice was poorly paid, but he preferred that to being shot at and bombed. Within just a few days, workmates started to call him Will, and it stuck forever.

Rebecca decided to move away from the town leaving Jane and Will as sole tenants at the house. While Alis was young, they worked shifts that allowed one of them to be with her constantly. When she started school, their working lives became fuller.

From the moment she went to school, she confirmed what Jane and Will had always known: Alis was gifted and intelligent; she made friends easily; she was happy.

As a new queen was prepared for her crown and ointments in distant London town, Alis passed her tenth birthday. She was trustworthy and sensible, so Jane and Will felt able to give her time alone, especially at weekends when she had friends to rely on for company. But Alis went exploring alone. She could wander down to Rhosson and that cottage. She vaguely understood its significance. Closer to the sea, the ruined chapel sent a chill through her, even on the warmest of days. There was an ancient energy beaming from its stonework, and small voices, using a language that meant nothing.

By the lifeboat stations, old and new, Alis climbed the steps down to sea level. The rocks and caves were slippery and sharp, but they were comforting, as was the sea as she paddled.

In another direction, it was no distance to the coast near St Non's relics. Whenever she reached it, she cupped her hands and drank water from the well. Then her roaming extended, around in a loop from these relics to Caerfai beach and back through St Davids to home. Long walks for a relatively young child, but she felt she wasn't, and never had been, young.

There were occasional family outings. Jane and Will took Alis to Solva by bus and, once there, they doubled the surprise by climbing on a boat to cruise out to Ramsey Island. The busy craft, filled with sight-seeing passengers eager for glimpses of sealions, all manner of birds and perhaps of dolphins, made its way along to the island. Alis saw many things in the faces of those people. They were strangers to her, in fact to the whole of this small corner of the county, yet she saw truth and lies, good and bad, happiness and sadness. And she saw a sense of renewal and confidence, despite the austerity they all endured. Hearts and minds were changing, eager to leave behind the terrible events that had marked the first half of a century. This short boat trip, across waters her grandmother had sailed, and in which she had perished, helped Alis find depths of empathy and intuition for the way she saw and interacted with strangers.

Jane and Will treated her to a second-hand bicycle, and it enhanced her curious, impetuous roaming. The quiet lanes presented neither risk nor danger and Alis often cycled to Solva, up past Middle Mill to Caerfarchell and back home via Whitchurch. The airfield was still guarded by men, machines and wire. An occasional flight occurred, but the place seemed like an antiquity to Alis despite it being of an age with her. She wanted to walk unhindered past the uniforms or climb through the wire to see what made those barriers necessary. Her mam and dad told her it would soon be closed, having played its part in a victorious drama. They also said they were glad to see the back of it: a symbol of how money could sometimes be found when it was needed, but only to suit those holding the purse strings.

As well as sating her curiosity, the cycling made Alis strong and fit. She was tall compared to her peers, but graceful with balletic movements. What she loved most about any of the trips she made, on foot or bike, was how her mam and dad loved to hear what it had meant to her. How it had made her feel. The things she had learned. Alis was lyrical and descriptive in the way she told these tales and they spoke openly about her feelings that these places were somehow known to her. Will and Jane knew only fragments of the history Alis was absorbing and often told her they couldn't answer her questions or calm her worries. But they encouraged her to write down her thoughts and feelings. This she did: sometimes in poems; sometimes in short stories. Words neatly scribed in pencil on the pages of an old notebook.

When she went to the big school, Alis continued to learn voraciously with a love for mathematics. She also proved to be adept with languages and asked for books so she could learn German and Spanish. She was viewed, by every teacher she encountered, as highly talented and gifted: more than enough to do the new-fangled A levels, and dream of a place at university.

These things overwhelmed Jane and Will with pride. Their child was almost always happy and now it was clear she also possessed exceptional skills. There was no longer any sense between them that Alis was a cuckoo. Will and Jane had successfully presented her to the worlds of authority and bureaucracy as their child. Alis James-Harty was judged to have been murdered and no one ever considered the coincidence that Jane had a baby girl with the same name. Alis' birth had been registered with amended facts about Jane's original pregnancy. The retrospective birth certificate for Alis Howells was waved through by a registrar, too harassed to dig deep.

But this was history, troubling no one's conscience. Terrible tragedies and losses had ended well. Alis was the apple of so many eyes and her parents revelled in it. Their jobs were secure, but their income was low and Alis could never be spoiled. There were occasional extra special gifts: the bike; the boat trip. But the one she was given to mark both her thirteenth birthday and the Christmas of 1955 remained sacred to her for the rest of her days.

The bus trip to Fishguard took more than an hour, making it an adventure all on its own. Alis saw the signs to new places, and subtly changing scenery. Compared to St Davids, this harbour town was a metropolis. Alis found it both fascinating and troubling, but it was their surprise arrival at Fishguard's Cinema that sent her into bubbles of delight. The matinee performance of *Lady and the Tramp* was a revelation. Jane and Will had been to the flicks before, at Haverfordwest's Cinema de Luxe. But those had been old monochrome films, worthy and dramatic, for adults who were probably lovers. The dazzling colours of an animated film and the newer, more vibrant sound and vision were astonishing to them. Whereas, for Alis, this was simply magical, and gave her the desire and ambition to see films as often as she could, no matter how complex the logistics.

Her teachers had not over-stated Alis's abilities. Instead of leaving school in the summer of 1958, she stayed as a sixth former, studying French, History and Mathematics.

Will had worked his way up to be a senior chef. Jane was head of housekeeping. Tourism was growing as more and more people discovered this part of Wales. The hotel was thriving, and it meant steady employment. The family home was increasingly filled with small things to indicate material and cultural gains. In some ways, they really had never had it so good.

In November 1959, Alis celebrated her 17th birthday. Will and Jane treated her to books about learning, but also to a record player and several 45rpm discs: Little Richard; Connie Francis; Ricky Nelson; The Everly Brothers; Eddie Cochran; The Platters. She was besotted by this new, crazy music. After they all shared a slice of birthday cake, lovingly baked and iced by Will, they danced together with joyful abandon to *It's Late* and Alis didn't think she could love her mam and dad more.

Alis also received a treat in the form of a much-anticipated kiss from Rhodri Lewis. They'd met at school and Rhodri was polite and undemonstrative, which very neatly matched Alis's cautious, reserved nature. In the few weeks building up to their debut, she had grown to like how, whenever he called round to ask if she'd walk out with him, he called Will *Sir* and Jane *Ma'am*.

It was a chilly December afternoon when they left school together. Rhodri said he had a birthday gift for Alis and asked if he could walk her home. She had no intention of saying no. Once clear of the school she took his hand and they walked to the old Celtic Cross to sit on the steps, which seemed a good place for

Rhodri to suggest a kiss. After all the months of smiles and stares, the moment made perfect sense despite any fumbling inexperience. That single kiss wasn't the end, and it was some time before they stopped to sit, close knit and holding hands.

Alis felt charmed and aroused by Rhodri's proximity and the calming waves of his voice. It seemed they both felt a desire to be together and to form new, deeper links. Everything he said was beguiling. Her responses were receptive and eager. She started to kiss him again, their mouths meeting in between her nibbles on his neck and ear lobe and temple. Two pairs of hands moved gently over places they both felt were safe to touch while avoiding more needy parts. For the first time in her life, Alis found the sensual; not only from his hands on her neck, back, hands and face, but also through her own fingers on Rhodri's body.

He broke the spell with an almost brutal change of subject.

Rhodri spoke, no longer calmly, of his frustration with life in this backwater, filled with small things and smaller opportunities. How could there be a future here? What could possibly be good for anyone this far from the modern world? Rhodri wanted to move away, and not just up the coast to Aberystwyth or along the way to Swansea or Cardiff. The lives of young people were taking off, rocketing towards new things for a new decade to come. Not here: in England; especially in the cities. That was his future.

He said it in a way that made Alis feel excluded and spurned. His kisses had been arbitrary and momentary. In the time it took him to say what he'd said, she saw there was no future in all the things they'd just enjoyed.

It made her tell him to go and never come back.

Alis cried herself to sleep that night, with a sudden

sense of loss and seclusion heaving in her heart. The next day, she rose to tell her mam and dad she needed to be alone.

She walked to St Justinian, and down the steps to sea level. Leaning back against the rocks, her feet in the searching waters as they lapped up to meet her, Alis cried in a way that she had never cried before; not even when she'd learned what had befallen Stina and Thomas.

In this place, between earth and water, Alis was entranced and had a sense of being elsewhere. Disorientation gripped her, as if the rocks behind her were liquid and the sea beneath her was solid. Her eyes flickered and she felt a growing, unbearable nausea. When she looked across at where Ramsey Island should be, there was an opaque darkness.

A cinema reel of images became projected on to the darkness ahead. Alis seemed to take off and float above, around and sometimes through the screen.

It started with cartoons and shorts.

Lines of trenches, khaki-clad men, a lifeless soldier snared by wire.

A beach, a pretty young girl cavorting, a crashing surge knocking her back.

Ruins, a cautious man, confused, fearful then terrified as blades flashed.

Astride a bomb, plummeting down at a child, terrified and lonely.

That's All Folks.

Nothing else to see.

Then the features began.

Weddings, across generations, smiling brides, simple finery, grooms in uniforms with medals and stripes. Some faces were vaguely familiar, but she wasn't sure how. Successive services, in a place she knew, spanned time, revealing older versions of the couples.

A change of scene, to clifftops above a harbour. A couple, perilously close to the edge. The man had been one of those uniformed grooms, but this wasn't his bride. This was more than love. They were fiery-eyed, their cries like rage rather than passion. Handcuffs and a truncheon lay nearby.

A different church, another uniformed, jittery man, his cap crushed under an arm. She'd seen him, older, demented and broken at the Bishop's Palace. A woman approached, her wedding dress pretty, in its way: simple; no head dress. Alis saw tension, and very few smiles. The same bride, years later, sneering at the swirling confetti, uninterested in the wedding party being captured in photographs. A cigarette drooped from her mouth; her hand shook when she reached to remove it. Her grand clothes seemed to be made threadbare by the dying soul they dressed. The groom called this woman *mum*. His bride's eyes held contempt. Alis zoomed in to the couple and captured their faces.

Then she flew away over land and water to see more happy family scenes. Words in a language she knew but couldn't translate. Her attention settled briefly on a short, dark-haired man with cruelty in his eyes. He seemed anxious to leave, to do other things, but there was also love in his eyes for the couple being married. Alis retained their features so that, when they reappeared, she knew them despite their greying hair. She glanced again at the anxious, furtive one, still cruel and contemptuous, with the cold disdain, perhaps of a killer. Then she focused on the couple being wed. These people filled one final scene, once more at a church, but this time for a baptism. Two infants in identical, flamboyant gowns, howled their dismay. One of Alis's surges towards the font caused the babies to become silent.

Then the reels flickered to blank, and Ramsey Island was back on the horizon, unmasked and bold.

It was a sunny, cold December day and the incoming tide was causing a deepening pool under her knees. Time to go. Back to mam and dad, and to make an apology for her rushed unhappy demeanour that morning. They were the best thing in her life and losing sleep over a boy, for he was still just a boy, was no way to behave. Alis was ready to be the perfect child for perfect parents, but also to find ways to honour the parents she had barely known.

Back at school, Alis made sure she politely but permanently avoided Rhodri. Nothing was left in her heart for him, and she wondered how she had ever missed his disloyalty to this place, their home. For his part, Rhodri was unhappy and more determined to find new pastures. In the time he'd known her, Rhodri had become terribly fond of Alis, enough to think of it as love. Her sudden loss of temper that evening was mysterious to him and to anyone he tried to discuss it with. But he took the hint, and left Alis to her own devices.

Alis wanted to see *Look Back in Anger* and, sensing her sad determination, Will took her to see the film. They sat in the stalls, captured by the monochrome tension before them, bewitched by the lilting beauty of Richard Burton's voice and diction. Will had felt uneasy that the film might be inappropriate for Alis but, when they left, she told her dad she felt happy now. He asked her why and, on the bus back to St Davids, she told him how she had fallen for Rhodri. How she had been hurt by him. How she hated him for wanting to run away from their home, town and community. How she felt rejected by him wanting to leave her behind. Will listened with baffled concern, then told her Rhodri had done nothing wrong. His ambition and restlessness weren't crimes, and it wasn't disloyal to look away from home. The important thing was to know that home is always there. Being able to return to it is the one thing that makes leaving it easy.

Alis linked her arm through Will's and rested her head on his shoulder. He'd said nothing to make her seek reconciliation with Rhodri, but she loved the fact that her dad had shown her what she herself felt. Should she ever leave their home, her heart would always be there. With Jane and Will. With Stina and Thomas. With Ava, Megan and Bethan.

Alis didn't get a place at university. But Rhodri did and, once he was in London, he wrote to her every week. His letters, increasingly affectionate and loving, were filled with news of things that seemed quite literally incredible. When Alis eventually wrote back, she crammed a dozen pages with the things she felt about Rhodri. He came home after his first term to spend Christmas 1960 with his family. Instead, he spent almost every day with Alis.

After leaving school, she had joined her mam and dad working at the hotel. It offered visiting families a service in which their children were tended and cared for, allowing the parents time to be alone together. Alis became part nursemaid, part parent, part teacher to these children while despairing that their mams and dads could leave them, even for an hour, to shirk their own responsibilities. Outside of home and work, she was a little lost and her correspondence with Rhodri became a sole, treasured diversion.

Towards the end of his first year, Rhodri wrote to suggest Alis should come to visit him. It would be good for her; for him; for them. Jane and Will didn't object, helped her plan the trip then travelled with her by bus to Haverfordwest, where her onward journey could begin. As the train trundled along to Cardiff, then over the border to England, Alis realised she was making a journey that her father had never been able to make in peacetime. Back to London, to the Thames, to a house and home and an endlessly grieving family. She became lost in this notion.

Rhodri met her at Paddington, then Alis stood with him in the crushed proximity of an underground train carriage and felt free. This was a world she wanted to know. Not just the pleasures of being with the young man she loved, and who she knew would soon be naked underneath her. But this place. This mass of people and ideas and constructs. Opportunity and threat. Strong and weak. A world apart from the places she knew, in another tiny geography. As they jerked and jolted through a tunnel of love, Alis felt she might not return to Goat Street. Part of her history, of her flesh and blood, was right here in London. Somehow, Will's words about leaving home made her heart feel torn, for perhaps there was a sad reality in which Alis had no home.

They spent more time in Rhodri's spartan room than in the pursuit of cultural or popular pastimes. A day and half lost in a place where desire and pleasure replaced whatever they had previously felt about each other.

When it was needed, they strolled out for refreshment; simple food at a café; a flavoured shake from a milk bar; a walk in Russell Square. These things refuelled their lusts for another evening and night.

Alis wanted to stay longer but, with no means to contact Jane and Will, her return journey couldn't be postponed. It was weeks later, at summer's end, that she and Rhodri travelled back to London for him to start his second year and for Alis to spend time in the capital. Each day she walked miles while Rhodri attended lectures and it seemed to Alis that she learned more than he did. She also realised that his fellow students called him Rhod, and she liked to gasp that in his ear when they made love. That lost syllable was a boon.

When she told Rhod she wanted to go and see the docklands, especially in the Isle of Dogs, he told her she was crazy. It was a dying, decaying place. Unsafe and unruly. Alis insisted and said she would go alone if he continued to resist her. They had quite a row. Rhod was adamant there was no more to see than disused docks, demolished housing and vanished prospects. In between their raised voices and frustrated gestures, Alis shouted that it was her father's home.

She hadn't meant to tell him, but now he knew.

During their bus ride through the city and Wapping to Tower Hamlets and finally into the old docklands, Alis told Rhod some closely guarded secrets about her real mam and dad. These were tales handed down to Jane by Megan and Bethan, whom Alis had barely known. But she believed it all: Thomas and Stina; a brave RAF erk and a skilled clothes maker; lives cut short; evil and injustice; unfinished business.

It was a saddening, awful journey. Rhod felt cut off from the history Alis revealed, and shocked by what it said about the community back home. His judging and unhappiness also upset Alis. They became silent and fractured by the revelations, but also by the decaying landscape at their destination. They left their bus near a large park and walked through the greenery towards the Thames. Holding hands, but without real conviction, they walked along the riverside with the smells and ships and certainty of the waters to their left. Alis had no idea what she was looking for, but she knew there was something to find. She didn't know her father's family had lived in Malabar Street and that he'd been a pupil at St Edmunds' school. She knew his name was Thomas Harty but that was it. It was a search against a backdrop of desolation for, in this place, the only life seemed to be in the hissing, tumbling waters of the river and the craft it sustained. They walked back to the main road and, when their silence became unbearable, Alis pulled Rhod towards her, asking him to hold and kiss her.

It recharged their affection, and they walked along roads bordering great swathes of demolition sites. Rhod asked how he could help her resolve this search. Alis told him she simply didn't know what she needed but felt better now she had him back. She agreed with his suggestion that they return to his college for food, comfort and a library full of facts and reference books. Their hand holding was back to being tender and intimate and they spoke happily of home as they passed the junction of Malabar Street and Alpha Grove. As they reached the bus stop, Rhod pointed to a telephone kiosk and suggested Alis might find people called *Harty* in the phone book. There could be hundreds, but it would be a start. Alis cuddled him tight and said she'd found what she was looking for.

There were two days left before Alis had to return to St Davids and, together, they read many accounts of what had happened on the Isle of Dogs since Thomas Harty left in 1940. They went to Westminster Abbey and spent time sifting through names in the Civilian War Dead Roll of Honour. By the time she sat on the train home, Alis felt sad but resolute about what she now knew of her father's home in E14. There had been widespread loss of life in bombings and V1 missile attacks. She had found the recorded deaths of several people called Harty, but some instinct made her dismiss any of those listed before December 1942. Perhaps the few who died after Thomas was murdered might have been his, and her, relatives. It was all inconclusive. She never knew a maternal grandma called Ava nor paternal grandparents called Jennifer and Joseph. Like Stina, she had formed a loving bond with surrogate parents. Yet these were people-sized silhouettes in all her thoughts and memories. Something, or someone, had removed her biological loved ones.

As the train steamed from the tunnel under the River Severn, Alis felt no sense of joy that she was back in Wales. She filled the remaining journey writing a long, loving letter to Rhod.

As her bus crawled up the hill out of Solva, Alis was bored and irritable. It felt as if she'd been travelling forever, not helped by the train's late running. She'd perked up a bit along that stretch of sea and sand past Newgale and again when she saw the pretty harbour. The tide was in, and the afternoon sun had flashed on the water and masts. She did love the sea. But it was soon out of sight, and she sighed deeply as the bus picked up speed.

Suddenly it braked sharply, and she heard the driver swear loudly then shout a question to the conductor.

The conductor confirmed that, no, he hadn't seen that. But Alis had. Over to the right, quite close to their road, there'd been three massive flashes. Like lightning, except none of the lights had been fork-shaped or a jagged strike line. What was imprinted on Alis's vision, even behind closed eyes, was an abstract letter A: one; two; three. Darting up from the ground at an angle, then again to intersect with the first, and then finally across from left to right.

The driver shouted an apology, then the conductor walked along the aisle checking everyone was all right. No one on board was troubled. But as the bus coasted down into the centre of St Davids, Alis was preoccupied and alert.

There he was. The fine figure of a man that Alis had captured and retained from those visions. Even in old age, he looked strong and quite powerful, his bearing proud and undaunted. Who was he? Why was he here? Why there, at the Police Station? The backslapping, handshaking, laughing throng of patriarchal oneness made Alis shudder. As she stared at the scene with these questions churning in her brain, she saw him watching the bus with disquiet.

Old Dewi had driven down to join in with another retirement celebration for one of the lads. His own retirement had been emotional not least because it had meant the loss of a home as well as the daily grind. But Claire had enjoyed being back in Fishguard. It had always been their destiny to return. Lizzie and Stephen were there, and they sometimes saw Gareth and Karen, whose recent wedding had been so joyful. David Junior and Kathryn had a home nearby, so it all felt like the family had regrouped.

Yet Dewi still missed the days at Tyddewi and the uniformed camaraderie he'd shared with many pals down the years.

Alis's eyes met Dewi's, and he frowned.

What did he know?

This was all gone in a few seconds and Alis climbed down from the bus to walk the final few hundred paces of her journey home. Jane was there and greeted her daughter with warmth and tenderness. When Will joined them, tea was served, and a very happy family reunited for their first meal together in more than a week. All Alis's news was of London's sights and sounds. Trips to the cinema, to see Lilies of the Field and Charade. The hot new music she'd heard with Rhod at Ronnie Scott's made her mam's eyes roll and *Kind of Blue* was soon revolving on the record player. As Will tidied and washed up, Alis asked Jane what she knew about the policemen in town from back when she was young.

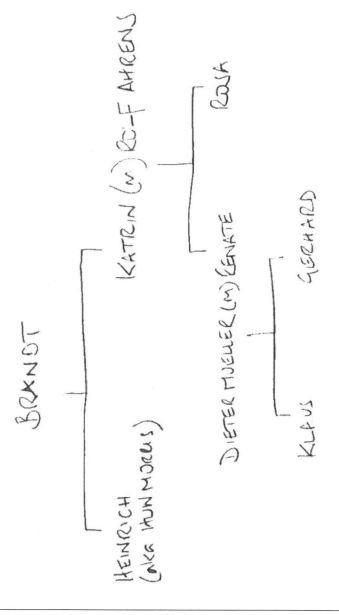

BRANDT

HEINRICH
(aka IRON MORRIS)

KATRIN (m) ROLF AHRENS

ROSA

DIETER MUELLER (m) RENATE

KLAUS

GERHARD

TWO

Heinrich Brandt still wasn't comfortable in the name and guise he'd taken back in 1945. His pride in all he had been as a young German and Nazi had been diluted these eighteen years and he hated this guilt-ridden nation and the powers that controlled and occupied it.

Yet he also chuckled to himself that, from his heyday as a spy and saboteur, his alter-ego in Wales lived on in the name he had fashioned for himself. Uwe Moritz had no accent, no limp and no love of that crazy game called rugby, but Huw Morris was alive and kicking somewhere in Heinrich's soul.

He'd seen the end long before it arrived, and the plan he formed that day in Barsbüttel was executed in haste several weeks before Germany surrendered. With help from a trusted fellow officer, papers were created to show his new name along with a credible history. They kept it simple and ensured very limited variation from Heinrich's real story. When his new history was documented and certain, he shot dead the trusted fellow officer.

They'd made his story simple. Born in 1905, orphaned by influenza in 1919, a citizen of Lübeck, working as a delivery boy for a shop that perished in RAF raids. He'd joined the Wehrmacht in 1938 and eventually been stationed in Northern France. When the British and Americans landed, Uwe fought heroically, but was captured near Caen and spent the rest of the war in a prison camp. He returned to Germany and settled in Hamburg. Then the fiction turned to reality. Uwe really did become an aid worker, helping the homeless and refugees to find shelter, food and clothing. In 1950, he formed a business with a family friend from Neubrandenburg, Rolf Ahrens, and their grocery store had been thriving ever since.

In 1963, Uwe turned fifty-eight and felt the heavy toll of pretence even though his sister, her husband and all their family, had agreed not to talk of their history as a family called Brandt.

He didn't expect to be discovered, yet Eichmann's capture, trial and execution by the Jews had left Heinrich jumpy and fearful. He truly didn't know if any records existed that declared Heinrich Brandt as a member of the SD. But if there were…

Events kept making him anxious. The death of his niece in that bombing raid might link him to Katrin. She was just a child, alone in a building, terrified and lost then blown to bits by a cowardly British bomb. Her death was a recorded fact, but he had no way of knowing if any lines linked Rosa to him via her mother.

When his niece was married, Heinrich had felt a chill all through the ceremony as if he were being watched or spied upon. There was no reference to anyone called Brandt, at any point during the service, yet somehow it felt that the name was piping from the organ or floating from the priest's book of prayers. That had been more than ten years after he'd killed those irrelevancies on the Island, but he couldn't shake the fear of being discovered. The British were everywhere in Germany, being directed and governed by their American overlords; like Pavlov's Dogs, conditioned by the stimuli of stars and stripes.

What if some chance meeting might uncover him as

a murderer and spy, for whom hanging wasn't good enough?

It was the same at the baptism. Uwe believed that these events, where he was part of a family that Heinrich had left behind in 1945, were somehow dragging him down into a deathly undercurrent.

These thoughts had to be dismissed. Here he was, walking hand in hand with his great-nephews, who loved time with their grey-haired old double uncle. That's what they called him: *Der Doppelte Onkel*. They knew nothing of his crimes, his Nazism or his pretence. He was just the man who spoiled them with treats and walks in the park. Someone who wasn't their dominating mother or uninterested father. And, best of all, someone who occasionally told them stories about the war.

He wasn't supposed to tell them, but they kept asking.

How or why could these two young boys, born twelve years after Germany's defeat, be guilty of anything? Heinrich dismissed it. Uwe dismissed it. They were part of a new Germany. It was divided and occupied, sure enough, but he knew they would be part of something bigger and better long after he was gone. He loved dear Klaus and Gerhard.

And they loved the open spaces here in the Hammer Park, where they could run and laugh and call out to their double uncle, knowing he would throw or kick the ball for them whenever they demanded it. But they also left him to think and reflect on a lovely spring day. These were good times. Hamburg was slowly evolving from all that had sought to destroy it. A strong, vibrant city and port with culture racing through it like a virus. Uwe didn't always approve of this new direction, but he never bit a hand if it fed him. Hamburg was feeding him.

They were close to the end of the pathway through the park that ended on Hammer Hof. His neat, clean Ford Taunus was parked there, ready to take them back to the boys' parents. Ahead of him was something else that fed Uwe, almost to a fault. The *wurst* vendor didn't seem to be trading too well, which seemed a shame for she was rather pretty in his eyes. Tall and dark. A Slav maybe? Or Celtic. These incomers were everywhere. Uwe called to his nephews to see if they wanted a *bratwurst* with some bread and a little mustard. This was his favourite, but he guessed right that the boys would decline. These were old-fashioned delicacies now and their parents were feeding them on the sops and saps of modern food from America, and the fucking Italians. Why were those peasants influencing German diets now?

He shook his head and felt he should resist the lure of the sausage he loved. The boys had returned to his side and walked dutifully with him. Playtime was over. Double Uncle Uwe was in charge. Then he changed his mind. The young woman at the stall really was strikingly beautiful and her dark purple eyes smiled at him, her eyebrows raised in a challenge and question.

Möchten Sie eine Wurst, mein Herr?

Of course he wanted one. *Sicherlich.*

Uwe asked the boys to stand obediently still while he took and paid for his *bratwurst*. The vendor happily smeared extra mustard on the paper plate and smiled when Uwe asked for a second piece of bread. This was an unexpected treat at the end of a lovely couple of hours in the company of his favourite *Jugend*. He would have to eat it before driving, so once again he asked the boys to wait patiently, then bit into the sausage.

Uwe didn't really understand what happened next, but Klaus and Gerhard were quite clear. They ran in terror from the large black cat, big as a panther, that leapt out at them from inside the Hammer Park and past the stall selling sausages. It had terrifying eyes and sharp, deadly claws. It was going to attack and kill them. With his mouth full of porky goodness, Uwe watched them dash away with surprise, then shock. The driver of an oncoming van also didn't understand what he saw. He couldn't brake in time to stop his van smashing in to the two boys as they ran from the pavement. They had seemed to do it for no reason. Nor did the driver understand why that old man was standing clasping his throat, his eyes staring maniacally, his mouth opening and closing like a silent film star dying on screen. Were the two things connected? By the time the driver realised his van had killed the two young boys, pedestrians were also tending the body of Uwe Moritz. A sudden wind had blown away the tissues and paper plate he'd been holding.

No one knew where Uwe bought the *bratwurst* that killed him, but no vendors had been licensed to operate in or around Hammer Park that day. It was assumed he must have brought it from home. Large traces of Botulinum Toxin were found in his system, consistent with the food poisoning that can be caused by poorly prepared sausage. The two boys, Klaus and Gerhard Mueller, must have been scared by the sudden muscle spasms and terrible noises their Great Uncle had emitted. In a blind panic, they ran away and into the path of an oncoming van.

All three deaths were declared as accidental and two weeks later, Katrin and Rolf Ahrens sat in the rear seats of a large funeral limousine with their daughter and son-in-law facing them. Everyone was stone faced, but their tears had all flowed.

The limousine didn't reach the church. It was found outside Hamburg's city limits on wasteland. All four occupants were dead because the car's exhaust had been redirected into the rear compartment. The company booked by the funeral director to supply the limousine told police the reservation for their car had been cancelled three days before the funeral. No one in the street where the Muellers lived had seen anything suspicious. It was the funeral of a man and two tragically young boys. Everyone knew. The arrival of the large black limousine had been unexceptional. The black-clad driver, with dark glasses and a large hat sat patiently in the car while the Muellers and Ahrens climbed on board. Then it drove off.

No trace of fingerprints or any other identifying evidence was found on the steering wheel, driver's seat, door handle or ignition key. It seemed odd that, despite being driven at least ten kilometres and the engine left running for some time, the car had a full tank of fuel and the engine appeared never to have been started. The police initially issued a warrant for a killer they couldn't describe but, in the end, the investigation into the incident concluded that one of the occupants had driven the car to its destination then joined the others in the back and committed mass suicide. It was the only credible verdict.

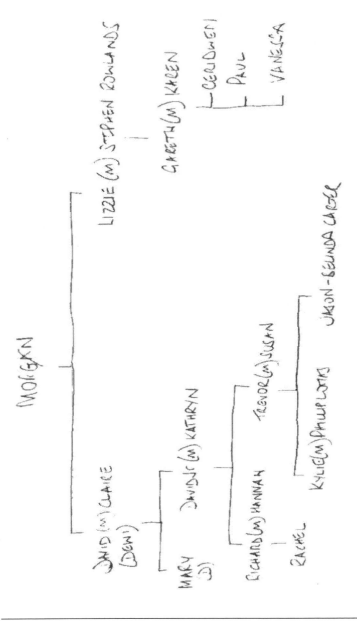

MORGAN

DAVID (m) CLARE (DEW?)

LIZZIE (m) STEPHEN ROWLANDS

MARY (D)

DAVID JNR (m) KATHRYN

GARETH (m) KAREN

CERIDWEN
PAUL
VANESSA

RICHARD (m) HANNAH

TREVOR (m) SUSAN

RACHEL

KYLIE (m) PHILLIP LLOYD-JONES

JASON - BELINDA CARTER

THREE

Alis

Alis married Rhodri Lewis in a small ceremony at the cathedral. It was a local affair, and the hotel provided a function room for the reception. Will and Jane joined with the groom's parents in wonder that their children had come home to be married.

For most of Rhodri's final year at University, Alis had been living in London and found work as an *au pair*. The couple she worked for often travelled and Alis accompanied them, even to occasional overseas destinations. As he stood with her outside the cathedral door, Will told Alis he'd only been able to travel abroad due to a war yet now, here she was, a seasoned traveller. She smiled and reminded him of his words about coming home. It didn't matter that she lived in London and had been to Brussels, Bern, Strasbourg and Hamburg. Here she was, home where she belonged.

The newlyweds soon headed back to a different home in London; the tiny basement flat Rhod had rented in Earls Court. It was close to the couple Alis worked for in South Kensington, and to underground stations that meant Rhod was in The City in no time, to grow his career with one of the high street banks.

Alis revelled in the proximity of dozens of cinemas and went weekly to feed her craving for films. She always saw the latest releases but loved older films too, especially those experimental French New Wave films. Rhod joined her occasionally, but she was happy on her own, especially when the films involved gorgeous actors like Peter O'Toole and Omar Sharif.

1965 was a very good year for Alis and Rhod.

The Police Sergeant

The detective constable turned off the main road down from Fishguard and slowed to a crawl in the narrow lanes that led to the coast. When he reached Porthgain, a uniformed bobby signalled him to halt so he pulled over then showed his warrant card and was waved through. The officer told him to make his way up to the clifftop cairn on foot.

As he parked his car, he could see activity up on the hillside overlooking the harbour. There was an ambulance parked ahead of him, backed up as near as it could get to the start of the path. He reached for his notebook and pen, then pulled on his overcoat before heading up to the cairn.

Another constable and a uniformed sergeant greeted him, and they exchanged introductions. There was a disturbing incident for Detective Constable Bessant to investigate, and a medical team was in attendance. He was told he needed a strong stomach. He noted that the young constable was visibly upset.

As they spoke, a woman approached and identified herself as Doctor Laing. In a tone that sought to be matter of fact, but which was filled with appalled distress, she confirmed that the body she'd just seen was dead. It was a middle-aged woman, perhaps in her late forties or early fifties. She was fully clothed. The cause of death was asphyxiation resulting from a blockage in her windpipe and mouth. Doctor Laing had found no personal effects on or near the body. She paused and took out a handkerchief to dab her nose and then one of her eyes. She said the ambulance crew would prepare the body so it could be carried with dignity to the ambulance, and she asked that nothing should be touched or removed from the body, pending a post-mortem. DC Bessant frowned at the word *removed*. Had she checked for personal effects or not? He remained politely silent.

The Doctor concluded her short briefing with the news that she would file a report and needed to know where to send it. The local sergeant provided those details.

DC Bessant asked if he could go and see the body and crime scene and Doctor Laing waved a hand in an expression of resigned *laissez-faire*. He shook her other hand and wished her well before walking over to where the uniformed ambulance crew was in action. He asked them for a moment to examine the scene and the pair walked away, lighting up cigarettes and chattering excitedly about the freak storm they'd seen on the drive over. Down St Davids way, it was. Or maybe out to sea.

There was a body lying on its back, fully clothed in flat shoes, trousers and a lightweight woollen jacket of some kind. She lay, or had been left, with her feet pointing to the south. Her arms rested above her head with the palms facing upwards. There was no obvious sign of a struggle. He noted this in his book and made a rough sketch of what he could see, paying attention to the proximity of clifftops and the cairn. Sweeping around the horizon, DC Bessant saw there was a similar cairn on the cliffs above the southern side of the harbour. Then he took out a small camera to take photographs of the scene. He was thinking constantly. Who was she? Was she local or a stranger? If a stranger, how far had she travelled? How had she got here? Did anyone see her walking up the path? When was that? Had she been alone or in company? Was she wearing clothes suitable for hiking? Who else had been in the area that might have witnessed any struggle or violence?

When he climbed back into his car, less than an hour after arriving, he had drawn a blank. No one had anything to tell him, but then no one was allowed to see the body, so they couldn't possibly say who it was and whether she was local. Once he'd finished his investigation at the crime scene, he knew he'd never seen anything like it. The cadaver, lying with apparent calm and no outward signs of violence, had a single horrifying signal of assault. He didn't want to look closer, but it was his job to look, listen and learn.

The body wasn't lying flat after all. There was a small log of wood, perhaps six inches in diameter, lying left to right under the woman's shoulders and it meant that her head was bent back almost at right angles to the spine. Her eyes were shut, and her pale brown hair was tidily arranged with a band, away from her face and ears. There was no sign of any wound. Doctor Laing had been right: this was a middle-aged woman. She wasn't wearing much makeup, not that DC Bessant was an expert. Earrings, a necklace and a simple bracelet indicated that robbery probably hadn't been a motive. As he searched the neck and face for signs of violence, his eyes kept gravitating towards the woman's mouth. It was open, with a strap or thong of leather falling away towards the right jawline. The strip of well-worn leather formed a loop, with a diameter that would allow a large hand to fit through it. There was a tight knot at one end. The loop of leather hung from a wooden implement of some kind, with a hole drilled through it. About an inch of this implement was visible outside the body's mouth.

Detective Constable Ceri Bessant knew what the implement was.

He'd written in his notebook that the body appeared to have a police truncheon forced into its throat, windpipe and chest via the mouth.

FOUR

Alis

Alis dropped Rhod at the railway station for his journey to Temple Meads. He kissed her on the cheek, then under her ear before squeezing her upper arm. She couldn't turn to kiss him properly, but she blew a fond kiss of farewell that he feigned to catch, before touching his palm on her straining tummy. He always told Alis that their baby deserved all her kisses.

He opened the car's back door to double check on the suitcase they'd packed, then confirmed Alis would pick him up from the early train. They'd be back home in time for Welsh cakes and cocoa before bed.

She waited outside the station until the train arrived and, once assured that Rhod was on his way into the city, Alis drove back through the town and on to the big house where she worked. She spent almost all her time alone humming a tune she hadn't thought of since she was a toddler. Whenever she came to a halt at a junction, she placed her hands on her tummy and hummed the tune loudly, so it passed into baby's mind. Two notes. Four notes. Two notes.

They'd moved to the west country when Alis was offered a job as a nanny by the owners of the big house. The London jet-set couple she'd worked for as an *au pair* became increasingly fractious and unpleasant during the second half of the sixties. They sometimes apologised and tried to make out it was due to pressures at work, but Alis knew it was the drugs. A summer of love hadn't ended at all well and, when some nice men in suits arrived to remove a television and some paintings, Alis left the house and never went back. They owed her several weeks' pay, but she and Rhod knew that any pursuit of the debt was a lost cause. Alis also missed out on any form of reference so her ability to work stalled for several weeks. Rhod's career was a continuing success, but they only just survived on his income. She'd had to pare back her visits to the cinema. It was a luxury they couldn't afford.

It turned out that the move away from London worked well for Rhodri. The bank offered him a transfer and promotion. There was nothing to keep them in the capital, and soon they found and rented a little house. As a couple, in love and as one, they settled into a much happier time in the thriving, growing town.

The change of location also meant they were closer to Pembrokeshire, which both of them still called *home*. Jane and Will had left the hotel to become managers of a small café in the town and Alis loved how happy they were. Once settled in Yate, Alis travelled to see her parents every month, with or without Rhod.

She loved being back in St Davids with her mam and dad, but also took every opportunity to walk to one of the beaches then amble barefoot to feel the sand between her toes and the water rippling around her ankles. She also walked to St Justinian and sat near the lifeboat station, imagining heroic launches to save souls. There was something flowing back into her, like fibres of history and family. When she was near the sea, or down near Whitchurch and Solva, Alis found she was humming that tune constantly.

During the spring of 1969, Alis had seen the doctor and learned she was pregnant. The news made Rhod incredibly happy, and he felt a surge of ambition and responsibility. Parenthood would make him work harder and be better. It didn't even trouble him that they would lose income again or have insufficient space for a family in their home. These things made Alis doubly happy. She was thrilled to be expecting, especially since baby was due on or about her 27th birthday.

That afternoon the roads seemed busy, and it took forever to get through the toll booth on to the Severn Bridge. Alis objected to paying, but Rhod said the two and a half bob was worth it. As they passed over the final part of the bridge, across the River Wye, they knew they were back in Wales and sang *Cwm Rhondda* with a boisterous swagger. But the great redeemer didn't guide them any quicker and it still took more than three hours to reach Goat Street and one pair of gleeful grandparents-in-waiting.

Alis had secretly hoped she might go into labour that weekend, but her 27th birthday came and went with her bump intact. There were cake and candles and a cumbersome group dance around Jane and Will's living room. The latest chart hits boomed out: her Mam and Dad loved The Archies; Alis sang loudest to Stevie Wonder and his yester-dreams. There was a lunchtime gathering at Rhod's parents the following day, and it was clear that Mr and Mrs Lewis objected quite strenuously to their son being called *Rhod*. It was also clear no amount of excitement was enticing the baby to be born in Wales.

It ended up she was born a week late, on December 11th, 1969. Alis had always known she would have a girl and Rhod loved the fact that he had a daughter. They called her Brigit, and she seemed content and calm in the arms of either parent. When her eyes opened, they were dark purple and soon began a constant search of both her parents' faces.

She learned to find fun and love in her father's eyes,

for he spent all the time he could holding his daughter and speaking or reading or singing to her. But all connection with Alis seemed to be shrouded, as if her mother were resisting any link or fusion: and she was.

More visions had started and Alis couldn't bear the idea that Brigit might see the things she saw: small ships sailing to and from a harbour; that tall, powerful man, smartly dressed, apparently enjoying life; a woman alongside him, kindly but nervous, bearing sadness like a cloak; another couple of similar age; some children, one tiny.

During a trip to visit Brigit's grandparents, Alis found a more powerful emotional bond with her daughter. They travelled alone and when Alis saw the love and joy her baby brought to Jane and Will, then to Mr and Mrs Lewis, it cemented that bond.

Rhod drove over to bring Alis and Brigit home. It was a time of great love and family unity, but it was over too quickly. When they left, Alis felt she'd been robbed of the time needed to show her daughter all the places that formed her birthright and history. It caused her to bicker with Rhod for almost the whole journey home. Brigit wailed from her travel cot on the back seat as her parents argued and complained, sometimes with shouts of rage.

As they crossed the Severn, the bridge was swaying in freshening winds. Her mam and dad became silent, but Brigit continued to cry. The conditions were frightening. Rhod gripped the steering wheel, his anxiety heightened by the howls from behind his seat. It wasn't busy, but no one had slowed down. Several vehicles swerved from the outside lane into their path. It felt like a disaster must be coming.

Alis hummed a repeating tune. Rhod joined in, without really knowing the notes. Brigit became calm and her crying turned to gurgling, giggling noises.

Alis placed her right hand on Rhod's left forearm while she watched their baby smile and laugh. The quarrelling was done.

Once they arrived back in Yate, they'd agreed on a return trip to Pembrokeshire in the early summer. At least ten days, perhaps a full two weeks. Brigit would be old enough to enjoy time on the beaches and with her grandparents. It would be their first proper holiday as a family.

Back home.

THE POLICE SERGEANT

It was never going to be an indulgence, but Dewi Morgan was determined to celebrate his golden wedding anniversary with something more than a glorified Sunday lunch. Claire deserved it; they both did.

When he talked it over with David Junior, they quickly dismissed the notion that it should be a secret and surprise for Claire. That couldn't possibly work. Instead, a plan was hatched bearing all the precision and structure that two soldiers could muster. A Morgan family conference - Dewi, Claire, David Junior and Kathryn - was held and agreement quickly reached. Everyone in the family, wherever they were and however far they needed to travel, must be invited and, if necessary, instructed to attend. Then, maybe, some old friends might also be added to the list.

Dewi and Claire spent a morning in residence at David Junior's new home to make use of their recently installed telephone. Claire called her sister-in-law, down on the south coast, all the time worrying that Stephen might not be well enough to travel. He did have his moments these days. But Lizzie loved a party and a good singsong: she said she wouldn't miss it for anything and was sure one of their sons would lend a hand with travel.

Dewi made the next call, to Richard. He wanted to be the one to ask his grandson, who was a fine young man studying hard up the coast at Aberystwyth University. It was typical of the lad to ask his grandpa's permission to bring his girlfriend. How could Dewi refuse?

More telephone calls ensued. Claire put some money in a tin on the mantelpiece to pay for them.

David Junior and Kathryn found and booked a small function room at an inn not far from the station, making it ideal for anyone coming by train. It was no time at all before everyone that needed to be invited had been contacted. No one declined until, with hardly any notice, Lizzie's son Gareth cried off, claiming their baby son was poorly and couldn't be left. Dewi had been furious and, when he called his nephew, Gareth half-heartedly offered to pop over on his own. But Dewi knew a liar's voice whenever he heard one.

It was a pleasantly warm summer's day when Dewi opened the front door, before calling one last time to Claire that David Junior would be there soon. He'd spent the morning pottering in the garden, watering the roses and borders out front. He knew all the planning and calls and arrangements were in place. A two-tier cake, with yellow icing and a golden *50* was in Kathryn's care at the venue. They'd put twenty pounds behind the bar for them that wanted drink; Dewi knew it was far too much, but Claire insisted.

As he called out to Claire again, Dewi felt the sun on his face and revelled in it. There was always a breeze from the sea, bearing the smells of a harbour and all its coming and going. It was noisy too; ship's horns; seagulls; an occasional sound from the railway across the bay. It didn't spoil the sun's radiant effect on his face and hands.

He was getting impatient now and turned inside to call more loudly. It wouldn't do to upset the neighbours, who'd been a bit frosty about not getting invited. As he said her name, he heard Claire gasp. It might have been a sob and it seemed to cause an especially brisk rush of sea breeze at Dewi's back. It was suddenly quite chilly.

Claire came out into the hallway, and Dewi could see she'd been crying. A dark line had marked a path down her left cheek, through the powder and downy hair. Fifty years they'd been married, and it was sixty since the day in 1910 when they met at the tea dance. There'd been that time, those few weeks of passion, when perhaps Dewi hadn't loved Claire, nor she him. Yet her tears were a powerful symbol of all they had been for more than half a century. In their Sunday Best, Dewi and Claire embraced, and she told him of the sadness she still bore about Mary. Drowned; dead all this time; she would have been thirty-five this year. In her prime, beautiful and bountiful. Claire said she couldn't celebrate the longevity of their marriage like this. What did those golden years mean against their shared blame for Mary's loss?

Dewi took out his handkerchief and dabbed at Claire's eyes and cheek. He told her the best way to celebrate was to make sure they remembered Mary at the party: openly and with pride. He, Dewi, would say a few words to reflect on all they felt about a long-lost daughter. It was something their children and grandchildren should hear; and Lizzie and Stephen's family; and all their guests. Mary would be part of today's celebration.

Claire looked into his eyes and smiled. He'd been a good man all these years, even when he wasn't being good.

A car horn indicated David Junior was outside and, after a final correction to her makeup, Claire told Dewi it was time to go.

As he opened the door to let Claire walk outside, a hand raised in a wave to their son, Dewi noted another blast of cold wind from the harbour. Was that a patch of ice on the path? It couldn't be. Not in summer. It must be patches of wet left over from his watering. Untroubled, Dewi locked up then took hold of Claire's arm to walk down the short path to its final few steps and gate.

Watching from the car, David Junior became mystified, then horrified to see his father suddenly slip with a cry of alarm and a simultaneous scream from Claire. As he fell, Dewi's firm grip on her arm dislocated it at the shoulder. David Junior could see his father's feet fly up above his head.

Dewi crashed headfirst to the pathway, breaking his skull and neck, killing him instantly. Claire fell too, still screaming but weakly now. She was flipped sideways by her husband's uncontrolled fall, over his body and into the rose bushes that formed a hedge between tarmac and grass. The thorns dug into and snagged her face and neck, tearing through her scarf to her blouse. A final wail of pain. Then silence.

David Junior leapt from his car to see what had happened. When he saw their bodies, weak, old, broken and bleeding, he rushed to hammer on next door's windows to get them to call an ambulance, cursing his father's refusal to get a phone.

A cat stared out impassively at him, then licked a

paw before leaping back into the room.

⚓

Lizzie Rowlands was still furious about her son declining to come to the party. They could have brought the baby, and he could have been cared for by any amount of family. It was an insult to their aunt and uncle. Her husband, Stephen, listened with ambivalence and wished he could still smoke his pipe. But it had made him breathe funny and he'd accepted ages ago that it wasn't a good thing to keep sucking on it. All that tar.

Along the line they went, up to Whitland and she'd been on about it constantly. Stephen hoped the change of trains would help. But it just got worse, especially now the carriage was busier. Lizzie clearly thought the volume of people sharing their carriage would mask the righteous diatribe about their son and daughter-in-law.

He finally got her to stop by recalling how long it was since they'd seen Claire and Dewi. The plans they'd all made to grow old together in Abergwaun had been disrupted by work, then family and finally by illness. Times had not been as good as they'd planned, back when Dewi retired.

But soon all would be well for a while. David Junior would be waiting to collect them at the station, then they'd all be reunited within minutes. Despite Stephen's reassuring calm, Lizzie made a huffing noise and said the reunion was incomplete and therefore imperfect. She would not forget the embarrassment their son had caused.

When the train slowed to begin its approach to their stop, Stephen Rowlands stood to take their suitcase from the luggage rack. Dutifully, they walked to the end of the carriage to wait by the door. Lizzie whispered that it seemed strange they were the only ones getting off, but he made a gesture with his head to show they weren't alone. A young, tall, dark-haired woman was walking towards them, smiling distractedly. She had no luggage or bag, and neither Stephen nor Lizzie could recall seeing her until now. Maybe she'd come through from the smoking carriage?

The train still had some pace but was cruising along towards its stop. When the large sign saying Fishguard and Goodwick glided past outside, Stephen slid down the window and gripped the handle he would twist to open the door. While the train was still moving, he inexplicably went ahead and turned the handle. The door flew open. Stephen swung out from the train and, still gripping the handle with whatever failing strength he could muster, was dragged along for several yards. Lizzie had screamed throughout these seconds but, when Stephen lost his grip and fell to the platform, her screams were loudest and filled with terror. Then a gurgling, gasping noise welled up in her throat and she clutched at it, then her chest. The sight of Stephen's body tumbling and disappearing caused Lizzie's heart to fail, suddenly and literally broken by what had happened to her husband.

She turned in a final pained moment of fading lucidity to look into the dark purple eyes of the young woman. When the train suddenly slammed to a stop, just a few moments after Stephen had fallen, the young woman stepped over Lizzie's body. No one saw her leave the train.

They sat on the quayside and watched the boats bobbing on a shimmering, glistening sea. The tide was in, and it was the prettiest scene anyone could want. Rhod had an ice cream cone with melting dribbles all down its side and on his fingers. It was a mess, but he was happy. Alis held Brigit on her knee, facing away so she could see the harbour scene and they were happy too. It had been a wonderful start to their holiday. The sun shone constantly and, according to the paper, the weather was going to get better still.

They were alternating, two days at a time, between Alis's mam and dad and Rhodri's parents. It made the grandparents happy. Jane and Will were still active and busy. Mr and Mrs Lewis were retired and stumbling towards old age. But all four of them seemed enchanted by Brigit's presence. She was less than nine months old yet had a mesmeric personality.

It was nearly ten years since either Rhod or Alis had lived in the area and, as the holiday progressed, it felt natural for them to walk the streets showing Brigit the sights and sounds. It didn't take long to tour the town, and, from her pushchair, she smiled and giggled at all she was shown. The hotel where Jane and Will had worked all those years. The police station. The Farmer's Arms. The school where Brigit's parents met and fell in love, even though they needed several more years to realise it. The Celtic Cross with its plinth of steps.

Alis told Brigit that was where her mammy and daddy kissed for the first time. The word *kiss* made Brigit smile at Alis, who kissed her to show what it meant. Rhod captured the scene on his tiny new instamatic camera.

There were days doing nothing, and days on the sandy beaches. A boat trip around the coast and islands to see the birds and sealions. A drive along the narrow lane to park near St Non's chapel and well, where Alis held Brigit so she could soak her hands in the water. Rhod said it was filthy and they shouldn't touch it. Alis scooped a handful of the well water up and dribbled it into Brigit's mouth. Then she smiled and laughed at Rhod, took his hand and kissed him.

Two days before their scheduled return home, clouds rolled in to spoil the fun. Rhod suggested a trip further afield, but Alis said there were still things to show Brigit, in the lanes and pathways to the east of the town. Those places didn't mean a thing to Rhod, but Alis wasn't willing to have her wishes denied. They had another argument, that ended with Rhod driving in a stony silence and refusing to leave the car whenever they stopped.

In each place, Alis took Brigit from her travel cot and carried her up and down so they could see things together. The houses. A church with its external bell. A woollen mill next to a babbling river and its pretty bridge. A quarry with its gate and silent buildings. A mother told her daughter these were places of consequence: one of them was where Alis had been born and where her real parents had died. She nearly choked on those words, and Brigit stared at then touched her mother's tears.

During the short drive back to Jane and Will's, the heavens opened. It made driving unsafe, and Rhod turned off the main road. He was muttering about monsoons and condensation and didn't really notice how quiet Alis had become. She was staring straight ahead at a vast bank of opaque darkness hanging over the fields, where she knew the old airfield lay. As the first line of brilliant white light shot up into the sky, Rhod swore about how a thunderstorm was all they needed. The second made him jump. And the third flash made Brigit laugh from inside her travel cot.

THE POLICE SERGEANT

Gareth Rowlands heard a rattle from the letter box and wondered why he'd heard no footsteps. He pulled the curtain aside to look out over the road, but it was deserted. Rightly so: this was Saturday morning; it was supposed to be quiet; and always was. He saw no postman walking away, so he must have sneaked across the front to next door. Gareth hated the fact that they did that. It was like trespassing. You're allowed on the pathway, but not our lawn and flower border, you bastards.

Then his wife laughed with pleasure and Gareth decided to stop scratching himself and check the cause. Joy had been in such short supply since his parents' deaths.

Accidental, they'd called it, and in the absence of witnesses no one could contradict the verdict. That was dad, increasingly too obstinate to take more care of himself, he'd been an accident waiting to happen. It was just past his seventy-first birthday, yet he decided he could lean out of a moving train like he was twenty. Mam's death was simpler: heart attack, despite no history of problems; no pains; no complaints. Fit and well, mam had been. Gareth gnawed guiltily on his bottom lip as he pulled up yesterday's underpants then a pair of slacks. His lie still troubled him. Baby Paul had been perfectly well that day, but his general frailty was an easy excuse. Truth was, they just hadn't wanted to go to the golden wedding.

The police had arrived to tell them the multiple bad news. Almost simultaneous with Mam and Dad's deaths, Uncle Dewi and Auntie Claire had also suffered a terrible accident.

Four years, it had been. The family had been united in grief and, for many months, there was constant dialogue, support and sympathy amongst them. Dewi and Claire's grandson had spoken eloquently at their funeral. There'd been no choice, for David Junior was overwrought. Gareth's eldest boy had made them proud by singing Lizzie's favourite hymn in church. David and Kathryn's Trevor, still just thirteen, had worn his grandpa's old police helmet and war time medal to walk in front of the coffins.

In just one day, their family had lost a generation. It was hard to understand, harder still to bear. But they'd borne it bravely, and then moved on.

Karen held up a card to show him. Gareth frowned and shook his head, but she was peering into the envelope, as if searching for something else. When she passed him the card, he saw it was a wedding invitation. It was Cousin Richard. Him and Hannah.

RSVP.

The boys were happily shouting through a noisy match between Cardiff City and Peru on the kitchen table. They both loved their Subbuteo and were allowed to play it often, though sometimes Gareth and Karen regretted that they'd bought it. It caused all this noise and discord. Paul was the younger, but he was better with his flick-to-kick skills, and he'd already got Cardiff into a commanding lead over the hapless Peruvians. Their sister wanted to join in, but she sat patiently, often laughing at her big brothers with their crowd noises and incredulous commentator voices.

Gareth realised there was a powdery coating on the invitation and Karen showed him the residue of something white in the envelope. It was talcum powder, scented with lavender, she said. And perhaps there was another smell; another floral bouquet; lilies, she decided. Karen passed the envelope to Gareth for him to check but he wasn't paying attention and the package tipped up and shed some of the talcum on to the baize green grass of a make-believe Ninian Park. The boys howled with dismay, but little Vanessa giggled that it looked like snow. This met with agreement, and winter's match needed the orange ball. Their excitement redoubled, and Peru soon pulled one back after adapting surprisingly well to the sudden change of weather and conditions.

Gareth finally got hold of the envelope and, without any real clue about the smells, agreed that it probably was lavender scented. He enquired if they would be going, and Karen shrugged and pursed her lips. It sounded posh and it was a long trip to the coast. They probably should go, but they had months to decide not to.

He took another sniff of the envelope then left Karen and the kids to their various activities. As he closed and locked the toilet door, he heard Karen ask Vanessa if she wanted to smell the lovely flowers in the envelope. Then the boys asked for more snow on the pitch and there was laughter from them all.

Gareth dropped his slacks and pants then turned to sit on the lav. His Saturday morning routine was back on course. A shit, a shave and a short walk to the shop for his Sun and the boys' copy of Shoot! Karen would tell him what glossy she wanted, and he usually picked up a small gift for Vanessa to keep her happy. A Milky Way: that was her favourite.

A week later, the shopkeeper realised he'd missed Mr Rowlands' daily visit for his paper. Ever since the family had moved here, Mr Rowlands had been a loyal customer. Yet here was a second consecutive Saturday without his morning visit for the family's reading essentials. The Rowlands' bill was overdue too, but this was a constant, albeit minor dispute. He quite liked Mr Rowlands, and those two young boys were polite and kind unlike many of the local louts whose shoplifting knew no bounds. The shopkeeper decided to drop a bill round to the house that evening on his way home.

During his short walk he was surprised by a police patrol car speeding past him, up the road from Monmouth, lights but no siren. A Triumph 2000pi and that engine howled, tuned and powerful. There was a panda car at the Rowlands' house and officers were peering in through windows and banging on the front door. He joined the small group that had gathered and heard all the whispers that the Rowlands were away, so this was all a bit strange. Then the chatter was all about something being bad. One of the police from the patrol car was on his radio phone and must have been given a decision, because then they kicked in the door.

The local television news reported on the tragic story from a tiny home in rural Monmouthshire.

Family of five found dead.

Police uncertain, mystified yet suspicious.

Local vox pops: quiet, they were; kept themselves to themselves; but nice, you know; always stopped for a natter; lovely kids; it's quite worrying, really.

Then more spurious, slightly salacious rumours were exchanged. Journalists had been digging into off-the-record comments, extracted from distracted police. The family had all been found in their beds. The house was clean and spotless. One of those tabletop football games was set up, teams ready for kick off. The family wasn't local and didn't mix. No one knew where He went every day. Kids often didn't go to school. She was sometimes rude to people. They owed money.

Something wasn't right.

The shopkeeper had a bumper uplift in newspaper sales, and happily served his customers over copies of the local rag with its increasingly hysterical headlines about rural goings-on.

FIVE

Alis

They moved to a tiny place close by the border of Wales and England when Rhodri Lewis decided to leave them. It wasn't a sour parting, but he told his wife and daughter that their oneness was exclusive and had become too complicated for him to join.

They knew it was over and things had to change. The house in Yate had been a happy place. Brigit loved her school and made many friends in the thriving community. At eight, she was tall, like her mother, and she was upset at first by her father's feelings. But, also like her mother, Brigit knew they would survive Rhodri's decision.

There was no settlement or fuss about belongings. During a short period of living together but apart, Alis and Rhodri agreed on what they needed to do and then managed that plan to its conclusion. He still went to work each day and came home to a meal shared as a family. He still did all the things needed to prevent absolute breakdown.

But things were broken, and the strands that retained them gradually snapped until none were left.

Alis had to be decisive. Briefly tempted by the notion of returning to Pembrokeshire, she chose instead to be near a river, high hills and a different kind of history. One weekend, in the early summer of 1978, she got in the car with Brigit and drove over the bridge then on up the Wye Valley. Tintern caught their imagination but not for long, as Brigit didn't like the noisy, winding road. When that road reached a busy junction at Monmouth, Alis meant to turn right. She got stuck in the wrong lane and ended up on an even busier road with speeding cars and roaring trucks. In a kind of panic, she turned off at the first junction and was soon heading out of the town. Small places came and went, and Brigit was becoming bored and fractious.

She had never heard of it, but Alis liked Skenfrith. It was quiet and seemed imbued with solace and a hint of mystery. Brigit liked it too and they parked the car to walk around the church, then the ruined castle. From the river bridge, they saw fish gliding lazily in the shallows. They both loved it, but Alis sensed it might be difficult to make a home here. She found a phone box and called Rhodri at work then asked him to look in Yellow Pages for letting agents. Alis called the three numbers and all of them confirmed they would manage clients in and around Skenfrith, but currently had no vacancies. They could put her on a waiting list, if she cared to give a name and phone number. She told them her name was Alis Howells and asked for any details to be posted to the house at Yate, because they had no telephone.

When they got back that night, the house was unoccupied. The framed photograph of Alis kissing Brigit had been placed on the hallway table, like a statement of the obvious. Rhodri didn't return during any of the coming three weeks. Perhaps he would come back one day for things he'd left behind, but Alis didn't intend to be there if he did. The lack of any final fading farewell meant they would never see him again, but it didn't stop these from being troubling days. Alis, usually calm and confident, was filled with worry about their future. Staying here was not what she wanted, not just because it was the safe, easy option.

That pretty place by the river, with its old castle walls and quaint church, was what she wanted. Was she being too prescriptive?

Perhaps it was easier to go back home to St Davids? Was that her only choice? Would it be right for Brigit?

Did she need to find a new man to create stability and an anchor? Maybe Brigit needed that? She had loved her dad, and Alis was uneasy that her daughter would never say that she wanted him back. Had she written Rhodri off too quickly, and without a care for her daughter's needs?

She thought of her own fathers, one who had loved her as his own, another who had only known her as a new-born and infant. She loved Will for his kindness, bravery and wisdom as well as for his undying love for Jane. She loved the faint memory of Thomas Harty's smile and how he smelled of Stina. Her biological parents had not seen her reach the age of two. Jane and Will had loved her as their own across four decades. If she got this wrong, would Brigit be deprived of something fundamental to her development?

These doubts and anxieties helped her pull through. To get what she wanted, Alis couldn't rely on luck or favours. She needed to graft. This couldn't be about her. In those last days in the Yate house, Alis realised that, at just thirty-seven, she must remain single to focus all her vitality and love on Brigit. Perhaps men would come and go for baser needs, but those must never be about dependency or growing old. Brigit didn't need a new father figure. The old one had proved weak and indulgent. He could have stayed and been loved forever. Instead, he chose to see his daughter and wife as too close and instinctive then viewed that as an excuse for flight, rather than a reason to love them more. To make things worse, he had tried to turn their empathy into a fault: the cause of his own weakness.

Alis became a regular at her local telephone box. She contacted an agency that specialised in placing domestic helpers and nannies. Her experience and references were well received and there was a quiet confidence that a client would be found. She phoned the education authority for details of schools and picked the one with plenty of buses to and from Skenfrith. Brigit would need to become independent quickly and without fuss.

Several interviews, conducted over the phone, resulted in Alis being dismissed, sometimes rudely, as a time waster. Too far away. No home in the area. A single mother. No real experience and, worst of all, no qualifications.

People had changed from what they had been when Alis first worked as an *au pair*. They were different; aloof; haughty.

Then the agency told her a client was reconsidering and wanted to speak to Alis again. She walked back to the phone box.

The call started with an apology, then lasted nearly an hour during which the two women warmed to each other. They travelled to meet, vaguely halfway, and Claire Clifton apologised again for being quick to judge. Her husband was ill, which was why she needed help and support with a young family, but that was no excuse for the way she had originally spoken to Alis. Claire had checked with the family at the big house near Bristol and she wanted to offer Alis an initial trial period. The Cliftons' home was near Monmouth. Ideal for Alis. A short drive, but regular buses too. It would be long hours on weekdays and probably some weekends. If necessary, Alis would stay overnight. Would she be comfortable driving Claire's large estate car? That was essential.

Alis knew this seemed too good to be true and was nervous about it being a trial with no commitment. She couldn't possibly travel from Yate every day. She decided to turn it down, but Claire could see in her eyes that Alis didn't want to reject the offer. They agreed not to be hasty, and Alis was invited to visit Rockfield with Brigit so the two families could meet.

It proved to be a success. Claire's husband, Steve, had multiple sclerosis and was increasingly frail and unable to work full time. Their children were all under ten and seemed uncertain about Alis and Brigit, and whatever part they would play in their family life. Steve and Claire clarified that role and how much it would mean for them to have some additional help. The uncertainty thawed a little. Steve asked Alis if she'd tried looking for holiday lets as well as regular rented property. When she admitted it had never crossed her mind, Steve held out a copy of the local paper opened at a page with several advertisements circled in blue ink. It had been a redundant question. Alis was told she was welcome to use the phone.

There was a cottage available in the hills near Skenfrith.

It was enough for them to move, for Alis to start and complete the trial period with the Clifton family and for Brigit to confirm a place at school. They packed whatever could be fitted in to the car and drove over to the cottage. Alis went back alone for another carload, then a few days later returned to Yate and left the car. There was no one at the house, but she knew Rhodri had been there.

It had produced a wonderful, loving child but their

life together had been a mistake. Alis had loved him and enjoyed each moment of the passions and joys they had shared. They had almost always agreed on every aspect of the choices and decisions needed for Brigit to be happy and well. Yet it was a truth that, from the time of their very first kiss, Rhodri had signalled he would move on. He wanted more, above and beyond whatever he might have at any given point in time. Perhaps she was supposed to rise to this challenge and love his restless soul and wandering curiosity.

Alis walked to the station and a few hours later left a train at Abergavenny to catch a bus. The framed photograph of Alis and Brigit's kiss was still on the hall table at Yate.

With employment assured, Alis found it easier to secure a permanent letting on a small house in Skenfrith. She supplemented her wages with part time work at the local pub and, at last, Brigit and Alis were settled. Back in Wales, remote, but with links to bigger things when needed. There was a train line nearby that meant they could visit St Davids, albeit with long journeys and brief stays. These were happy times, for Jane and Will loved to see them and doted on Brigit. They also encouraged Alis to spend time with Mr and Mrs Lewis who, it seemed, had also been deserted by Rhodri. He was overseas, they said, forging a career in the world of money and finance. He sent occasional letters filled with news and things they didn't understand.

In the space of a few months at the start of the 1980s, Alis and Brigit returned to St Davids on four occasions that were tainted with the sadness of loss.

Will died suddenly after a stroke and, six months later, Jane didn't recover from influenza. In between these tragedies, Rhodri's parents succumbed to the general frailty of old age. Their son didn't return for any of the funerals.

Alis bore the loss of her father with bravery but was distraught when Jane died. That final link to all that she was had been snapped. Jane had raised Alis alone despite her own pain and loss. But more than that, it was Jane who had stepped in to fill the gaping hole in Alis's history, soothing the waves of shock and grief that the baby and infant Alis felt but didn't understand. In the last few days at the house in Goat Street, Alis knew Brigit must be told about Ava, Stina, Megan and Bethan. About Cissy and Owen James. About tiny places surrounded by vast unyielding seas. About those who brought destruction and must be named and shamed: Hoppe; Morgan; Cottam; Morris; Brandt; Bevan; Rowlands; Moritz.

After Jane's funeral, Alis and Brigit walked in silence down to the cliffs overlooking Caerfai. It was overcast, making the sea a dull charcoal colour, capped by flashes of white effervescence. The steady breeze and the streaming, relentless lines of waves pouring onto the beach were the only sounds. Alis knew it was the last time she would be here. Brigit knew, for the first time, that her future was impossible to disconnect from this triangle of land and sea. She took her mother's hand and led her back to the town.

⚔

The Cliftons were good to Alis as she mourned. She was a trusted part of their lives, had helped them bind a growing family together and then set it on a new course to cope with Steve's illness. Alis repaid their decency and empathy by working harder still to assure that stability. When the time came that they no longer needed her services, they gave her a glowing reference and a generous *ex gratia* payment. It was intended to be closure but, within a few weeks, they all met up as friends. Those gatherings became a regular feature of all their lives.

Alis felt no desire to carry on being a domestic servant, no matter how friendly and inclusive the arrangement. She chose a different kind of servitude and asked to work full time at The Bell. This was welcomed by the landlord for her presence seemed to be an attraction for a certain kind of clientele. Alis also started to make small batches of homemade jams, pickles and condiments from the fruit and vegetables available in local farms. These delicacies were bartered, traded and sought after.

Brigit was working hard at school and, sometimes, it felt they were too busy for each other. Whenever these feelings took hold, Alis and Brigit spent time away from work and education. A weekend trip to the seaside at Tenby, uncomplicated and fun filled. Closer to home they learned to capture and absorb energy from the history in the old castle's ruins and the sacred grounds near the church. Alis took Brigit to wade in the Monnow, flowing close by their home, and to feel no fear about the water and being immersed in it. They travelled over to the Brecon Beacons and walked miles into the hills to look at the lands stretching out in all directions, sometimes staying overnight in the open to watch the sun set and rise. She wasn't yet fourteen, but Brigit had become imbued with the knowledge and emotional strength to cope with the fact that change was coming.

New visions had begun, and Alis shared them with Brigit.

There was someone she'd seen before, as a pretty young bride then as an older, chain-smoking drunkard. Now, wizened and skeletal, lying motionless on a sofa with an empty bottle next to her, a trail of ash down her front.

Then strangers, from a different era to that of her youthful visions. A sun-drenched man, middle-aged but carefree, at the wheel of a sailing boat. A younger, tanned blonde woman at his side, both with hair streaming behind them.

Another couple, with more bogus tanning, well dressed and all smiles in a fast car with no roof. They were waving enthusiastically at a small group of people outside a small business property of some kind.

Alis nodded, then smiled at Brigit. There was work to do.

THE POLICE SERGEANT

Detective Inspector Ceri Bessant placed his phone handset on its cradle. He hadn't expected what he'd just heard. The call had started with an introduction: DS Bowen, from Tenby; got his name from a mutual colleague; wanted to pick his brains about something; did he remember the Alwen Bevan case?

Eighteen years it had been, and still unresolved. So, how could he forget? It was one of those crimes that lives with you. In all his years on the force he'd seen three murders, but Alwen Bevan's had been the first.

He retrieved the file. There was the sketch he'd made that day. His photos were there too, but despite these *aides memoire*, Ceri still struggled to understand what had happened to that poor woman. They'd identified her eventually. A former boyfriend had come forward and testified it was Alwen Bevan. The boyfriend had seemed reliable at first but his testimony in the coroner's court was mumbled and rambling. Liked a drink, he did, and kept referring to his boat trips up to Anglesey and how Alwen had borne him a child back in the thirties. Hadn't seen her or the boy since the war. Wasn't even sure if it was his. This testimony was nearly rejected, such was its lack of clarity.

Ceri re-read the file without really needing to. An open case, for sure, with no doubt about cause of death. Alwen Bevan had died as a result of a wooden baton *of some kind* being forced into her mouth, down her throat and into her chest.

Medical opinion was unclear about whether this had been done while the victim was still alive, but death was caused by asphyxiation.

Police opinion was relieved that the word *truncheon* had been omitted from the verdict.

DS Bowen took the call and listened to Ceri's succinct description of Alwen Bevan's death and the unresolved investigations that ensued. Less succinctly, for he was still unable to comprehend what had happened, DS Bowen explained that it looked like a copycat killing had taken place. Two killings, in fact.

The victims were a popular part of the maritime fun to be had at Tenby. They'd developed a thriving business in which, for a large fee, they sailed small groups of people around Caldey Island. The fare included breakfast and hot drinks on the outward leg, with a cream tea and bubbly on the homeward stretch. These trips on the *M&T* were popular, especially with customers that liked to look down their noses at more fundamental voyages to the same island.

They were known to be a loving couple, who had

never married and were happier for it. They had a home in the town but quite often spent the night on board *The M&T* to ensure it was shipshape.

When he'd finished talking with his colleague over at Fishguard, DS Bowen read the report again. Complaints from disgruntled, out-of-pocket customers led to the police dinghy being used. Officers sped over to the *M&T*'s mooring, but their shouts were not answered. When they boarded the boat, they found its owners below deck. They were dead and each of them had something rammed down their throat.

He had been given the task of establishing the man's true identity, as it was quickly established that their names were pseudonyms. During a search at their home, a birth certificate was found for Geraint Bevan, born in 1933 at Porthgain in Pembrokeshire to Alwen Bevan, housewife, and Stanley Jones, of no fixed abode.

The house search also revealed that the couple had a child, and a statement was broadcast that police were keen to hear from anyone who might know the whereabouts of Sylvia Griffiths, believed to be the daughter of Terry and Martha. Sylvia was also urged to contact the police as a matter of urgency.

The open case from 1965 was inextricably linked to the two deaths onboard the *M&T*. Post-mortems on Terry and Martha revealed the same cause of death. The truncheons used were old, the kind of stick used by officers in the 1940s. No one had seen their like for decades, yet two had been found and used to kill.

COTTAM

GEORGE — SHEILA
(D)

JACK (m) TARA

JOHN HAWS (m) MICHELLE

JAKE

LEON (m) DEBORAH

SIX

Brigit

Brigit and Alis kissed goodbye at the station with no tears or sadness. Their embrace was loving and longing, for it was their last. Each walked to different platforms to board a train, and both went home.

Alis needed to change trains more than she wanted. It was nearly dark when she reached a deserted Kirkham & Wesham station and, seeing she was alone on the platform, some swearing lads descended from the street level booking office. They egged each other on with verbal and suggestively physical filth until Alis said something none of them understood but that somehow made their dicks so much less impressive. Her connection to Lytham arrived and the last fifteen minutes of her journey were soon past.

It took Brigit several hours to reach Hereford and she couldn't bear the thought of being stuck on the train any longer. She wandered towards the city and found a small inn on Commercial Road and curled up in the tiny room. It didn't feel very safe for a young woman to be alone here, but she was learning that was true about almost anywhere. The following morning, she walked back to the station and saw there were plenty of trains to Abergavenny, so she decided to spend some time exploring.

There was a fading grandeur about the city. She quite liked it and when she reached the cathedral, she absolutely loved it. Inside, it seemed different to the other cathedral she vaguely knew. There were smells she couldn't place, and something seemed less homely. Yet it was intimate, and it had an old map she gazed at for minutes on end. Outside was a complete cloister, which had people's homes in it. Best of all, there was a Bishop's Palace in leafy lawned grounds, like the country seat of an aristocrat. Brigit's long walk back to the station, over an old stone bridge then along a riverbank and back through the city, left her slightly lovestruck.

THE LANCE CORPORAL

Jack Cottam pulled on his finest pair of Italian shoes and made a final adjustment to his cuffs. In the mirror he watched Tara smoothing down her dress and felt a jolt in his cock and balls: she was still a remarkable, desirable, fuckable figure of a woman. Later, he hoped, they would have a tipsy, flirtatious night of all that he craved. By then, she'd crave it too.

The clattering clamour of Kirkham Club Day was still a perennial joy for the Cottam family. Not even his mum's death six years earlier had squashed this enjoyment and, in fact, had made it less of a bind. She had been complaining about how it wasn't the same any more for as long as Jack could remember.

They all met up for breakfast at Jack and Tara's home out on the road to Wrea Green and there was the usual intense discussion about business or money or assorted iniquities. Then they all trooped out into a taxi and, once dropped off, grabbed a place on the grassy wooded area near the station to watch the parade.

A minor celebrity in the town, Jack enjoyed the smiles and nods they received. Mostly it was his employees, but some of the handshakes were with strangers who'd clocked him. He felt this annual festival was something he had to own, not in a grasping or acquisitive sense but as a local citizen of note, even though he hadn't lived in the town since the early seventies. His father, long dead and forgotten, had been born and bred in Kirkham and that was enough for him to say the town was in his blood.

His mum had disintegrated over the same decades in which Jack and Tara had set up then grown the caravan park. They'd developed this tourist haven so there were static vans too, and then he set up a company running open-topped buses taking customers along to Lytham St Anne's or into Blackpool.

Tara was a huge part of it all. They'd met in their twenties at the Winter Gardens and Jack had to fight his way out of the ballroom that night. She was all that he wanted, but others wanted her too. Blackpool could be wild and being from out of town was a curse. Mainly you needed to use your fists and feet, but he also carried a knife, just in case. They fell in love and married in 1957. Her folks gave them a bit of a nest egg, enough to take a share in the tiny campsite. They'd worked diligently ever since and put business before family.

Jack and Tara owned the business outright by '65, when Michelle came along, and Cottam's was a sought-after destination when Leon arrived four years later. The family was complete and the electricity between Jack and Tara was the envy of their whole set.

Today's parade around the streets was filled with the usual smiles. Great banners divided up the marching line. Brass bands, from near and far, provided a soundtrack. But it was the simple innocence of the children, proudly representing their school or church that never failed to make the procession a joy. Jack often shed tears as he watched, drawing teases from his wife and daughter about his soft heart. How on earth could he be such a thorough-going bastard in all his business activities, and yet well up at a few poor kids in their uniformed finery?

When the procession ended, almost everyone was off the leash, out into the pubs and screaming on the rides at the fair down by the graveyard. Jack and Tara enjoyed a drink with Michelle, but she was far more interested in her fiancé. It was a match with parental approval from both families. The Wallises had a few bob from the building trade. The marriage would be the talk of the coast when it happened, and Tara was already making all manner of plans for that day. No one needed to doubt that this lovely young couple had already mapped their own future together. Fit, lithe and sexy, they soon waved goodbye to Jack and Tara and headed away from the town for a more appealing date with their newest best friend, Charlie.

Leon's whereabouts were unknown, but it was expected and accepted that, like most of his peers, he would be drinking illegally somewhere. Perhaps that might also involve looking for a fight with outsiders. Tara half-cared but fully didn't want to know. Their son was wild, and Jack encouraged his feral nature. There was a time and place for lads to have these urges, Jack said, and the school would eventually smooth away those rough edges.

They headed home to shower and change shortly after three, and spent the next few hours watching television. Once the warm day had cooled, Tara and Jack headed back to Kirkham to spend time at the fair.

The sun was down below the trees and buildings on the horizon, making the fair's lights more evocative and its music more intoxicating. Dressed in what they liked to think were more casual clothes, but which were still ridiculously over-indulgent, Tara and Jack dived in among the stalls and rides. Their favourites were busy, but they managed to get a waltzer to themselves and Tara shrieked through the whole five minutes of kaleidoscopic, hallucinating mayhem. Then they had to wait through three sessions before a dodgem was free. It tried their patience: queueing really wasn't for the likes of them.

Jack stepped into the tiny car with the same hauteur he used to slide behind the wheel of Tara's Range Rover. He worried he'd get shit on his chinos from the mucky last lot and bore this fear with ill-concealed dislike. Tara's heels made it even harder for her to climb in but there was a long wait while everyone paid, and she eventually settled down. The music made conversation impossible, so Jack ran his hand up the inside of Tara's thigh and tried to stroke between her legs. A sign of things to come, he hoped. She let him do it, but it wasn't a turn on for her not least because her legs were squeezed tight together in the dodgem's cockpit. Jack pulled his hand away abruptly when the woman collecting payments walked by. She was tall and dark, and even Tara had to admit she had a gorgeous arse. But perhaps she was quite old for that kind of work? The woman bent down to take the tokens from Jack, and her dark purple eyes looked calmly back into his. Tara could see he'd like to get his hand up between her legs too and, as the woman passed behind their car, she jumped up on to the rubber bumper, holding the pole for a moment. Then she disappeared.

The siren cranked up; it was time to bump things. Jack rammed the throttle, simultaneous with every other driver.

Witnesses were shocked, some terrified by what they'd seen. There were always plenty of police on duty. If there was violence, and sometimes there was, it was usually later in the day at the fair. But the officers struggled to cope with the mass of panic and rushing crowds, desperate to be clear of the fairground. Something terrible had happened.

Simultaneous with a massive blue flash from the dodgem arena, each ride at the fairground had stopped working. Every light went out. All the music stopped. People were left dangling; others were injured by the sudden halts on their rides. There was an especially terrified panic erupting on the dodgems as drivers and passengers leaped from their cars, unable to tear their eyes from the single dodgem and its smoking inhabitants.

For many minutes, there was no control or order. The police at the scene were caught between helping people with injuries and calming the rush. The arrival of more senior uniforms brought stability, and ambulances were called. Those who had witnessed whatever had happened at the dodgems were asked through a loudhailer to report to the police.

None of the witness reports made sense. All anyone could say was that there had been a massive blue flash, down from the canopy over the dodgem arena. A young woman and her friend had seen the impact of the flash on Jack and Tara's dodgem. It felt as if the instant she'd pressed the pedal for go, nothing happened except that flash. It had sounded like a huge burst of static. Did that make sense? The police officer said it didn't.

The dodgem controller had no idea what had caused it but, together with the fair's general manager, eventually stated that, inexplicably, thousands of volts of electricity must have been channelled in to the one car that was still occupied. All the power from the generators providing electricity for each ride had been diverted into the Cottam's dodgem.

How was that possible? No one could say.

Had it ever happened before? Never.

Don't the cars have rubber wheels to prevent shock? Yes.

Medical staff found Jack and Tara Cottam dead: presumed cause, electrocution.

The witness reports continued to be confused and confusing. One man, drunk beyond words, kept grabbing a police officer's arm to insist he'd seen something incredible. He was told to go home, politely at first but increasingly firmly until, over-frustrated, the officer gave the man a punch in the face to shut him up. His colleague, keeping watch by the gates so ambulances and other emergency vehicles could come and go unhindered, nodded with approval. They agreed the bloke had been pissed and a nuisance, but no one was watching so that slap was a done deal. And, anyway, what the fuck had he been on about? There were death and horror over there at the fair, and this twat was on about a woman he'd seen in the graveyard.

When he recovered from that blow of arbitrary justice, the drunk man walked off telling anyone who would listen about what he'd seen. A tall, dark-haired, dead fit woman. A real looker. Body to die for. Anyhow, she'd walked out from among the rides and, like an athlete, vaulted over the cemetery railings, spikes and all. Then, he said, she'd gone to lie down next to the most recent tombstone and quite literally dissolved into the earth.

They were more than 120 miles away, due west from the castle, with countless hills and valleys in between. But Brigit saw the tiny flashes and the bubbling of a darkened sky against the late summer afterglow. She continued to stare long after it all ended, then put her head in her hands and wept.

The house where she had lived with Alis for more than eight years was just metres away, but that darkness and those streaks of light also seemed to denote a place called home. They also conveyed the news to her that her mother was gone. And it meant that some of the people who had connived in Stina's death were also gone. Brigit didn't know how, or where, but Alis had finished her work.

It was dark now, and she remained seated on the grass inside the castle's walls. Brigit was sixteen and had the confidence and certainty Alis had given her since birth. Yet something left her feeling like a child, lost and lonely, subdued and subordinate. There would still be school to go to, and lessons to learn. A house and home to maintain. None of that had ever bothered her so long as her mother was there. Now there was just a colossal hole in her self-belief.

Brigit couldn't decide why it was like this and when her efforts to rationalise it failed, she fell back on what she knew. Her crumbling confidence wasn't about lack of intellect or wisdom. It wasn't about poor social skills, or imperfect competency. It wasn't about money, or food, or dealing with authorities.

She was going to survive. She simply couldn't bear the idea of survival without her mam.

It turned out that Rhodri had done something

unexpected, but in a second-hand way. All those letters to his parents had contained cheques. Mr and Mrs Lewis had banked them but never told anyone. After they died, their wills revealed that an amount of cash had been banked, to be given to Brigit on her 16th birthday. It wasn't a life-changing sum, but it was life-sustaining; enough for Brigit to keep living in this place, with food to eat and bills paid.

SEVEN

Today

Ben lay in the silence and felt the darkness oppressing him. For all he knew it might have been one hour, one day or one week since he had been imprisoned. Nothing made sense and, whenever he tried to make sense of it all, it felt like his brain was fried, scrambled and poached.

The only thing he was certain about was that Erin was going to kill him.

During her story about Alis, Erin had become occasionally erratic and lacking in detail. She'd even contradicted herself. There were spells when her eyes and gestures seemed deranged, out of control, remote. And, occasionally, he sensed it was someone else talking, in a language that was indecipherable. But that could easily have been his own mania and fear.

She hadn't repeated the syringe episode, nor done anything else that might be physically life-threatening. If anything, Erin had shifted her whole manner away from being a gaoler or torturer and instead had become more flirtatious. In between her tales about death and murder, Erin was teasing and lascivious. She seemed to desire him. Or desire something.

His loss of any real understanding, particularly about time, meant Ben was inert and insensate. Could he even begin to get it up for her if she demanded it? Yet he was preoccupied by the notion that he might have to, whether he wanted to or not. In the darkness, he tried to think about the lines of her arse and legs, then the outline of her pussy through the tightness of those shorts. It made no difference but caused a brief diversion, in which he sailed into an internal discussion about the correctness of words like pussy. Soon he was riffing a sequence for his act.

His loud snort of laughter turned instantly to copious tears. What on earth was he achieving? He could be dead at any point soon. This was not and could never be a routine.

Earlier, while she was still talking about Alis, Erin had left the room without ending her account. He heard her descend the stairs, then pound back up them as if rushing and excited. It turned out that she was indeed excited. She put something, he couldn't tell what it was, on the table to his left, then started unbuttoning the top of her waistcoat. Smiling down at him, she'd thrust her chest forward so her breasts were straining against the material.

'Shall we play, Ben? It's a rhetorical question, Ben, so no blinking needed.'

Then she put on a cockney accent. 'No blinkin' naffink needed, Ben. No effin' blinkin' bleedin' anyfink. Lord love us.' Erin laughed, with a kind of warmth. Then the playful mania of her face and smile fell away abruptly.

'Wax, Ben. That's what I brought. I saw you wondering. Wax. For play. Not foreplay, Ben. Or it could be, I suppose. Wax Play.'

She reached across to the table and picked up a stick of red, about a centimetre square and perhaps the length of a pencil.

'If only we were lovers, Ben. Imagine how much this would be turning you on. To have this ultra-fit woman - me - standing here in my lycra shorts and PVC top, with you lying there naked at my mercy. Doesn't anything turn you on, Ben?'

She reached over to pick up something else. 'Don't forget, Ben, that it's one blink for yes, two blinks for no. Staring with wild-eyed fear is not an answer of any kind. So, let's try again, Ben. Doesn't anything turn you on?'

He blinked once.

'Goooooood. You see? That wasn't hard. Now, of course, I realise you can't tell me what a filthy fucker you really are underneath that charming boyish naïveté. But I'm going to guess that you'll get a boner when we do Wax Play.' Erin stared into his eyes, then along his torso until her gaze rested on his groin. 'Still woefully underachieving in the old wedding tackle, Ben.' She sighed crossly, then a click ensued, and she held up a butane gas lighter. Its flame created a soft-focus zone of light above where Ben lay.

As the first drops of hot wax dripped on to his left nipple, Ben made a small cry of pain through the tape mask.

'Isn't that just the best, Ben? The pleasure of that heat?' Erin released the trigger on the gas lighter and the room's light seemed almost dark by comparison. 'Well, the wax has gone hard, Ben, but not you. What is a girl supposed to think?'

The gas lighter clicked and flickered again. More hot wax dripped between Ben's pectorals, then down in a line until a small pool filled his navel. He shook his head and groaned. The lighter went out again. She waited then poured some cold water on to his chest and tummy, before pulling the line of solid wax away.

'I had hoped it would remove some hair, Ben. But nothing.' She lit the gas lighter again. 'Ready for especially hot action? Don't forget what I told you about terrified eyes not being part of our coded signalling system, Ben.' He blinked twice and she suddenly raised her voice in fury.

'For fuck's sake, Ben. You can't say no to me about this. I'm going to melt hot wax on to your scrotum and all around your cock and because you've been so naughty, I'm going to pull back your foreskin and it's going on your glans too. It might even go up your crack.'

Ben let out a muted wail and tears filled his eyes. Erin let the gas extinguish and looked with a semblance of pity into his eyes.

'Don't cry, Ben. Please.' She placed the red stick and lighter back on the table then took a pace towards the bed, before bending over to lick Ben's tears. 'I said don't cry, Ben.' Then she nuzzled her nose into his neck and whispered it again into his ear. She nibbled his earlobe too then whispered, 'Wouldn't you like to fuck me, Ben?'

Her hand ran down from his throat to his abdomen, then grabbed at his cock. After a moment, she bit him on his jaw line.

'Why can't you get a hard on? What's wrong with you?'

In a fury, Erin screamed more frustration and rage at Ben then simply turned and stormed out, switching off the light and slamming the door shut as she left. Moments later, the small slit of light under the door disappeared and all Ben could hear was silence.

The oppressive darkness was not his friend, and Ben wondered if he'd ever had a real friend. All those audiences looked and sounded as if they loved him, but it was an ephemeral, vapid kind of love. He knew they were all fickle. The next mover and shaker would soon be on the circuit, young and happening and wowing the punters.

Not friends. Any of them.

His nana had raised him since he was five and told

him constantly his mum and dad had deserted them. He could vaguely remember his dad, Tim, who his nana doted on till he'd taken up with Ben's mum. Nana hadn't liked Ben's mum. She was a piece of work and nana blamed her for his dad's death. Ben didn't really know how his dad died but that was the last time he'd seen his mum. She'd come rushing back to England to see him and nana, barely registering that the news of Tim's death was so terrible. She just wanted to know Ben was all right and when it was clear that he was, gave nana a bag of money, and said there was more in the bank, enough for them to forget about her. Then with instructions about maybe sending Ben to a boarding school but with neither affection, nor words nor touch for her son, she left the house and disappeared forever.

And it was worth noting that he wasn't called Ben, then.

Maybe that was what this was all about. What had Erin said that time? About Ben being his real name?

Nana had married Ben's grandad two years before Ben's dad was born. They were a happy family until Tim left school and disintegrated. He joined a band playing synthesisers, with drum machines popping and thumping away in the mix. Nana and Grandad put up with his drug taking and lack of contact for a few years. Then he met Ben's mum and went gallivanting off to France.

All Ben knew was nana's version of events. His mum and dad had formed a band, gigging in and around the holiday destinations in the South of France. They'd returned to England in mid-1989 so Ben could be born, hung around for a while, trying to do conventional jobs to create some family security. But Ben's mum was constantly nervous about being in Britain, and soon convinced his dad they should return to France where they could make so much more money in the sun.

Ben was left with his nana and grandad. Not long after he passed five, grandad died so it was just Ben and nana.

That was it. That was all he knew. Nana reverted to her maiden name after grandad died and there was the other thing his mum had told them to do. Change the boy's name, she'd said.

Ben nodded off with these stories, from nearly thirty years before, still swirling around like clues and taunts. When he heard the door open, the bedroom was filled with a two-metre orb of light. Erin was holding a candle. Her waistcoat had been buttoned up.

Ben recoiled from her as she sat on the bed, but he needn't have feared. It was time now for more tales and Erin spoke of her mama, and all her acts.

This tale, slow at first, was a haphazard, quite scattered narrative. Perhaps Erin was making it up? There was a catalogue of surreal happy accidents: car crashes; drownings; illnesses; suicides. These things had saved the daughters' time and energy.

Was she repeating herself? This sounded like stuff she'd already been around.

EIGHT

Brigit

Surrounded by such a small, curious community, Brigit feared there would be one or more interventions. At best, the stifling nosiness of neighbours. At worst, a social worker or some other agent of conformity, in or out of uniform.

When that summer's school holiday ended, she got up every day and jumped on the bus. It was the start of her final two years at school. She was bright and intelligent, but academically disinclined. Brigit saw value in the learning, but not in what it gave her. She wanted to know how to negotiate and agree terms to buy and sell. To argue without quarrelling and be as contented with conflict as with comfort. The study of literature, science and a language was a journey that ended with a sheet of stiff paper and a stop sign. Brigit didn't intend to rebel or revolt. She just didn't want to join in with the indulgence.

Alis's absence had been noticed but Brigit rebuffed any attempts to investigate. Her mum had travelled to Pembrokeshire to deal with enduring problems in her late parents' affairs, she told them. Important for me to complete my A levels without a change of school and home, she told them. It's quite common for a sixteen-year-old to live without another adult, she told them.

In the end, the community rallied round. This remarkable young woman was to be respected and supported, and everyone did.

In the cold December of 1986, Brigit passed her 17th birthday. A week later, she caught the bus home at the end of term and when she arrived at the cottage, for the first time since Alis had gone, felt overwhelmed by emptiness. She tried to read but the chosen book was just a jumble of letters on pages. She tried to sketch something, pencil on paper, but the clouds and sweeping lines of landscapes were vapid and futile. She turned on some music, in the forlorn hope that something she loved would be a buoy. The taped copy of a Billy Bragg album left her cold, despite how much she'd loved it once. Then she slid the compact disc of *So* into the player and went straight to the last track to sing along with *In Your Eyes*. It made her go back to the beginning of the album and felt calmed by it until she reached the haunted, haunting devastation of *Mercy Street*: tugging at the darkness was a cause; not a cure.

Brigit sat in silence. Music had always been in this house and home. Music; and films. Maybe that was it? Watch one of mama's favourite films. But as she hunted for something in the big box of old video cassettes, all she could think of was Alis dancing with her to *Kiss*. So, she listened to *Parade* and, by the end, when Prince sang about love not being love until it's past, Brigit felt even more alone.

She spent the following day just losing herself in the mundanity of chores and it made her wild with frustration. Brigit needed to go. It didn't matter where or for how long. Something was calling to her and it was a chorus with a crescendo. She packed inadequate things and threw the bag containing them over her shoulder. A bus ride took her to Abergavenny station and a kind of T-Junction of choice; left, up the line to Hereford; right, down to Newport then who knew where.

Brigit bought a ticket to London and took the right turn.

To her unaccustomed eyes, Paddington Station was like a whale consuming plankton. Brigit watched as her train rolled in from the fading light of a winter's day to the arched innards of the beast. Then, within just a hundred or so steps, there was another gaping mouth, ready to suck her in and ingest her in tubes of gaudy colours with complex names.

She felt caged and had done ever since joining the Inter City train at Newport. It was fast, but noisy, and fellow travellers were also tediously loud. Now she was here, Brigit didn't know where she was going but knew she couldn't bear being in another airless canister. She followed an exit sign and stepped out into London to find it filled with the rushing, blinded consumerism of the final weekend before Christmas. Even here, remote from the more popular retail oases, there was madness to avoid.

The sky was darkening, but endless streetlamps created a dazzling radiance. She set off without fear down Praed Street, watching for signs that might indicate the peace of a place without traffic. She needed somewhere that would calm her growing sense that she'd made a wild, unstructured decision to come here.

Brigit reached the entrance to Hyde Park, and it seemed like half an answer. The park's footpaths were quite busy, but that helped her to stop feeling lost and disoriented. There were trees and a lake and even though the ambient traffic noise and whining of aeroplane engines made silence impossible, Brigit felt this was a place to process incoming codes and signals.

The park's footpaths were lit, and the horizon held a permanent halo of light. It didn't feel like night-time was close.

She needed to be still and in shadow, so Brigit moved off the path towards the lake, which seemed intrinsically murky, almost black. She dropped her holdall so she could lean back against a tree. Ahead of her, ripples on the dim water picked up tiny glittering reflections.

She looked up into the tree's branches and felt waves of detail surging through her. She saw Alis and a catalogue of scenes in which her mother was present. These scenes didn't shock Brigit and, as she returned her gaze to the lake, she was confronted by an aura of opaque darkness. Suddenly, something unseen had projected images on to the obscurity ahead. One scene added to the next until a grid of small screens was there. Brigit frowned, looked around and could see people walking back and forth on the paths. She wasn't invisible to them, but none stopped or smiled.

The video was just for her. It started with a short trailer.

Recent, colourful fashions in a half full church. A couple, formal but joyful. This faded to the same couple hugging a baby. Another shift of scene, to a view from the back seat of a car. Brigit saw the bride and mother from the previous scenes. While this woman drove, she sang a song, accompanied by giggles and words in a high-pitched voice. The woman turned to smile at whoever was in the passenger seat. The car veered into the path of an oncoming truck. Brigit saw the violence of collision, blood on a windscreen, smashed bodies. Outside, shocked despair, heads in hands. More on-screen glimmers and crackles. There was the groom and father, seated at a table. Small bottles, one on its side, were scattered in front of him and he held a larger bottle. He was alternately eating, then drinking. Before each mouthful of tablets, he made a despairing wail, throwing his head back so she could see the darkened, bereft eyes, sunken cheeks and shattered demeanour.

The screen went blank. Brigit gave a small snort then reached out towards the darkness. Symbols appeared. Chevrons pointing left and right, either side of a large arrow pointing right. She pointed at the large arrow, and a story unfolded.

A middle-aged man surrounded by people and gifts. A woman was addressing everyone, then handed the man a small rectangular package. His eyes filled with tears. Then he was walking with an affectionate woman across tarmac towards an aeroplane. He held a holdall and seemed nervous.

Brigit made a small gesture with her right hand, and it made the video advance. Now there was a beach, lapped by an azure sea with tiny craft bobbing on its surface. Her perspective flew into a couple, walking hand in hand, tanned to a deep shade of brown. Their hair was braided into dreadlocks and the man's was bleached. Then they appeared under a canopy, performing to a large group gathered around them, many of them dancing. But this scene switched, to show the man writhing in agony, occasionally clutching his leg.

She tried her gesture again and when the fast forward stopped, a young couple were strutting arrogant and proud through lines of people waiting by a luggage carousel. Brigit zoomed in on them and felt the man was vaguely familiar, but not the woman: not at all. While the mass of people reacted to a siren, the couple just kept walking, pulling their cases on tiny built-in wheels.

Another right hand signal and Brigit's line of sight

flew over a pretty village green, with a pond and cars winding around it like clockwork toys. On she went, towards a large house, in through glass doors. A well-dressed, well-manicured middle-aged couple was kneeling at a glass table, each with a silvery tray in front of them, with lines of white powder.

The next fast forward ended in a green valley with cloud shadows rippling across the hills. Brigit swooped to track a man and woman hiking up this vale, stopping frequently to take photos or to point and laugh at something on the little rectangles in their hands.

Brigit made another gesture, but the video had finished.

She had no idea how long it had lasted but, when she picked up her bag and turned back towards the path, she realised it was neither darker nor less busy than before. She felt disoriented about how she'd got here. Over to her left was a gathering of people around something illuminated. She hadn't passed anything like that on her way into the park, and this compounded her confusion. The way out was to her right: back to the mania of those roads and dazzling emporia.

But what were they all looking at?

Brigit walked towards the throng surrounding the statue of Peter Pan. She stood at a distance and looked at the figure, the crowd of people preventing her from seeing all of it. Brigit, who knew the tale of the boy who could fly, smirked and squinted her eyes with a kind of menace. They loved being in Neverland, didn't they? They believed that stuff. A faerie story bringing smiles and contentment, joy and mystique. But why? Did those ice creams and hot dogs taste better? Were those funny luminous wrist and neckbands more special? Maybe those cuddly Rudolfs could fly too?

Her eyes softened. She was being harsh, which was

unusual. And, anyway, Brigit had more pressing concerns: she needed somewhere to stay and was alone in the heart of a gigantic city. She walked on through the park and left it near the Royal Albert Hall. Still drifting, Brigit walked until finally she ended up at a small bed and breakfast. She lay in the comfortless room listening to the sounds she hated. Being lonely in this urban cacophony was worse, infinitely more terrible, than being alone in the pastoral silence of Skenfrith.

But she slept well and felt better the next morning. There were cafés and other places where she could eat just about anything she could imagine, and she sat happily in one of them, watching rivulets of condensation create bars on the window. The waitress was petite and shy, so Brigit smiled and arched her eyebrows when she ordered. When it arrived, her plate seemed to have extra sautéed potatoes, more scrambled egg; and now she smiled to herself.

From in amongst the hurly burly of chatter, Brigit knew the voice. It had always been calm and composed yet there it was sounding strained and defensive. She looked up at the giant etched mirror over the steaming, groaning monster that made coffee, and saw them: the back of a man's head and shoulders sitting upright in his seat; a woman's face, harsh and defiant under a neat mess of hair. Her face a series of lines, none of which hinted at joy. Even where there was colour, darkness ruled. Her voice was lowered then silent and, once more, his voice filtered across the steamy atmosphere.

It was her father.

Brigit kept staring up at the mirror watching the ebb and flow of a dispute. She'd finished a plate of food and mopped up the smeary remnants with a last triangle of buttered bread. The tea tasted good, and she wanted more. But, instead, Brigit stood and went to pay then threw a few coins on the table for the especially cute service. Rhodri had been deserted now, and his shoulders were hunched over whatever he was eating. A large cup and saucer sat opposite him, another near his left hand.

Brigit slid on to a chair at the table next to him, so she was facing him across an angle. She dropped her bag on the floor between them and his sideways glance seemed sly. It wasn't one of acknowledgement, recognition or welcome. She smiled and raised her eyebrows again, then feigned interest in the menu. He didn't used to eat the way he was eating now: her dad had always wolfed his food; huge mouthfuls that mixed any combination from his plate; a sandwich gone in two bites; a whole Welsh cake in one go. As she watched this man slice a sliver from the end of a sausage and dip it in the band of ketchup smudged across his plate, Brigit wondered what was wrong.

She asked him if the sausages were good, and he told her they were and went well with the smoked bacon.

He didn't know it was her. Not a clue.

She told a different waiter she needed longer to choose, then started small talk with her father.

He was here on business, personal and corporate.

What's the difference between those? Isn't everything just business, in the end?

Maybe so. He stopped chewing, put down his knife but used his fork to illustrate how his job would soon bring him back to Britain. He was buying a place in Canary Wharf. Had she heard of it?

She was just a tourist but, yes, she knew of it and some of the history that preceded it. And is that a hint of lilting Welsh in your voice?

That's perceptive. Hardly anyone notices it anymore. Wales was once a home but hasn't been for years.

A home?

Yes.

She lived right on the Welsh border – perhaps he knew the place?

He didn't, but now Rhodri was engaging in eye contact and not just staring at his food or looking towards the door with the toilet signs.

Was she here with her parents?

Yes, in a way.

That made him frown then giggle, and Brigit had to breathe in sharply to suppress a sudden sense of love and loss.

Then the door opened, the one across the room with the toilet signs. A face held above well-padded shoulders seemed to have become calmer since before, but those dark lines hardened when they zeroed in on a man talking to a tall, dark-haired, young woman.

Brigit stood, placed her hand on Rhodri's and, loud enough for most people in the room to hear, told him it had been good to see him again.

As she left the café, swearing had erupted in earnest.

During the walk back to Paddington station, Brigit analysed what had happened. She berated herself for not saying who she was. Then she berated him for not knowing her. Maybe he had never known her? Was that it? For those few moments of interaction, her father's face transformed from a cynical, broken hangdog boredom and became briefly curious, then engaging. It was as if he'd never had a day's fun in his life before their encounter. Was the curiosity also fake? An act? He hadn't shown even a glimmer of recognition, not even when she indicated they had met before. Instead, his eyes had glazed over with confusion and seemed to have quickly calculated that Brigit was perhaps troublesome; part of something he shouldn't share.

It had been more than ten years since he'd held her, yet that brief touch of his hand caused memories to flood up through her arm, reigniting all the synapses that bore details of a happy childhood. It was as if the skin of her palm had bonded with the veins and bristled hair on the back of his hand. Brigit held that palm up to her face, hoping for a lingering scent of their bond. There was nothing at all.

She took her seat in the no smoking carriage, then changed so she had her back to the direction of travel. Staring out at the lines of bored looking travellers and groups of uniformed workers, Brigit's eyes filled with resolve. Since Alis left, Brigit was stronger, not weaker. Their tiny home was all she needed to raise herself with no interference. She would finish her schooling, then stop needing books and lectures and raised hands. She would do the one thing, the only thing her father had given her to do.

Business.

THE POLICE SERGEANT

Ever since his mam and dad died that day, twenty years it was, David Morgan Junior had been nervous about steps and ramps. Despite Kathryn's loving guidance and encouragement, he felt a desperate sense of panic almost as soon as they arrived at the airport. The shuffling along through lines and barriers, being processed and validated, helped make him a little calmer. But the instant they walked out from the gate onto the noisy tarmac, David Junior felt it welling up.

Kathryn kept telling him that deep down it was a fear of flying, and nothing to do with steps or falling. But it wasn't. Each step up made him feel he was about to stagger backwards or tumble over the handrail.

When they finally, successfully reached the aeroplane's door, he felt better for the warmth of Kathryn's hand in the small of his back. The crew was welcoming, especially that one in the bright yellow jacket with her clipboard and ear protectors around her neck. Her dark purple eyes told him all would be well. Later, he watched her from his seat, a model of efficiency it seemed as everyone was boarded quickly, even the gang of lads who had already had too much to drink. Kathryn was in the window seat, he in the middle and it seemed the aisle seat was free so David Junior began to take small actions that would make it his. The beautiful woman in her luminous attire had been in the cockpit, but now she was by the door again making a final assessment of some sort with the stewards, then an exchange of paperwork. Soon, she was gone, and the curved door was pulled shut.

Four hours later, they arrived at their hotel. This trip was Kathryn's retirement gift to David Junior, but partially it was for her too. So many tragedies had befallen their family. The difficult times seemed to have ended after Gareth, Karen and their poor children had been found dead. It still beggared belief that a family living in the back end of nowhere could have died from anthrax poisoning and no one had ever explained how they came into contact with the spores. Kathryn, in particular, always felt Gareth had been up to something and the deaths had been his fault. But then she'd had their son's wedding to supervise, and it didn't take long for everyone to feel that, at last, there was renewed joy for the Morgan family.

The general happiness lasted more than ten years. Despite his age, David Junior rose to be quite senior in his company's management team. Kathryn didn't need to work but held down a nice job, four hours a day at the florists. Number one son, Richard, and his wife Hannah spent a few years growing their careers, then decided to start a family. Little Rachel was the most adorable child. Then Kathryn had a health scare, and David Junior had to postpone his early retirement, just in case.

It seemed incomprehensible that Hannah and Rachel were killed that day. The poor child was not yet five and her mam just thirty-four. Richard was nearly destroyed by it. His world imploded. The people at his job were sympathetic to a point, but eventually they lost patience with his grieving, and he was kicked out on some trumped up disciplinary. Kathryn got better but Richard never really did, despite all the love from his parents and brother. He was more or less on level ground when David Junior retired and seemed happy that his mam and dad would take this time away. It felt like it was his blessing, but David Junior still didn't want to leave his eldest son alone.

After three days, their time in Spain had become relaxing and contented. They'd done next to nothing except eat royally, watch people and admire that magnificent cathedral, inside and out. Today's trip, though, was going to be special. A walk on the route of the Camino in the footsteps of countless pilgrims. It was to be the highlight of the whole trip. A coach would take them to a pre-designated point outside the city so they could walk back and see the city and cathedral as the pilgrims would have done.

Once back in Santiago, these modern-day wayfarers would join to share sangria and some grilled food. It was exciting.

David Junior sat quietly in the small lounge off the reception area while Kathryn got sorted in their room. The coach was supposed to arrive at just after three. They had more than twenty minutes, but he was still fretting about missing it. It wasn't all he was fretting about, but he muted those anxieties with a further check on his small rucksack to ensure the contents were still there: water bottle; fruit; first aid; a spare hat and socks. With his attention inside this small sack of essentials, his worries were suppressed. As soon as he zipped up the fastener, all those burdens bore down on him, like gravity.

He couldn't explain to Kathryn that retirement might be the end of him. So long as he was working, it was much, much easier to file away all their troubles and focus on life in the fast lane. The burden of Kathryn's illness, the possibility it would return and whether they could afford the care she might need. The burden of grief for Rachel and Hannah. The burden of a son who was so lost and broken that no amount of love could find or mend him. The burden that their other son, Trevor, felt excluded by the attention poured on his older brother. The burden of time lost that should have been shared with parents, aunts, uncles and cousins.

The greatest burden borne by David Morgan Junior was something Dewi had told him.

Shortly after his retirement, they'd travelled back to St Davids so Dewi could pay his respects to the family of a former colleague who had died suddenly. After the service and wake, they'd driven back up the road, but Dewi asked his son to turn off and go to Porthgain. Sitting by the harbour, staring out over a gloomy sky and bubbling, frothing sea, David Junior was surprised to hear his father start to cry. He tried to put his arm around his dad who recoiled petulantly and told him to listen. It wasn't what David Junior expected. Instead of an outpouring of grief for a dead colleague, Dewi spoke hesitantly about his part in a great injustice. He'd never felt any remorse for the dozens of enemy soldiers he'd killed in the trenches. But without firing a gun, throwing a grenade or lunging a bayonet, Dewi had sent innocent people to their deaths. He also feared that he had colluded in the deaths of others, by failing to act on the festering imperfections of another man. He told David Junior he couldn't go to his grave with this knowledge trapped in his head. He swore his son to silence and refused to provide more details when questioned.

David Junior assumed that the whisky might be causing this. Yet something nagged at him constantly. What had his father done? And when? And to whom? And why? Hadn't Dewi always been a pillar of rectitude?

Kathryn appeared in front of him, wanting to know if he'd covered himself in sun cream. It would be hot, and they both needed plenty of protection.

The welcome party for the returning modern day pilgrims was being held in a small park area on the outskirts of the city. Standing next to the empty coach, the tour's guide checked off the names and handed each arrival a small ribbon and medal confirming completion of the route. Guests were mingling, chattering away excitedly about how it had felt and reviewing aches and pains in their feet. Two names remained without a tick mark, but it was early evening now and the guide was eager to join in with the drinking and eating. He assumed Sr and Sra Morgan had decided to avoid the party and head back to their hotel.

Their sunburnt, shrivelled bodies were found, several days later, well away from the Camino, miles from any village or town. They bore no markings and no injuries. No substance was found in their bodies. Their packs contained half-full water bottles and rotting apples. In the absence of any clear evidence to the contrary, it was assumed they must have become lost after setting off in the wrong direction when they left the coach. Perplexed, perhaps, unable to relocate the right path, they must have tried to find help in a village or town and simply ended up more lost with every step. No one else on the tour had noticed them after leaving the coach. The last people who saw them alive turned out to be a family from Toulouse, who came forward after appeals and said the couple seemed happy and well. Mr Morgan had even spoken to them in French.

Within a week, Richard Morgan took an overdose of diazepam and paracetamol. His brother found him slumped over a table, curtains drawn, empty bottles and tablet strips strewn around him, an empty vodka bottle on the floor. He was dead and, from that moment, Trevor Morgan began to believe something more than bad luck was in play for his family.

NINE

Brigit

After she returned from London and reflected further on Rhodri, Brigit was in no mood for the mounting Christmas celebrations in the village. It would mean more rounds of cross-examination about Alis, and her story about family problems was wearing thin. Some instinct told her, nonetheless, that she should engage and when everyone stood near the church to drink mulled wine, eat mince pies and bawl along to carols, Brigit joined them and enjoyed herself.

Another instinct clicked in when she was asked whether Alis would be home for Christmas. It was an easy lie and would buy her several months without needing newer, more expansive lies. She told them that Alis had met her estranged father while they were both in St Davids. There had been a kind of reunion and, when Rhodri returned to London, they had started to speak occasionally by telephone. It was why she, Brigit, had travelled over to London that weekend. To try to play a part in her parents' attempts at reconciliation. If everything went well, they might all live together again, in London – or even close to Skenfrith.

Her deceit caused an outpouring of joy and good wishes.

Brigit returned to school, relieved that her routine was back in play. The year just finished had been tough for her and she wanted new diversions. She'd been good at netball since junior school, but had now become a powerful wing attack, helping the school team to town and county honours. She worked hard too, scoring high marks in her mock A levels. Above all, Brigit loved hard. More specifically, she discovered a penchant for sex that led to many encounters over the months before the end of exams in early June 1987. The convenience of having her very own home made this too easy, and all through that summer her neighbours became scandalised by the parties being held at Brigit's cottage. She didn't care. Something deep within her had been awoken and it made her a demanding, impatient lover. In turn, she became disenchanted with the young men of her age group and sought liaisons elsewhere.

Brigit passed her A levels with grades that should have seen her join a university, but she was intent on a different journey. Alis had taught her how to cook and the cottage was filled with accessories for making jams, pickles and condiments. Brigit travelled around the local fruit and vegetable farms and made deals to be given excess or mis-shaped products in exchange for work on the farm. In some cases, the work was fucking and that got her extra produce.

She posted flyers through every door in the village asking people to retain their jars and lids for her to collect. Each day thereafter, she knocked on doors asking for empties and was given plenty. It would seem that the same neighbours who were scandalised by her antics in the bedroom were more than happy to benefit from her endeavours in the kitchen. Back at the cottage, she spent hours cooking and sterilising. She created a small business plan and, as the second summer of love drew to its close, Brigit was a regular at local markets with a small stall, loaded with the fruits of that plan.

When the 1980s shuddered to their close, Brigit was paying farmers solely with cash and had contracts in place with several local shops for the supply of her produce. She still made it all at her cottage, and had certificates to prove it was a safe, healthy environment for food production. And she still spent as much time as she could spare fucking grateful men.

During the summer of 1990, Brigit jumped on the train at Abergavenny and, after several changes and more hours than she could bear, got off at Carmarthen and boarded the bus to St Davids. She had a reservation at the hotel where Jane and Will had worked and, after checking in, she set off for a tour of the old town. Later that evening, she had dinner with the hotel's manager, and they agreed she would supply the kitchen with branded products that were unique and would complement the manager's plans to offer guests an artisanal, local menu. They agreed that Brigit's produce would be labelled 'made in Pembrokeshire'.

Neither woman was concerned by the deception. These things could easily be concealed. No one would ever know. What couldn't be concealed was the way the manager, Louise, kept looking at Brigit. As they finished their meal and concluded the business discussion, she suggested they share a drink in the bar. Within an hour, they were in Brigit's room, aroused, naked and writhing from the assortment of new sensations they unleashed on each other.

They awoke the next morning and did it all again, prompting a bang on the wall from a neighbouring room. Their laughter was unwelcome, and a shout of rage went up about calling the manager. Louise pulled on a robe and went to enquire what the problem might be.

Later that afternoon, the couple walked from the hotel down to Caerfai beach and made love in a cave.

Brigit felt something strange about the space. Neither their gasps nor screams caused any kind of echo. It was as if the cave was dead in some way. Louise seemed too absorbed to notice.

On the drive back to Carmarthen for Brigit's train, she asked if they could make some detours. They stood together looking down the old runway, then at the church and its bell tower. Past the mill and the river then on past the quarry. Outside The Wool Merchant's House, Brigit was moved to tears, a reaction she couldn't explain to Louise, who held her close. The warmth and tenderness of that touch caused more tears.

Moments later they parked up in a remote spot and made love until it was too late for Brigit to catch her train. In the moments that she came, Brigit saw the opaque darkness. As she arched her back, almost blacking out with pleasure, she recalled it was the third time she'd seen those three lines. She'd laughed the first time, cried the second. Now it seemed those flashes were just an A grade in recognition of Louise's oral skills.

The Police Sergeant

Tim Thomas took a long draw on their joint and looked at Sylvia as she pedalled their craft across the Mediterranean, about a hundred metres off the beach. Last night's gig had been excellent, and the bars and fast-food shacks had given them more cash. Their recycled pop and club hits, pumped out from synths and drum machines, always got people jumping. Sylvia had a great voice across multiple registers, and he could back her up when needed.

Every week they spent time reviewing what was

happening in the British charts and chatted to new arrivals about what was hot, but also to the Dutch and Germans and Swedes about their music scenes.

SG & TimTom, they were called. They were never going to be millionaires doing this, but they loved what they did, and they did it brilliantly. And everyone loved them.

Sylvia reached over and put her hand on his stomach, a sign that she wanted the joint. He passed it to her and said he was going to take a quick dip to cool down. She stopped pedalling and finished the joint. It made her horny, it always did, and when Tim reappeared, she told him they needed to head back to the van. He smiled, then winced. He said he thought he'd hit his ankle on the side of the pedalo when he dived in. It was sore, but he hauled himself onto the boat with relative ease. Back at the shoreline, they beached the pedalo and Chabane refused payment, as he always did.

During the short walk to their campsite, Tim felt increasingly uncomfortable and when they got inside their old VW, his lower leg had a series of red wheals and was swelling. Sylvia gave him some paracetamol and told him to rest and keep his foot off the ground while she went for something to make a cold compress. When she returned, Tim was in distress, breathing rapidly and in pain.

At the campsite pharmacy, the staff said it looked like a jelly fish sting even though Tim was adamant the problem was an impact wound. Perhaps it was infected? The sea was polluted, despite being clear. The staff were sceptical, were resolute with their sting diagnosis and recommended antihistamine tablets with an accompanying cream. Neither stopped the pains and discomfort. Within an hour, Tim was struggling to breathe and sweating profusely. The whole of his right leg below the knee had become swollen and had turned a deep maroon. Back at the pharmacy, Sylvia was told Tim must see a doctor and should be taken to hospital.

Now she was panicking, frantic with worry and numb with uncertainty. Manu from the bar saw her and brought her a Perrier and she asked him to come and look at Tim. When they got back to the van, Tim was still distressed and occasionally confused. Manu shook his head then went and got his jeep. They helped Tim into the back seat so he could lie down, then pulled up the soft top to create shade.

The road was quiet, and Manu soon pulled up at a hospital. Tim was no worse, but wasn't improving. Manu told the medics what had happened and, after they'd listened and done a quick examination, Tim was put on a trolley that they pushed away quickly.

Manu said he'd come back later to collect them and told Sylvia not to worry. She sat in the waiting area and ignored his advice. What if the worst happened? She'd have nothing to do. He was the musical brains behind *SG & TimTom*. She could hit keys and buttons to make a contribution, but Tim was the one who made it all hang together. He always had been.

But it was okay. He'd be fine. Earlier, as they wheeled him away, he had smiled at her. He'd be fine.

She was soon back to what if…?

It would mean going back to England to tell their son and Tim's witch of a mother. More things to drag Sylvia down. The child had been an accident that she and Tim knew from the start was a mistake. So, they'd cut him adrift, leaving Tim's mum to raise the boy. They sent money and sometimes talked with Simon. But the bond was limited, and their son didn't really understand who they were.

Sylvia shook out these thoughts. If Tim didn't make it, or was chronically ill, she'd have to begin a new career, perhaps using a karaoke machine. Yes: that could work. The same places would have her for that stuff. She could rock the joints. Maybe sell the camper van and quit the grass. Smarten up too. Lose the hippy chick vibe and cut a new look. They were in the second half of the nineties. She still looked like she had on Ibiza in 1988.

The nurses found someone who spoke English and who came, with a voice full of condolence, to tell her Tim was dead. Jelly fish toxins had caused anaphylaxis. Despite the oxygen and fluids, the antihistamines and steroids, despite all they had tried to do, Tim had suffered a massive physical shock that kept stopping his heart. His system couldn't cope with the reaction. Finally, his heart didn't restart.

They were very sorry.

Sylvia was broken and hadn't recovered when she rushed back to England. She was fine around people, or when there was stuff to do. But any amount of just sitting and waiting made her jumpy and anxious. At Marseille Airport, with too long to wait, she developed a troubled theory about family history. She hadn't seen her parents since her 16th birthday when she upped and left them to their loved-up life on the ocean wave. It hadn't stopped the old bill tracking her down with news of their deaths: the bizarre, macabre killings and how they linked to another identical murder in the sixties.

What if Tim's death was not the tragic accident everyone believed? It made her so worried that she was scared to board the plane back to Leeds.

He was still a child. Simon was seven. He had hardly known his father and seemed unaffected by the news of his death. Tim's mum, Simon's nana, was beside herself with upset. The fact that it was Sylvia bearing the news made it much worse. Nana hated Sylvia. It was her fault her son had gone off to another country, become a drug and sex addict, and was now dead.

He was still a child, but Simon was old enough to see how much his mother was panicking and frightened. She wouldn't say why she was nervous and worried about being in Britain but was unequivocal that she had no intention of staying, nor of taking Simon with her. Sylvia patiently fielded nana's insults and shaming by keeping on track about her plan. She was going back to France in a matter of days. There was some money in a bank account for Simon that would continue to be supplemented, as well as the several wads of notes she'd tipped from a bag on to nana's table. Sylvia didn't want the names Thomas or Griffiths to be used for Simon and was relieved that nana had reverted to her maiden name. Sylvia didn't really care what he ended up being called so long as it wasn't Simon. Above all, no one was ever to mention Sylvia Griffiths. To anyone.

Nana had snorted with contempt and said there was no risk of that name ever being mentioned again.

He was still a child and Simon wanted his mum to hug him, kiss him, give words of kindness and love. She might be going for good so this would be the last time they ever saw each other, and that made him feel confused and slightly guilty. Sylvia didn't even tousle his hair. She just told him to forget her and be good for his nana. He didn't know how she'd got here and where she was going.

He was still a child, and his nana's hugs and cuddles helped a little. His tears fell hard and fast. Simon didn't know what or who he was any more. Five days after his mother abandoned him, permanently, he went with his nana for a day trip to Harrogate. Despite her hatred for Sylvia, nana had taken her worries at face value and wanted no risk for Simon. They had a proper afternoon tea and, accompanied by sandwiches and cake, they talked about what name Simon might like.

TEN

Brigit

Life in Skenfrith had run its course for Brigit, and her feet itched for new horizons. A chance encounter with Claire Clifton in Monmouth had been a catalyst. She'd known Claire instantly, despite her increasingly aged appearance. They met at the small bus station and caught the same bus out of town. Claire told Brigit she was exhausted so much of the time she didn't dare drive. Steve, who was increasingly frail and immobile, had retired on medical grounds. It meant Claire was the only earner.

Brigit tried to steer the conversation to concentrate on the Clifton family. Was Steve getting care? How were the kids? Was the garden still as lovely? But inevitably Claire had questions too. She was shocked and visibly emotional when Brigit told her Alis was dead: there was no point saying otherwise. She kept it simple. Alis died in a car accident while visiting friends down near Bristol. It led to several moments of quite forensic questions and Brigit nearly contradicted herself twice. She was glad when the bus arrived at Rockfield, and Claire had to leave. She almost broke down when Claire told her how much she and Steve and all their children had loved Alis.

For the remaining miles, Brigit was gazing out of the bus window, unable to stop tears falling. The thing she had eradicated, history, had caught up with her, in a way she hadn't expected.

That night, she phoned Louise and cried her heart out.

Hereford's thriving market, held each Wednesday, had become a regular trip for Brigit. All over the city, she was constantly making deals that expanded her business. She found a stall in the Butter Market that agreed to sell her produce. The city had a growing alternative retail scene and café culture. Small shops wanted and happily took local artisan products.

She began to see Hereford as the place to be. To go and live there and set up a small operation to make her products and engage a wider customer base. It wasn't a retail and manufacturing powerhouse, but she loved the city and its people. It was charming yet closed. It was almost of another time, possibly even of another world.

Then she met Gerard.

Brigit was down by the river, enjoying a lunchtime sandwich and drink. It had been a hard morning's work and the break was welcome.

He wore espadrilles, baggy shorts and a ragged tee shirt. A net shopping bag full of produce dangled from his left hand, and he had a music player with headphones. He seemed lost in whatever he was listening to, and Brigit could hear the percussive hiss of something she knew. It was *Heroine*, by Suede. She hadn't made up her mind yet about that album. Louise hated it; said it wasn't a patch on the debut.

Brigit hadn't been with a man for more than a year. Louise had made her bored by the fumbling physical and mumbling mental incapacities of the male psyche. Yet there was something joyously preposterous about this man and she vaguely wanted him. He was a mess, but perhaps it was a construct? The Walkman was top of the range. And that watch looked weighty. His face had a weathered finery and he looked in good shape. Suddenly, he said something aloud. It wasn't far short of a shout. *Bloody piccalilli*. That's what he said. He spun around and stumbled on his cheap shoes. Then he realised he was being observed and tore off his headphones to apologise for his outburst and any offence he might have caused. His voice tried to conceal its Hereford accent, but it was too easy to detect in his vowel sounds.

He was struck by two arched eyebrows and the dark purple eyes beneath them. Then, with an enigmatic smile, the woman said she knew just the place for the best piccalilli in town.

Gerard bought three jars of Brigit's Genuine Herefordshire Piccalilli at the cheese stall. He grabbed some tasty cheddar too, then walked to a different outlet to buy four pork pies. They ambled back through the streets to the Old Bridge and sat in a bar having coffee. It was a pleasant afternoon, so the occasion merited a shared bottle of wine with some nibbles. He seemed well enough known by the bar's owners for them to take his bag of shopping and keep it in their fridge.

Brigit listened and learned. He took the hint that she tended to avoid questions and, instead of asking more, Gerard rambled through the bits and pieces of his own life story.

He was fifty-three. He was married. He lived in Tupsley, in an old tumble-down house, and was minted. Brigit had been most interested in two parts of that story: that there was a place called *Tupsley*; and what on earth *minted* might mean.

It was early evening, and they both needed to be elsewhere. He walked her back to the station, having explained that *minted* meant he'd inherited a fortune when his parents shuffled off. He used phrases like that a lot, as if he lived in a Wodehouse novel. *Tupsley*, it transpired, was a suburb to the east of the city where all the best people lived. Brigit told him she hoped he didn't have far to walk. He wafted a hand away to the right and said Bodenham Road was very close. As if it meant something to her.

It seemed like an encounter that was charming and innocent. Brigit forgot about it within twenty-four hours.

He called her the following weekend. Gerard had done some digging and got her details from one of the retailers in the city. Her piccalilli was rather splendid. It went perfectly with blue cheese. So, he'd tried her spiced plum chutney too. It was ripping. Would Brigit be back in town soon? He had a proposition.

Louise told her to go and find out what he had in store. Brigit was dithering. The man could be dangerous. Louise laughed and told her she'd come over and be a chaperone, or one of those covert surveillance people, tracking all the places Gerard took Brigit. They ended the call laughing and Brigit felt so loved that it was like a shield; no harm could possibly befall her. She didn't need a chaperone, but she adored the idea of Louise watching her doing things.

Gerard met Brigit at the station, and they drove for around ten minutes. He was still in shambolic clothes and the inside of his Mini Metro was littered with mess. Brigit noted that he smelled deliciously of a fragrance. It wasn't like the colognes she'd encountered on the necks and chests and abdomens of the men she had slept with. This was a subtle blend of floral and spicy. Something exotic.

Small talk agreeably filled the time until he drove into a small trading estate and parked his car in a space facing a sign saying, *B.Rhodes – Owner*. Brigit made a joke about whether Hereford had any A roads, and Gerard gave a hollow laugh before explaining that Bernard Rhodes was his late father. After glancing across and seeing her discomfort, Gerard told Brigit not to worry. He'd heard the joke before, and no harm had ever befallen the comedian. It burst the momentary bubble of tension.

The air outside had an inexplicable putridity, and it was a relief to get inside the unit. They climbed stairs and Gerard sat at an oval table, indicating that Brigit should sit oppositive. The room was furnished with modest things. A much smaller table with a telephone and a comfortable looking swivel chair. Several spiral bound notebooks and stacks of A4 paper sat on the shelves of an otherwise empty bookcase. The floor was covered with squares of carpet, black and grey like a shady chess board. To Brigit's left, just beyond the end of the table, the wall held a whiteboard. Underneath it was another table, waist-high and sturdy. It held a large box, like the ones used to contain grand cutlery sets. At the other end of their table, a window looked out over the main working area of the unit, which was empty and silent.

Gerard explained this was the hub from which his daddy had run a small business empire. This and that. The other. Brigit told him it felt cold, calculating and slightly unnerving. He told her that he disliked clutter in the workplace and when her face showed puzzlement, he laughed and said his car wasn't ever a workplace. But none of that mattered. What he wanted to know was Brigit's business model. In her own words.

She spoke quietly about it. No one had ever asked her to be like this; to sell herself and her business. She knew it was successful and every detail of how it operated. She had contingency plans for any eventuality. She re-invested most of her revenue, but still made a small profit. She used a series of suppliers, not just for raw materials but also to make her produce. She avoided big company buyers, even though one or two had been sniffing around.

He sat forward with his palms flat on the table. Gerard didn't speak or make any sound during Brigit's speech, and held her gaze throughout. When she finished, he nodded then stood and pushed a button on the telephone. When a voice said *hello*, he smiled and asked for some drinks and food to be brought to the unit. The voice asked if there were any dietary needs, and Gerard raised an eyebrow at Brigit who shook her head. She noticed that Gerard smiled constantly at the handset speaker, and his tone of voice was friendly. In closing he used a forename to thank the voice. Christopher also used Gerard's forename when he confirmed how long the delivery would take.

Gerard brought some paper to the table, then opened the box under the white board to take out a handful of pencils and three coloured marker pens. They'd been starting to digress a little from Brigit's recount, and small talk was on the rise too. But now, Gerard asked her to remain quiet for a while and to make notes of anything she wanted to say while he worked. Then he began to draw on the whiteboard. Over the next fifteen minutes he created a graphical view of Brigit's business. Every few moments, he stopped and took a pace backwards to look at what was developing. He also changed colours often, using orange to indicate something different to green or blue. Brigit occasionally scribbled something on the paper in front of her, but otherwise sat and watched his work.

When he returned to sit with her, Gerard asked what

she had written. Instead of answering in words, Brigit went to the white board and altered some of the descriptions, redirected lines between boxes and added what she had heard him refer to as *a process step* which he had missed from his flow chart.

Christopher's arrival was announced with knocking, and Gerard went to help with the trays of food and drink. After a smiling round of intros, Christopher wished them Bon Appetit and left for his next delivery. Gerard unwrapped and uncovered things and told Brigit to get stuck in.

They ate and talked, and Brigit wondered what Gerard's proposition was going to be. He was very calm, to the extent that he seemed to lack focus. But, occasionally, he would drill deeply into something Brigit said, seek details, demand more clarity. Each of these episodes involved note taking or sketches on a piece of paper and, sometimes, Gerard revisited the white board to amend or add to his illustration.

Once they'd grazed through the food, Gerard suggested a walk to clear heads, stretch legs and talk about something different. They walked along a street of terraced houses then on to a busy road. He explained it was the Ledbury Road, one of the main routes into the city. They crossed over a small stream, and Gerard explained it was the cause of the unpleasant smell she'd noticed, since the brook ran alongside the trading estate as it flowed along the last mile of its journey into the River Wye. Soon, they turned into a small cut between buildings and strolled between the comforting houses of a cul-de-sac called Brookside. Fifteen minutes later, they arrived back at the trading estate via a different entrance. Instead of returning to the office, Gerard led Brigit into the vacant space of the unit and without any preamble outlined his proposition.

'Let's make this the place where all your products are made and packaged, then stored ready for despatch. It means you can cut out multiple, time-consuming steps in your supply chain and allow you to focus on customers, who you can also impress by bringing them here if they want to see the operations. You can assure larger batch sizes when needed to meet demand. It also gives you a place to run your business, instead of doing it in today's slightly haphazard way. You create a sense of place for your trading, and people will buy in to that.'

Brigit kept her feelings concealed and asked Gerard what his involvement would be. His offer was simple: he would invest in the development of his unit as a food production site: machines; safety; hygiene; access; security; recruitment; marketing; logistics. Then he would be a director of her company and recover his investment from its inevitable success and growth. He could also provide additional sites, once expansion was required.

It didn't make sense to Brigit. Why her, and why her business?

Gerard shrugged and told her it's what he did. He also said he didn't expect her to agree right here and now; he didn't have a contract conveniently ready to sign. But there would be properly drawn up terms and conditions for this proposal once Brigit agreed in principle and their negotiations were complete.

It was some time until she needed to be back at the station, so he suggested he would leave her at the unit so she could make calls and reflect on his offer.

Brigit phoned Louise. They spoke for ages through questions and answers, doubts and certainties. By the end of the conversation, everything was clear. Brigit had her own proposal. When Gerard returned, with a bag of doughnuts for good measure, he smiled broadly when he saw that Brigit had wiped clean the white board, and written the following:

"Contract - including financial commitments

Terms of Business Conduct for board members, old and new

Statement of Operational procedures and creation of manager role for new site (I don't want to live in Hereford)"

Then she'd drawn a line to a final sentence, in capitals: "Do these things, and I can agree to your proposal."

When he dropped her at the station, Gerard suggested Brigit should return soon so they could continue and conclude negotiations. She repeated that once he'd drawn up all the contract terms, they could continue with the things she'd listed on the white board. It could be completed quite quickly. Gerard nodded and smiled again. This was a meeting of minds, and a warm handshake assured it.

Back at Skenfrith, Brigit took out the folded piece of paper from her jeans and dialled the number she'd copied earlier while using the phone in Gerard's office. When Christopher answered, she asked if he'd like to meet next time she was in Hereford.

It took a week for Gerard to get the contracts drawn up and they met in the city to agree heads of terms. Then they jointly worked on drafts of the other documents Brigit wanted and it was a productive day.

With business concluded, and not much left to do, Brigit declined Gerard's offer to join him and his wife for dinner. Instead, she met Christopher in the city centre and, after just one drink, they walked to the hotel and had a productive night.

Everything Gerard did for Brigit's business was a success and it meant she had the option to live just about anywhere she chose. In the end, the choice she made was for her child to be born in Pembrokeshire.

Christopher had been enthusiastic and bold during each of the dozen or so nights they spent together but he was resentful and tearful when Brigit told him she needed to end their affair.

He didn't see why she needed to leave him just because she was moving away from the area. Brigit felt vaguely wretched about how he reacted but was quietly pleased that he didn't dig deeper. If he knew the real reasons for his rejection, Christopher could easily have been plunged in to a deeper, more lasting despair.

He had done what she needed. The sex and attention he'd enjoyed had been merely a functional act for Brigit and, while her pleasure was sometimes genuine, it too was utilitarian. She needed a baby and this handsome, toned young man had helped to create one. Now, since his work was done, Christopher would no longer be a part of Brigit's, nor her baby's life.

Brigit had found it hard to tell Louise about her need for a baby daughter. The only person she could explain it to with any clarity was herself. In the end, as she so often did, Louise made things easy for Brigit by telling her to do whatever she needed, so long as it didn't mean the end for them. After each session with Christopher, Brigit called Louise and they had phone sex that was frantic, feverish and left Brigit wondering how a man and his dick could ever make her come so much and so hard as she did with Louise. This was the second item on her list of reasons to move back to St Davids.

The place Louise found was fine on paper but, when Brigit travelled to view the property, she knew it was perfect.

Leaving Skenfrith held no complications. Brigit wasn't remotely sentimental and took the opportunity to leave behind or dispose of many accrued items and trinkets. She hired a car on the company's account and Louise travelled over by train to help load it. They travelled back on the slow roads.

In mid-January 1996, Brigit picked up the keys to her new home, in the place that had always been her home. Her business was in safe hands and required her guidance but rarely her presence. Her pregnancy was safe and sound. Her partnership with Louise was now permanent and infinitely more intense. Her reacquaintance with this place was an abiding treasure. When she gave birth to the baby girl she'd always known she was carrying, Louise was constantly at her side and, together, they decided the beautiful, tiny baby would be called Erin.

THE POLICE SERGEANT

Sylvia took her own advice and ditched Griffiths. She'd subtly amended her forename, too. Both real names were still on her passport but now all her bookings were in the name of Sylvie Smith.

It had taken nearly a year for her to come to terms with Tim's death. The stuff with their son back in England was the least of her worries and had felt like the one good thing to have happened. Deserting him, leaving him to a life he knew well and in which he could thrive, ensuring she made a financial contribution to that growth - all that felt like closure. She had done good. For Simon, and for Tim's memory.

The steady flow of work *SG and TimTom* had built up was gone. She'd tried to set up a final show in which she might perform some of what had made their act so popular. But the bars and holidaymakers had no appetite for such a memorial. It was time to quit, move and rebuild.

Her sadness over this was made worse by Sylvia's terrible paranoia about what had happened and how it sat alongside what she suspected about her family's history. Whenever she relived Tim's final few hours something pricked and stabbed at her. He'd done a clean, shallow dive but, despite being stoned, Sylvia's memory was clear that she'd heard no impact or knock on the pedalo to indicate he'd hit his leg. The sea often did have jelly fish, sometimes a lot of them, and people did get stung. But they'd been gliding over the water for more than an hour that day and seen no jelly fish. Not one. Tim hadn't dived deep, where the gelatinous horrors might have been waiting. It just didn't seem real. Sylvia was certain something else had caused his death. These impish pricks of malice wouldn't go away and let her rest. Not even a certificate with *anaphylaxis* as cause of death settled her fear of something more terrible at work.

Her re-branding made a small difference at first. Having a different name, and a completely new act meant that Sylvie edged towards freedom from the feelings she had about Tim. She was entertaining a different kind of tourist. Slightly more chic. Slightly less interested in music as anything other than a background accompaniment to their food and self-absorption. Probably wealthier, and easier to relieve of their money.

So, Sylvie Smith gigged and gigged up and down the Côte d'Azure. Like *SG and TimTom*, the money wasn't a fortune, but it was enough for her to afford the rent on a simple flat in Le Lavandou. She quit the drugs, stopped drinking and became vegetarian. She realised she was happy to be single but, if she got hornier than DIY could satisfy, would phone for an escort.

Each month, she transferred as much as she could to Simon's account but never wondered what had become of him, or what he was called now. As the end of a century approached, Sylvia knew he had passed his tenth birthday. She sent double the usual money that month, but no other acknowledgement.

Sylvia felt no sense of motherhood, nor of pain from its loss.

When she was invited to perform at the festival that would celebrate a new century, Sylvie saw the possibility that newer, bigger things might be on the horizon. She was still young and craved success if it was available. There were nationally celebrated performers at the same show, which would mean agents, managers or producers must be there. She was in an early slot on the schedule, but Sylvie decided to give this her best possible shot and began practising and rehearsing in earnest.

Each of the four songs she sang was met with enthusiastic applause and, as she left the stage, the house band and audience stood as one to acknowledge a fine performance. Sylvie Smith had delivered.

It was a wonderful evening, but she soon felt crushed by the lack of any lucrative connection. Men floated by to tempt her with drinks, but Sylvie was sober and therefore poor company. These suitors returned to their tables. She was ready to leave and erase the memory of something that had ended up flat and fruitless. By the time an organised fireworks display and then a gunfire salute were finished, a parade of noisy vehicles overwhelmed the promenade. It was clear that any attempt to break through that gridlock would be impossible.

Sylvie decided to accept the next offer of champagne. Despite her abstinence, it seemed churlish not to celebrate the triple bonanza of a new year, decade and century. Sure enough, another suit appeared, so she flirted with the guy and let him fetch her a second glass. As they chatted with increasingly lustful intent, Sylvie decided she liked the look of the front of his trousers. She would take him home to bed as soon as they could get out of the building. A really good fuck with a stranger might make up for the evening's lack of musical achievement.

As Sylvie searched for the moment to suggest taking things elsewhere, a woman appeared and ran her hand up the neck of her suitor. His wife, probably, or perhaps his lover. Tall, with long dark hair and a dazzling frock. About the same age as Sylvie, give or take a year. She wore those glasses that were *à la mode*: like sunglasses; clear lenses coated with colours that changed depending on how the light hit them. Sylvie could just make out that the woman's eyes were a striking shade of purple and when they searched into Sylvie's own eyes, she sensed twin chills of attraction and fear.

Another flattened prospect. Oh well. A night alone with her trusty dildo would have to do. It was a pale substitute, but she knew how to make it seem like the real thing, especially since the real thing was a rare treat these days. It would categorically be the best cure for her sudden horny thoughts. She would make use of the picture she'd captured of the way that guy's packet swelled so impressively below his belt buckle. As much of that, inside wherever he might have wanted to put it, could have been divine and that thought was increasing her sense of arousal. She tried to suppress it with more champagne.

Sylvie ended up drunk, but someone was kind enough to arrange a taxi that whisked her home. It was well past four am when she closed and locked the door. The effects of alcohol, after years of abstinence, had made her feel so tired and disappointed about her future. But none of that had changed her need to come, as many times as she could make herself. She unzipped and stepped out of her dress then left it to hang itself up.

She lay in the pitch-dark room, her hands by her sides for now, and closed her eyes to picture the guy undressing. With each item he removed, tuxedo, shirt, trousers, her breathing deepened. Sylvie parted her legs slightly then ran the fingers of her left hand over the lace of her bra, imagining it was his tongue making her nipple harden. She repeated the same motion on each of her breasts then slipped the bra off. Now she saw the guy standing in his pants and the bulge had become a peak. Sylvie kept one hand stroking her breasts and nipples and felt a more powerful surge of wetness. She ran the fingers of her right hand down between her breasts. Slowly, and barely touching her skin, she moved that hand onwards over her tummy where she made small circular movements around her navel. There he was at her side, removing his pants and climbing to be above her, raised up on all fours. She opened her eyes now and moved her hand, millimetres at a time, until the fingers reached the short bristles at the upper edge of her Brazilian. With a new vision of him lying underneath her, she got up to sit on her haunches, moved her fingers down and, as she slid them into the warm wetness, Sylvie moaned. As she quickened the pace, her moans turned to gasps, then cries as she imagined him coming inside her.

Her drunkenness made her want more and she reached over to the bedside cupboard. After grappling in the dark for a while, and nearly tumbling off the bed, she finally found and took out the dildo. It slid inside with ease, and her moans and gasps quickly resumed. The slow, familiar rhythm made her think once more of a partner, but now it was that tall, dark-haired woman with her eyes of purple, such intensity in their gaze. Now the woman was kissing her with great passion; then her mouth breathed warmth onto Sylvie's neck, then her shoulder, then her breast. Purple Eyes was between her legs, licking and nibbling. It made Sylvie pull the dildo out so she could move her free hand down to touch the wet heat then taste what that woman was tasting. She resumed the sliding, and now she didn't need to think of Purple Eyes, or of anything other than keeping things moving to cause the eruption that was welling up.

Sylvie lay there, slowly emerging from the ecstasy and felt her breathing return to normal. Perhaps it was her abstinence from alcohol that had caused her to miss out on coming like that. Those five or six – or was it seven? – glasses of champagne had made her horny in a very different way.

Something had felt slightly different about her dildo. In a drunken haze, it hadn't felt strange but now she sensed it might be longer, and perhaps more rigid. It had helped, hugely, with the way she'd just come. But as she started to withdraw it, Sylvie became certain that it wasn't a dildo. When she switched on the bedside lamp, what she saw in her hand was a police truncheon.

Sylvie giggled and used a mock police voice to say *come quietly now, madam*. Then she laughed aloud, just as the light went out, and everything suddenly seemed much darker.

ELEVEN

Brigit

Erin's infancy was troublesome, and it caused things to go wrong. Many of those problems were essentially trivial, but these were overshadowed by a vein of simmering complexity. Whenever that vein bled, Brigit was diminished, alone in a vacuum. Worst of all, Erin's problems became so unmanageable and errant that they eventually caused the breakdown of her mother's relationship with Louise.

Brigit was happy that she was a mother and, from the start, constantly exuded that joy. She had never revelled in her tendency to be a winner, but it felt now as if whatever she touched was destined to succeed. Motherhood would be no different. Louise loved Erin too and, as a couple, she and Brigit became devoted parents. It wasn't always easy for them to be seen together as a family, especially in public. This didn't stop both women referring to Erin as their daughter.

There were small signs during her first thirty months that Erin could be hard work. She had extremes of emotion and moments of being withdrawn, as if in another place. Brigit, with Louise's encouragement, changed nothing and sought no external advice. This was parenthood: times could be tough; nothing about Erin was disturbing; she just needed extra care. These issues faded, apparently, once there was regular contact with other children, which seemed to make Erin more settled and calm. It appeared she was sociable and enjoyed having a part to play in any kind of group activity.

More complex problems arose when Erin started at the small nursery school. At first, she adapted but after a few weeks one of the teachers called Brigit to ask that she collect Erin, who had been disruptive and had slapped another pupil. When they got home, Erin became tearful and apologetic. Brigit let it rest and soon took her daughter down to the beach so they could paddle. Then Erin fell asleep in her mother's arms, which reassured them both. She returned to nursery after two days and was good as gold.

Over time, more minor infringements were reported, and it began to worry Brigit. It felt as if something she couldn't understand was slowly splitting apart the decades in which her family had gained strength and certainty from itself and its legacies. Her relationship with Alis had sometimes been stretched taut by disputes, but it never snapped. The tragedies Stina and Alis had known, the desperate loss of never knowing their mothers, could not possibly happen again. Brigit sometimes couldn't drive the demons from her mind; the ones whispering that Erin, like Stina, was conceived without love.

Louise supported all Brigit's efforts to manage Erin and sometimes created calm, laughter and smiles when Brigit had given up. But there were more troughs than peaks, and the succession of troubles prompted a trip to see the family's GP. It brought mixed results.

Doctor Bowen seemed unwilling to offer much more than scepticism, and her tone could be condescending when Brigit spoke of home or family. But the doctor spoke to Erin, asking questions about how she felt, and what made her feel those things. Erin replied politely and seemed composed. She told the doctor she liked other children, and that two of her peers were close friends. Erin said she loved her mother and loved

Louise. She said she didn't always feel happy and felt no one understood her. She said she missed her daddy and wanted to see him more often. Doctor Bowen's eyebrows shot up at this revelation and she made rapid notes on a sheet of paper before continuing. Erin seemed perplexed by the next question, about whether she'd like to talk to someone else about her feelings. She replied that she had plenty of people to talk to. Her parents. Teachers. Doctor Bowen. The twins and all her grandmas. Best of all, Erin said, she had herself to talk to.

And now it was Brigit's eyebrows that were raised.

The doctor nodded through the answers Erin gave, then told her she meant someone new. A different kind of doctor called a health visitor. Someone who understood young children. Erin gazed at Doctor Bowen with her dark purple eyes, then squinted before shaking her head and saying that no one except young children understands young children.

The consultation soon ended, but Doctor Bowen asked Brigit to stay behind for a few moments. The doctor struggled to make the progress she'd wished for, as Brigit was silent for most of the short discussion. Doctor Bowen ended up as troubled by a mother's eyes as she had been by a daughter's and quickly concluded their discussion with a recommendation that Erin would benefit from seeing a health visitor. When Brigit asked if that would make Erin stop being difficult, the reply was evasive. It might but, without it, the problems couldn't be properly assessed or treated. Brigit said she'd consider it after discussing it with her daughter and with Louise.

Erin was smiling broadly at Brigit when she retrieved her from the small reception area. Whatever failures of medical due process had occurred, the consultation had created a happy bond. Their walk home was joyous, filled with giggles and many comments making fun of Doctor Bowen.

Later that night, Louise and Brigit lay sated in each other's arms. They discussed what had happened and agreed that they both needed to understand what Erin had said: about not being understood; and about her father. They also agreed that the interview with a doctor hadn't ended anything, and Erin's problems might not be over. But until they really understood more about Erin's feelings and behaviour, a health visitor seemed unnecessary.

After a period of calm at the nursery school, there was a significantly more worrying incident. In the nursery's small playground, Erin somehow climbed up the frame holding the swings and perched herself on the top beam. Her balance and control seemed precarious, but her demeanour was nonchalant, almost to the point of provocation. No one could get her to come down and even when Brigit arrived with Louise, Erin resolutely refused to move or speak. Eventually a ladder was found and leaned against the frame allowing Brigit to climb up and cajole Erin into returning to earth.

For several days, Erin was taciturn and silent. Brigit could get no kind of response from her daughter and the silence and lack of joy felt corrosive. Louise's efforts, so often a success, were met with something akin to contempt in Erin's eyes. It left Louise frustrated and, for the first time ever, she and Brigit had a tense exchange of disagreement, ending with raised voices and a slammed door.

When Erin heard her mother crying, she went to lie with her and brushed away her tears. She said she didn't mean to be horrible but didn't know how to stop.

They lay together into the early hours discussing Erin's feelings about being understood and her father. The young child in a mother's arms seemed to accept that Brigit would do all she could to be better at understanding her, but that her father was an irrelevance.

The parents of other children at the nursery had been busily making their views known about that wild child and her degenerate mother. It left Brigit with no choice other than to withdraw Erin from the nursery. The row with Louise was short lived, and now they agreed to work hard to show Erin she was loved and could still learn and play outside any formal establishment. The two women also found friends who wanted no part of the short sighted, ugly attitudes that had been all too readily accepted by the nursery. It meant Erin had more love, more to do and more friends to make than she had known. They'd all turned a corner.

Within a year, Erin went to school and Brigit felt whatever had been broken was now mended. Erin had responded well to the time spent learning basic skills with her mothers and had become a happy sociable character who was liked by her small collection of friends and their parents. Erin took well to school and adapted to being back in a formal environment with its learning and soft discipline. Teachers found her easy to teach, full of genuine curiosity and capable of achieving more than most. Erin looked around her and saw no competition. She knew she was good but cared little for being top of the class.

With more time on her hands, Brigit re-engaged with her business and, in particular, with the people she employed. One day each week she travelled over to Hereford for meetings and reviews about growth, reach and clients. At first, she made it a day trip. But she realised she was beginning to feel love for the city and its surrounding countryside, so she started to stay and revel in that love. Business was booming and Gerard's enthusiasm for expansion was all consuming. They'd worked effectively at a distance, but Brigit saw how much more effectively they could operate face to face.

At school, Erin's calm outlook and adept learning skills lured everyone into a false state of complacency. Louise was left in charge during the days when Brigit visited Hereford, and that time together was uncomplicated for more than a year. Louise sent text messages to Brigit with news of what Erin had done and said that day. Each evening at bedtime there was a call, in which Brigit told Erin a short, good night story. Before she was seven, Erin had learned how to send texts from her parents' mobile phones and Brigit was frequently distracted by her daughter's loving messages.

One day a message Brigit received wasn't loving at all.

When she replied to Louise asking what she was on about, her screen very soon displayed the message: *It's me, Mama. I wish you could see me*. Brigit quickly reviewed the first message, about looking down at all the teachers and classmates. Without explanation, she packed up her things and raced back over the fastest route. Within thirty minutes, Louise called in a breathless fury that Erin had taken her mobile phone from her handbag and was now ruining a school trip to the Bishop's Palace by sitting at the highest point she could climb to above the old abbey. Soon Brigit was driving with dangerous tears blurring her vision. Louise refused to offer any support or comfort.

Erin was out of reach. No one could get any sense

into her. It was only when Brigit had calmed down enough to think straight that she realised she could phone her daughter and try to talk her down.

It was an unnerving conversation. Erin's manner was unflustered and tranquil. Brigit was barely in control of anything, least of all her car. After less than ten minutes, Erin said she was bored now and was going to throw the phone away. The line went dead.

As Brigit accelerated out of Carmarthen her phone warbled through the car's speakers and the school's head teacher informed her that Erin had now climbed down and was being tended by Doctor Bowen. She asked if she could speak to her daughter but was told it would be better if she could get back home quickly to take charge of her child. The head teacher also told her that Erin was repeatedly asking to see her father.

Brigit drove the last thirty or so miles much too fast and with scant regard for the rules of the road.

The next day, with Louise holding her hand, Brigit called Doctor Bowen and told her it was time for Erin to see the health worker.

The Police Sergeant

The disappearance of Sylvie Smith, singer and musician, was cause for concern. It was a matter of fact that she was often away performing at venues all along the coast. But, when a worried club manager reported his concern that Sylvie had missed two engagements, it resulted in a warrant being issued to break into her home, where a woman's body was found. The body was on the bedroom floor, with a block of wood under its shoulders so the head was stretched back at an angle.

It was presumed to be Sylvie Smith and the officers

called in for someone to identify her. While that was being arranged, the discovery that something appeared to be stuck in the body's mouth caused an escalation of activity, and the area was designated a crime scene.

The shock was soon mingled with confusion, because the only documents found in the property were a passport and UK driver's licence in the name of Sylvia Griffiths. It took time to establish that *Sylvie Smith* was a stage name, and that Sylvia was originally from Tenby, in Wales.

The police followed the procedures for reporting the death of a foreign national, and the British Consulate in Nice was informed. Sylvia Griffiths was legitimately living and working in France which made things simple, and the machinery began to process a search for her next of kin to arrange repatriation of her body. A picture emerged in which Sylvia was linked to Timothy Thomas and their work as musicians until his accidental death. Records also showed that Timothy and Sylvia had a son, Simon Thomas. He was registered at a school in North Yorkshire and child benefit was being claimed for him by Mrs Joyce Budd.

The connection to Terry and Martha, and the open murder cases for them and Alwen Bevan, created a sensation about Sylvia's murder, and the tabloids on both sides of the English Channel were suddenly screeching their hysteria.

His nana wrapped her love around Benjamin Budd and refused to have anything to do with his mother's affairs.

The Lance Corporal

The fairground accident that killed his parents

changed Leon Cottam. A cocky, aggressive teenager became more sociable and compassionate. He stopped playing rugby, left the school CCF and chose humanities as his A level subjects despite being a more gifted scientist. His school was outwardly supportive of this altered personality and outlook, especially in light of what caused it. But, behind closed doors, he was deemed to have bottled it and to be cut from entirely the wrong cloth.

His sister recovered more quickly from their parents' deaths. She comforted and loved her young brother, and they became closer. But there was a company to run, and Michelle was plunged into the twin complexities of being out of her depth in business, but with a seemingly bottomless supply of cash.

Leon didn't care. Michelle was going to marry John Wallis and he knew the pair of them would make an abject mess of the company his mum and dad had built. He assured his own financial security from his parents' estate, then left John and Michelle to their fate.

After finishing his schooldays, Leon took a gap year with his girlfriend. He was hopelessly in love with Debra, and it was a long-term thing. They'd been sweethearts almost as soon as they met. She was eleven, he was twelve and she instantly loved Leon's extrovert wildness. He was practically feral. But where others were drawn to Leon's money and connections, even as a young teen, Debra just adored the brash way he converted dreams into reality.

They had their ups and downs, break ups and reunions, stormy rows and periods of calm intimacy and, by their mid-teens, these things had made them a perfect couple.

It was Debra who found Leon, drunk and disorderly with his mates, at the school playing fields. She bore the news that his parents had been killed and, for the next several weeks she held him whenever she could and sucked out every ounce of his screaming, grieving devastation. She stood next to him at his parents' funeral as he read a short speech and took him in her arms when he broke down after less than a minute.

Their time spent on trains, visiting the great cities of Europe, cemented their relationship. It helped Leon to convert his grief into the kind of wan memories that eradicate shock in favour of cuddly, rose-tinted melancholy. The trip was wonderful, and neither of them wanted it to end.

But they returned home, and it turned out that it had been a gap year for Debra, but not for Leon. She went ahead with her plans to go to university. He invested money in a pub, newly renovated and re-opened. He quickly developed a taste for wheeling and dealing in get-rich-quick schemes.

This success didn't stop Leon fretting that, when she returned from university, Debra would have changed, have new aspirations, and perhaps no longer love him. But when she returned to her parents' home, Debra hadn't changed at all. She simply wanted Leon to change. To revert, maybe even regress into the bold, spirited boy she had fallen in love with a dozen years before.

It caused periods of on/off, off/on uncertainty between them. Neither took solace with another lover, and both sought to repair things whenever there were breakdowns. But even when he proposed to Debra, there was a sense that it was a bow being tied, rather than a knot.

Debra's cold feet continued to chill their bed and, twice, she took off her engagement ring and placed it on his bedside table. It was back on her finger within days, but they were spending too much time dancing around the problem. One didn't like what the other wanted him to be. One couldn't bear the idea that she might end up unhappy with the wrong version of her man.

Leon spent hours each day fretting about what he should do. He saw his old life and mannerisms as part of a time when his parents had reined him in if needed, but more often encouraged his excesses. It was the 1980s: like greed, excess was also good in any given context. But when Jack and Tara died, Leon couldn't stay like that. He needed to be something new.

Now, for Debra, he needed not to be nice.

There was no overnight transformation. Leon practised his reversion to type via small moments in which he erupted with malice or abuse or, at best, over-assertive contempt. In business and social settings, it worked. People backed off, or backed down, or ran to hide. Occasionally there were murmurs that he had a drink or drug problem, which suited Leon; he never took narcotics, and only ever drank fine wine with Debra. He was clean as a whistle, but increasingly fought dirty.

When they married, Leon and Debra swaggered from the church and never saw the tall, dark-haired woman taking photos, or gazing disdainfully at the wedding party.

Leon truly didn't care about anything external. He loved Debra, née Walsh, now Cottam. His regression into his former self meant that she finally loved him too; utterly; inescapably. But above all, Leon loved himself. He was back where he was born to be. Son of Jack - his hero and mentor. Grandson of George - a distant war hero he'd love to have known. Grandma Sheila had always told Leon he was cut from that same cloth.

The happy couple spent a wild night at a hotel and jumped on a plane to Malaga just after lunch the next day. When they landed in the blazing heat of the Costa del Sol, Debra and Leon swanned through baggage reclaim pulling their neat little bags with wheels and extending handles. While the plebs were hopelessly trying to spot their scabby luggage on the noisy, stuttering carousel, Mr and Mrs Cottam had the keys to their hire car, and soon raced along the motorway.

Shortly after seven pm, Leon listened as the receptionist confirmed their luggage had arrived and was already in the room. Then the porter unlocked and opened their door so Leon could pick up his loving wife to carry her across the threshold and in to the first night of their three-week honeymoon. The hotel in Puerto Banus had everything they could wish for, and their third-floor suite had a balcony commanding spectacular views over the sea and the seething over-indulgence all around the pools and bars beneath.

Late in the afternoon of their second day, Leon's phone pinged an announcement that a message was waiting for him. It was from Michelle, telling them to expect a treat from her and John. Not much later, a tall woman in the hotel's uniform wheeled a trolley into the room and out on to the balcony. Dinner for two, a gift from Mr and Mrs Wallis with a complimentary bottle of vintage Rioja courtesy of the hotel's management. The woman showered them with congratulations and hoped that Mr and Mrs Cottam would return to the hotel time and time again.

Leon tore his gaze from those remarkable dark purple eyes, looked at the trolley of treats with astonishment and, after tipping her extravagantly, asked the woman if she would take a photo of them alongside the feast. While Leon explained how to work his camera, Debra uncorked the wine and poured two large glasses.

The camera, had it been found, would have contained two digital images. One, the smiling confidence of young newlyweds, holding up their glasses of carmine liquid in a toast that dripped with a kind of taunting arrogance. Second, those same faces, terror dawning as their bodies tumbled backwards from the balcony and down to their deaths in the sun.

TWELVE

A Child in Time

The health worker reported back that Erin was a curiously ambiguous child. She was bright, confident eight-year-old with plenty to say. She could be smart and perceptive yet seemed to harbour some strange hidden complexity. The two episodes in which Erin had climbed up high indicated an absence of any sense of risk, and this was borne out by some of her answers to questions. She understood danger but perceived it as something that wasn't physical or rational. Danger was everywhere, Erin told the health worker, but a child climbing high was much less threatening than someone in a car, or in a plane or sailing on the sea.

After each of her meetings with the health worker, Erin told Brigit and Louise she was getting nothing from the process. She'd made up her mind that *they* were evil and filled with no good purpose and it troubled her that neither Louise nor Brigit could see this.

The tension being caused in their home became too much for Louise. Neither the moments of passionate pleasure she still enjoyed with Brigit, nor the contented domestic environment they'd created, provided any comfort for the fact that Louise increasingly felt Erin was malevolent and destructive. When she discussed this with Brigit, it ended in a terrible but inevitable resignation. A loving couple concluded they could only remain together at arm's length. Louise couldn't stay in what had been a happy family home. Brigit couldn't bear the knowledge that the love of her life would go back to being a date, not a partner.

Erin sensed the resentment she'd caused and tried to make amends by inviting Louise to dinner every day and encouraging her mothers to meet and enjoy time together. It made no difference. The health worker, when confronted by the news that Louise and Brigit were no longer co-habiting, seemed torn between relief and inexperience. Like Doctor Bowen, he had limited understanding of how a child could flourish in a family without a father. But his suggestions about ways in which Erin could prosper in a single parent household fell on deaf ears. Erin kept up her commentary that the professionals overseeing her problems were fools and therefore dangerous. Brigit, increasingly, believed her daughter.

But Brigit was also bereft. Her love for Louise had been deep and wild for more than a decade. They were still lovers, but the decision to disconnect from living together was really a separation, and it caused great waves of sadness and hurt. She began to have paranoid visions that Louise was seeing others and having more fun and better sex. Their love making became less spontaneous, more difficult and, somehow, it lacked all the easy intimacy and fun it had always held.

When the upset overwhelmed her, Brigit took a long walk along the coast. At journey's end, she dropped down to the beach and, sitting in the shallows, tried to commune with what she held dear. For the first time in more than fifteen years, Brigit spoke aloud to her mother and grandmother to ask for their love and guidance. The sea held her captive, soaking her clothes and rushing around her legs and hips and waist. She lay down flat in the rippling shallow surf and let it flood over her and found herself laughing that she was soaked from toe to top. The laughter was short lived. Brigit was wrapped up, as if mummified. She was Alis's daughter, with Stina and Ava, Megan and Bethan watching over her. Yet that powerful legacy was lurching towards what might be a messy end. She wanted Erin to be the child that grew into that legacy. That was the plan. That was the idea. But there was question after question that made Erin's part in the legacy seem remote.

When she was in her thirteenth year, Erin ran away. She left home to walk to school and, instead, caught the bus that took her to a rail connection that ended in Hereford. She stole money and a debit card from Brigit's bag, but neither was enough to allow her to stay at a hotel. She looked older than she was, but still couldn't pass as eighteen. It left her with one last hope, the address on her mother's business card.

The trading estate was busily industrious, and the manager of the production plant quickly realised she had a problem to solve when Erin arrived, asking to see Gerard.

His battered old car pulled up and parked outside the unit, and he greeted Erin with great warmth. An hour later, Pauline Rhodes was helping Erin find something to wear among the content of her daughter's over-subscribed wardrobe. Gerard was speaking to Brigit who was shocked and angered by Erin's actions and insisted she would drive over to collect and berate her errant daughter. Gerard proposed a different strategy. Let him and Pauline take the strain for a couple of nights. Make Erin feel at home. Create some room for her to be whatever she needed to be away from her home. Then bring her back and enjoy a reunion and some seafood down there on the coast. Gerard finessed this proposal by calling Louise and suggesting Brigit might need company.

Erin spent the next few days with a family she didn't know but suspected was somehow a huge part of her life. She became great friends with Pauline and Gerard's daughter, Jessica, and developed an unbearable crush on their son, Will. It was Gerard and Jessica that accompanied Erin back to St Davids. All the way, they sang songs, old, new, borrowed and blue. When they reached the long stretch of sand at Newgale, Gerard pulled into a car park and suggested a paddle. A well-timed text ensured that, as happy splashing was in full flight on the beach, Brigit arrived and ran at top speed into the surf and an unstoppable embrace with Erin. It seemed completely natural that five fully clothed people should be like this, soaked and chilled by the waves yet happy and overjoyed.

That evening, Louise served them all a simple meal and Erin sat glumly as everyone tucked in. It was a reunion in many ways, and it felt like good company and simple family ties had been joined.

Erin was exhausted, physically and emotionally, and told Brigit she needed to be in her bed and for her mama to read her some poetry. Later, as she lay listening to Brigit reciting a poem about wild geese, Erin became mute, then tearful. She told Brigit she believed Gerard was her father and that was why she had gone to find him. They hugged and kissed, and Brigit said Gerard might be the best father anyone could want, but he was simply one of their best friends and a powerful force for good in their lives.

Over breakfast, Gerard told Erin she should come to

stay often and spend time in the finest city this side of the North Sea. Everyone smiled, and perhaps everyone agreed. But there was a journey to make and school to attend. Erin said she needed Gerard and Jessica to stay but finally accepted they must leave. They all wanted more times like this. And maybe there would be.

Or maybe there wouldn't. While Erin performed well at school, both academically, in sport and in drama, her wild, complex being was slowly causing cracks in all she touched. This complexity was made worse by her ability to switch on and off the more destructive sides of her character. An adept scientist and gifted poet, she seemed to view academic achievement as worthless. She performed well in each year's exams and constantly achieved the best results but cared less. Her disciplinary record was dreadful, not least because she could be arrogant, abusive and aggressive towards her peers. Erin matured quickly and socialised with the older pupils at school, developing a reputation as a hoochie. Brigit didn't object too strenuously to this until she found out that Erin was having unprotected sex, often and wherever it could be had. She had also begun to flirt openly with older men whenever she encountered them.

One evening, Erin arrived home with a bruised eye, lacerations on her face and neck and a torn blouse. She had stepped over a line with a man visiting the city, and his wife quickly attacked. The police arrived to investigate a complaint that Erin had attempted to lure the man to have sex with her. It was a serious matter, because Erin was a minor. She made no attempt to defend herself and she was given a formal warning about her future conduct.

Brigit was furious, sent Erin to her room and told her not to come out again. Ever.

A long conversation with Louise didn't dissipate Brigit's rage. The two women sat at the kitchen table, one with her head in her hands, the other staring with dismay and chewing her lip.

Louise refrained from saying what was in her heart. That she might not be able to keep going. That Erin was deliberately driving them apart. But she loved Brigit and was torn by contrasting needs: for some normality away from her partner; and her desire, passion and love for Brigit. Louise stretched out her hand, took hold of Brigit's and told her they needed to try again with Erin. Something would work, eventually. Brigit shook her head. Her daughter had gone too far this time. It wouldn't be long before she did something disastrous.

Louise told Brigit she doubted it.

THE LANCE CORPORAL

Michelle Wallis often counted the ways in which she hated her life. She'd have hated her family too, if any of them was still alive. Apart from Jake, of course. He was very much alive. She didn't hate her son, but she didn't love him enough to keep him here at home. The boarding school in Wales had been a strange choice. Michelle and John had never really agreed it was the right school for Jake, but he'd started there the previous September and, in all their discussions and emails, said he was happy and blossoming. Each parent presumed the other had made the decision and acquiesced in it. The removal of their son to a college, in a small community in the hills between Brecon and Carmarthen was, in the final analysis, a sign of their love for him. An investment in him. A way to ensure he was cared for.

Otherwise, *care* was a word she struggled with. Deep down, Michelle knew she didn't care for people and had never once cared for her forebears, such as they were. Sheila Cottam, just sixty-four when Michelle was born, had become a raddled old lush by the time her granddaughter was old enough to really know her. Reeking of cigarettes and whisky, her grandma was prematurely aged with a streak of bitterness about her life and past. It defined how she behaved in every family relationship, young or old, and infected any family occasion with joyless gloom. Jack and Tara always put a brave face on it, but Michelle knew that her mother despised Sheila, especially for the ways in which she controlled Jack.

Then, by the time she was ten, Michelle realised that Sheila also stank of piss and BO and churned out an eternal dialogue about how her husband George had been an evil bastard that deserved his fate. No one was listening and everyone was dancing around the problem. The solution, as with so much of the family's way of working, was financial and cold rather than emotional, and Sheila was consigned to a care home for her last few years.

Ironic, that word *care*.

Michelle had learned to love her parents, especially the ruthlessness with which Tara had managed Sheila's demise and cut her out of everyone's lives. But Michelle saw plainly that Jack and Tara placed wealth and business above love of their children. Her brother was given slightly more attention, for Jack connived in his son's laddish belligerence and favoured that over Michelle's need for solitude and space. In their parents' eyes, the children were accessories: a sign of success; feted in their social lives; dressed up in the finest, newest threads; free from defects; educated at whatever cost, regardless of quality; and ultimately more perfect than everyone else's perfect offspring. During her teens, Michelle's love for her parents slowly diluted until all that was left was duty.

The day they died, fried by whatever freakery caused that accident, Michelle inherited no legacy of happy family times or memories. She was handed responsibilities she was ill-equipped to manage: a business, an unhappy younger sibling, a rushed marriage. And more money than she could count.

Her care for Leon, especially when she saw the depth of his grief for their parents, was real but with a short shelf life. She diverted all her love into his well-being, and they found ways to move on. They also found a kind of entente, in which they accepted they didn't really love each other and had nothing in common. The one thing that united them was a shared knowledge and unhappiness about their parents' lack of love for them. This made them relaxed and on good terms, without the need to be close or dependent. But, with some notable exceptions, they ended up having almost nothing to do with each other. When Leon gave Michelle away at her wedding, it was a proud moment. When Michelle asked Leon to be one of Jake's godfathers, he accepted with pride. When they asked Michelle to play a part in Leon and Debra's wedding, she was delighted.

Nine years later, Michelle still struggled to believe that her brother never returned from his honeymoon. An investigation concluded that a terrible accident had happened, resulting from extreme drunkenness. Several empty bottles of wine and another of brandy were littered around the room's balcony. Fast-food boxes were piled up inside the room. No official ever used the words, but Michelle's take was that Leon and

Debra had indulged in a colossal and uncharacteristic bender. She cared even less about her brother and sister-in-law when the whole business of repatriating their bodies fell to her.

She'd stopped using coke when Leon needed her in 1986. His death, and all that it entailed, led her back to it. Nine years since the end of the Cottam line. Now there was just her, Jake and John and it was all about the Wallis line, but Michelle wasn't sure she cared much about that either.

Sitting under the parasol on their balcony, she gazed across the green. The dinner party later, with friends over near Southport, was something to look forward to and she sipped on her tea to wash down another benzo. Really, she just wanted to be elsewhere. The ever-present irritation of constantly circling traffic formed a backdrop of noise and exhaust fumes. At the far side of the green, the small pond had its usual gaggle of folks chucking things to the ducks. Dogs yapped. Kids screamed.

What was her life for? How many more lies could she live in? She'd married John because of his money and compelling sexual delivery, but away from the glittering prizes and his splendid cock, he'd proved to be a bad partner. Between them, they'd turned Cottam's into a shambling mess in which they always seemed to be just one step away from litigation. It had failed miserably within twenty years of Jack and Tara's deaths, though they'd kept their heads and money out of the problem by executing a hasty exit via the bankruptcy ticket. John had come up with that solution, and they'd suffered some indignities as a result; name calling in the street; threatening letters and phone calls. She didn't care about the people who were cut loose by the failed company, nor by anyone affected in similar fiascos. But she did fret about the rising levels of hatred poured on her in the latest on-line craze, social media. They'd been called all sorts by people, some of whom threatened to tip off the police about their drug use and tax evasion. It all got nasty, and they'd needed to threaten the people involved with legal action if it continued. The warning worked for a while, but an undercurrent remained and, reluctantly, Michelle quit the sites. Yet she found herself riven by paranoia about what might still be being said.

Alongside these trials, the thing that felt right was those moments when she and John ingested their little white lines. They made everything seem sane and nothing really mattered except another hyped-up discussion on the phone with whoever would listen.

A message popped up on her mobile. It was John. He was leaving the office and would be home soon with a nice surprise. Michelle replied that she liked surprises, especially if they'd marched all the way from Bolivia. John confirmed they had. She finished her tea then floated inside to get things ready for her man and his packages.

The surprise was twofold. When he walked into their living room, John had a hand behind his back. The other waved a small bag. There were at least five grammes in it, but before John could confirm it, he pulled his hand from behind his back to reveal an inky black kitten.

She told him off for not remembering that a pet was too much for them to care for, but it was clear that John meant well.

Even better news, John told her, was that the five grammes he'd brought were authentic, pure and clean. They'd get a fantastic buzz, every line, and the guy in Lytham had assured it, like he always did.

While John prepared the accoutrements for their ritual, Michelle took the kitten and felt quite drawn to its improbable beauty. Such perfect eyes and fluid movements, even for such a young kitten; she was quite adorable. The animal was less enamoured and lashed a paw at Michelle, slicing a laceration across her hand. With violence, Michelle knocked the tiny creature away. It landed on its feet just before it hit the glass doors leading to the balcony. Unperturbed by its rejection, the kitten sat and watched as the man and woman began cutting lines of their executive class cocaine on silvery trays, then inhaled it through silvery tubes. The ritual included an extravagant, almost theatrical post-inhalation performance: mutual acknowledgement of the quality and effect of the drug.

Before the man and woman could bend to ingest their next lines, the kitten saw them start to shake and fit, as if they'd been electrocuted. Blood suddenly streamed from their noses, then their performance was nothing more than a collapse.

The kitten, now a cat, licked its paw and slunk away from the bodies in their last act.

THIRTEEN

Erin

Louise had got it wrong.

Brigit had got it right.

Like the final act in a tragedy, it was always going to happen. The misery Erin caused was unspeakable. The end of a line. Yet, as in any good drama, the means justified the end.

That incident with the police made Erin pliant and quiet at home but resulted in difficulties at school, mainly involving taunting and bullying. Once, she would have fought back. But now she was potentially subject to prosecution if she stepped out of line, Erin kept her mouth shut and her fists behind her back. The unpleasantness died down and, as she approached her GCSEs, the school sent positive messages to Brigit about how well Erin was going to perform in the coming exams.

Out of school, Erin was being very good. She didn't go to parties and abstained from any form of contact with men, young or older. In fact, she imposed her own curfew and began to be more helpful around the house. Brigit and Louise felt the benefit of a less complicated daughter and, in the months leading up to Erin's 16th birthday, there was an air of contentment.

When her exams were finished, Brigit and Erin took a holiday in France. For a week, they hiked in the Ardèche, swam in rivers and lakes and slept in the open air. Then on to La Rochelle for a second week of sunshine, sea and a little luxury. It was a happy union. Brigit felt closer to her daughter than at any time and

Erin saw how much she had missed. Her mother was beautiful, talented and loving. Erin had neglected all the things Brigit could have been for her. As they walked, they talked and learned many things about each other. Erin finally learned to love her mother.

Louise joined them for the last few days on the coast and saw a transformation. The mother and daughter that greeted her at Bordeaux airport seemed more like sisters. Erin had gained a kind of gravitas and lost all the spiked, sharp, rough edges. Brigit was back to being the woman Louise had fallen in love with. Physically more lithe and loose, Brigit's face showed freedom from the all-consuming tension that had for so long seemed to define her. Louise had seen, in all these sixteen years with Erin, how the greatest weight Brigit bore was that her daughter somehow represented loss.

Louise had never stopped desiring Brigit but maybe she'd lost a little love for her. The years together had become marred by Erin's problems. Too often there was silence when there should have been words. Louise and Brigit always agreed they had equal responsibilities for Erin, to be her parents at all times. That agreement ended up as something less, in which Louise saw she bore none of the pain and ended up with none of the influence she'd once believed might exist. The wild, sensual beginnings of Brigit and Louise's relationship had been a foundation for everything they did, yet lately Louise sometimes wondered if she could bear to be with Brigit if she was merely an afterthought; secondary; a passenger. The fact that desire remained while love waned seemed too functional, too ephemeral. Shouldn't both be equal in a true partnership?

These feelings sometimes made Louise fill with

doubt. But the burnished, sun-kissed woman she took in her arms after all those days apart made Louise feel their love could not be questioned.

Erin passed all her GCSEs with one or two exceptional results. She celebrated with friends at the mass party they held on Whitesands beach, but when some started smoking weed and the sounds of fumbling and fucking filled the air, Erin walked home and drank tea with Brigit.

As the summer of 2012 blended effortlessly into autumn, Erin, Brigit and Louise travelled to Hereford and stayed with Gerard and Pauline to join the celebrations for their son's wedding. It was a joyful and perfectly low-key day, made doubly happy by Jessica Rhodes' announcement that her boyfriend, Joe Bishop, had proposed and they were engaged. It was a long weekend of celebration.

On their return trip, Louise watched Brigit driving and wondered if she should propose. She knew they should marry; had done for weeks. Her hesitation was driven by what she'd seen in Brigit's eyes while she watched Sophie and Will Rhodes posing for photographs. Louise's gaze kept returning to Brigit's face. The love of her life seemed consumed by sadness. Brigit's eyes held the dull despair of the dying, as if this tableau of love was the last she would see. It made no sense. After all the reignited joy since the holiday in France, Louise felt anxious that the silence in the car was significant. The closer they got to St Davids, the deeper her disquiet. Not even Brigit's frequent, prolonged strokes of Louise's thigh cut through the anxiety.

What Louise had failed to spot outside the church was the change in Erin. All the months of self-control and peace were dissolving. Her crush on Will Rhodes had itself been crushed. Her bubbling friendship with Jessica, in which they'd become correspondents on social media and in letters, had never mentioned Joe Bishop. Why would that be? Why would Gerard, the powerful force for good in their lives, have kept all these things from her?

Erin was wild with spite.

She sat in the back seat of Brigit's car and observed the uneasy silence in front of her with a combination of malice, knowledge and glee. Unlike Louise, Erin understood the sadness in Brigit's eyes. She knew what it meant, and where that sadness would end. She should feel the same, for that end involved her. Her own feelings were submerged, for Erin had been consumed by the rage she felt about the way two dreams had evaporated back there in Tupsley. Will and Jessica. How could they? All those smiles for the cameras. All that sickly sweet love and affection. Who was it for? What did it achieve? All the gambolling, unremitting joy of weddings, one in the present, one still to come, had left Erin's composure shredded.

As they dropped down the hill in to Solva, Erin made up her mind. Something had to be done, and she had to be the one to do it.

Brigit went back to Hereford a few weeks later to complete a transaction Gerard had set up. She was gone most of a week and, when she returned in the early hours that Friday morning, there was an eery quiet in the house. Louise's things had all gone from their bedroom. Clothes. Luggage. Jewellery. Not one room in the house retained any trace of Louise.

Then Brigit found a room that did. On the kitchen table, where so many conversations had made their lives stable, Brigit found a padded envelope on top of a sheet of paper. Louise's untidy writing covered the middle third of the page. The words cut a slice out of Brigit's heart.

"My Love,

Except you're not, are you?

Nor am I yours.

Not anymore. How can we be whatever we are supposed to be when something like this can happen?

Look inside the envelope, Brigit.

Your daughter has finally won. It makes me physically sick to recall that, once, she was supposed to be my daughter too. I need to forget that. I need to forget her. I need to forget you. I need to forget us.

There is a life for me to live away from the uncertain mania you and Erin represent. I know I was never part of your lives. I can't forgive you for making me your pawn."

Brigit folded the paper in two and sat down to peel open the adhesive flap on the envelope. It contained something cylindrical and when she peered inside, Brigit sighed with upset. A tear squeezed from the outside of each eye. It was Louise's dildo, the one they had used often. More than a decade of visions flashed before Brigit's eyes. The writhing, passionate, unstoppable ways she and Louise had made each other come. It had never once been imperfect in any way. They had been the utmost of lovers, whenever and wherever it could be done.

Now the tears were rolling, and Brigit's mouth dropped open, her jaw shaking. She put the package down, wiped her eyes and re-read Louise's words. And now, she knew. This wasn't a memento of their times together, a way to recall all the love making and desire. It wasn't a gift, perhaps still bearing the final scent of Louise's most recent orgasm. "Your daughter has finally won."

Brigit slid the dildo out from its padded haven. It had five words written on it in black, indelible ink. "This is not my father."

She suppressed the howling scream of rage and dashed up the stairs to Erin's room. It was empty, the bed made, the floor free of its usual piles of discarded clothes. The small desk held her daughter's laptop and phone.

Brigit found Erin sitting on the stone steps of the Celtic Cross. In the dead of night, their eyes met, and a mother's anger melted away as she captured a daughter's thoughts.

You knew this had to be done, mama. You couldn't keep that alive alongside all that needs to happen now; alongside all that is still to come. It seems like pain but, really, I made her happy. She just doesn't know it yet.

They sat in silence and held hands, staring up the street from which Megan and Bethan had carried baby Stina away. Where Cissy and Owen James had been killed. Where Thomas Harty had fallen in love with Stina, for all the world to see. Where Alis and Rhod had shown Brigit their home town, capturing a kiss at this very spot.

It was time to go.

They parted in London. A fast train took them there from Cardiff and another train in a tube carried them to Canary Wharf station. Amongst the glass and metal, the water and stone, and in the great curve of a river, Erin held her mama. No words or tears came. Their dark purple eyes met, and they kissed one last time.

THE POLICE SERGEANT

Susan Morgan opened the curtains at the small B&B and gazed out over a developing Lakeland scene. It was just before six am, first light on an early autumn day. Trevor's light snoring continued to fill the room and she pulled on her noise reducing headphones then selected an old Genesis album from her music app. The tunes and words seemed to sit nicely alongside the pastoral scene entangled before her: rolling hills; a verdant valley; distant peaks, silhouettes against the rising sun.

It was their last day here in Eskdale. Today's walk would be a modest one compared to the last three days. Around eight miles; along the valley; then a steady climb up through the forest; the Tarn; back down into Boot. Then, a freshen up somehow and into the car for the trip back home. First, though, there was breakfast then packing. She calculated that, once they'd loaded up the car and checked out, they'd be ready to walk by ten.

Trevor looked at Susan. She was serene and glowing, very much in love with the view and, perhaps, with whatever music accompanied it. These few days in the Lakes had been restful, a balm to soothe away the pressures they'd both felt in the build up to, and aftermath of their daughter's wedding. Those punishing days had induced a kind of mania. In between coping with Susan's increasing bouts of panic about the big day, and with his daughter's own distress about committing to marriage at twenty-three, Trevor had very nearly lost the plot completely at work. Something he'd seen in the faces at meetings, that whole *you're too old for this aren't you, Trevor?* motif had finally been made more explicit at a one-to-one with his boss. *It's a young crowd here, Trevor, so there's no shame in admitting you've lost a step. I know fifty-five doesn't seem old, but alongside these young guns, you've got to consider your options.* It had made him resentful and hurt.

It also made him forget something he'd set his heart on - a fitting celebration for their silver wedding anniversary. But that simply became another thorn in his side; something else he felt slipping through his fingers every time he tried to convert his thoughts into actions.

The last person he'd expected to impart wisdom about these stresses and strains was his son. They were at the pub so Trevor could practice his father of the bride speech and Jason stopped his dad after less than a minute and told him to relax. It made Trevor start to cry, which made Jason hug him and ask what was wrong. It all came out. All the things Trevor and Susan couldn't cope with, and which threatened their marriage. All the reasons why Kylie's marriage to Phillip Lomas felt wrong. All the things that the family had endured since that day, forty-two years previously, when Dewi and Claire, then Stephen and Lizzie had died. Such inexplicable and seemingly unending tragedy.

When Trevor became speechless with a kind of grief, Jason held him more tightly. They rarely saw eye to eye, but his dad was his dad, and his dad was crying in public. It was time for simple affection, empathy, a child's love. The love eventually included going to the bar and ordering a bottle of rum, which the two men started to sip at and, slowly, Trevor calmed down. He had another go at his speech, and Jason applauded constantly and shouted *more*. In the end, Jason giggled his way through two expansive ideas. One -

that Trevor should get hammered before delivering his speech at the wedding. Two – that the silver wedding celebration was too soon after Kylie's big day; therefore, keep it simple; do something grand later in the year.

By the time they'd finished two thirds of the rum, a walking holiday in the Lakes was deemed a perfect way to both rest and celebrate. A couple of days later, Jason had found and booked a few days in the tiny hamlet. All he needed was his father's credit or debit card.

The walk took them past the church of St Catherine and across stepping stones that seemed almost magical in their haphazard shapes and sizes. It was a cool day, but the walk was warming, and the last few days had been good for Susan and Trevor. They stopped often to share moments. Photos. Selfies. When signals allowed, announcements were made on social media about their whereabouts and sights seen. The walk became a joyous event, binding a couple whose lives had seemed torn.

Susan linked her arm through Trevor's and pulled him to a halt. They kissed, tentatively at first, and then with passion. It was twenty-five years to the day since they married. It was twelve years since his mum and dad had died in Spain, followed by Trevor's grisly discovery of his dead brother. They had recovered, rebuilt and there were still many years to come in which they could be happy. The selfie they took, arm in arm and doe-eyed in love, was soon receiving likes, loves and adoring commentary in the assorted places they uploaded it.

The forest trail was open and bright, but the trees either side were dark. It felt good to escape from it as they climbed quickly to a small promontory then across boggy ground. When they reached Blea Tarn, both drew in a breath at the understated prettiness of the scene. It was a small, vaguely oval lake in a kind of aquatic amphitheatre.

Susan soon took off her boots and socks to dabble her feet in the lake. It was clear and the icy-cool of its touch was invigorating. Trevor took her photo, laughing in the shallows. More selfies then, reshod, they began to walk along the shore towards the higher ground. Their map indicated they had about a mile to go, across marshy terrain, then down into the valley. Above them, as they climbed away from the waterside, a figure appeared. She was tall, with dark hair and seemed transfixed by their progress. Trevor waved, then hailed her. She waved back half-heartedly, more of a dismissive flap of the hand than anything. Then she bounded off in the opposite direction.

As they began their descent towards Boot, they reached a small wooden fence. About tummy high, made from solid posts and strips of four by two, the structure formed a barrier to a hole in the ground. A small sign informed them to take care, since this was a mine shaft. Looking down into the hole, Trevor could see it was not that deep; about fifteen feet down there was what looked like solid ground. But then, as he looked more closely, it was possible to see that a smaller tunnel dropped down into darkness. These details didn't trouble Susan, who was more concerned with the wonderful scenery, where hills and clouds seemed to mesh together in grandeur. Taking out her digital camera, she took photo after photo of the landscape, sighing with joy and wonder as she snapped. This was a perfect end to their celebrations.

They agreed that the view was a worthy background for yet another selfie and spent several moments composing the right position for their faces and the scenery. Then they captured endless selfies, with smiles, kisses and hugs and soon Susan held her phone up especially high to capture them in an embrace. Trevor lost his footing and stumbled backwards, throwing his arm out to use the wooden barrier to steady their fall. There was no barrier. Just a hole in the ground.

Down by St Catherine's Church, two walkers heading out on their hike passed a tall, raven-haired woman who took no notice of their greeting. She seemed distracted and rushed as she explained her destination was the other side of the stepping-stones. The couple shrugged and wished her well, but the woman's curt demeanour had upset one of them. As they walked along the riverside, admiring the pools and crystal waters, she kept looking back to see what the woman was up to. Her partner's thoughts, that it wasn't worth bothering about an ignorant old woman, led to a minor disagreement about the dark-haired woman's age. She couldn't have been more than forty – forty-five tops. The annoyed one looked back towards the stepping-stones, and she saw the object of her annoyance slowly balancing on and pacing across the stones between the banks of the Esk. Her partner, indifferent and eager to make progress, was already several paces further along the riverbank. With a final look back at the stepping-stones, she was surprised to see the tall, dark-haired woman step down into the river and, as she immersed into the water, she dissolved.

FOURTEEN

Today

Ben watched Erin start to cry but she turned away from him. She'd slowly filled up with something akin to rage. The time spent in narration of her mother's demise seemed to have overwhelmed her. It wasn't rage in the end. It was unstoppable sorrow.

Her voice was shaking. 'Do you believe what I've told you, Ben? Have you followed what all this means, and understood your part in it? I can't tell whether I should keep going with all the stories and explanations or go straight to the fiery dénouement.'

Now she turned and walked to his side. 'I know you think I've done evil, cruel things to you. But I've cared for you too. Cleaning up the bed. Feeding you. Washing you. Reading these bedtime stories to help you sleep. Or narrating them, I suppose. I mean, Ben, I've kept you alive. This is a good thing, surely?'

Erin's gaze was fierce now and she looked up and down his body before locking her eyes on his. 'I think I've even started to desire you, Ben. Which is troublesome, isn't it? Problematic. Especially since you don't feel the same.'

She took his hand. It was the first time she'd touched Ben without him feeling a chill emanating from her fingers. 'I wish I could change that. Make you see me as desirable. But I totally get that these things between us - abduction, imprisonment, torture - might be a barrier for you. Totally.'

With a sigh, Erin dropped his hand and waved her own dismissively at him before walking over to the table. She brushed her fingers over the assorted items, like she was wondering which type of chocolate to buy and indulge in.

'Shall I finish the story then, Ben? Tell you how we closed down all the terrible things that happened to my ancestors? Cancelled out those families and their right to live on when my family had been denied their lives? There isn't much left to tell. Apart from you. There's a lot to say about and do to you. Let's dim the lights. We will start with the business of Business.'

Gerard looked at Erin after he'd read, then re-read the letter. It was a deed in which Brigit signed over all her company shares and ownership rights to her daughter. It instructed the board to accept Brigit's resignation as managing director, explaining that she was embarking on a lengthy leave of absence in which she would be travelling overseas unable to fulfil her role and duty of care to the business.

Erin could see the disbelief in Gerard's eyes and suspected it was mingled with distrust.

Whatever troubled him was converted to shock when Erin said she wanted to negotiate the sale of her shares, either directly to Gerard and other major shareholders or perhaps by finding a buyer for the whole company. The news in the letter was a complication. Erin's desire to quit was like a slap in her mother's face, which Gerard bore in Brigit's place. He felt it was appropriate to take one for the team now that Brigit had made herself incommunicado. Erin was in charge. And her first act as MD was to sell. If he hadn't been so dazed, Gerard might have admired Erin's bold start. Once he recovered, his main concern was to take urgent steps to protect his own investment.

They worked hard together and found a buyer. The sale netted a lot of cash. After that was done, Gerard and Erin parted company with neither fanfare nor sentiment. Her final request, pretty much as an afterthought, was that Louise must be tracked down and given some of the money. It was the first and only time Gerard wondered if there might be a heart beating in Erin's chest.

During the process of the sale, Erin also sold her family home. She felt a growing, intense need to travel; to have no roots; to be stateless; to be elsewhere for real, not just as a state of mind. She felt all the same things, the tremors of legacy that had been felt by Brigit and Alis. But in her head, these were irritants. Whatever needed to be done was a mission she found distressing. Here she was: the end of a line; pointed at a single objective; to find all the places where the last few seeds had been blown to and landed; those weeds were nearly all gone; but what then? Ever since Brigit had explained all this, Erin hadn't been able to process the reality that, when she'd found the last Morgan, Cottam and Bevan, her time also ran out.

'It really started to get me down, Ben. Mama told me what to expect. *Visions* she called them. But what I got was nothing of the sort.'

She left the room and clattered down the stairs, soon to return holding a tablet. 'It all happened on this thing. I could be happily selling my soul to the demonic masses on social media or fooling with willing beaux. My god, some men like a virtual wank don't they, Ben? They probably think it's fucking, I suppose, if you scream long and loud enough for their benefit. Anyway: I could be doing bad things of one sort or another and these items would randomly pop up, like on one of those machines they used once upon a time. What were they called?'

Erin looked askance at Ben. He kept his eyes as wide open as he could manage. 'A telex. Yes! That's the very thing, Ben. Thank you. It was all incoming. Tickertape. Rat-a-tat-tat. Here's a name, a place, another name and a smiling face that you need to know. Or whatever. Detail. Data. You know what to do, Erin. Realise, resolve, repeat. Yet despite this perfect technology it all seemed scattered and inconclusive. Like something wasn't reaching me. Like there was a broken signal.'

She turned the tablet round so Ben could see the screen. It was blank. She threw it on the bed near Ben's legs. He could see that mania simmering up. He knew it now.

'And there was all of mama and grandmama's handywork, like I had never been told it. Weddings. Boring. Funerals. Double boring. Crying. Smiles. Sometimes together. Sometimes unconnected. Couples. Families. Mama there, with a camera or camcorder.'

Erin made a yawning motion with her hand.

'And then my targets. One crying because his drug addled parents were dead, and their funeral left him all alone to go racing off in his toy car to be a man. Another with his woman in their mobile home, at it like rabbits. The last of them safe, or so they thought when they fucked off to France.

Why was this my problem, Ben? I don't mind telling you I thought long and hard about doing a runner. Who'd know? Just think. If I'd ignored it all, you'd be downstairs right now pacing up and down, entertaining imaginary masses with your dubious wit and wisdom. Blithely ignorant of all the pain and misery involved.

So, I did fuck off. Once mama's company was off my hands, and I had no home to manage and some money to waste, I jumped on to trains. Retracing things. I needed the knowledge. I needed the certainty that this was all real.'

Erin stepped from the train at Glasgow Central and watched her fellow passengers make their way to the barriers and exit. This was another country, bold and yearning for independence, but the building looked the same as any other railway terminus. The announcements were a little different. More lilting? But the same language; the same imparted knowledge; the same ennui. This could be anywhere. A place where you arrived or departed. Where you were welcomed. Where you waved goodbye.

She'd left London five and bit hours earlier, and the time on the train had left her feeling compressed. Even in first class there was no freedom from a herd. Almost from the start, she'd watched the suited, booted creatures pounding on laptops, expounding on phones, compounding everyone's misery. Whenever the males of the herd turned their grazing to gazing, she smiled back, wondering if they understood she was the hunter. But she was quickly bored by that sport and diverted her attention to the scenery flashing past her window. Out there, less ridiculous herds could be seen, and Erin hated that she was stuck inside when she wanted freedom to roam with all those wild creatures.

Then the day darkened, and the rain and mists left her feeling all she had was a countdown to the end of the line.

A slow stroll along the platform eased some of the tension, then she bought coffee and a pastry from one of the vendors in the concourse. The predictable tastes, processed to perfection, made Erin calm. She had nearly two hours to wait for her next train, followed by another five hours in a cylinder, so she went and mingled among the city crowds.

It took no time at all to reach the Clyde, and Erin walked along the riverside. It was many miles to the sea, but she walked towards it, breathing in the splendour of a mighty river's history. The Waverley steamer sat proudly at its mooring, ready for its next cargo of eager sightseers. Constant traffic noise blasted overhead and made her gaze up at the bridge, as if hoping it would dissolve to make the sounds stop. They continued to roar, and it made her snarl across at the far bank and its glassy visage. If it wasn't for *over there* no one would need this tumultuous cacophony.

Erin's snarl turned to a squint of malice as three young men drawled something at her. Their limbs were slack and gangling, like marionettes. Instead of strings, these puppets were loosely empowered by lager. Another torrent of wordless sound gushed towards her, like liquid. It might have been threatening or flirting or just about anything. Erin replied and what she said made them recoil. She headed back towards the central station, unhindered.

The statue appeared as she emerged from the dark shadow of yet another road bridge. A woman's figure, arms aloft, fists clenched. A mottled face, pock-marked but noble. The ankle-length dress of stone failing to hide a determined pose. Erin stopped and stood in the lea of this striking effigy and felt a surge of belonging. Then she shook her head as she read the statue's dedication. The only words she registered were *Better to die...*

It was no distance back to Queen Street station. Erin passed a shopping mall, like a giant glassy slug barring her way, then strolled on into an area with grand, sandstone buildings and their countless mercantile tales. Something here oppressed her, and she rushed onwards, to get on a train and leave subjugation behind.

When that train crawled out from Queen Street station, Erin was staring with astonishment at her phone. It showed there were twenty-four scheduled stops on the second leg of her journey. It beggared belief. Then she studied their names and loved that many of them were lyrical and evocative. Erin began to imagine what life could be like in Arrochar & Tarbet, or Arisaig. And what would await her when she crossed the Bridge of Orchy. This reverie kept her happy, as did the increasingly powerful landscape the train was bisecting. All that water. All those hills and mountains. An emerald wilderness with an apparently unlimited horizon.

The rain closed in again making the ferry crossing gloomy and unexceptional. It didn't take long and, more than thirteen hours after leaving London, Erin reached the island she'd needed to visit. The short walk to a bed and breakfast took a little over ten minutes: half a mile of comfort; the only comfort she'd felt on the entire trip.

It was a cosy, relaxing place to rest and she slept well.

With kind hospitality ringing in her ears, Erin walked back up the road and caught a bus to Broadford, then another to Portree. As a bright, sunny day unfolded, she became a little lost in love with all she could see.

The island seemed alive with simple beauty. She really didn't want this journey to end.

At the Portree and Raasay registry office, she found she had no idea what questions to ask or what answers to give. She'd made this journey without preparation of any kind. It was an impulse to retrace voyages, to seek understanding and to make sense of all the hand-me-downs and bequests. The clerk wasn't busy but didn't know how to help when Erin's sole reference point was someone called Ava. Both of them became tetchy and impatient.

It was clear she needed time to collate her thoughts, so Erin smiled at the man and calmed the situation. She said she'd return later with more details, then left the building and walked along the quayside to the ferry terminal. This wasn't a pretty place, but the lifeboat station was there too, and Erin cocked her head to look at it, as if it might hold clues.

What did she really know about her great-great-grandmother? Actually: what did anyone really know about a relative that far removed in the family of things? Erin was shaking her head. All through her childhood and schooldays she'd got to know a few peers, and none of them ever mentioned a generational bridge spanning a gap of nearly one hundred years. People talked of what they knew: of mam and dad; of siblings; of nana and grandpa; cousins; aunts and uncles. That was it: the limit was three generations. Not four and categorically never five. Yet she had been required to know Ava and Stina, as if she had met them. Why? Somewhere in a box, at one of the lockups she rented, there was an old shawl that mama told her had been passed on through the decades - twice as a result of tragedy. That was a part of the answer. An embodiment and cause. But a well-preserved wrap of wool wasn't a photo, a conversation, a hug redolent of scented sentiment. Those were the things she heard other kids saying they had with their grandparents. Something warm and calm, different to the stricter codes of parents. Erin hadn't even known or been held by Alis, her own grandmother.

The stories she knew, about events that ended more than fifty years before she was born, were the scripted narrative for her life. Stranded and adrift, hundreds of miles from home, Ava's search for Stina's father had been fruitless. When she sought to return to her birthplace, so her child could be safe from harm, here on this island, her journey ended abruptly and with violence. Then, with the love and devotion of strangers, Stina became strong, passionate and dedicated. She found love and revelled in it. But she perished, like her mam, when it was ordained as necessary. Their deaths were tiny, forgotten parts in wider acts of war. Not even a statistic.

Erin shook away these thoughts and gazed across the water at the Isle of Raasay, a couple of miles across the loch. What facts did the man at the registry office need? A surname? Not known. Parents' names? Not known. A date of birth? Not known.

But maybe she knew a year. Ava must have been twenty-seven in 1915 when the Strathnairn was torpedoed and Stina was born. That was a fact, for it governed all their births.

The register of births from 1888 had no entries for a baby girl called Ava, or any other name that might be similar or could lead to a diminutive. Several births were registered on Skye that year and slightly more than half of them were girls. But the man told her there was no certainty that a family would obey the law about registering a birth. The person Erin sought quite possibly never existed in the eyes of the state.

Defeated, Erin thanked the clerk and headed to a café.

With hindsight, this failure to find answers had always been likely. Whoever her great-great-grandmother had been, she wasn't a matter of record. Erin's sense of doubt took several steps up its scale.

She headed back to the mainland and, when she reached Glasgow, decided to catch the first train to London instead of spending another night in Scotland.

Erin had a small place in London. It was a short-term let, enough to give her the time to work out what to do with her growing sense that, maybe, she should make it her home.

The train eased out from the station and the early evening brought many new colours into the sky. As she crossed the bridge, these hues rippled on the river's surface like a glassy, liquid rainbow. Erin's sense about London turned into an urgent certainty.

She'd expected to leave Scotland armed with details about her ancestry. She'd wanted to retrace Ava's journey across the water from Skye. By train to Glasgow then on to England and finally through the Marches down to Cardiff and Tiger Bay. She'd even considered the idea of hiring some sort of boat to sail out into the Bristol Channel, and onwards up the coastline back to Scotland. That expectation had been dashed and it made the idea of the journey to South Wales less desirable.

But Erin still found herself reflecting on the necessity of that journey in 1915. War was raging across the continent back then. Travel must have been, at best, slow and, at worst, dangerous. What did Ava believe or know about the man she sought, other than that he was Stina's father? He meant something that caused Ava to create huge risk to herself and her baby during all that time spent rattling along in third class. And, with no evidence or discovery of him, even greater risk travelling back as a stowaway.

Then she narrowed her eyes. Who was Stina's father? Had he deserted Ava? Or had she made use of him solely to be a mother? In which case, why had she tried to track him down? She must have needed to tell or show him something. Maybe plead with him to join her and celebrate their baby's birth.

Erin glared at the man sitting in the seat opposite hers. He had taken no notice of her when he sat down. Once comfortable, he'd fiddled with his phone for a few moments, then reclined his seat and fell asleep.

In the gathering darkness outside, the journey seemed to have no movement. The occasional jolt or bump from below her feet reminded Erin she had a destination. One particularly alarming shake made her traveling companion wake up and begin a soft-spoken conversation with someone on his phone. When he left the train at Warrington, Erin was the only passenger left in the carriage. She used the remaining couple of hours making scribbled notes and shaping mental ones about where she would live and what she would do.

Erin took out a longer lease on the apartment she'd found in London. It was close to Paddington station, which she'd decided was essential. It was sparsely furnished and couldn't really be called a home. But it had a pleasant view of the canal and was sufficiently insulated against the sound of traffic on the nearby A40. It was possible for her to be almost invisible here and, to all intents and purposes, she was. No one would ever join her in this place, except by phone. She found people online who liked the idea of written, then audible sex. Whenever it suited her, those encounters led to more substantial acts conducted using video calls. It was enough for her, but it was also boring and led to long spells of abstinence from pleasure and desire.

The walls and rooms of Erin's small existence gave her comfort and purpose.

The plan she devised during that journey from Glasgow took shape during the early part of 2013 and involved several journeys along to Pembrokeshire. She paid cash for three dwellings there, one each in Solva, Caerfarchell and St Davids. The website she created allowed her to let these places as holiday homes. The revenue started to flow and easily covered the maintenance and management costs. It was a popular destination, all year round.

Erin took out another long lease on a house overlooking the harbour at Solva, a base from which she could manage and control whatever was needed at the holiday homes. It was a place where she increasingly learned to feel belonging but, like her London base, the accommodation lacked homely or material things. The solitude and isolation suited her. Erin's life was neatly packaged into simple compartments from which she occasionally departed to travel further afield. To Scandinavia, the Adriatic, Portugal and an especially bittersweet reprise of the time she'd spent in France with Brigit.

The journeys made her content, perhaps calm. The wild, complex, scattergun behaviour of her childhood and adolescence was still a feature. But, during most of these days, no one ever saw it or suffered its consequences.

'I spent a lot of time online, Ben. There was always some poor little man out there that needed me for something. The things I did for them! Increasingly, I needed extra technology and gear: cameras; clothes; makeup; tools; toys. Occasionally, I met them in person and walked up and down their egos in my seven-inch heels.

But these things were interrupted. I just didn't like it, Ben. Sex. I mean how could I possibly like something that I would need to do to begin the countdown to my death? And why would you give a fuck about that?'

She put her face close to his and brushed her lips against his eyebrows, then kissed him several times along his jawline. 'You see, Ben? Nothing. I make a gently arousing physical statement like that and nothing happens. Mr Floppy remains in his comfort zone.'

Erin sighed. 'Something more important interrupted me though. You guessed it, Ben. I was distracted once again by the need to tie up the remaining loose ends of my ancestors' problems. It was difficult to keep up my enthusiasm, especially when the past wasn't clear. It all seemed so disconnected. Mama had always been so unequivocal. Her innate certainty was unstoppable, and that's how it had been for my grandmama too.'

Erin looked at Ben. 'Can you remember their names, Ben?'

He blinked once.

'That's good. Where was I?' Erin walked to the

window, opened its blind and looked out, perhaps at something hiding in the dark. 'Yes! Disconnection. That was it. Alis and Brigit had something inside them that made them so powerfully committed to their actions. Whereas I felt that the signals I needed were somehow lost, broken up by interference.'

She handed the bottle to him again and told him to drink. 'You'll need sustenance for these last few stories, Ben. And for what follows, because it's nearly time. One more history lesson, a few final closures, some sweet moments...' Erin looked at Ben and made a flourishing hand gesture accompanied by a small, percussive oral sound. '...then boom! I go down in flames, Ben.'

Terrified, he tried to break free from the bed. Ben had gradually developed a sense of relief in which Erin had seemed softer and less deadly. But there it was. At some point in the next few hours, or maybe days, she was going to do something terminal. That hand gesture and those words left him in no doubt: Erin was planning something incendiary.

FIFTEEN

She crawled through the traffic, away from the station and then across the Isère. She was soon clear of the city and accelerated hard up the steady incline of the road that would eventually reach their home. The three-day trip to Paris had been tiring, made worse by the fact that she disliked being away from Phillip. They'd been in touch constantly by phone and Facetime, and he was safely, busily getting on with his own work as a freelance writer. It didn't change Kylie Lomas's terrible, constant sense of foreboding.

It was the thing that made them leave England so she could take the job in Grenoble. Since her mum and dad had been found in that disused mine shaft, nothing had happened that felt like a threat or a continuation of the long history of terrible accidents and deaths in their family. Yet her anxiety and fear that something would happen to them, or to her brother, were constant.

It made her slow down. Phillip had called her just as the TGV pulled into Grenoble. He was okay. She was okay. It was only thirteen kilometres to their home, but the road had some tight turns. Racing made no sense. At a steady 60 kmh, she had time to be calm.

While they were still alive, her mum and dad continued to speak often about how grandad and grandma had been found dead in Spain. Kylie was less than a year old when it happened, and it was many years before she understood that those deaths had caused all the troubles that haunted their home. For all the years that she knew him, the same distress never left its place behind her father's eyes.

The circumstances were inexplicable, by any number of measures. But alongside all that had gone before, it seemed impossible to see David Junior and Kathryn's deaths as an unfortunate accident, or due to a bizarre loss of reason. And that was the thread; it was stitched through all the losses, right back to Dewi and Claire.

Why hadn't the police got involved? Dewi was one of their own. Wasn't he? A lifelong pillar of constabulary fortitude and rectitude. Wasn't he? But the same old platitudes were rolled out, time and again. Terrible, tragic accidents had occurred. Unforeseen and above suspicion. Kylie spoke aloud as she drove: 'How the very fuck could exposure to anthrax spores not cause curiosity?' She was getting stressed now and the final few moments of her journey were quite dangerous, for she was barely in control of the little car. It meant that, when she turned in to the short lane that led to their house, she didn't notice the tall dark-haired woman standing on the road's edge with a large dog sitting attentively at her side.

But Phillip welcomed her home and soon they were sitting, relaxed and stress-free on the small, paved area between their house and the forest. He'd warmed up some food, a plate of canapés that went very nicely with the Provençal rosé which, in turn, went very nicely with the fish stew. Kylie told her husband about the time she'd spent in Paris, and how it had been relatively easy despite her not wanting to be there. Her expert advice about how her American company could bypass French employment law had been accepted. Job done. Objectives achieved. Jobs taken away. Then Phillip told her about the copy he'd written for his newest client and delivered well before the stated deadline. He'd received a small bonus for that effort. They'd had a successful week, with much to celebrate. As the evening turned to night, their celebrations spilled over into an outburst of passion lit by the pale, discreet lighting en terrasse. Despite any fears or woes, this was something they had missed. Things intensified and, eventually, there were several moments in which the darkness was filled by their moans, then by shouts and wails of pleasure. These sounds echoed back at them from the trees, then mingled with another sound: a chorus; savage; and dangerous.

From the very start of their relationship Belinda Carter and Jason Morgan liked sex. With each other. It was the activity that defined them. Their appetites had to be fed frequently and without regard for anything else that might need to be done. The only rule they lived by was that it must never involve anyone else. This helped them to believe that their unstoppable libidos were, in fact, love. Enduring. Permanent.

When he was sixteen, she was nearly twenty. She'd liked him instantly, and that meant he was allowed to stay at the party he'd gate-crashed. On the walk across town to her flat, they had their first fuck. It didn't matter that it was on the bonnet of a parked car, nor that it barely lasted two minutes. It simply felt perfect, and long into that night they began to learn the things that would become their unbreakable habit.

Jason left school and got a job as a dogsbody doing errands for a local gardener. Belinda worked at the Town Hall. She was quite senior, and Jason liked that she often looked pristine and smart in her work clothes. He liked it even more when she sneaked him on to official premises for sex.

When his parents were declared missing, Jason and Belinda drove to the Lake District to join the search. Kylie and Phillip joined them, and they all tried to help the rescue effort by joining up the dots of photos their parents had shared on their last day in the area. It just seemed impossible that two people could go missing, especially in such relatively benign terrain. Brother and sister sat together one evening in the cosy pub and each expressed the terror welling up inside them. About the loss and pain that had broken their family for forty-two years.

The last place Susan had posted a photo was near Blea Tarn, and a check-in on social media was agreed to be indisputable. The search focused on the area between the tarn and Boot, where the Morgans' car was still loaded with their belongings, ready to head home. Not far from the small lake, the dogs began to bark their certainty that there was something of note connected to the mine shaft and its sturdy wooden fence.

At the coroner's hearing, the deaths were deemed to be accidental without third party involvement. The bodies showed no signs of injury beyond those caused by the fall. When Kylie cried out that it couldn't be that simple, and the result didn't take account of all that had happened to generations of Morgans, she was shown sympathy and asked to remain calm. Her continued agitation eventually caused a recess and a more emphatic request to respect the court's proceedings. She didn't return to the room and sat outside with Phillip. Their status as newly-weds seemed to have lost its ring.

Jason felt a strong sense of blame for what had happened because, after all, it had been his suggestion that his parents should take that walking holiday. Worse, he knew that the rum-fuelled evening with his dad had quickly been shrugged off as nothing special, despite the hugs and oneness. As soon as he got back to Belinda's flat, the only thing he cared about began again. He didn't need any duty or responsibility regarding his parents and family. All that mattered was the immeasurable pleasure he'd found with Belinda.

He bought a VW minibus and amused himself by calling it the Camper van Beethoven. Belinda was made redundant by the council so she also quit her flat and they set off on an adventure in which they marked off all the different places they could expend their desires. When they needed money, Jason hustled work as a gardener. Belinda offered a supplementary service as a cleaner to his customers. It kept them safe and sound.

Several years later, they decided to try west Wales. It was a place that formed a huge part of his family history, and Jason needed to be there. Yet it didn't stop his awful sense of something indefinable about the land of his great-grandparents.

It was a long drive, and both needed the facilities of a proper site. It seemed everywhere was full, and Jason was making increasingly frantic calls. The only place with vacancies was some distance from St Davids: up the coast; too far away.

As they passed a sweeping beach, his phone rang. A site down near Rhosson had got his voice message and had a spare pitch for their van. They pressed on, and soon drove across the bridge and stopped to look at the pretty harbour. Darkness was rolling in, so they kept moving. Great clouds were amassing to their right, with sheets of lightning almost constantly flashing. Belinda and Jason reached the city's outskirts without seeing those sheets turn to streaks.

They cruised down the High Street and Jason couldn't tear his eyes from one of the buildings. He had a sense of shock in his chest, like you'd get after a couple of espressos. He was glad he wasn't driving. Belinda seemed to be going too fast, and someone on the pavement gesticulated that she should slow down. Jason was transfixed by a cross on its plinth and by pubs. Then a glimpse of a cathedral and the substantial ruins nearby. When they finally pulled into the campsite, Jason was in considerable distress.

Belinda made him put on some boots, and they set off to the coast to find some calm. She pointed at two large birds gliding in the distance and it broke Jason's distraction. They watched the serene swoops, without being able work out what breed of bird they were watching. They were black, jet black, with strange, angled wings. Belinda joked that they looked like giant bats.

Down by the lifeboat station, they looked at the sea crashing on the rocks. Ramsey Island glowed serenely in the distance, the sun setting behind it. The hedges didn't completely hide the ruined walls of the chapel and they both instantly knew they had to ignore the signs about private property, get inside that rectangle and have sex. So, they did and later both claimed they'd never known anything like it. There'd been a sense that something was watching over them, driving them to greater heights, during which Belinda had bitten Jason's cheek. This was new. It utterly turned him on.

Over the next few days, there was amusement at the sounds emanating from the old VW. This turned to frustration, then irritation, when it was clear it was never ending. One afternoon, the shouts and screams were especially loud, and it was too much for one resident who went to complain. A tall young woman with dark purple eyes expressed regret and gave assurance this would be dealt with. They walked together to where Camper van Beethoven was parked, its windows shrouded with drawn curtains and blinds. The woman knocked on the side door in vain. There was silence.

The frustration and irritation turned to concern when neither of the young couple was seen for three days. More strenuous knocking on the van's doors and windows yielded nothing, and when they called Mr Morgan's phone, its ringtone could be heard inside the van.

The police arrived and smashed a window so they could see inside. There was a great deal of dried blood smothered over the two pale bodies that were locked together in the missionary position. It appeared, so far as the crime scene folks could determine, that they had bitten each other forcibly during sex. The gaping wounds in both their necks had caused terminal blood loss. Their terrified, lifeless eyes suggested this bizarre act had been far from pleasurable.

SIXTEEN

Jake Wallis knew the tales of old George Cottam's time as a soldier and Military Policeman. His great grandad may not have been a hero, but it had always seemed he'd been given a bad press by his successors. Being murdered by some dangerous old bitches was hardly his fault, was it? Jake wasn't one for jumping to conclusions, and despised conspiracy theories, but he often thought something odd had been going on in the family.

The fairground owners had never admitted culpability in the deaths of Jack and Tara. Odd.

A cursory investigation proved nothing that could dispute their innocence. The machinery had not been tampered with in any way, yet somehow all those volts had been diverted through his grandparents and barbecued them. Odd.

Uncle Leon and Aunty Debra had been on the lash in their €300 a night hotel room in Puerto Banus. Odd.

They rarely drank and no one had ever seen them drunk. Jake was barely three when the news had been broken to his mother that her brother's body had burst, and his skeleton shattered when it hit the ground beneath that balcony. He didn't understand her tears, but he cuddled her anyway. She didn't seem to want his touch. That, he soon learned, wasn't so odd.

He was twelve, that day, when the school's head teacher had come to take Jake out of his physics class. The matron was in the head's study and there was a strange man there too, who only introduced himself as a copper after they told him his parents had been found dead. Odd.

Jake always expected to hear they'd died in one of their too-fast cars. Odder still to find out that your parents were hopeless coke addicts whose final lines had been written by a poisoned pen.

They'd messed up his life and messed up his head. Jake had been sent away to a ridiculous school not far from the arse end of Narnia and he'd hated them for it. Then he hated that they'd snorted all that money up their immaculate noses. Then he hated that it never occurred to them that someone might have them killed for their abject lack of fiscal care and shamelessly projected material excesses. Finally, he hated them for not loving him.

On the plus side, there was still enough lying around in assorted accounts and funds for Jake to thrive. They'd made a kind of provision for him to be cared for, and for his endowment to be protected until he was eighteen. It was very odd indeed that the person nominated to protect Jake's wealth behaved with razor sharp integrity. Perhaps his parents loved him enough to find the one person on the Fylde coast that wasn't a complete and utter chancer.

When he left the school at eighteen, Jake was an orphan with a reasonable fortune that would gloss over the undercoat of his missing parents and their disgusting habit. A year later, he read the runes right, bet a huge wedge on black and found that a referendum result meant his investments in small English breweries kept bringing dividends.

He settled on Manchester as the place to live and opened a bar in the up-and-coming Northern Quarter, pumping out ales from his breweries or cocktails for the more aspiring clientele. Drinks got supplemented by a nostalgic menu of Real English Fare and the punters loved it. No one dared ask for a Heineken or Crème Caramel. On his 21st birthday in 2018, he opened a replica bar in Nantwich and, for a year, watched the money pile up. The loving reviews in traditional and social media never stopped. Then he read the runes right once more. A chance discussion with a customer revealed that a plague was sweeping the globe, killing and disabling all in its path. Jake sold off his shares in the bars and breweries and rented a remote country cottage out towards Buxton. This was the place for him to ride out the fifth horseman of the coronavirus.

Recovery was slow, but Jake became used to his solitary bubble. No one could burst it and he emerged during the summer of 2022 safe in the knowledge that his wealth had needed no vaccine to keep it fit and well. What he needed now was a fast car and a way to find hookers wherever he might travel.

In the months that followed, his thoughts kept returning to George Cottam and the place he had died. Jake decided he could do worse than to spend some time down there in Pembrokeshire. He found a terrific place to stay with a panoramic view of a harbour and beyond. He scraped and haggled his way through a process that got him a reduced rental. He decided the crazy sounding bitch that rented out the house could probably be suckered in to even more discounts after he got there and, eventually, he set off across country.

His night near the alma mater was a lively one and he paid the whore extra for some special attention to detail. Then he'd raced down the last few dozen miles to the coast where he found the house was everything it had advertised. Jake was so made up by its quality and finery that he sent a cheeky text to the crazy sounding bitch wondering if she'd like to join him for a schooner or two of bubbly. She never replied. At least he'd tried.

After a couple of evenings being utterly bored by the nearby, futile options for food and drink, he looked online and found there was a world-famous fish and chip restaurant not far away. Jake jumped in his M4 and told the satnav his destination. It took him down past the harbour then along a tiny road called Prendergast, lined with pretty houses and curious stares. When he reached Middle Mill, the voice told him to bear left towards a place the artificial intelligence couldn't interpret but the map said was Caerfarchell. He wondered how the fuck that was pronounced then laughed with a degree of respect at his car's computerised navigator for giving it a go.

His laughter made him speed up and the massive power of the BMW's engine responded. He'd flashed past sixty mph when the sky darkened up above the high ground to his left. Jake nearly hit the woman standing on the grass verge to his right and now he accelerated at full power up the hill, away from the hamlet. With flashes of lightning making the sky white, he was suddenly disoriented by a flock of black birds swooping at his car. He was still accelerating as he steered to avoid the birds. Out of control, at a speed in excess of 80 mph, the car veered off the road and ran over the grass verge, crashed through some undergrowth and dashed towards the area near a disused quarry. The earthen, grassy roadside slowed him down but the impact with a derelict two-story concrete building caused his airbag to deploy.

Instead of saving Jake's life from the collision, it exploded, showering him with shards of razor-sharp metal. Shards shaped like birds.

SEVENTEEN

Today

'And that's where you come in, Ben. More to the point, it's where I come in. To this happy holiday home, that you are letting from me.' She smiled with gleeful triumph.

Ben shook his head and tried again to break himself free, to escape from the impossible terror welling in his gullet and throat.

'Endings. Closure. The last notes in the last bar of this symphony. You and me together, Ben. A chord.'

Erin was standing on tiptoes to look out through the skylight. It was light out there, a brilliant blue sky was visible beyond her head. Ben still had no idea what day it was. He felt strong enough to keep trying to snap the bindings, yet weak beyond words. The tales Erin had told him seemed implausible, from a different plane. Avenging angels, or imps, or whatever they were, consumed by their cause, with hate and love and peace and war and compassion and ruthlessness fuelling all they did. How could he possibly believe these things? In the world he inhabited there was a kind of peaceful co-existence. He lived in his simple terraced house among good people who minded everyone's business as well as their own. Ben's audiences and fans flocked to see him, laughing with unreserved pleasure at the routine. He was never fêted as a maestro, but the media cognoscenti were generally kind to him. Nothing in his life, nor in the lives of those around him, was controversial or skewed. People had fights, for sure, usually about the nothings they'd always fought over: but there was no death or glory battleground for most of them; not even on the killing fields of Twitter and Facebook. On any given day, walking along the streets of Clitheroe, he might pass the very best and the very worst of humanity, searching out their needs in the town's shops and bars and cafés. Ben saw those poles of good and bad as multi-faceted, layered and complex. He knew the country was run by terrifying wealth that steered its tiny prophets through their political careers, but he kept all that out of his shows, out of his ideas, out of his mind. Nana still loved him, and he loved her. Grandad had loved him too. That love was constant, borne out of Ben's rejection by dissolute parents. He'd never known his mother and father. They'd loved each other above all else, leaving no room for Ben, or Simon, or anyone.

'Imagine that. A couple having a wildly liberating fuck so that, in those moments, they could forget all they feared, and just as they were ready to let it all go, a pack of wolves bounds up and tears them apart. In 2015, Ben. Grey wolves! Roaming the wilderness, cheek by jowl with the domestic bliss dotted in and around their habitat. It's unthinkable. Isn't it? *Incroyable*.'

She turned back to face him. 'Isn't it, Ben?'

He'd had enough. It didn't matter anymore. There was no need to fear her and whatever she planned to do to him. He was dumb, so his insolence came from his eyes. Ben squinted, then opened his eyes wide and blinked repeatedly.

Erin burst out laughing. 'Oh, Ben! Maybe you do have a spine. But perhaps not balls. From where I'm standing, Ben, that collection of items between your legs still lacks any kind of certainty. Maybe I need to make something happen there.'

She turned back to the window and opened it slightly. 'Poor Jason and Belinda. Such a perfect life together. Nothing of any consequence except constant, fulfilling sex. No stimuli except... well, coming. Magnificent. What a design for life, Ben. Such perfect passion, such endless indulgence. Until it got a bit wild. One taste was all it took. That time in Justinian's Chapel: a playful nip on the cheek; a tiny puncture and just a drip of blood; that was all Belinda needed, Ben. And, whatever she wanted, Jason wanted it more. Their sad, lonely existence was over because literally any form of arousal had to be tried: mutually; exclusively; terminally.'

Erin made a frustrated hissing sound. 'What a fucking stupid way to kill yourselves. Wasn't it, Ben?'

She spun around and raised her eyebrows in support of the question. He wasn't looking. Ben had decided to ignore her, or at least to look away instead of letting her eyes dominate him. He turned his head to look over to his right, out through the window with its view of trees and a bit of the building next door. It didn't release an ounce of fear or relieve the dull pulsing in his chest. Erin left the room and soon he heard noises. Things being moved and dropped. The front door being unlocked, opened and closed.

For the first time, Ben realised he could hear sounds from the adjoining house.

What the fuck?

No, I mean what the actual fuck?

So, she had an accomplice in there? Was that it? How many of them were there?

And those noises. What made that noise when it was dropped? Something heavy, yet not so dense that it couldn't bounce slightly. There was no ring of metal, nor the sharp crack of rock. It had to be something organic. Wood, therefore. Or flesh and bone.

The front door made its opening and closing noises again. Her voice cried out. She'd never done this before. 'I'm home, honey.' Her laughter was getting crazy again.

More sounds of industry, of the processing of objects through a system so they ended up on the floor beneath his room. Then a smell wafted through his senses. Sulphurous. Something acrid, pungent and gaseous. Was it sulphurous? It felt like the right word but maybe some pedantic fucker would point out he was wrong. Ben decided to stick with sulphurous.

She was back, wiping her hands on a towel that was then launched, discarded into the far corner of the room.

'It's time for you to drink some more. You need your strength. And you can ignore me all you like, Ben. But sulking isn't a good look for a thirty-something.' She pulled the line again to restrict his movements then put the bottle in his hand, like she had all this time.

Once she'd pushed the tube through the tape, Ben squeezed some fluid from the bottle. That taste hadn't changed. Whatever it was, it had kept him alive.

'I know your name. Maybe you've forgotten it now, thanks to your wicked mother. The funny thing is… your name could've been one from several. Jones. Bevan. Morgan. Thomas. Griffiths. Quite cute that you went with Budd. It suits you. It didn't matter though. We knew you, even though it took more time to work out how things had worked out.'

Ben had another palpitation. Nana. On that cruise ship, somewhere up near the Arctic Circle.

'But I wonder how much of this you know. Your parents didn't want you, did they? Maybe you've accepted that. If you've been paying attention, it's possible you might have joined up the dots. Just up the road from here is the place where it all began for you. A funny little harbour with haphazard houses scattered around it, plus a pub, a restaurant and weird deserted factories. Your great-grandmother was a strange one. I quite liked her, or what I was told about her. She knew what she wanted and generally got it. Your great-grandfather was a bad man. I'd go so far as to say he was evil. Quite impossibly evil, Ben.

Strange meets Evil: a compelling combination, as usual. They liked each other despite all the reasons that society frowns and tuts about. An out-of-town affair. Wild and unrestrained fucking, soft grass massaging her back with every push and thrust he made. It got pretty wild, so much so that they made someone up there on the clifftops. They conceived your grandpa in a final act of dazzling desire. But that was wrong, wasn't it? A married man and a semi-detached woman making babies? Very wrong.

Even though they had no future together, your great-Gs went ahead and created a future in which you would be a part. Strange had made up her mind that it was over, regardless of what they'd created. Evil accepted that and walked away: back to a wife; back to his law and order. He never knew what they'd made. But it had happened.

Strange went back to the drunken sailor she didn't ever crave but who could be made culpable for her baby. She never told him it was Evil's son and the drunken sailor cared for her; proudly certain he was the real father. They'd done it a few times, so why not? Stanley Jones, he was, but she didn't take his name. Bevan got the nod.

'The Strange/Evil offspring was born, and she decided to call him Geraint. Geraint Bevan. Isn't that a name to conjure with? A bastard, obviously, but that was inevitable.

Drink some more please, Ben. You look tired.'

Erin smiled. It was kind, that smile. Her eyes were filled with the same gentleness. Ben glanced down at his hand, squeezed the bottle and drank some more.

'Is the drink helping you, Ben? Do you feel all right?'

He was still trying to avoid her gaze if he could, but Ben had been drawn to the smile she'd given him. So, he looked into her eyes, gave a miniscule nod and blinked once.

She reached down to his head and stroked his hair. 'Good. Very good. Where was I? Yes: bastards.' Erin walked back to the skylight and gazed out, breathing in the air through the small opening. 'Alwen raised Geraint until he went off to do his national service and then never came back. Seems he'd inherited his real dad's non-existent moral compass. His pretend dad was away. Another non-existent man. Poor Alwen, Ben. Your Great-Grandma was all alone.

But the boy didn't care. Your granddaddy, having deserted his poor mother, went a bit wild. Had his time on shore and offshore with all those other unwilling young men, pressed to serve their country. Learned how good it felt to be in a gang and all the things that could teach him. Decided to dress himself in whatever mode made him part of a gang. Took a few punches. Slashed a few cheeks. Fought vicious battles with people in other gangs and sometimes, ironically, with the police: what would his real father have thought?

He drifted and floated, then Geraint got in with the wrong crowd. He changed his name and bolted back this way, to be nearer home. But he still didn't go to see his poor mam. In fact, he never saw her again.

When he met your grandmama, the lovely Martha,

his world was suddenly alive with new things. He took her name, and she took his wild side; tore it up into tiny strips and re-assembled them so Terry had a future. A life on the ocean wave, Ben.'

She lifted her hand and placed it across her eyebrows, then surveyed an imaginary horizon. This was strange. Ben was deeply troubled by the sudden appearance of a kindly-sounding, quite pleasant Erin. Now, she was giggling: a preface to a hugely theatrical 'Ahoy there!'

Ben returned to his attempts at ignoring her. She wouldn't like it, but it was his strategy now and he owned it. He must have nearly finished the bottle of liquid. It felt light. When he turned his head back to look at it, his eyes noticed something new among the items on the table to his left.

'Geraint was Terry. And when Martha had their child, that was your mother. Sylvia Griffiths. And a couple of hundred miles away your daddy was also born. 1967. The summer of love, Ben – although it wasn't quite like California. Not in Tenby and Richmond. And the proud parents of these two babies didn't do drugs, making it hugely ironic that your parents were routinely off their tits on something.

Is that karma, or kismet? I never know the difference.

Timothy Thomas had so much talent. He was quite staggeringly gifted. You should have heard him play, Ben. Your daddy was a ridiculously skilled piano player. Learned all his scales and arpeggios, got his pieces learned so he passed all his exams. He was the pride and joy of an entire community and the apple of his parents' eye. They loved him. And his mama was right: it was a desperate waste that he fell in with Sylvia. She knows a thing or two, your nana.'

Ben flinched and tried another go at loosening his

restraints. Erin's recent good humour snapped off.

'You really are stupid. After all this time, what on earth makes you think you can break free? It's not fucking possible, Ben.'

She turned away from her lecture. 'We were starting to get along well, I thought. Your ingratitude has really upset me.'

Erin picked up the hammer. It was the first time she'd ever touched it.

This was it. He'd pushed her over an edge and after all the hints about what she might do to him, now the chips were down she was just going to smash his skull in.

'I'm going downstairs to fix something. When I get back, I want you to have finished your drink. There can't be more than a mouthful left.' There was another change of expression. All he could see in her eyes now was rejection. The kind he'd seen when his teenage friends got dumped. Her work as a captor, gaoler and executioner seemed diminished. He'd been scared since all this started. He'd felt in grave danger. The new look on Erin's face made him terrified. Not because she was more dangerous or evil or deranged. It was because a last chance had come and gone. Ben's last chance. The one that, somehow, she might change her mind and release him unharmed. Worse, it was he who had closed that door. Every single nerve and cerebral pulse seemed to fail. With a silent snort of frustration Ben squeezed on the bottle and finished what was left of what might be his last ever drink.

That last mouthful did taste different.

'I'm back and I've been thinking about why you suddenly got all stupid just now. It's because I mentioned Timothy's parents, isn't it? Your grandpa and grandma. Except you call her Nana, don't you?'

She sat on the bed. 'I don't want you to worry about her, Ben. I promise no harm will come to her, or any of her friends up there in the Fjords. Well, obviously she'll get a shock and feel huge sadness when you fail to get in touch ever again, lost without trace, whereabouts unknown.

Ah-Haaaa: you've finished your drink. Bravo, Ben. I'm so pleased and glad you did as I asked. We can finish off some loose ends while all those good things get to work in your system.

You know the lovely thing about Sylvia and Timothy getting together? They both attended a young people's music festival as teens. Sweet, eh? Except they didn't meet there. Your dad heard your mum singing, tracked her down and wrote to her. Double sweet. I mean that was hard in 1981. No social media then, was there? So, your lovely, sweet dad contacted the organisers with a made-up story about how he'd found some music with her name on. This was before privacy laws made everyone terrified of everyone else, and they just gave him her address. He wrote full of praise for her singing, and how she shouldn't worry about not reaching the finalist stage.

She didn't write back for ages, so he wrote another letter.

When she finally replied, it was the longest letter your dad could ever have wished for. Full of thanks and chat and questions about his musical talents. Then about her school and friends and home. The music she had started to love, all that punk played on synths: Visage; Heaven 17; Ultravox. And right at the end, Sylvia told Tim that she couldn't stand her parents and as soon as she was sixteen, she would leave school, go and live alone and find work as a professional singer. She signed off with her name, a string of kisses and her phone number.

Your dad fell in love with every word, sentence and page.'

Ben was in a quandary now. This was all news he had never known and wasn't sure he wanted to know it. It was nearly thirty years since his father's death and more than twenty since his mother died. Yet here was a stranger, to him and to them, turning their lives in to a cute novel for his benefit.

And how the fuck does she know all this?

Wait. A novel. Is that what this is?

'Anyway, the rest is silence. We covered the jelly fish and the truncheon/dildo mash up quite recently and we don't want to dredge all that up. The thing is, Ben, and maybe you really do need to know this bit: your mama and daddy loved each other very deeply. Your nana gave them both, but Sylvia in particular, the worst possible reviews. It's true they didn't really love you and never showed you any kind of love. Which is wicked beyond words. They loved each other so much there simply wasn't room for anyone else. And, in its way, that's sort of hopeful.'

Erin was standing at the foot of the bed, staring down at the floor. She seemed to be calculating something, perhaps completing the workings out for a problem she'd always done one way but now saw a new result from a different reckoning.

'I wonder if there should always be hope. It's led a lot of people into dead ends, I think. We hope that justice will prevail and be true to itself. We hope that governments will make their country fair and equitable. We hope that business will act in good faith across all its activities. We hope that science will concentrate on discovery that enhances and enriches life. We hope that humans will see their failings as a reason to change, rather than a reason to lash out with hatred and blame. We hope that hope matters.

From where I stand, Ben, every single quote about hope is plainly lacking in hope. Whoever says something profound, in a holy book or on the hustings or via some mighty work of art, about how hope must win quite possibly has their fingers crossed behind their back. And perhaps their conviction is really a luxury derived from their place on the side lines.'

She stopped pacing the room. 'Look at us, Ben. What hope do we have? You might be hoping all this is a massively exaggerated practical joke and at some point, soon, I'll set you free to walk peacefully into the sunset, all threat and fear banished.

I might be hoping that strange forces will send signals to me that none of this is needed, and I don't have to die or have a baby. A child who will never know her future because all she can think about is a history that diminishes her because she has to keep changing it.'

Erin raised an eyebrow at him, and he couldn't stop himself blinking once. 'There you go, Ben. You might also be hoping that some powerful agency is homing in on me, ready to take me out with a drone strike. Robotic, black clad agents of fortune will burst in and release you and let you begin your life all over.

Maybe I'm hoping I can just do the right thing. Pick up my phone and call for help, perhaps give myself up or send an anonymous tip-off about where you can be found. Release myself from this imprisonment. End the retribution while the record can still be put straight.

We are both in confinement, Ben. We are both victims. I just hadn't realised, until these last few hours, how much that was true for you, as well as for me. All the same injustices and wrongdoings that we have been avenging these last sixty years have hurt you equally, possibly more profoundly.

I hope you realise I can see that.' She reached out and touched Ben's foot. Her touch was familiar now, almost tender in its warmth. He felt something else, too. Regret? Complicity?

'I need to leave you alone again.'

Ben decided to count the time she was gone. A rough approximation of seconds past, literally just ticking them off in his head. He passed 1,250 then lost track because he started trying to work out how many minutes that was. But then he heard a sound he hadn't expected.

Erin was coming.

It started with the tiniest gasps of exhalation. Then she made sounds as if she was humming and laughing in tandem. Suddenly, she said 'Fuck', then after more of those build-up noises, shouted it again. After that she just made louder and louder and louder cries and screams. Then finally she just screamed 'Yes, oh fuck, Ben. Yes.'

It almost beggared belief that Ben had a hard on when she returned to the room. She was wearing an unbuttoned blouse and knickers.

'Well, isn't that a sight for sore eyes? It's quite impressive, after all. Although I should probably admit that it's had a helping hand.' She reached across to the table and picked up a bubble pack of tablets. After a deft squeeze, a blue tablet popped out from one of the indents. 'Sildenafil. I ground up three and put them in your last drink. I'm guessing you don't suffer any cardiovascular disease, because the side effects can be risky for your ticker, Ben. But the plus side is right there. And since we're both ready, I'm going to make the most of it.'

Ben was powerless. Restrained by chains and tape; drugged with a chemical that he once spent time researching for his act. He'd been amused by the side effect that could cause priapism. He'd written a short monologue about the ways a permanent hard-on might be explained away. It didn't go down too well.

Erin was on him, guiding his cock inside. She kept saying she needed him to make her pregnant. She didn't care about her own satisfaction, she just wanted Ben to shoot all he had into her. Ben was trying everything he could think of to stop this being the result. Every cliché under the sun. Nothing worked. She was too beguiling and beautiful. He was charmed, like a mortal sailor hearing the sirens' songs.

'This feels good, Ben. But I meant it. Pleasure isn't the idea. I want your enjoyment to be about one thing.' She stopped talking and closed her eyes, as if side-tracked into pleasure. 'One thing, Ben. That's the plan. We do this, you give me the best juice you can muster, I get pregnant, and the process moves on to the next step.'

She moved her face down so she could whisper into his ear. The change of position made Ben grunt through the masking tape. It felt good. 'Except there's a change of plan. I don't want this. Don't want another baby, another daughter. These are the motions I'm going through, but the truth is there's a get out for both of us.'

Ben stopped moving. Her skin and hair smelt of that same sulphurous smell, except it wasn't sulphur. It was petrol, or some derivative of petrol. And now he could smell fire. Smoke seeped in from the landing. Now he could hear the crackles of burning wood.

'You can stop this if you want, Ben. I've played the part I had to play. I've known for a while that it would mean the end for both of us. Such a shame. And just as we had started to feel such a special connection.

And just as we had discovered a strange but special bond between us.

And just as we had realised what we meant to one another. What a shame. Isn't it, Ben?'

He looked into her dark purple eyes and blinked. Once.

EIGHTEEN

The Grand Theatre, Blackpool

The new routine was electric from the start.

His famous one-liners and puns remained, peppered amongst longer tales that demanded attention. There was complexity in this work and, since the tour started, local and national media reviews had eventually decided that Benjamin Budd had spent his time off to good effect. He was taking risks with bizarre and unusual material. It relied a lot more on narrative than anything he'd done before. And it was dark.

There'd been grumbling from his more traditional fans about all that. Complaints bubbled to the surface: that the laughs were few and far between; that it was no longer comedy.

But what was it?

Ben was oblivious. This audience cheered and laughed and applauded loudly. More than usual, perhaps. It was Christmas Eve. Joy to the world? Something about the season made comedy somehow funnier and apposite. People seemed more ready to forgive.

And this was a local boy, more or less. That counted. It helped him bring the house down.

The set was stark. A large screen was suspended behind his microphone, occasionally used to flash up a scene or a photo of a social media post to reinforce the routine. Otherwise, it remained dark and therefore barely visible. The stage was hung with diaphanous material, draped so that it created the sense that the performer had just emerged from the mouth of a tunnel. He was lit by a single beam of light, so narrow that if he stretched out an arm it became invisible to many in the audience.

There'd been no warning that something might go off piste. No signs in the foyer, or hints on social media. There'd been that weird thing where the initial posters and adverts for the tour had a watermark saying, Not Cancelled. It caused some curiosity. But that didn't last. The words were soon removed.

When the theatre plunged into darkness mid-sentence, a rumble of concern was mixed with a smattering of chuckling expectation. Maybe this was a special Christmas joke? But it didn't sound like a joker's voice. 'Forgive me, everyone. Something unexpected has come up. I might need to....'

Before his sentence was complete, the large screen flashed to life and sounds crackled from the PA speakers. It was momentary, but plenty of people saw it. Three jagged white lines flashed back and forth, up and down, side to side. One from bottom left of the screen, diagonally across to top right. The second and third lines bisected it. Anyone in the audience who'd watched these drawings on the screen had a brief imprint of a flattened letter A on their eyesight.

The houselights stayed down, but a calm announcement was made. 'Please don't be alarmed, ladies and gentlemen. We have a minor technical problem, and your show will resume very shortly.'

Not so many chuckles now. Murmurs and whispers instead. Then a drunken voice: 'What the fook is this? C'mon Ben, for fook's sake. This is my money you're pissing away here.' There were reactions around the room, some vaguely assenting.

The spotlight on the microphone flashed back to life, and Ben was there. He was smiling nervously into a large phone, occasionally looking at the audience whenever he spoke. 'I'm sorry to spring this on you, my friends, but it is actually incredibly special to share something amazing and unbelievable with you.' He poked the phone and looked back at the big screen. 'If I can get this fucking thing to work...' A burst of laughter erupted, tension and relief combined in exhalation. '... I will be able to show the thing... the things that are so amazing.'

When the screen finally came to life, a woman was there. Muted for now. Her hair was tied up and she was visibly exhausted, lying on a bed apparently.

'Hello, Erin. It's so good to see you.' Ben's voice was shaking.

'Don't cry. Please, Ben. It will set us all off.'

Ben turned to the audience. 'I better not, had I?'

Now Erin was being handed two bundles, each with a tiny pink face. She looked into the camera's eye and said, 'Ben and I wanted you to meet our beautiful babies.'

A massive cheer rent the air. Applause and whoops. A few started singing *Oh Little Town of Bethlehem*. Ben tried to create calm with hand gestures, but he was losing. Eventually he shouted, 'Can everyone just sit down and shut the fuck up?' It just caused more laughter and a smattering of jeering non-compliance. The carol singing was now quite infectious.

Then tiny baby voices could be heard over the speakers, and those did the job that Ben couldn't do. A kind of calm was restored.

'Thank you, everyone, for being good enough to listen to my children. The show will restart soon, I promise. But I didn't think you'd mind giving me some time off to see our very special Christmas gifts.'

He turned back to the screen. Erin was holding the

babies, so their faces were up against her cheeks.

'Is everything okay, honey?' Ben's voice was shaking again.

'I think the phrase is *mother and babies are doing well*. And these two beauties can't wait to see their daddy when he's finished work.' More squeaks affirmed it.

'Can we get a close up somehow? Can you ask the nurse?'

Erin smiled and nodded at the camera. It slowly zoomed in on her face, so her dark purple eyes flashed across the ether and penetrated the theatre. 'Here you go then, Ben, and everyone there in Blackpool. Our gorgeous twin baby girls.'

The video moved between the bundles in turn, as Erin said, 'Please, everyone, say hello to Megan… and to Bethan.'

REVENGE, RETRIBUTION, JUSTICE

UNENDING

ACKNOWLEDGEMENTS

I'm lucky to have an English teacher as a friend and I'm grateful to **Andrew Budd** (no relation) who spent hours reading the manuscript, correcting my grammar and punctuation. He also provided invaluable commentary and insight, in turn creating immeasurable impact on the quality of Justinian's Daughters. I love you, my old friend – and thank you for all you did.

During 2021, **Ellie Hawkes** reviewed the opening 20,000 words of the manuscript and provided some terrific feedback both in a written report and during a meeting. Her help played a huge part in structural changes I made, and I will always be grateful for her honest, sometimes quite robust comments. Ellie is a really, really wonderful person.

I'm hugely grateful to **Lynne Walker**, who proofread the opening few pages of the book in one of its early drafts. It was fantastic to get a professional's focus on the detail and she provided a lot of guidance and made me see how often I make mistakes. I'm very proud to know she is my friend.

For their help, guidance, support and love, thank you Nikki Rees-Harries, Petrea Carton-Kelly, Diane Jones, Sophie Lockwood, Martin Lewis, Viv Ainslie and Gary Potter. Thanks also to the judges of the 2022 Cheshire Novel Prize who provided some hugely important feedback and guidance about the opening pages of my submission.

A mention, too, for The Old Tailor's Shop in Caerfarchell. A magical holiday home where I stayed twice to combine writing retreats with walking. It was on the large comfy sofa there that I first jotted down the ideas that became Justinian's Daughters. The cottage is just a short distance from that imperfectly drawn letter A and all the spirits and magic it contains.

My parents took me to St Davids in 1973. I wondered, during one of my writing research trips to the city, if their spirits were guiding me as I weaved and meshed all the ideas that surged through me to create this tale. Thank you, Mum and Dad, for that childhood journey to Tyddewi. You showed me a place I've grown to love very deeply indeed.

Printed in Great Britain
by Amazon

18325727R00217